Other titles by S. Usher Evans

THE LEXIE CARRIGAN CHRONICLES
Spells and Sorcery
Magic and Mayhem
Dawn and Devilry
Illusion and Indemnity

THE RAZIA SERIES
Double Life
Alliances
Conviction
Fusion

EMPATH

THE MADION WAR TRILOGY
The Island
The Chasm
The Union

THE DEMON SPRING TRILOGY
Resurgence
Revival
Redemption

THE VEIL OF TRUST

Princess Vigilante

Book 3

S. Usher Evans

Sun's Golden Ray
Publishing

Pensacola, FL

Cover Design by Jo Painter
Line Editing by Danielle Fine, By Definition Editing

Sun's Golden Ray Publishing
Pensacola, FL
www.sgr-pub.com

For ordering information, please visit
www.sgr-pub.com/orders

DEDICATION

To the girls who reach out

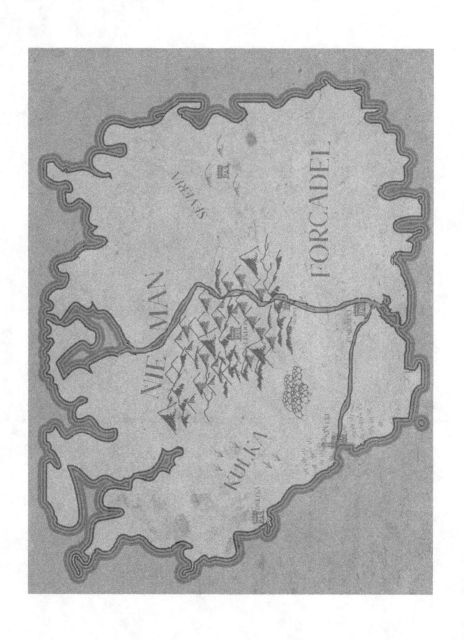

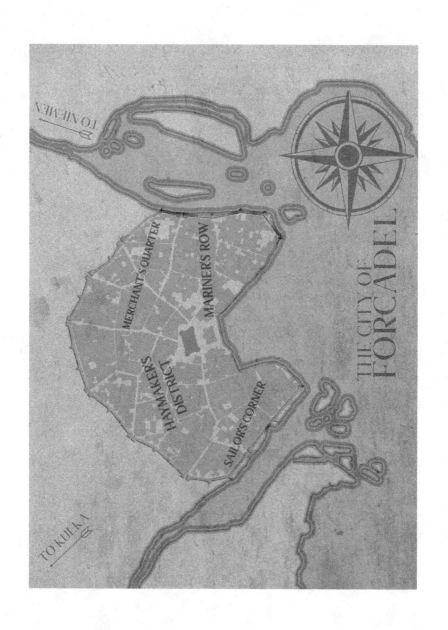

THE CITY OF
FORCADEL

Chapter One

"Hundreds of explosions! Wouldn't stop. Fifty dead in twenty minutes!"

I turned my head slightly. Two old men were grousing over their tankards in this busy tavern, filled with travelers on their way to and from Forcadel. Being so close to the city was dangerous— sitting out in the open even more so. But I was desperate for information, and my hood covered much of my face.

"Never seen anything like it, not since the desert-dwellers invaded."

I straightened, inching closer to hear better.

One of the old men shook his head. "Whoever did it was a monster, that's all I'm saying. You heard they took out Zuriel's family? He hung himself."

The mayor of Forcadel. I shifted closer to them, but any further conversation was drowned out by another pair of merchants who sat at a table between us and started a loud conversation on the price of beer.

Cursing softly, I averted my gaze to the empty bowl of stew. I had gotten wisps of conversation about some attack that had just occurred in Forcadel, but other than the general death and destruction, these patrons had given up nothing more—nor had they shared with me their knowledge of what had occurred upriver.

"...Neveri..."

My ears perked up again.

"Haven't been there myself in an age. Hear that gate is something to see."

"Yeah, I've only seen it from afar, but my cousin—he's assigned to Neveri's fortresses—he said it's pretty magnificent."

Something uncomfortable slid down my spine. If this man's cousin was at the fortress, he was probably dead. Along with sixty Severians and forty-two Forcadelians. Some with families—

I exhaled softly, clearing that train of thought before it got too far down the path. It was done; there was nothing I could do about it now except to keep fighting.

It had been less than a week since my small army had taken Neveri in the name of Forcadel, though it felt more like a lifetime. The question was—had news of this event come to the capital city yet, or more importantly, to Queen Ilara? If so, it would complicate matters significantly. Hence my precarious position here at this tavern, eavesdropping on half-drunk conversations and trying to piece together contexts.

I thumbed the two pendants hanging from a chain around my neck. One had belonged to Lieutenant Riya Kellis, one of my most loyal soldiers who'd died in the ensuing battle in Neveri. The other was Captain Felix Llobrega's, who was beyond the city walls in Forcadel, as was Katarine, my sister-in-law, and Beata, her girlfriend. Getting the three of them to safety was my top priority, even before I thought about dislodging Ilara.

But instead of retrieving them myself, I'd sent along a pair of soldiers—Jorad and Aline. In Neveri, around fifty Forcadelian soldiers had turned against Ilara and sworn fealty to me. Only Jorad and Aline had accompanied me here; the rest I'd asked to camp to the north of the capital and await further instructions. I'd thought the two I'd chosen would be more flexible of my independent ways, but Jorad, looking very much like his cousin Felix, had made a strong case that until we knew how much Ilara knew, it would be better to make myself scarce and let them handle it.

Still, delegation wasn't something I really had a taste for yet, and I didn't like being idle, especially with the pressure of time sitting on my chest. So to make myself useful, I planted myself in the center of this tavern with the hood over my head, listening and waiting.

Two old ladies at the table next to me started a lengthy conversation about Mayor Zuriel and his family, ultimately deciding that the traitorous bastard deserved it. I couldn't disagree; he'd been one of the few to betray me during the initial invasion. But his family should've been spared.

"...Felix Llobrega."

I turned my head, spying an older man talking with a group of women. He looked slightly familiar to me—perhaps he was a merchant I'd seen in town before.

"I can't believe he'd betray Her Majesty like that," he continued. "Or that he'd kill innocents."

"Are you saying he was framed?"

"Absolutely he was framed. Ilara's been looking for a reason to get rid of him."

"Surprised she needed one."

My heart began to thud in my chest. *Get rid of him? Betrayal?* What in the Mother's name had happened in Forcadel since I'd been gone? Last I knew, Felix had donned The Veil's mask in my absence to make inroads with the rebels causing trouble in the city.

Clearly, something had gone very, very wrong.

The man who'd been speaking rose to his feet, telling his female counterparts that he was off to relieve himself. I followed behind him, keeping a healthy distance as he stumbled into an alley and untied the front of his pants. Once his business had been concluded, I revealed myself.

"Evening," I said.

He cursed and jumped backward, splashing into the puddle he'd just made. "Mother above! What do you want? I have no coin."

"The bartender will be sad to hear that," I said, walking into the alley. "I want information. What happened to Felix?"

He shook his head slowly. "I don't know."

"I don't believe you," I said, flapping my cape to reveal my knives.

"I swear, I don't," he said. "The word from the castle was Felix was seen wearing a mask and cavorting with a known pirate."

I swept my tongue over my teeth. *Kieran, I swear if you screwed Felix...* "And what do you think?"

"He wouldn't have betrayed his kingdom like that. He's loyal to Forcadel, through and through." He swallowed hard. "As am I, I promise you."

"Where is he now?" I asked, after a few moments.

"The dungeons," he replied. "No date has been set for his...his execution. But the conditions down there might just do the job anyway."

The urge to march into the castle and wring Ilara's neck was strong. The dungeons were in the basement of the castle, and it would take more than just knockout powder to extract him.

"What else have you heard?" I asked, taking another menacing step forward. "Anything about Neveri? Or Princess Brynna?"

"P-Princess Brynna? She's dead. Unless..." He squinted in the dark. "That can't be... Is it you?"

"Shit." I reached into my bag and grabbed a bag of knockout powder, throwing it at his face. After a moment of blinking, he fell to the ground, out cold.

"You could have at least let him fall away from his piss."

A shadow moved in the alley behind me. Jax sauntered into the moonlight, wearing a smug grin. He belonged to the feared forest pirate Celia, and she'd loaned him to me as I took the city of Neveri. I wasn't exactly sure why he remained in my employ, but I'd use him as long as I could.

"Why'd you have to ask him if he knew you were alive?" Jax said, nudging the merchant with his toe.

"Did you discover anything interesting?" I asked, ignoring his comment.

"Nothing about Neveri," he said. "Everyone's talking about this attack on Forcadel last week. They say your boyfriend is gonna hang for it."

"Not if I can help it," I said, looking at the merchant on the ground.

"What are you gonna do, storm the castle?" Jax asked. "Your army is currently a day's ride to the north."

"Did you hear anything about this attack that killed Zuriel's family?" I asked.

"Sounds like it was more an attack on Ilara loyalists than anything," Jax said. "From what I hear, it sounds like they used ond for it."

"That's impossible," I said with a scoff. "Ariadna only let us take that small bag we used in Neveri. The Severians had something similar they used during the invasion, so maybe that's what did it."

"The rumors say it was Niemenian," he said.

"They also say Felix was responsible for it." I crossed my arms over my chest. "What about Katarine? Have you heard anything about her?"

"As far as I can tell, she's still in Ilara's good graces. For whatever that's worth."

A whistle echoed through the alley, and a few moments later, Elisha, all of thirteen years old, jumped down from a nearby roof. She was the only other body Celia had provided to take Neveri. Although she was young, she was an effective lookout, and a pretty good shot with a crossbow. I'd sent her along with Jorad and Aline, and seeing her alone scratched at my already raw nerves.

"Where are they?" I snapped. "You're late."

"Jorad told me to tell you that things were more complicated than he anticipated and that he was working on it," she said, then began ticking off her fingers. "And to give him until sunup. Also to tell you that Captain Llobrega was arrested." She paused and thought. "And that they aren't sure they can do what you asked, but they'll certainly try."

"Great," I muttered. The two soldiers were capable, but vigilantes they were not. "This is ridiculous. I shouldn't have sent them by themselves. I should've just gone."

"Eh, what's the worst that could happen?" Jax said with a devilish grin. "They get captured, give up your location and plan, and everything you've worked toward goes to hell? I mean, you're doing a good enough job of that on your own, what with getting made just now."

My gaze fell to the man on the ground, and a small voice whispered that Jax was right. I dug into my pocket and found a gold coin, flicking it at Jax. "If they asked me to give them until sunup, that's what we'll do. Go get us a room for the night so we aren't sitting out here in the open."

"Fine by me. I could use a good night's sleep." He nodded toward the man lying in the street. "What about him?"

"Leave him," I said. "Maybe he'll just believe he had too much to drink and hallucinated the whole thing."

"Hope does spring eternal," Jax said, whistling as he walked away. I glared at his retreating back. Perhaps he was just sticking around to watch me fail. He did seem to delight in it.

"What do you want me to do?" Elisha asked, breaking my attention. "Keep lookout? Find some soldiers to interrogate?" She punched her hand, ready for a fight. "I'm ready to do whatever you need, Your Majesty."

I winced as her young voice echoed in the alley. "Why don't you follow Jax? Make sure he doesn't get us a room with one bed and we have to sleep on the floor."

Chapter Two

Katarine

I never liked being summoned to the throne room. It reminded me of being called to my father's back in Niemen for some youthful infraction. But at least his temperament was even. With Ilara, I never knew what I was going to get.

My nerves were especially frayed recently since Felix had been outed as the masked vigilante who'd been patrolling the streets and causing anarchy. The secondary charges were complete nonsense—at least, I hoped he hadn't been involved in spreading ond and killing Forcadelians. Where the rebels had gotten their hands on the Niemenian ore, I had no idea. Access to the mine was tightly controlled. I'd already penned a note to my sister, Queen Ariadna, asking her to look into it.

But even Ariadna's latest note to me had left my mind with more questions than answers. She'd written about the first snowfall of the season, and included some minor details about her pregnancy, as was normal for our regular correspondence. At the end of the note, though, she had a line that seemed out of place for the rest of it:

Even though winter is descending, spring may yet be on the horizon.

If my instincts were to be trusted, and if I knew my sister as well as I hoped, Brynna had made contact with Ariadna, and help would be arriving soon.

I prayed it came sooner rather than later, as Beata had already received reports of Felix's mistreatment in the dungeons. He was tough, but if Ilara found out Brynna was alive... I shuddered at the thought.

"Good morning, Katarine," Ilara said, her face a bright, contented mask. One could scarcely believe her city had been viciously attacked a few days before. "I hope you're well. You look a little pale."

"Merely the stress of the news these past few weeks," I said, forcing myself to smile. "I trust the cleanup is going well?"

"I suppose. I'm not really interested. Captain Coyle has taken it upon himself to oversee all of it."

Captain Coyle. That certainly hadn't taken long. "He is very on top of things, it appears."

She made a face. "Shame to hear that Felix betrayed me so."

"I don't know what to say," I said softly. "Perhaps he suffered a mental break. He didn't seem right after August died, and with Brynna..." I shook my head. "He never allowed himself to grieve."

"Perhaps you should've pressed him to," Ilara replied, eyeing me intently. "Because now...now I don't know what to do. Shall I leave him to die in the dungeons like Garwood? Or have him executed?"

"There are still many in the city who adore him," I replied, as my pulse ticked upward. "It might be better to keep him out of sight."

She cast me a coy smile. "I know you care for him deeply. You don't have to pretend otherwise."

I quieted, not trusting that I wouldn't say something to get me in trouble. Finally, I settled on, "I just wish he'd made a different choice."

"As do I, my dear. As do I." She took my hand. "I'm just grateful you had no part in it. I don't think I could stand it if I lost both of you."

I had my doubts about that. My position with Ilara had always confused me. I'd obviously been loyal to her predecessor, and Ilara had killed my husband. When Brynna had been deposed, Felix and I had both agreed to stay and serve the kingdom as long as Ilara would let us.

But while she'd spent months surgically removing all Felix's protections—first, he lost his oversight of the cadets, then she began reassigning his allies to the farthest reaches of the country— she hadn't done the same with me. She still sought my advice on strategic matters in our weekly sessions, I gave it to her, and she ignored it. Perhaps she considered me of more value, as my sister was the queen of a potential ally. Or maybe she was just biding her time.

Either way, I remained on guard.

"Did you want to discuss something with me?" I asked, as politely as I could.

"Oh, yes, of course." She handed me a thick stack of papers. "I reviewed these requests for waivers and none of them seem truly in need. They're all denied."

I took the stack, a half-smile of disbelief on my face. Within them were shippers who'd been loyal to the Forcadelian crown for generations, and even some who had helped ferry Ilara's own forces into the city.

"Your Majesty," I began slowly. "There are some excellent cases in here. People whose very livelihood depends on earning an income from what they transport. Surely, we can allow some of them to dock in port and unload their wares?"

"If they wish to unload, they can do it in the east," she said. "Do the people out there not need to eat as well?"

It wasn't about feeding Severians; it was about economy. One shipload of food could net a shipper a hundred gold coins—more than enough to pay for the trip. But if they were returning with nothing but Severian glass, worth a fraction of the cost, they would soon run out of money to fund their operations. Already half a dozen shipping companies—some spanning generations—had gone out of business.

"I worry that we're squeezing the life out of our merchants," I said softly.

"It's merely a change," Ilara said, rising to her feet. "Soon all will be revealed. I promise you that."

But I don't trust you. For Felix, however, I would have to pretend otherwise.

"As you wish, Your Majesty."

My mind was heavy at the end of every day, weary of watching my tongue and thoughts, filled with anxiety for my best friend and fear for my adopted homeland. Unanswered questions about what the future held echoed incessantly.

But all of that seemed to ebb away when I opened the door to my suite of rooms and found my love waiting for me.

Beata grinned when she saw me, popping up from the settee and rushing over to greet me formally. A Forcadelian beauty, her dark hair had already been let down from the tight braid she kept it in, and her eyes, the color of dark pools, were framed by the longest lashes I'd ever seen on a woman. Although I was a head taller than her, I fell into her arms, pressing my face into her neck and inhaling her sweet scent. Everything I'd been holding back came rushing to the forefront, then disappeared in her embrace like mist in the sun.

"It will get better," Beata whispered, unpinning my hair and letting it tumble down my back.

"It's just so absurd," I said, straightening. "I speak about Brynna and August as if Ilara wasn't the one who'd killed them."

It pained me not to tell Beata that Brynna was alive, but Felix had made me promise. And although I trusted her with my life, we had trusted others. And Brynna's secret was too precious to gamble.

Beata brushed the hair from my forehead. "I've made some tea. You haven't been sleeping, and if you aren't at your best, you may..." She bit her pink lip.

"I will try to relax tonight," I said, resting my head on her shoulder. My eyes grew heavy and my pulse slowed. I slid my hand on her knee and she covered it with hers. "I promise—"

A knock at the door jarred us both from our stupor. Beata gave me a panicked look, but I patted her knee and rose. "It's probably a servant."

I gathered my hair into a makeshift braid and opened the large door.

"I don't..." The words died on my tongue. Felix stood before me—no, not Felix. His younger cousin, Jorad, a man who'd been assigned to Neveri with Riya. My heart raced in my chest as a thousand scenarios dashed through my mind.

"Your Ladyship," he said, bowing. "Miss Beata."

"What are you doing here?" Beata asked, joining us at the door.

Jorad pressed his finger to his lips and stepped inside. "I'm here to take you two out of the castle."

"I'm sorry, what?" Beata said beside me. "On whose authority?"

He grinned and flashed the Forcadelian seal under his hand. "Princess Brynna."

My knees grew weak as I braced myself on the door. Brynna was not only alive, but she'd made contact with the soldiers in

Neveri. My hopes, which had been so far in the darkness, lifted slightly.

"That's a terrible joke," Beata said beside me, mistaking my relief for horror. "Jorad Llobrega, your cousin would have you flogged within an inch of your life if he heard you carrying on this way."

"Bea," I said, giving her a look. "It's the truth. Brynna's alive."

Just like that, she turned her formidable ire on me, her cheeks growing ruddy. "Ex*cuse* me? You *knew*? And you didn't *tell* me?"

"We can discuss this later," Jorad said. "I only have a few minutes before the next shift and—"

"I'm not going."

The words tumbled from my mouth as the thought echoed through my brain. Brynna still needed my help. I could still gather intelligence about Ilara's weaknesses and plans. And I couldn't even dream about leaving Felix behind.

"You go," I said to Beata. "Go to Brynna and help her."

She spun on her heel. "I'm not going without you."

I took her hands in mine as Jorad turned away to give us privacy. "Bea, I have some measure of immunity from Ilara right now. But you? She could use you against me if she had a mind to. It's better that you get far away from her."

"She could use you against Brynna, as well," Beata replied pointedly.

"No, not if you go," I said softly. "If Ilara is to trust me, she has to believe I've been forsaken by all whom I love. Felix is in the dungeon, and my love has run to Brynna's side." A tear leaked down my face. "She has to believe I'm without allies and at her mercy."

"And you will be," Beata said. "She's unpredictable, Kat."

"She doesn't always make the most obvious decisions, but I know her." I brushed the hair off her cheek. "I can make her believe me, I swear to you. And whatever new information I can glean from Ilara, I will bring to you when...when I find a way to get Felix out."

"And what if you don't?" Beata asked, a tear leaking down her cheek. "What if Ilara doesn't believe you and you end up down there with him? Kat, I don't know what I'd do if—"

"Do you trust me?" I asked her.

She opened her mouth, her soft lips opening in surprise. "Of course I do, but I don't trust her."

"Trust me when I say this is the best place for me. As I trust that you'll help Brynna as well as you can." I cupped her face. "Please, I'm begging you. Go."

Beata covered my hands with hers, sending warmth from my fingertips to my toes. She closed her dark brown eyes, allowing a few tears to leak out. But when she opened them again, there was determination in her gaze.

"If you don't return to me, Katarine, I will be most cross with you," she said.

"And if you don't leave right now, Beata, I will be most cross with *you*," I replied with a watery laugh. "I love you with everything I have."

She stood on her tiptoes to capture my lips. "I will see you very soon."

"I'm counting the days," I said.

Jorad cleared his throat loudly. "I hate to break this up, but we really must get moving."

I helped Beata quickly gather her most personal effects—her mother's silk petticoat, her father's compass—and pack them in a bag. All the while, her eyes were wet and her lip trembled. I couldn't look at her, in danger of falling to pieces myself. But I needed to be strong for her, or she wouldn't leave.

She disappeared into the back and Jorad came up beside me.

"Her Highness won't be happy that you stayed. She was counting on your strategic help, now that your brother has returned to Niemen."

As much as I wanted to know every detail of Brynna's journey, I held up my hand. "Tell me nothing more. It's hard enough to keep my tongue." I paused, chewing my lip. "But do pass along my love for her. And please...just tell her to trust me. This is the best place for me right now."

"I will." Jorad nodded. "And I swear that Beata will arrive safely and remain out of harm's way until you two are reunited." His eyes flashed as he turned away. "I only hope you'll be able to keep Ilara from hurting my cousin too much."

"He was proud to be led to the dungeons," I replied with a half-smile. "It was the least he could do for his country."

When the coast was clear, Beata led Jorad to the hidden servant's door across the hall. She paused, only briefly, to give me a final look, then she was gone. I shut my door and leaned against it, holding my aching chest as tears leaked down my face.

Then, with a deep breath, I steadied myself. There was no time for tears. I had work to do.

Chapter Three

Jax paid for a room on the first floor, and I was able to climb in through the window to avoid being seen. Jax took one of the two beds in the room, and I gave Elisha the other, knowing I was too jittery to fall asleep. After sitting there for a few minutes, I couldn't take the silence. Carefully, I opened the window and crawled out onto the streets again, then used a nearby stack of crates to climb to the top of the inn. The city of Forcadel was a dark mountain in the distance, but even without light, I knew it intimately.

Thick, high walls surrounded the capital and two rivers flanked it on either side, depositing into a large bay that was heavily protected to the south. It was the perfect capital for trade, and nearly impenetrable. For centuries, kings and queens had tried, and Forcadel had always been victorious.

Until one dumb idiot decided to let Ilara in the front door. I doubted she'd offer me the same courtesy.

But that seemed to be my only move. If we tried a full-frontal assault on the city, we would most assuredly fail—and all the soldiers who'd given up everything to follow me would be slaughtered.

I ran my hands across my face, allowing the perfect storm of worry to batter my consciousness. Felix was in the dungeons, Katarine perhaps not too far behind him. The city was being destroyed by someone with ond, perhaps. Ilara had done nothing except make matters worse by closing the borders to trade. And I, the only person who could solve all these problems, was sitting on a rooftop, unsure what to do next.

Conquering Neveri had been a confluence of dumb luck and Luard's brilliance, both of which I no longer had. Katarine's mischievous brother, who'd always been around to kick me back on track, had returned to Niemen with his soldiers, and I wasn't sure when or if I'd see him again. I could've guessed what he'd say —get back to my troops and be a queen. But it was easier to hide out on rooftops, especially when I had no idea how to tackle the mountain at hand.

Movement on the road below caught my eye. My heart fluttered to my throat as I scrambled over rooftops, catching the three figures as they came into the stables behind the inn.

"Psst!" I called, walking through the hall. "Jorad?"

The figures appeared in the moonlight, but the smaller one broke free, rushing toward me with wet cheeks.

"*Brynna!*"

A second before she slammed into me, I recognized Beata's face in the scant light. I hadn't seen her since before Ilara had invaded —and based on her reaction, she hadn't known I was alive.

"You're really here," she said, gripping my face so tightly it was painful.

"I am," I said, unable to keep from smiling. "It's so wonderful to see you and..." My gaze slid behind her, but there was no one else. "Jorad..."

"She wouldn't come," he said, taking a step forward. "I'm sorry."

My arms slackened around Beata. "W-what? You told her that I needed her out of the city, didn't you?"

"He did, and she still... She wouldn't... She said she wasn't going," Beata whispered. "She said it was better if she stayed behind to keep an eye on Felix. And...well..." She dropped her voice. "To keep tabs on the queen."

"That wasn't the plan," I said, throwing a dirty look at Jorad.

"The plan had to change," Aline said, appearing by his side. "When we got there, we found out that Captain Llobrega had been arrested for treason. Nearly all the soldiers in the castle are Severian. Jorad was only just able to get inside the castle by claiming he'd left something in his barracks."

I rolled my eyes. *Amateurs.* "There are other ways inside the castle."

"But not to the dungeons," Jorad said. "I know it's hard to admit, but Captain Llobrega...he's a lost cause."

"And Kat told you to trust her," Beata said.

I scowled at all three of them, unwilling to admit they were right.

"Your Majesty, if I may," Aline said. "Perhaps it's time to return to the rest of the soldiers. You left them with nothing but vague direction. We should plan for our strike against Ilara, especially since she doesn't know you're alive, nor does she know that you have an army."

"I'm not ready to make a move against her yet," I said, buying myself some time. "Besides that, I need the Kulkan and Niemenian armies ready to assist. I'm sure Luard's just now arrived in Linden."

Jorad nodded. "Then we should get out of the city. Return to the camp and prepare. We can send riders to Skorsa and Neveri to make contact and open lines of communication."

"Yes, do all that," I said. "Take Beata with you to the northern camp. She'll be safe there. Perhaps even see if you can get her passage to Linden. Ariadna would be glad to have her until this is all over." I straightened my spine. "And I'm staying here."

Jorad and Aline shared a look. "But Your Majesty—"

"Someone is blowing holes in my city," I said. "They framed Felix for it, but I'm going to find out who it really is. And along the way, I'll get a good look at Forcadel's defenses and where Ilara's putting her soldiers. We'll need all of that."

"We can find that out for you," Jorad said.

"You won't even know what you're looking for," I said. "You are soldiers. I'm a vigilante. This is what I do."

"This idea is unimaginably risky," Jorad said. "You need to return with us to the camp. It's safer there, and we can come up with a strategy to defeat Ilara. If you stay here, Ilara could catch you. If that happens, it's all over." He licked his lips. "I know you care for Felix, but I'm not sure you're thinking with your right mind."

"I said nothing about Felix," I snapped, grateful the night hid my blushing. "You're right, he's a lost cause. And Katarine said to trust her. So that's what I'm doing. But I also know this city better than any of you. So give me a few weeks."

"You can't go in there alone," Jorad said.

"I'll have Jax and Elisha with me."

"With all due respect," Jorad said, "he's a criminal."

"And with all due respect," I said, turning on him, "so am I."

Aline and Jorad looked behind them to where Beata stood, as if asking for her help. She just shrugged. "I thought she was dead until about two hours ago. You're on your own."

"Jorad," Aline said, after a moment. "I'm sure Her Majesty knows her limits. We can take Beata to the camp and be back within a few days. Jax and Elisha have proven to be excellent guides. I feel confident that Her Majesty is in good hands."

Jorad made a face that was too similar to Felix's, but he

nodded. "Fine. Just please...be careful."

I turned to Beata and took her hands in mine. "I wish we had more time to catch up," I said. "But I'll be back up to the camp soon."

"I'm sure I'll find some way to keep myself busy until then," she said, kissing my hands. "I'm so glad you're alive, Brynna. You don't know how much hope you've given me."

And when I delivered Felix and Katarine to her, I would give her so much more.

I walked them to the edge of the small city then gave Beata a long, firm hug before sending them off. Jorad kept his objections to a silent scowl, and Aline promised they would return soon. They disappeared over the pink horizon, and I headed back toward the village.

Obviously, I wasn't giving up on Felix and Katarine. Jorad might've thought his cousin was a lost cause, but I had made my name getting in and out of tricky situations. Besides that, I knew more about the castle than anyone. And what I didn't know, I could find out quickly.

I climbed through the window of our rented room then made a beeline for my pile of things on the floor.

"Where are you going?" Jax said, watching me with one eye open.

"To Forcadel," I said. "Clearly, I'm the only one who can get anything done around here." I tossed his still-full bag onto the bed. "You're coming, too. Help me get inside."

He kicked the bag onto the floor. "Didn't you manage it before?"

No, I'd fallen into the river and nearly drowned before swimming to the docks. But I wasn't going to tell him that. "Cut the crap. You're still here, which means you still work for me. So tell me how Celia gets in and out of the city."

"I know!" Elisha said, sitting up.

"Shaddup," Jax snapped. "You don't know nothing."

"I hear things," Elisha said with a sneer. "There's a grate on the eastern side of the city that's big enough for a few people to get through. Not enough for product, but people. That's what Locke said when he came back from the city a few weeks ago."

"Well, at least one of you is useful," I said, eyeing Jax. "Can you show me the way?"

"I can try." She beamed.

"I know the way," Jax said, kicking the covers off and reaching for his boots. "At least if I go, we won't get caught trying to get in."

Elisha melted a little, clearly afraid she was going to be left behind. "But—"

"When we get there," I said to her, and she perked right back up, "I need you to listen very carefully and do exactly as I say, understand?"

"Yes, ma'am," she said with a nod. "But will I get to do any fighting this time?"

"If I can help it, none of us will," I said.

Jax snorted. "I'll believe that when I see it."

Chapter Four

With the high city walls and dark castle, Forcadel was almost invisible against the cloudy sky. Jax, Elisha, and I kept close to the Vanhoja river rushing from Neveri toward the bay. The last time I'd attempted to break into the city, I'd fallen into that river and nearly drowned. I hoped Jax had a better way.

"Are you sure you know where you're going?" I asked as the space between the city wall and the river narrowed.

"No, I don't," he said, stopping in front of a large boulder. "I'm just fumbling through the dark and hoping I find something."

Elisha cackled, but quieted with a look from me.

Jax leaned down and tugged at the rock, which was smoother than I'd thought previously. "See?" He pulled the grate from the rock, revealing a thin opening I'd have to crouch to walk through.

"How does Celia get stuff into the city through here?" I said, peering into the hole.

"Very slowly." He gestured to the gate. "Are we going to stand around here all day or are we going inside?"

"And you're sure nobody will be on the other side?" I asked. "They aren't guarding this?"

"Not yet, but you know, every day's a surprise," he said, his teeth glinting in the low light.

For his smart remark, I made him go first, and when he motioned that the coast was clear, Elisha and I filed out. From the buildings, I recognized Merchant's Row, the middle-class section of Forcadel.

"The Severian patrols do a tight round in this section of the city, so we need to get moving," Jax said.

"To the roofs?" I asked.

He sighed heavily. "Why? Why can't we just walk on the streets like normal people?"

"It's efficient for keeping out of sight," I snapped back, walking past him and finding a stack of crates. I pulled myself up, showing Elisha where to set her feet. After some loud grunting, Jax joined us and we kept toward the city center.

I moved with ease, reacclimatizing to the feeling of being in the city I'd once called home. Climbing the snow-capped mountains of Niemen and walking through never-ending fields in Kulka had made me realize just how much I loved the salty, muggy air, the roads, the buildings, the people.

"Oi!" Jax whispered harshly behind me. "Slow down, will you? I can't keep up!"

"I think he's just dragging his feet," Elisha said beside me. "He can move faster than this. I've seen him."

"Perhaps," I said, hiding a smile.

"What happened over there?" she asked, pointing at what should've been another building.

My brow furrowed, and I walked to the edge of the roof, staring down into rubble. My first instinct was that it had been destroyed during Ilara's invasion, but it was too far from the water.

This must've been one of the casualties of the ond attack.

A hot surge of anger rushed through me. Someone in this city —a Forcadelian, most likely—had killed their own countrymen. And for what? What had killing Forcadelians done for their cause?

You also sacrificed forty-two countrymen in Neveri.

That serpentine voice slithered around in my mind, and the weight of the pendant at my neck grew heavy again.

"Well?" Elisha asked, drawing me from my thoughts. "What happened here?"

"Ond happened," Jax said, wiping his brow. "But I saw a couple Severians nearby. It's gonna be hard to avoid them if we keep stopping like this."

I nodded. "We're almost there."

We came to the Forcadel town square, the center of life and activity in the capital. In the morning, it would be filled with vendors and farmers selling everything from clothes to baked goods. Beyond the square, the castle loomed in the darkness. Lights flickered from some of the windows, but most of it disappeared into the night. By instinct, I searched for the tallest tower, where Felix had imprisoned me so many weeks ago.

My gaze drifted down to the high walls that protected the castle from the rest of the city. There were secret passages all over, connecting royal rooms to servants' halls. But to my knowledge, there was only one secret exit—and based on the two guards standing next to the door leading out to the gardens, I supposed it was no longer that secret.

I came to the side of the church and the bell tower. A section of wood covered a rickety door, revealing the entrance to my secret Veil lair.

"And we're sure nobody's gonna be there waiting for us?" Jax asked as we ascended the dark stairs.

"No, we're not sure," I said. "But that's why I've got two fighters with me."

He made a noise. "One-and-a-half."

"Hey!" Elisha cried.

"Ssh," I said. "The sisters may not come up this way, but your voices echo."

When I lit the lamp at the top, the soft glow illuminated a mostly-empty space. A few trunks were open, but other than that, it was empty. I hadn't expected Felix to do much, but some part of me wished he'd made his own Nestori contacts in the city.

"Spacious," Jax said, brushing by me. "Which piece of hard floor is my bed?"

"Pick your favorite," I said, settling down and yawning. "In the morning, we'll—"

I was answered by his loud snoring.

"He's an ass," Elisha said, covering herself up with her threadbare cloak. "Goodnight."

"Night," I said.

I waited until I heard her soft breathing before opening my eyes again. At the top of the bell tower, the faintest bit of sky could be seen. It was still dark, but growing pinker.

Silently, I sat up and watched Jax and Elisha, but they didn't stir. They wouldn't notice my being gone for an hour or two. So with care, I grabbed a few things from the mostly-empty trunks and crept down the stairs.

If I was going to retrieve Katarine and Felix, I needed to know how to get in and out of the castle without being seen—and for that, I needed the castle schematics. I'd seen them only once, and I wanted a refresher on the litany of secret entrances, hallways, and doors—some of which had been unknown to anyone except for me. It was housed under lock and key in the archives.

This effort might've been easier with Jax and Elisha, but I wasn't sure they could be trusted. After all, Jax still worked for

Celia and telling her there was a detailed map to get to my royal bedroom seemed like a bad idea.

The building was a short walk from the church on the other side of the square. Two large, oak doors met me—formidable and immovable. But with a little work, the front door lock turned over with relative ease. I came into a large, dark room filled with books, some of which Katarine had used to instruct me on the history of the country. The map of the castle would be further in the back, behind yet another locked door. So I bypassed the books and kept walking toward a back hallway.

I froze at the soft clearing of a throat, and I reached for my knife. But the sound had come from the front, not the back, and as I peered around the corner, I found the source—a Severian guard standing in front of the archivist's office.

At least he was alone, which was good. I reached into my slingbag and attached a small bag of knockout powder to one of my arrows on my crossbow. Then, with another glance around the corner, I aimed and fired the arrow to just above his head.

The bag ripped and the powder fell on top of him. He blinked for a moment, then slumped to the ground. I had about half an hour before he woke up, but I wanted to be long gone by that point. The door was loud as I scraped it open, but clearly no one else was in the building.

I dug through the archivist's desk, finding maps of the city and requests for books from Katarine, but no map of the castle.

I paced the room, opening every drawer and cupboard and finding no other maps. The castle schematics were a highly secured state secret, so perhaps it had been silly to think it would've just been sitting out.

I sat down on the archivist's chair and rolled the chair over the wood. To my ears, it was solid, until I heard the faintest echo. Near the brass wheel was the smallest hinge.

"There you are," I said, pushing the chair out of the way and kneeling down. But the end of the board was under the corner of the desk, probably on purpose.

Hoping that the knockout powder was still working its magic, I braced myself against the desk and pushed hard. It was solid wood, but with some effort, it scraped forward just enough to allow me to pop up the loose plank, revealing a small alcove.

There, I found an assortment of books—including a description of the defenses of Forcadel, which I happily stashed in my slingbag—and, as I'd hoped, the map of the castle I'd seen before.

With care, I unfurled it onto the archivist's desk. I put my finger on the secret entrances to the royal chambers. It would be so easy to slip in and kill Ilara. But that wasn't the ending I wanted for her—not yet, anyway—and it wouldn't remove the hundreds of Severian soldiers swarming my city. Besides that, I didn't know if she knew this map existed. If she did, she might've already placed soldiers at the royal bedchambers.

I shook myself and refocused on my original task. I ran my finger along the edges of the castle walls, praying to the Mother she would guide my gaze to the right spot. There was the main entrance, the gate entrance, but every other wall was solid.

There.

I blinked, rubbing the sleep out of my eyes. I had missed it the first time because it was a faint mark, almost an errant scratch on the page. But when I brought the paper close to my nose, there was very clearly a small door behind the barracks.

It wasn't incredibly helpful, though. From the barracks to the kitchen was about two hundred feet of open greenery usually filled with drilling soldiers. Crossing it would be difficult, but it appeared my only option.

The guard moaned on the other side of the door. My time was running short.

If I took the map with me, someone might sound the alarm

that it was gone. So I grabbed a spare quill and a piece of parchment and began sketching my own version, adding just enough detail that I'd know what it was, but if it fell into the wrong hands, someone else wouldn't be able to decipher it.

Then, quickly, I replaced the floorboard and pushed the desk back into place. Everything else, I righted as if I hadn't been there —even the guard, who I hoisted back onto his chair. I gathered the evidence of the knockout powder, including the arrow and bag, and dashed around the corner, waiting for him to awaken fully.

He blinked a few times and rubbed his eyes then jumped to attention, as if realizing he'd fallen asleep on duty.

I slipped out of the archive with the map and a smirk.

Chapter Five

There was a gloomy, overcast sky, but a definite warmth to the city when I awoke the next morning. Winter in Forcadel consisted of long stretches of balmy weather and the occasional rain to wash the mugginess away. Down below, the town square was fairly busy, although there seemed to be more soldiers than people.

"Good morning," Elisha mumbled, sitting up with her dark hair in tangles. "Or is it afternoon?"

"Midday," I said, gazing down at the town square. "Feel like getting us some food?"

She nodded and took a silver. From above, I watched her dart through the vendors and talk to a few of them before coming back to the tower. Although there were Severian guards in the square, none of them paid her any attention. One of the perks of having a child spy.

"A silver wasn't enough," Elisha said when she came back to the top of the stairs. "So I had to steal a loaf."

"It should've been enough," I said with a frown.

"Not with Ilara's new edicts," Jax said, eyes still closed. "You saw how bad things were in Neveri. They're worse here."

I shook my head. "Today, I want the two of you to patrol the town. Find out what you can about all of this—the merchants, the edicts. All of my knowledge of the city is at least half a year old. Help me get up to speed."

"And you're just going to...what? Stay here?" Jax quirked a brow. "Since when?"

"Since I promised Jorad and Aline I'd stay out of trouble," I replied with a sweet smile.

Jax didn't believe me, but he and Elisha left anyway. Once their footsteps died down, I uncovered a pair of sticky gloves underneath a floorboard. I used them to climb the wooden wall up to the top of the bell tower, where I could look over the city without being seen. Down below, Jax and Elisha made their way out into the city square, and I cracked a smile. Suckers.

I settled myself onto the ledge and gazed out into the city. In the daylight, Forcadel was beautiful. Buildings of all different sizes and shapes rose from the cobblestone streets. People walked to and fro. The bay glistened in the sunlight. I had seen some magnificent things in my journey through Niemen and Kulka, but nothing compared to this view. Nothing compared to home.

A fine-looking carriage rolled out of Mariner's Row, pulled by two cream-colored horses. They trotted around the perimeter of the market square before pulling to a stop at the foot of the tower in which I sat. When the door opened, a woman stepped out.

My mouth opened a little; was that Councilwoman Vernice? She was still in town? And by the looks of it, still the proud owner of her title.

I quickly climbed down the wall, landing in a crouch on the floor. I took the stairs two-by-two down to the bottom of the stairwell but didn't continue out into the street. There was a small door in the shadows that led to a hallway. One way led to Mother Fishen's apartment, and the other, along this very wall, into the confessionals. If Vernice was coming to the chapel at this hour, she was surely in need of some guidance.

And if she were amenable, she might help me get inside the castle.

With care, I pushed open the door leading out to the main nave. Vernice was sitting in the front row, her head bowed in prayer.

I hadn't seen her since the day Ilara invaded. She'd lost her rosy, round cheeks and perfectly styled hair, and her dress looked a little less new and fashionable. Her lips, which had been a shade of vibrant purple the first time I met her, were a dull pink, giving her the appearance of a much older woman. But she still looked like a Councilwoman, so it appeared she'd taken the same path as Katarine: trying to make Ilara into a better queen for the benefit of Forcadel.

I closed the door just as her eyes darted up. Through the mesh on the door, I watched her stand and walk to the other side of the confessional. The door unlocked and she stepped inside.

"Mother, are you there?" she whispered.

I swallowed, unsure what to do or say. Being there under false pretenses seemed like a spiritual bridge too far for me. But at the same time, perhaps I could learn something from Vernice that I couldn't anywhere else.

Mother, forgive me. "I am one of the sisters," I said, lowering my voice. "Mother Fishen sends her apologies."

"It is just as well," Vernice said. "I suppose I need someone to talk to."

"Then speak," I said.

"I'm torn," she began. "It's only by the Mother's grace that Ilara hasn't made a terrible decision that's plunged us deeper into war. But I suspect it's a matter of time. She's ordered the merchants to bypass the city entirely. Now goods and food will go directly to Severia, leaving very little for us. That, I fear, is why the usurpers attacked the merchants they did. They were hoping to disrupt this new edict." She sighed. "Unfortunately, Ilara's undeterred. If the merchants refuse, she'll commandeer their vessels and throw them in the dungeons."

I couldn't help the groan of misery that came from my lips. Through the mesh, Vernice shifted.

"Please, continue," I said.

"My brother in Kulka has begged me to come to him, to live in the guest cottage on his property." She smiled, sitting back. "It was the farm where I spent my summers as a girl. He inherited it from our great uncle. Beautiful land, lush with apples and berries. Horses running wild. It's magnificent."

"And far away from the turmoil of Forcadel," I finished for her. "Why haven't you left yet?"

"Because my duty is to my kingdom," she said. "I thought it would be no different than when Brynna was in charge. A young, brash woman who needed a little guidance."

"You call what you did to me guidance?" I snapped before I could stop myself.

Vernice gasped and turned to the grate. "I'm...sorry?"

"I meant what you did to the princess." I winced, cursing myself for being so careless. "She spoke to me often about you. Said you were harsh and untrusting. Doubted that she was even the real princess."

"I never thought that in my life," Vernice said, and I couldn't help but roll my eyes. "She was a little rough around the edges, sure, but I knew she wanted what was best. She just didn't know what that was. And unfortunately, none of us could see the impending invasion coming."

I seem to remember you telling me to kick Ilara out a number of times. "What do you think is best for your country? To stay and try to sway Ilara until she forces you out, or just go now?"

"Stay," she said. "But it's hard. I'm scared for myself. I don't want to end up like Garwood."

I jumped. "Garwood? What's happened to Garwood?"

"Surely you heard? He refused to submit to Ilara and she had him thrown in jail." She exhaled softly. "His days are numbered."

"She's going to have him executed?"

"She'll let the conditions in the dungeon take care of that," she said. "He hasn't seen the light of day in months, let alone had proper medical care. He's not the youngest man either, not like Captain Llobrega." She paused, fussing with her hands. "Lady Katarine insists that poor Felix has had a mental break, what with losing August and Brynna so close together. I don't know how she maintains her stoicism. Must be the frigid northern climate where she was born."

I sat back, chewing my lip. Garwood was down there with Felix, and had been this whole time. He was my mother's brother, and while we weren't exactly close, he'd been a stalwart ally. But he'd sacrificed everything for me—his house, his husband, and possibly his life. And Felix seemed bound and determined to do the same. It was all so unnecessary.

I didn't care about the cost—I'd get all three of them out. Today.

"Stay," I said after a long pause. "Stay and fight for this country. You've still got some sway with Ilara, clearly, so you should use it until there's no more left. The citizenry need you to temper her."

"If I can."

"You must," I said. "All we can do is the best with what we have. And hope the Mother judges us fairly."

She nodded. "Thank you, Sister, for your guidance. I will return to the castle."

And so would I.

After leaving the confessional, I kept to the side streets around the church, my gaze focused on the ground. I left the town square and continued along the perimeter of the castle, avoiding Severian patrols. I'd only have a few minutes to test the wall, so once the soldiers turned the corner, I darted across the street. I moved quickly, running my fingers along the rough, bumpy plaster, inspecting every crack to see if it hid something more. A brief flicker of fear echoed in my chest as I considered maybe they'd bricked over the wall.

But then, as I'd almost given up hope, something moved under my palms. A false door opened just wide enough for me to slip through. Something thorny dug into my pant leg, and I received a spiderweb to the face, but I shut the door behind me and exhaled softly.

My eyes adjusted to the different light. I'd squeezed myself in-between the wall and the barracks. Placing my feet surely, I moved toward the end of the building. Soldiers were drilling on the green, nothing new—except that they weren't Forcadelian. They were Severian soldiers with Severian colors. I could picture Felix standing where the Severian lieutenant was, barking orders to his troops.

I waited until they started their jog around the castle to move, crossing the green toward the kitchens and keeping my head down. My breath came in short spurts until my hand touched the kitchen doorknob. But to my horror, it turned over in my hand.

Thinking quickly, I ducked out of sight behind a nearby bush as a maid came walking out with a basket full of refuse. She didn't see me, too preoccupied with balancing the basket of smelly bones and rotting meat on her hip to be mindful of anything else. I didn't recognize her from my time in the castle, but she seemed Forcadelian, so she'd probably recognize me.

However, she was about my size.

I stalked her as she headed toward the refuse pile on the eastern side of the castle. Keeping an eye out for the jogging cadets, I waited until she came to the back of the castle—near another drainage grate—and dumped the trash before I knocked her out with powder.

"Sorry," I whispered as she slumped over. I undressed her, leaving my cloak to cover her while she slept. Then, smoothing the lines of my dress, I walked confidently toward the kitchen door.

Walking the halls of the castle brought forth a rush of memories, none of them warm. I'd never felt at home here, not as a girl, not as a woman, and definitely not now. Still, it was hard not to feel nostalgic, remembering conversations with Katarine and slipping through secret hallways with Felix as I left for my vigilante activities.

But memories could wait; I was in an open hallway with a recognizable face. Twice, I had to duck behind a pillar to avoid being seen by passing guards or maids.

I turned the corner to find the dungeon door about a hundred feet away from me and two guards out front. I passed by them, glancing at the door out of the corner of my eye, and kept walking until I turned the corner and waited.

"...not sure this is suitable. It's dirty and dangerous down there."

"I appreciate your concern, but it's Felix."

My heart stopped in my chest as familiar voices echoed down the hall. Ilara and Katarine, arm in arm, were headed straight toward me, deep in conversation.

I turned, spotting a bucket next to a painting, perhaps where a maid had left it, and grabbed the rag, dunking it in the gray water and scrubbing the gold frame of the nearest painting.

Chapter Six

Katarine

It was hard to balance both joy and fear as Ilara walked me down to the dungeons. I could scarcely believe she'd granted my request to see him during our daily walk through the gardens. From what I'd heard, the guards hadn't been able to find out a thing from him, and I'd convinced Ilara that, as his best friend, I might have sway where others didn't.

"I do hope you can get through to him," Ilara said. "It pains me to see him down there. Then again, I suppose you've not had much luck convincing your sister."

There it is. "I have sent her yet another letter requesting her to reconsider your stance. I have done everything I can to convince her. Forcadel and Niemen used to be such close allies."

"Perhaps it's time to make an in-person plea," she said. "Perhaps you can send Beata."

My pulse sped up. It was the first time we'd broached the topic of Beata since she'd left in the middle of the night, but I had been spreading rumors through the wait staff. I was just surprised it took her this long to bring it up.

Ilara jumped at my silence. "Is there something the matter?"

"Nothing that needs your attention." I offered her a fake smile, knowing she could see right through it. "I'm sure Beata will be happy to act as your official envoy once she returns from... wherever she went to."

"She...left?" Ilara stopped in her tracks. "Why?"

I cleared my throat, allowing the pain of her leaving to come to the forefront. I was honestly distraught, and I could use that to convince Ilara.

"I don't know, really," I began softly. "We did not part well."

"Oh, I'm so sorry to hear that," Ilara said, turning to me fully. "You two seemed so very happy."

I nodded and covered her hand with mine. "I'm sure she'll be back soon and we'll be mended. But our parting conversation has left me a little..." I forced a watery smile onto my face. "Unseemly."

"You know you can talk to me about whatever you like," Ilara said. I almost believed her. Since she'd unceremoniously announced our relationship to the court, she'd been heavily invested in it. At times, I thought her concern and interest genuine. But it was hard to reconcile that with what I knew about her manipulative nature.

"I didn't wish to burden you with my romantic troubles," I said. "Especially as I'm sure they'll be resolved on her return."

"Do you know where she went?" Ilara asked.

At that, I hesitated, as I'd practiced. "That was...the source of our disagreement. She wanted me to go with her but wouldn't tell me where we were going. I fear there's something..."

Ilara's gaze bored into me. "That's odd."

"I know," I said with a small shake of my head. "She's been agitated lately, like she was hiding something from me. I thought it was just my imagination running amok, but clearly..." I sighed.

"Clearly, I should've listened to my instincts."

"And you've no idea where she's gone?" Ilara asked quietly.

"I wish I could tell you she was merely going to the southern shores, perhaps for a week away," I said. "But I fear that would be a lie."

She patted my hand on her arm. "I will continue to hope for the best. You two were becoming quite serious. Perhaps she's just getting cold feet."

"Perhaps," I said, swallowing my indignation at the very thought of it. "But I won't trouble you with more of this conversation. Not when you've given me something to be so joyful about."

Ilara gazed at the dungeon door. "For his sake, Katarine, I hope he gives you something useful."

When the dungeon door slammed shut behind me, I jumped a little. My nerves were already on edge from a restless night, worry about Beata heavy on my mind. It had been made painfully clear that Felix's time was running out—and mine, perhaps, was too.

As I reached the bottom of the dark staircase, I was overcome with the smell of human excrement and Mother knows what else. I'd never been down here, not even when August, Felix, and I were rebellious teenagers in search of thrills. This was reserved for true traitors to the crown, however few of them there had been before Ilara took over.

Now it seemed every cell contained at least ten people, cramped together in living situations that weren't even remotely sanitary. The torchlight reflected in the whites of their eyes, following me as I passed. No one said anything, but their animosity was palpable. I had no friends; they all thought me a traitor. But they wisely said nothing, as there were Severians posted every few feet.

"Halt," said the guard closest to me. "You can't be down here."

"I am here to see Felix."

"On whose orders?"

"The queen's," I replied with cool steel. "She's asked me to try my hand at convincing him to speak."

He grunted and rubbed his chin. For a moment, I thought he might turn me away, but instead he waved me on. It didn't escape my notice that he'd taken me at my word. Lying about Ilara's approval would work only once, so I'd save it for when I really needed it.

At the end of the hall, two guards stood in front of iron doors. One, I assumed, held Felix on the other side.

"Who's in that one?" I asked the guard.

"Garwood," he said. "Traitor."

"Yes, I'm aware." He was August and Brynna's uncle, and the only one on the Council who refused to swear fealty to Ilara. He had been down here for months now, and I feared his time was running short. "May I see him as well?"

The guard gave me a look. "You said you were here for Llobrega, not Garwood."

"Can't I see both?" I asked.

"No." He motioned to the guard on the left. "Llobrega only."

So my word did have limits. I hadn't expected the guard to allow me in, but I'd needed to know where his trust ended. "I suppose that will do."

The door to the cell opened and I walked over the threshold. Here, the disgusting scent that permeated the dungeons was more prevalent, but there was another smell—metallic. Blood.

"Felix?" I called softly.

"Kat?" He sounded weak, and my heart did a somersault in my chest.

As my eyes adjusted to the lack of light, I edged into the darkness, until my toes hit metal and I made out the shape of something sitting against the wall. I knelt, reaching out to touch the damp cloth of his shirt. His face was shrouded in darkness—no…it was covered in purple bruises. His eyes seemed swollen shut, or nearly shut, and blood oozed from his nose and lip.

"Oh, Felix," I whispered, the sight of him breaking down the wall that I'd built up. "Felix, what have they done to you?"

"They tried to do something to me," he said, cracking a wry grin that seemed tinged with pain. "They forget that I used to endure worse from the castle guard in training."

A lie, if I'd ever heard one. I'd never seen Felix earn a single lash. I brushed my fingers along his grimy forehead, lifting the hair stuck there.

"What are you doing here?" he asked.

I pressed my fingers to his lips, hoping he'd know I wasn't alone. "Ilara wants me to ask you about the rebels in the city. She believes you know who they are."

He opened his other eye, casting a glance behind me. "I'm afraid I can't tell you."

"Have you considered the possibility that you don't know who did this at all? That perhaps you're just deluding yourself into thinking you met with them?"

He met my gaze again, and the corners of his mouth twitched. How lucky that he could read me like a book. "I am not delusional," he replied, turning away from me. "And I'm honestly offended you'd think me so weak."

"I can't stand to see you this way," I said, covering my mouth. "Not with Beata gone."

Felix started, concern evident on his face. "What happened to Bea?"

"She left," I said. "She said she was going to visit family, but… the way she asked me to go with her. Something's wrong, but she wouldn't tell me what it was."

He opened an eye, staring into mine, understanding dawning

on his face. I wasn't just telling him this, I was also letting the guard behind me know. "Why didn't you go?"

"I don't know. Leaving Her Majesty seems like a bad idea," I said. "And I can't leave you, Felix. Why won't you talk to me?"

Felix sighed. "Fine, I'll talk to you." He looked behind me. "But only if this guy leaves."

"No," the guard said. "I stay."

"Please," I said, turning to him with pleading eyes. "This may be my only shot to get through to him. I promise I won't tell Queen Ilara that you left me alone."

He sighed and looked behind him. "Five minutes. Then you're out."

"Oh, thank you," I said, standing and walking over to him. He refused to take my hand, instead slamming the door in my face.

"Rude."

"Be careful of your tongue or he'll lock me in here, too," I said, returning to Felix's side.

"I doubt it, not with that acting job," Felix whispered, a smile growing on his face. "I actually believed that you think I'm crazy."

"Maybe I'm the one who's crazy," I said, grateful we could speak honestly. "Coming down here the way I did. Felix, you look a mess. And you smell atrocious."

"Tell me what's happening up there," he said. "Did Beata really leave?"

"Jorad came to get us," I whispered, barely making a sound. "Our girl sent him."

"Jorad?" Felix sat up. "He's supposed to be in Neveri. And she was supposed to have gone to Niemen. What in the Mother's name is going on?"

"I don't know," I replied. "I asked him not to tell me. It'll be easier to be surprised that way."

"You should've left when you had the chance."

I made a noise. "Are you joking? And leave you here to die? I would never."

"Kat…" Felix swallowed, his throat bobbing in the dark. "I'll probably die here. And if you aren't careful, you could join me."

"I have a plan," I said with a weak smile. "I hope. But it's better for B…our girl if I remain in Ilara's good graces, at least for the moment. When I decide it's time for us to go—"

He covered my hand with his bruised and bloody one. "Then you go. Leave me."

"Tell me you aren't making things worse for yourself," I said, gingerly touching his purple eye.

"I don't see how I can be," he said with a dark chuckle. "They keep asking me the same questions about the ond attacks. You'd think they would've gotten the message the first thousand times I refused to answer."

"Felix, why are you protecting them?" I asked.

"If I don't talk," Felix said, looking at the darkness before him, "perhaps they'll be more willing to work with our girl."

"That's…" I shook my head. "You don't know that."

"I told them she was alive and they weren't interested," Felix said. "This is…this is the only thing I can do for her. I failed in everything else."

"Tell me who it is," I said. "I'll get the message to her somehow."

"I can't. The only thing I have is…" He sighed. "I just can't."

"Then give me something," I said. "Something to prove to Ilara that allowing me down here wasn't a mistake. If you won't let me help you, at least help me stay in her good graces." I licked my lips. "Please."

He closed his eyes. "There's a woman called Ruby. She's the one who put me in contact with them. Is that enough?"

"It will have to do," I said, leaning in to kiss his bruised cheek softly. He grasped my hand with his swollen one again, but his grip was weak. Some of his fingers appeared to be broken.

"If you need to leave me behind, I understand. Just tell her that I love her."

"And I'm telling you, Felix Llobrega, that I love *you* and I refuse to leave this castle without you by my side," I said, as a tear fell down my face. "We're in this together, Felix, so you might as well just get used to it."

"I think," he said with a groan, "I might have gotten the shorter end of the stick in this together business."

"Time's up," the guard said, opening the door behind us. "What'd you get from him?"

"I got that she's a stone cold bitch," Felix said, wrenching his hand from mine.

I allowed the hurt to dawn as if his words were true, and I got to my feet. "I will pray for you, Felix. And hope the Mother provides you some sense soon."

Chapter Seven

Katarine's conversation with Ilara had been enlightening, mostly because it had proven just how capable a liar she really was. She was using Beata's absence as a way to get closer to Ilara—even I felt bad for her. But if I was successful, it wouldn't matter. She and Felix would be leaving with me today.

Ilara waited by the prison door for a long time, void of the fake smiles she'd shared with Katarine. My knives sat under the maid's dress, but I didn't reach for them. Just scrubbing, scrubbing, scrubbing.

Finally, Ilara turned to leave, and I turned back toward the painting as quickly as I could, scrubbing harder with shaking hands. She stopped behind me, and for a moment, I thought I'd been made. Could she recognize me from behind? Had I accidentally turned and revealed my face?

"I think that frame is clean enough," Ilara snapped as she walked by me. "And get a new rag, that one is filthy."

Her footsteps echoed behind me and I didn't quite breathe until she was gone. I closed my eyes and said a prayer of thanks— that had been close. After a moment, I turned my attention back to the door and the two guards. I had one bag of knockout powder left; that would get me in the door. But what might I find beyond that? I could wait until Katarine came out, or I could throw caution to the wind. The guards were already eyeing me suspiciously.

The door opened and Katarine walked out, wiping tears from her face. My heart dropped into the pit of my stomach. Felix was surely dead, or close to it.

"Well?" the guard barked. "What'd he say?"

"He said that the last person he visited prior to his arrest was a woman named Ruby," Katarine said. "That might be a good place to begin an investigation."

The guard rolled his eyes and brushed past her, slamming the door behind him, but I lost my breath. Ruby? My old informant had entrapped Felix? It was insanity, but...at the same time, she had consorted with criminals like Beswick.

Katarine wiped her cheeks, losing some of that doe-eyed fear in favor of her sharper, more familiar gaze. She was playing the guards —perhaps to help Felix? I'd find out when we spoke.

But before I could catch her gaze, a hand covered my mouth and pulled me backward. I didn't fight, allowing whoever it was to pull me toward the secret entrance. Mostly because I recognized the calloused hand.

Jax released me and I stumbled forward in the darkness. "Let me do what I came here to do," I whispered at him. "She's right there. I can get her out—"

"Then what?" he asked, his voice barely above a whisper. "Barge into the prison and take on all the guards by yourself?"

"There can't be that many," I said.

"I'd tell you to go look for yourself and see if you get captured, but unfortunately, those soldiers who gave up their commissions to follow you into battle might have a problem with that." He crossed his arms over his chest.

"Five minutes, then we can go," I said, inching back toward the door. "I'll just get Katarine—"

"The Niemenian told you to let her handle it," Jax said, throwing his arm up to block my path. "She seems like a smart broad and she had the opportunity to leave. You might as well let her dig her own grave if that's what she chooses to do."

"It's not just about saving them," I said, glancing at the door again. "It's about reducing vulnerabilities. Surely you can understand that."

A whistle broke our conversation—someone was coming. I motioned for Jax to follow me into an alcove that would hide us both. We stood in the darkness as a maid wandered by, humming to herself and lost in her own world. She paused to check the bottom of her shoe, then kept walking.

"See? It's stupid for us to be here," Jax said with a disgusted shake of his head. "Get your head out of your ass and come with me."

He started walking, but I didn't follow. "I'm not leaving them, Jax. Felix is being tortured down there, and Katarine could end up in the same predicament."

"Look," he said, sighing loudly, "The Niemenian is keeping herself close to the queen because she knows it's the best place to help you." He pointed to the wall. "The captain can afford to be thrown in jail. But you? If you get caught? It's all over. Nobody left to pick up the mantle. And all those people you killed in Neveri would've died for absolutely nothing—including your friend whatshername."

"Riya," I said softly. "I'm not going to get thrown in jail, Jax."

"You were nearly made just now," he said. "It's a good thing Ilara was too busy barking orders to recognize you."

My face flushed. How long had he been watching me? And how had I not known he was there? Perhaps I was rusty.

"I'll be more careful," I said.

He rolled his eyes, as if he couldn't believe he was still doing this. "Look, you wanna be queen, right? That means you have to delegate and trust that people are gonna do what you want. They may not do it the way you wanted, but the job'll still get done. You have to believe that they know what they're doing, so that *you* can take care of the shit only a queen can take care of. Get it?"

I wasn't sure I liked this new version of Jax. "Since when did you become so perceptive?" I asked, taking a step back. "And care about what I do?"

"Celia's orders. She promised me quite a reward if I kept you from making a monumental mistake."

My jaw fell open. "*Celia*? Why in the Mother's name would she do that?"

"You got debts to pay," he said. "Debts you can only pay if you're queen. Ergo, here I am. Saving your ass when you obviously don't want to be saved and telling you things you ought to know already."

It sounded so believably like Celia. Besides Luard, Jax was the one person whose opinion I begrudgingly listened to. Even if he did insult me while delivering it.

"Fine," I said, walking toward him. "But that doesn't mean I'm giving up on Felix and Katarine. I will rescue them."

"Of course you will."

I didn't like his snide tone, but I let it slide. "In any case, it wasn't a complete waste of time. I know who Felix was speaking with before he was arrested."

"Yeah? Who?"

My gaze darkened. "Someone who's about to regret what they've done."

By the time we were able to sneak out of the castle, it was already dusk, which suited me perfectly. Knowing Ruby was even partially responsible for Felix's predicament set my blood boiling. I wanted to find out what she knew—tonight.

"If I were you, I'd take things a little more gently," Jax said, crouching beside me on the roof. "She sold out your boyfriend, but she also has information you could use."

"I know that," I snapped. Like the rest of the town, Ruby's café was closed after dark, but she was inside, cleaning. There didn't seem to be anyone else there. "Doesn't mean I can't have a little fun with her, though. Make her sweat her decision."

I made my way across the street to the alley behind her shop. With ease, I picked the lock and let myself inside the large kitchen with stone ovens and wooden tables. I padded quietly across the floor, thumbing my knife hilts at my waist, as I walked into the front of the cafe.

Ruby didn't notice me, humming to herself, so I cleared my throat. She spun, a knife appearing out of nowhere, before clattering from her hand.

"Holy Mother…"

"Glad to see you, too," I said softly. "Seems the usual crowd is a lot harder to track down these days."

"And you've got a copycat running around," she drawled, the shock leaving her face as she returned to wiping the counters. "Captain Llobrega seems to have really missed you, Princess."

I licked my lips, surprised that I was surprised she knew the truth. "Clearly, he ended up in the wrong place at the wrong time," I said, taking a threatening step forward. "Know anything about that?"

She shrugged. "He came asking questions. I can't help that you didn't tell him how to do things around here."

I dug my nails into my palm, debating continuing this line of questioning or pivoting to something more productive, as Jax had suggested. If I had a mind to, I could make Ruby regret selling Felix out. Or, if I kept my temper, I could possibly find out what he hadn't been able to. Ruby might trust me more than Felix, and that could be enough to tip the scales.

"Unfortunate," I began, walking forward toward the bar. "But as it stands, I'm back to reclaim my kingdom."

"Ah..." She shrugged. "I don't think so."

"What do you mean?" I blinked, shaking my head. "Ilara needs to go."

"Well, that's true." she turned back to the counter. "I don't think that we really want you back on the throne. Someone else, perhaps, would be better."

My heart skipped a beat. "Is that...a prevailing attitude or just yours?"

"My alliances have shifted," she said with a shrug. "Unfortunately, if you want to reclaim your kingdom, you'll have to do it alone."

Not the welcome I'd been expecting. Hadn't Felix been trying to make inroads for me? How badly had he screwed things up for them to be so ambivalent about my return?

There wasn't time to dwell on that. I needed information from Ruby, and I wasn't about to let my pride get the better of me.

"Just tell me one thing: who set the bombs in the city? And why?"

"Lots of questions," she said, getting that familiar look on her face. "Do you have coin to pay for the answers?"

I scowled at her, taking a step forward. "I don't think you understand how things are going to work around here. I ask a question, you answer. No coin, no bribes. Just you getting to keep your fingers."

She examined her nails, clearly unbothered by my threats. "I could answer your questions, or I could let the person behind all of it answer them for you. Which would you prefer?"

This is a trap, but I don't know how. "Let me talk to them."

"Bring me that person's name, and I'll arrange a meeting," she said with a shrug.

"Bring you their name? How am I supposed to find the name of the person if I..." I chuckled, understanding dawning. "It's a no-win situation. I'll only get a meeting if I know the leader's name, and I'll only know the leader's name if I've met with him." I shook my head. "Clever."

"Felix figured it out eventually," she said. "Perhaps you'll do it quicker. But until then, I'd make sure to steer clear of Mariner's Row. We've still got plenty of Niemenian ore left and it appears Queen Ilara hasn't gotten the message."

My levity evaporated. "That stuff kills people."

"Which is the point, Veil," she said harshly. "Because nothing else seems to be working."

A whistle echoed in the shop—soldiers were coming. I opened my mouth to tell Ruby so she could escape to safety, but I stopped. She'd helped me in the past, but her betrayal of Felix was unforgivable. So for now, at least, she was on her own.

"I suppose I'll just have to find someone else to talk to," I said, offering her the ghost of a smirk before disappearing through the door.

Chapter Eight

I made it out of the kitchen and up the stacked crates just as a pair of royal soldiers came running into the alley to seal the exits.

"That was close," Elisha said, crouching next to me. "Good thing I was paying attention."

"See?" I nudged her. "Lookouts are just as important."

"Were we followed?" Jax asked, looking behind us. "I don't think so."

"Maybe just bad timing," I said. "I..."

My lips parted in surprise. Coyle, one of Felix's most trusted lieutenants, stepped out of the shadows, flanked by Severian guards.

I suppose I should've known. After all, he'd been the one who'd poisoned my brother and father. And now, a shiny captain's badge glinted on his chest.

"You're under arrest for treason," Coyle called as Ruby came out flanked by two Severian guards.

"Treason?" She scoffed. "You ain't got no evidence."

"Felix Llobrega says you were the last person he spoke with before he was taken by the rebel leader," he said. "He won't give us the name of your boss, but perhaps you will."

Ruby stared daggers at him. "I don't talk to traitors."

"Put her in the carriage," he said. "Perhaps a few days underground will loosen her tongue."

The Severians tossed Ruby into an iron-barred carriage with very little ceremony. To her credit, she didn't cry out or show any sign of fear. But she'd always been tough. I just didn't realize how loyal she was to whomever she was working for.

"Guess that lead was a dead end," Jax said beside me. "What's next?"

"Maybe not," I replied, eyeing Coyle. He stood in Ruby's shop to oversee the final investigation, leaving no table overturned and no drawer not dumped out. Whatever they were hoping to find, they didn't, so they gathered in the street.

"Fan out to see if anyone else is skulking around," Coyle said. "And in the morning, I want every single neighbor and beggar questioned about what and who they saw coming in and out of here."

Six of the Severians gave him a half-hearted salute and dispersed. Two remained behind to keep watch over him, although they didn't look too enthused with their assignment.

"What are you thinking?" Jax asked.

"I'm thinking I want to have a chat with him."

"Did we not just have a long conversation about..." He exhaled loudly. "You know what? Do what you want. I'm done doling out advice for today."

And with that, he folded his arms over his chest and closed his eyes.

After failing to break either Katarine or Felix out of prison, then being deprived of the pleasure of taking revenge on Ruby, I desperately wanted to beat someone up. Perhaps I still had some hang-ups about killing people, but I had no issues with maiming and threatening people. Especially ones who so deliciously deserved it.

"Help! Help!" I cried, knocking over a pile of nearby crates with the tip of my foot.

"What was that?" Coyle asked. "You two, go check it out."

"We need to continue our patrol," said one of them.

"Fine, I'll go myself."

The other two peeled away from him, and I waited until they were almost to the end of the street before sitting up and making my way toward Coyle. I found him in the alley, lifting the overturned crates with a sour look on his face.

Gathering my cloak in my hands, I sailed off the building, the air billowing in my cape as it broke my fall. I landed in a crouch, then rose slowly, letting my fury radiate as he took me in.

"O-oh..." His eyes grew three sizes, fear evident in their depths. "You're alive."

"Indeed," I said, taking a step toward him. "You, on the other hand, may not be for much longer."

"The Veil doesn't kill," he said, inching backward.

I smiled. "She didn't. But that was before her guards betrayed her and she was forced to rethink some strategy."

In one move, I pulled my knife from its sheath and flung it at his shoulder. It sliced through his shirt, pinning him to the wall. I walked toward him, pulling the other as if to slash his throat.

"W-wait! I have information that can help you," he stammered, holding up his hands in surrender. "Please, just listen."

"How original. You're willing to sell your loyalty to save your skin," I said, sheathing my other knife. "Very well, speak."

"I know who Felix was meeting with," he said, his voice

shaking slightly. "The person who's been bombing and destroying the city."

"Oh?" I crossed my arms over my chest.

"That's why you're here, right?" He licked his lips. "Trying to pick up where Felix left off?"

"Suppose I am," I said, tilting my head to the side. "But why not share this tidbit of information with Ilara?"

"Biding my time," he said, shifting on his feet. "On the off chance that you were alive."

I quirked a brow. "That's an awfully big assumption."

"Not really. Felix might've been broken up by your death, but he wouldn't have allied himself against the crown unless he had a good reason." He shifted. "And you, Brynna, are the only thing that makes him lose his mind."

I couldn't say I believed him. It was far too convenient. "And so you held onto this information on the off chance you'd run into me again?"

He nodded. "You'll be joining forces with them, right? That's what Felix was trying to accomplish."

"You seem awfully knowledgeable about what Felix was up to," I said. "I doubt he shared any of this with you."

"He was taking a lot of meetings in the city," Coyle said. "I'm not the only one who's willing to sell their loyalty. People aren't as noble as you royals. We're all doing what we have to do to survive."

I didn't feel like arguing that point. "Who is it?"

"I need assurances that you won't kill me if I tell you," he said.

"That's rich," I said. "You asking me to show good faith."

He hesitated. "You won't get what you want otherwise."

"Here's the thing," I said slowly. "I could tell you that I won't kill you, but slice your throat anyway after you tell me what I want to know. So in the end, all you have is my word." I smiled. "And at this point, it's worth a whole hell of a lot more than yours, considering only one of us has betrayed the other. So you'd better speak before I lose my patience."

"Fine." He straightened. "Beswick. He was meeting with Beswick."

My brows knitted together. "Beswick as in...Johann Beswick?"

"The very same," Coyle said with a small, hesitant smile. "Which probably explains why he was so reluctant to accept Felix's overtures."

He was a thug, a lowlife. Why in the Mother's name would he be fomenting rebellion in the city?

"Power vacuums are dangerous things, and the wrong person with the right sway can screw everything up."

Luard's words rang true in my mind. Beswick certainly had the pull, the intellect, and the muscle to cause trouble in the city. And he had the ego to believe he should be in charge, no matter how ridiculous it sounded to my ears. But as with Ilara, he was more interested in self-enrichment, not the people's wellbeing. My people would be better served by a ruler who had their best interests at heart.

"If that'll be all..." Coyle said, inching toward the open street and tugging at his uniform.

"Oh, Coyle, that's far from all," I murmured, catching his gaze. "Because, you see, I won't kill you, but there's nothing stopping me from getting this juicy bit of information to Ilara myself— along with the fact that you also knew and kept it from her."

He swallowed. "I won't speak a word of meeting with you, I swear. She has no idea you're alive."

"I don't care if you tell her or not," I said, walking forward and pulling my knife once more. I ran the blade along his cheek, pressing just hard enough to leave a light mark but not break the skin. "What I need you to do, Lieutenant, is make sure that Felix doesn't die in that dungeon."

"I don't control the Severians—"

"I didn't ask what you control," I said, leaning in closer. "If he dies, I will dismember you, starting with the most sensitive parts." I ran my knife down his leg. "Am I clear?"

He nodded.

"Good boy." I released him from the wall and began walking away.

"I tried to help him, you know," Coyle called.

"Did you?" I squinted over my shoulder. "Like you helped me?"

"I warned him that Ilara was getting annoyed with him, had him trailed to prove he couldn't be The Veil. But he pressed on anyway." He pressed his hand to his shoulder, coming away with a thin strip of blood. "I couldn't hold her off any longer."

"And you consider that help?" I asked.

"If Ilara'd had her way, Felix, Riya, and Joella would've been strung up in the town square a week after she invaded," Coyle said. "At least now, Riya and Jo are safe in the border cities."

I flinched but recovered before he saw. I wouldn't tell him Riya's fate before I told Felix. "And you will see to it that Felix remains safe. Or else."

He nodded and took a step back. Then, like the coward he was, he scrambled out of the alley and into the dark streets.

"You look like you enjoyed that," Jax said, jumping down from the rooftop.

"It served a few purposes," I said. "Coyle's scared, I got a name, and now I get to threaten some other people."

"I doubt he's going to look after your captain," Jax said. "Sounds like he can't really do a whole lot in the castle. Those guards were making fun of him the moment they left his side. Surprised Ilara gave him the command at all."

Perhaps she valued loyalty over competence. Even though it was clear Coyle would flip the moment things went sour for him.

"Do you think he's going to tell his master that you're alive?"

I shook my head. "He's the sort of rat that keeps information like that to himself until it suits him. And Ilara's not a tyrant who'd allow him to walk after seeing me and letting me live. So his fear of her will keep his mouth shut."

"Until it doesn't."

"She's gonna find out sooner or later," I said with a shrug. "For now, we have bigger things to worry about. If Beswick's behind the ond attacks, then that means we need to find him before he kills more people."

He laughed a little. "Didn't you try that already? Failed miserably and ended up losing your kingdom in the process?"

"I'm not going to kill him," I said, my cheeks warming. "I want to talk to him. See if he's willing to work with me."

"That makes sense," Jax said. "I'm sure Beswick would love to do all this work to overthrow a queen and hand it to someone else. Especially to the little twerp who tried to gut him."

I ignored him.

Chapter Nine

"Beswick gains power through favors and alliances. So if we put pressure on the people who owe him favors, we'll get to him."

We returned to the bell tower, and I wouldn't let either Jax or Elisha get some rest. Not when I had a juicy new lead to investigate. Forward motion was still motion, even if it meant putting Felix and Katarine on hold for now.

"And how do we find those people? Knock on doors?" Jax said with a yawn.

"A few years ago, when I first started investigating Beswick, I compiled a list of all his known accomplices and business partners, " I said, walking to the wall and running my fingers along the wood. When they slid over a bump, I stopped and pulled it, revealing yet another secret hideaway—this one containing a notebook. "I'll bet you anything these people are still connected with him."

"Ilara's flushed a lot of the criminals out of the city," Jax said.

"Beswick's not one to let people just walk away, even after an invasion," I said, reading through the names and notes. "Besides that, he had as many aboveboard contacts as criminals. Some of them can't uproot their businesses and leave. I bet I can get them to talk."

"And what if he wants nothing to do with you?" Jax shrugged. "May be something to consider before you go through all this work to find him."

"I thought you were done doling out advice," I said, returning to the trunk.

"Not advice. A question."

"Then I'll make myself valuable to him," I said, after a moment. "But first we need to figure out what he's up to—and find him. Most of these are businesses, which means we'll need to investigate during the day—"

"You can't leave."

"There are hundreds of names here," I said. "You can hardly expect to go through all of them by yourselves."

"And about half the city has left for greener pastures," he said, plucking the journal from my hand. "Remember what I said the other day about delegation? This ain't something a queen needs to handle. Especially a queen everybody recognizes. Do you think you can just walk into these places and ask them what they've been up to?"

I scowled. "Well, no, but—"

"Just stay here during daylight hours," Jax said, lying down to sleep on the floor he'd claimed the night before. "Because I can only do one thing at a time—babysit you or go through this list. Your choice."

⇒————

In the end, I opted to stay behind. Jax was clearly being motivated by money, and taking his job seriously. So instead of moping, I spent my time crafting arrows from raw material I had and searching for the names of alternate Nestori suppliers. It distracted me from the gnawing feeling that the two of them wouldn't do as good a job as I would. That they'd ignore certain details or wouldn't understand context.

At dusk, Jax and Elisha returned together with a loaf of mostly-stale bread and loud complaints about how they'd been on their feet all day.

"How much of the notebook did you get through?" I asked.

"All of it," Jax said, throwing it at me.

"R-really?" I opened the notebook to find nearly every name scratched off. "All of it? There's a bunch of names in here. Are you sure—"

"Your Queen Ilara made it real easy. Half the businesses in the city are shuttered," Jax said. "So all we had to do was walk around and mark them off."

"Oh." I put the notebook down. "How many are left?"

"Fifteen or so," Jax said. "Couple businesses, couple seafaring merchants. A few I couldn't figure from looking at them."

My conversation with Vernice became a bit clearer. "Apparently, Ilara's ordered all Forcadelian merchants to bypass the city. They're picking up whatever produce they can from the farms along the border and sending it straight to Severia via the eastern ports. The merchants have been instructed to return with glass."

"And why do I care?" Jax asked.

"Well, in the first place, it means less food for Forcadel, which will further inflame tensions," I said. "And it means that the merchants are effectively losing money on every shipment, because they can't make the same from glass as food." I put my hands on my hips. "Any who don't follow orders will join Felix in the dungeons."

"I think Ilara is severely overestimating the number of prison cells she has," Jax said.

"Perhaps," I said. "Or perhaps she'll just expedite the executions."

I let Jax and Elisha sleep away the final hours of sunlight while I thumbed through the very short list of targets for the night. Some were spread out, but a cluster was within a few blocks. It would be safer to hit those first then see what information we'd found.

After darkness fell, Jax, Elisha, and I headed toward Merchant's Quarter. There, every other building had been boarded up, and those that remained seemed to have let maintenance go. Forcadel was dying.

"I liked that place." Jax pointed to a boarded-up sweet shop across the street. "Wonder what happened to her?"

"Hopefully, she just decided there were greener pastures," I said, but in the pit of my stomach, I knew otherwise.

The first stop was a man who owned a few parcels of land around the city. Although Beswick had built his wealth obtaining property and charging exorbitant amounts of rent for it (and when the tenants couldn't pay, blackmailing them into helping with his criminal empire), he'd allowed a couple of other landlords to thrive in the city—if only to hide his more heinous crimes and disloyal dealings.

This particular landlord, Waldemar, had ten properties in the city, but his own house was modest in size. Like its neighbors, the windows were dark and the hedges overgrown. So while Elisha played lookout, I picked the lock and the three of us slipped inside.

"This doesn't look promising," Jax remarked, gesturing to the sheets over the furniture. "How long you think he's been gone?"

"You said he was still around," I replied, walking to one of the sheets and lifting it.

"I said his tenants were still sending him money." He opened an empty china cabinet. "Either they're sending it pretty far, or they ain't sending it to him."

I filed that idea as another thread to pull, and Jax and I went upstairs to find something we could use. On the second floor, there were two small bedrooms—both empty—and an office overlooking the street. The office was small, with a large desk in the center facing the window, and stacks of wooden drawers lining the wall.

"Jax, Elisha, go through the drawers," I said, nodding to the wall. "I'll work through the desk."

I sat down on a squeaky chair that was stiff from disuse and rolled forward. There were a handful of papers on the desk, but all of them were dated at least six months before—prior to the invasion. The drawers on the side were similarly empty—just pens and a few jars of ink. But I did find a list of his current tenants, fifteen in all.

"This is a dead end," Jax said, after going through the first drawer. "And this place gives me the creeps."

"Fine, we'll go," I said. "But this isn't a dead end. If they aren't sending their rent checks to this guy, smart money says it's actually going to Beswick. So we follow the money and we'll find him."

"Tonight?"

"Later," I said, getting to my feet. "If the other leads don't pan out. Always good to have some backup plans in mind."

We set out for the next target, Halbert, one of four shipping magnates on the list. His home was dark, but there were two guards outside.

"Are you going to take them out?" Jax asked as we watched from a nearby rooftop.

"I don't know if I want to announce myself just yet," I said. "Check the notebook. Weren't there two addresses listed for him?"

"Yeah." He squinted in the dark. "This one's a little closer to the water."

The second address turned out to be Halbert's office, which was unguarded. It was a small two-story building overlooking the docks and fairly easy to break into. The first room was a clerk's office with about five desks crammed with papers and thick books.

"Fan out," I said to them. "I'll go upstairs to see if I can find anything up there."

"What am I looking for?" Elisha asked.

"Shipping manifests, employment ledgers," I said as I walked to the back. "We need more names and addresses of people to investigate, and I want to know what's come into Forcadel over the past six months—and what's coming."

Much like at our first stop, Halbert's office offered very little of value. Still, Elisha did unearth a shipping schedule buried in one of the many drawers of papers, including one that would be coming in the next week.

"Hang onto that," I told her.

We continued to the next house, which belonged to the owner of a shipbuilding operation to the south of Forcadel. The entire top floor of her fine townhouse was lit up, and the merchant herself paced in her office. On the floor below, her two children were playing in their bedroom. I didn't feel right about breaking into her house with her kids there.

"Oi," Jax said, pointing to the street. Two large men sat on the stoop, curls of smoke coming from their lips. "Seems to be a pattern for those still in the city."

"Indeed," I said, although the security was probably more for her kids' sakes than hers.

Our next mark was a Niemenian-born ore trader named Goossen. He helped facilitate business deals between Forcadelian businesses and Niemenian metalworks, and per my notes, did most of his business from his house. His townhouse was two blocks over, but unlike the shipbuilder's, this place was dark and deserted.

I easily picked the lock on the front door and quickly discovered why. Someone had ransacked the place. Tables were overturned, and a desk in the corner had all the drawers pulled out and dumped onto the floor. Yet all the fine china and gold place settings were still intact in the china cabinet.

"They weren't after this," Jax said, pocketing one of the gold forks and a spoon. "What were they after?"

"This guy was Niemenian, right?" I said. "Maybe it was the royal guards. Ond is from Niemen, after all. Maybe they thought this guy was responsible for getting it into the city."

"I doubt he'd be so dumb," Jax said. "More likely, they were looking for a scapegoat."

I walked into Goossen's office, sitting down at the desk and drumming my fingers on the wood. Those who worked with Beswick didn't worry about the repercussions of their actions—not from the royal guards, at least. Something had spooked him enough that he'd left all his worldly possessions behind.

I came back downstairs to find the china cabinet empty.

"Jax..." I called behind me. "Where's the gold?"

"What does it matter?" he said, adjusting the visibly heavy slingbag on his back. "He's not gonna be using it anymore. And we need gold if you don't want us stealing food. We can't just make bread and meat magically appear."

I couldn't argue that point. Besides, most of the finery in the house had probably been purchased with money stolen from the citizens of Forcadel.

"Just...don't be greedy," I said with a look. "I'm going to go check the back rooms."

I ignored his comeback as I gently pushed open doors along the back hallway. Closet, closet, small sitting area, then, I supposed, the master bedroom. And on the floor, bleeding out of the side of his head, was our merchant.

"So...still think it was the royal guards?" Jax asked over my shoulder.

"No, this was Beswick," I said, walking over to the guy. His skin was slick with sweat and his color was pale, but as I knelt down next to him, he moaned.

"He's alive," I said, pressing two fingers to his neck. "Maybe he'll talk with us—"

"Erm, you guys?" Elisha called from downstairs. "We might want to get out of here."

"Why?"

"Remember that stuff we used to blow up the gate? There's some of it in the kitchen...and the bag is on fire."

Jax and I shared a wide-eyed look as my heart stopped in my chest. "We have to get him out of here," I said.

"Are you mad? Leave him!"

"He's a lead!"

"He's as good as dead, and so are we if we don't get the hell out of here!"

I hesitated, but Jax grabbed me by the shirt and practically dragged me out of the house. Elisha was already waiting on the other side of the street, wringing her hands.

"Jax, we have to go back for—"

The house exploded in a fireball, sending debris flying. I grabbed Elisha and pulled her to the ground, shielding her head with my hand and waiting for the initial blast to die down. Across the street, doors opened and people ran out, gasping and pointing at the explosion. In the distance, more shouts—perhaps the Severian guard on their way.

"Go back for him, my ass," Jax said, wiping soot from his face. "We nearly got ourselves killed. And I'm not getting paid if you're dead."

I stared at the burning wreckage of the house as the twin emotions of relief and guilt swam through my mind.

"He was already dead," Jax said. "What was the point in blowing him up?"

"Because it wasn't about him," I said darkly. "It was about sending a message to all the others in Beswick's circle. If you cross him, that's what'll happen to you."

"And you're sure you want to keep poking that monster?" Jax

asked.

"If he continues unchecked, more people will die," I said, as five Severian guards ran down the street. "Let's get out of here."

Chapter Ten

Katarine

My anxiety for Felix was a constant hum in the back of my mind. I'd taken the name he'd given me to Ilara and it had bought him a temporary reprieve. But the woman refused to talk and was promptly put to death. I'd thought for sure the gallows would shake her tongue loose, but she'd died silently. Whomever she'd sworn allegiance to was clearly more terrifying than death.

More importantly, she'd been a dead end, which meant Felix was back in Ilara's crosshairs. When I asked if I could visit him again, she was clear: my one chance to get him to talk had been used, and I wouldn't get a second.

Still, Felix and Ruby had proven a nice distraction from Beata's departure. In my private moments in the mornings, I would roll over to the space beside me, expecting to find Beata there. When she wasn't, the hole in my heart ached. I wasn't a crier, but I found myself on the verge of tears more often than not. I had to hope she was safe and far from Forcadel. Perhaps even with Brynna, giving her a stern lecture for almost dying.

Jorad had given me some hope that Brynna was moving in the right direction, and Ariadna's letter (*spring is coming*) was similarly optimistic. But it was hard to maintain the hope when Severian forces marched everywhere I looked.

How in the Mother's name could Brynna fight such a thing? And would Felix last long enough in the dungeons to see the light of day again?

I calmed myself, pressing my hand to my heart. Brynna had been a masked vigilante for years, and before that, a feared thief. She was smart and capable, and had clearly learned the value of delegation and teamwork. If she could only put her ego aside, she would be unstoppable. I also had faith Beata would put Brynna in her place if need be. That woman could tame a fire with a glare if she had a mind to. And Felix was too stubborn to die.

There was a soft rap at my door. "Lady Katarine, a message for you."

I pushed myself out of bed and walked to the door, running my hand through my disheveled hair and smoothing my nightgown before opening the door. A young Severian messenger had a note on a silver platter. I didn't need to open the invitation to know who it was from.

"Tell Her Majesty I will be down as quickly as I can," I said, placing the opened letter back on the tray.

The messenger bowed and walked away, and I hurried back to my boudoir to finish my makeup. Ilara wouldn't wait for very long, so I quickly applied my eye and face creams and swept my hair into a simple braid down my back. Without Beata here to sew me into a dress, I had to opt for a looser version, a periwinkle blue number that slipped easily over my shift.

After a final look in the mirror to check my mask, I met the servant in the hallway and accompanied him to the throne room.

When I arrived, someone was already there—a Severian woman wearing a light yellow dress, her hands folded neatly in her lap. I'd never seen her before and the hairs on the back of my neck stood up.

"Good morning, Your Majesty," I said, curtseying.

"And a wonderful morning to you, Lady Kat," Ilara said. "I'm so glad you're here. I have wonderful news for you."

Wonderful. "Oh?"

"This is Luisa," Ilara said. "Since Beata's left, I thought it prudent to give you a new assistant. Lady Luisa was my closest confidante in Severia and was handling business for me there. She arrived just last night."

Odd, as Beata had only been gone a few days now. It took at least two weeks to reach the eastern cities of Forcadel, let alone get a letter all the way to Severia. This move had been planned for some time.

"I appreciate the offer," I began slowly, "but I'm confident Bea will be back soon. It was only a small quarrel."

"I share your confidence," she said with a simpering smile. "But in the meantime, it's not right for you to manage all your duties by yourself, on top of keeping your home running. Luisa will merely stand in until such time as Beata returns from her journey."

I curtseyed a little, even though I didn't want to. "Of course, Your Majesty. Thank you for your generosity."

"The two of you should get to know one another," Ilara said. "Luisa, please take care of Lady Kat as you took care of me."

"It would be my honor," she said. "Come, Lady Katarine, shall we go for a walk?"

Even if I didn't want to, I had a feeling I wouldn't have a choice. "Lead the way."

⇒———

The Severian walked in lockstep with me, clearly used to this role. She was older than Ilara—closer to my age, in fact. Her walk was confident, yet demure, and although her focus was straight ahead, she was observing everything. I couldn't trust her, but I would have to bring her closer than I would've liked to keep her from raising the alarm.

"So," I began, "tell me about yourself, Lady Luisa."

"Please, Lady Katarine, just Luisa," she said. "I'm not sure what there is to tell. I grew up in the capital in Severia as the fourth daughter of a pair of councilors."

"How long have you served Her Majesty?" I asked.

"Since we were children," she said. "I was her playmate first, and when it became clear she would not accept just any servant, I stepped in and offered my services. When she assumed the throne, she asked me to continue as her confidante and advisor."

And was it you who guided her to invade Forcadel? "You must be quite close. I'm sure you're glad to be back with her."

"I would prefer to be back in Severia, but this place will become home soon enough," she said. "It's been nearly a year since I've seen my queen. She has truly grown into her role."

"She has," I replied.

"And you, my lady? How did a Niemenian arrive at the Forcadelian palace?"

"I was married to Prince August in a treaty between our countries," I said. "I have lived in this castle since I was thirteen."

"How is it that you fare so well here in the south?" she asked, tilting her head toward me. "It must've been such an adjustment."

"I certainly had help," I replied. If she wanted to poke around in my relationships, I would offer a little taste, just to sate her. "When I first arrived, August noticed my dresses were all wool, so he had a brand new wardrobe commissioned in cotton and linen. It was the first time that I really felt I would be at home here."

"August seems like he was a wonderful man." Luisa's smile was anything but genuine. "Your capacity for forgiveness is incredible."

My step faltered a bit. "I'm sorry?"

"Well, clearly Queen Ilara ordered his death," she said, a mixture of innocent curiosity and strategy dawning on her face. "And your other best friend, Felix, is down in the dungeons by her orders. And yet...here you are."

My blood ran cold in my veins. "My duty to my adopted home is more important."

"Mm."

I turned away from her, uncomfortable. Ilara had never outright mentioned the oddity of me staying after Brynna supposedly died, and I'd just assumed she hadn't been bothered by it. But perhaps, like me, she was biding her time, sussing me out to see what my end goal was, and if it was in conflict with hers. Luisa, on the other hand, wasn't fooled. She was just as enigmatic as her queen.

"In any case, I'm sorry for your losses," Luisa said with a bowed head. "I couldn't imagine losing so many people so quickly."

Oh, but it was hard to hold my tongue. "Indeed," was the only thing I could force out.

"And your...Bea, you called her?"

"Beata."

"She has left as well?"

I licked my lips. "As I told the queen, only a small fight. She will be back soon, so I hope you aren't offended if our partnership is short-lived."

"Of course not," she said. "We're all waiting with bated breath for Lady Beata to return. In the meantime, I hope I will be an apt substitute."

I caught myself before I continued further down this path. It was understandable that I'd be upset about Beata leaving, but I decided to rein in the attitude. I chose my next words carefully. "So you traveled here to help me?" I asked. "That was very kind of Her Majesty."

"Oh, I don't believe that was the original reason," Luisa said, turning to face the front. "But just the Mother's good timing. It's as if She sent me here to help you in your hour of need."

"Then what role were you to take had Beata not left?"

"Confidante, perhaps, maybe even a friend," Luisa said. "Per Ilara's instructions, I have instilled a fiercely loyal contingent of councilors in Severia to guide the kingdom. But I daresay there aren't very many people left in our country. Most of them have moved into the eastern Forcadelian cities."

I didn't like the sound of that. Every Severian within our borders would have to be expelled—even the civilians. It seemed the more time passed, the more complicated regaining Forcadel became. I prayed Brynna would hurry.

"I look forward to getting to know you more," I said as we arrived back at my office. "But for now, I should get to work. Has Ilara given you a list of duties?"

"I've taken the liberty of making one for myself," she said, as if she were doing me a favor. "I saw that you hadn't had anyone clean your suites in some time."

"Ah, Beata preferred to clean herself," I said, clearing my throat. "And I can tidy after myself."

"Nonsense," Luisa said with a wave of her hand. "I've had the maids at work today, and your rooms shall be spotless when you return to them." She opened the door to my office, which had also been cleaned and tidied. A tray bearing a steaming kettle and teacup stood on the corner. "The maids here work quickly and invisibly. They told me you preferred to take an afternoon tea."

I forced a thin smile onto my face. "Thank you for the kindness."

"It is no kindness at all." She bowed. "It's my job."

And just like that, I was officially under Ilara's surveillance.

Chapter Eleven

"Beswick doesn't crush someone without a reason," I said, when we returned to the bell tower. "Blowing up the merchant's house was sending a message. The question is, what did the merchant do, and for whom was the message intended?"

"Unfortunately, he can't tell us," Jax said, picking his nails clean with his knife.

I ignored him, rubbing my chin as I thought. "I bet it had something to do with the ond being delivered. Ruby said more was coming. Goossen presumably had something to do with bringing it in."

"Well, as I said, he ain't around to tell us one way or another. Probably time to move on to something else. We picked up plenty of other threads last night. And we still got a few people left on the list."

I sat down in front of the various scraps of paper I'd laid out a few minutes before. One was marked *Waldemar's Tenants*, another

Halbert's shipping manifests, and the third *Goossen.* Further out were the targets we hadn't had a chance to question the night before.

Jax made a noise, as if he were growing tired of me. "Look, if you ask me, you gotta follow the money. Beswick's whole enterprise went up in flames when Ilara attacked. And yet, he's still paying people to do his dirty work. Where's that money coming from?"

"The tenants," I said, tapping on the paper.

"Probably some of it," he said. "You can have the kid go do recon. Find out who these tenants are and what they know."

"I can do that!" Elisha said. "I can go right now."

"Everyone's asleep," I said with a wave of my hand. "You can go at sunup."

She made a face and laid back down on her makeshift bed.

"And what about you?" I asked.

"I'm sleeping."

"Not tomorrow you aren't," I said, picking up the *Goossen* paper. "I'm not convinced there isn't a thread there. Go back to his house and talk to his neighbors. Find out who his business partners were in town, too."

"Me and the Severians will get right on that."

"I doubt Ilara will busy herself with that," I said. "But if she does, just stay out of their way."

"And what will you do?" Jax asked.

I swiped the third paper from the ground. "I'm going to take a look at this shipping manifest and see if anything looks familiar. I had a list of ships in my journal, too. It's boring work that will require me to sit here and not leave the bell tower." I flashed him a smile. "See? We've all got things to do."

It took me nearly the entire morning to go through the list, comparing each name with the notes in my book. A few matches, but not enough to draw any conclusions from. Even worse, the dates ended about two months prior, so I had no clue what he'd done to tip off Beswick. It was a dead end for now.

As the shadows grew taller outside, Elisha returned with a satchel of food.

"I used the spoon, like you said," she said with a proud grin.

"Okay, but you should've traded the spoon for gold first," I said with something of a grimace.

"Well, of course I did that," she said, rolling her eyes and handing me a coin purse. "I'm not stupid."

I blushed. "Good, I'm glad to hear it."

She settled on the ground and munched on an apple, looking exceptionally pleased with herself.

"What did you find out about the tenants?" I asked.

"I could only get to five of them today," she said, her mouth full. "But all of them seem on the up and up, you know? Just lawyers and businessmen in their offices." She wiped her mouth with the back of her hand. "But I'll go back tomorrow."

"Good," I said as Jax made his appearance.

Jax fell onto his makeshift bed. "I'm beat. Can we take a breather tonight?"

"No can do," I said. "We've still got one more name in my journal we missed last night."

"And it has to be done tonight?"

I pulled my slingbag on. "Let's go."

We set out, Jax grumbling the whole way. The final few names on the list were on the eastern side of the city in Mariner's Row. In this part of the city, most of those who could afford to move had done so, heading to Kulka and Niemen and cities outside Ilara's purview. The Severians had taken their empty houses for themselves —with Ilara's blessing, of course—but since there didn't seem to be much in the way of activity, the patrols were lighter here.

Clearly, our target was enjoying the perception of safety, because she was at home with no guards out front. Jax and I hovered in the alley across the street, watching through her open windows as she worked.

"I'm going in," I said, cracking my knuckles. "See if she can't tell us what we want to know."

"You think you're intimidating, but you really aren't," he said. "You're about as terrifying as a flea."

"Well, if she's not scared, I'll just break her arm. That seemed to do the trick with you."

I crossed the street between patrols and jimmied the window open, hopping inside and closing the window behind me. My footfalls were quiet on the floor as I walked down the dark hallway. My foot pressed on the wood and it creaked loudly.

"Who's there?" came the woman's terrified voice. "I have a weapon."

I waited, wanting to draw her out and see this supposed weapon before I approached her. After a long, pregnant pause, the scratching of her pen to paper resumed, and I continued my prowl.

I reached her office and peered inside. She was facing the window, a small knife by her left hand. Her gray hair was twirled in a bun, and she was hunched over her desk, writing furiously. A candelabra gave off a halo of light, but other than that, the room was dark.

I pulled my crossbow from the slingbag and added an arrow, pointing at the light and firing. The arrow knocked over the candelabra, sending it crashing to the floor.

"Wh-who's there?" Claudette jumped to her feet, waving her knife around and ignoring the small fire that had lit on the rug.

I walked into the low light, the flames from the rug casting an orange glow around the room. "Where is Johann Beswick?" I purred.

Claudette dropped her pen and spun around, her green eyes

wide. "W-who are you?" She shook her head. "There's no way. Llobrega was arrested."

"Do I look like Llobrega?" I snarled. "Tell me what I want to know."

"He'll kill me," she said, her eyes filling with tears. "Or he'll kill my daughter and send me her severed head."

I swallowed my disgust. "He doesn't have to know that you told me anything," I said softly. "You can fill in some gaps for me. I promise no word of this conversation will come to Beswick."

She nodded nervously. "I'll do what I can."

"Last night, Goossen was killed in his home," I said. "Do you know why?"

She shook her head. "I didn't even know he was involved in this. Isn't he an ore trader?" She licked her lips. "I bet he's the one Beswick was having trouble with."

"Trouble?"

"His first shipment of ond, the same that was used in the attack a few weeks ago, well, that came pretty easy."

"Who brought it in?" I said.

"I don't know the specifics," she said, although her wide eyes said she knew the name. "But there was supposed to be a second shipment shortly thereafter, and it never arrived. Apparently...well, apparently, it never left Niemen."

"Stopped at the border?" I asked.

"I have no idea," she said. "All I know is that Beswick's usual avenues are closed, so his man came to me last week and said that I was now his main ond supplier." She swallowed. "I don't know if that's true, but that's what he told me."

I waved her off. "When's the next shipment supposed to come in?"

"I'm not... Please, I'm the only one who knows..." She shook her head wildly. "He'll know I spoke with you if you get it."

I sighed, pinching the bridge of my nose. "Is there anything else you can tell me about your shipment? Something I might've come across on my own, that wouldn't necessarily point the guilty finger at you?"

"The ond is..." She licked her lips, thinking. "There's always a copy of the shipping manifests at the dock master's office. I submitted the papers for the shipment this afternoon." She chewed her lip, now red with worry. "Just make it look like he's been robbed."

"I will," I said.

"To be honest..." She swallowed. "I don't like what he's doing in the city. The ond attacks a few weeks ago killed one of my very dear friends. But I'm in too deep with him. If I don't do what he says—"

"I understand," I said. "And you have my word that your involvement will remain a secret."

"Just please try not to destroy the ship," she said. "It's one of my fastest, and it would be such a burden to find another that fast. You do have a reputation, you know."

I stopped and looked behind me, pondering all the things that could go wrong. Not for me, but for this merchant. Especially after seeing Goossen dead.

"You should leave," I said. "Tonight. Take nothing but what you need to survive somewhere far away from here."

Her eyes widened. "But I can't...I can't just leave. I have a business, a life here."

"You don't have it anymore," I said. "Unless you want to end up like Goossen. At least if you leave now, you'll have your life." I went to the window. "Don't say I didn't warn you."

⇨————•

"And you're sure she wasn't lying?" Jax asked.

"Yes, I'm sure," I snapped for what felt like the hundredth time. "We just have to be patient."

Two nights ago, I'd found the pre-arrival paperwork for Claudette's ship still on the dockmaster's desk. The shipment, whatever it was, had been scheduled to arrive tonight. Though just to be sure, I'd made Jax skulk around the docks.

Tonight, I had a feeling we'd get lucky. After waiting for a pair of Severian guards to pass, we crossed the street onto the wooden docks, the decks creaking under our weight. In Forcadel, the docks were a maze of slips and wooden pathways, allowing for hundreds of ships to be in port at one time. Now, most of them sat empty.

"Take the closer-in routes," I said. "Whistle if you see anyone."

He grunted and disappeared into the shadows, not bothering to soften his footsteps. Clearly, he wasn't a fan of this new plan. But besides his grumbling, he really hadn't vetoed any of my plans thus far. Was he biding his time, or did he trust me? Perhaps a little bit of both.

Without a moon overhead, it was hard to see where the dock ended and the water began. What was clear, however, was that most of the slips were empty. I moved slowly, touching each post and setting my feet before walking. All the while, I kept my ears open for the sound of conversation.

"Our agreement was twenty coins for the journey."

I froze, then carefully moved toward the sound. A boat—smaller than the usual vessels docked out here—was moored in one of the last slips. Two figures stood talking nearby, and so far, they'dd been too focused on each other to notice me. I crouched and kept low as I moved closer.

"I'm not paying you forty. We had an agreement."

"Things got harried up north," came the response. "Cost more than I thought to get past Neveri, and cost three times what I thought to get in port. It took us an extra three days to even get here. The price has gone up."

"I don't think our mutual friend will like that very much." I didn't recognize the other voice, but Beswick had hundreds of lieutenants and seconds at his disposal. "I have twenty in hand now, so you'll get that. If you need more, you can take it up with him."

"Or I'll just take the twenty now, keep the stuff, and when you have the rest of it, you can come back."

There was the unmistakable sound of metal being drawn and I instinctively went for my knives. This wasn't my fight; if they killed one another, it wouldn't mean anything to me other than a dead lead to Beswick.

The boat captain clearly thought better of his price gouging. "Fine."

He disappeared beneath the hull with his coin then reappeared holding a small bag. Ond, I would've bet my life on it.

"Take it. But tell your boss the price has gone up for the next shipment."

A new idea sprang to mind. Perhaps I couldn't find Beswick in this city, but maybe I didn't need to. If I took his precious ond, he might find it beneficial to come to me.

I reached into my slingbag, finding it empty, save a few arrows for my crossbow. As much as I would've preferred to do this with knockout powder, perhaps I'd have to do it the old-fashioned way.

I aimed my crossbow and fired. The weapon whizzed, then the man on the left cried out in pain before falling backward. He hit the water with a loud *splash*.

"What the—"

I reached in my bag, but there were no more arrows. So I stashed the crossbow in the bag and rose to my feet, walking into the dim light and making myself known.

"Who are you?" Beswick's man asked.

"I could be a friend," I said, putting my hands on my hips. "Be sure to tell your boss that when you swim back to him."

"When I—"

I dropped to my hands, swinging my leg around and knocking

him into the water. Once he was out of my way, I ran onto the ship where they'd been conversing, grabbed the small, metallic-smelling bag, and hurried off into the lightening city.

Chapter Twelve

"Beswick noticed you took his powder," Jax said, walking into the bell tower. "Four bodies washed up on shore this morning."

My jaw dropped. "Four?"

"All with their throats slashed. Including your merchant Claudette and someone who looks like her daughter."

It had been days since I'd taken the ond from Beswick. I wasn't sure what I'd expected, considering we were both supposedly dead people in a city under siege, but maybe my great idea hadn't been so clever after all. I'd sent Elisha and Jax to sniff around some of his usual haunts, but we hadn't seen hide nor hair of him.

Until now. "We can't let it deter us. We still have the ond hidden in the city, and Beswick's going to want it sooner or later."

"Or he's just going to bring more in," Jax said. "I mean, it's not like he hasn't found a way to do it before. Maybe he already has."

I picked up the book of Beswick's contacts. "Then we'll just have to pay a visit to all the others on this list. Maybe go back to

Claudette's house and see when her next shipments are. Or we can start canvassing all the places he might be hiding—"

"You could just leave it be," Jax said. "It's been a few weeks since we've seen your little soldiers. I bet they miss you."

I gave him a sidelong look. "I'm sure they're fine. We need to take care of Beswick first."

"I just don't see the value in focusing all your energy on this one person when you have so many larger fish to catch. Isn't that what got you stabbed?"

"Because if I don't get Beswick on my side or out of the way, there is no next step," I said. "You see how big his operation is. Even with Niemen and Kulka, I will lose if I have to go against Beswick *and* Ilara in these city walls. So even if it takes me a month, this must happen before anything else can."

"And your soldiers? Do you think they'll just stay up there and wait for you?" He crossed his arms over his chest. "Wouldn't be surprised if half of them left already."

"As soon as I make contact with Beswick," I said, my face flushing, "I'll meet up with the soldiers."

"And tell them what?"

My cheeks grew warmer. "I haven't figured that out yet. But if you want to earn some more gold from Celia, why don't you come up with something I can use to find Beswick?" I walked to the open trunk where my mask and cloak were waiting. "And in the meantime, I'm going out."

I hadn't meant to snap, but my patience was growing thin. It wasn't just that the soldiers up north needed my attention; it seemed everything I was trying lately was failing. I sat on the roof next to the church, looking at the castle and wishing for the umpteenth time that I'd been able to get Felix and Katarine out. I would've liked to hear their opinion on things. I missed Luard, too, and the unique way he'd managed to keep me both laughing and on track.

But more than anything, I wanted to see Beswick get justice for all he'd done.

I paced the city aimlessly, but I ended up down at the docks, perched on a roof across from the dock master's house. Three guards stood in front of the house, watching the empty streets. They hadn't been there before, but perhaps all of the shippers dropping dead in their houses had been cause for alarm.

That, or they were hoping to intercept something. The minutes passed slowly. Every fifteen minutes, another patrol passed by, waving at their compatriots and chatting quietly before moving on.

"Riveting," Jax said, sitting down next to me.

"Better than nothing," I said. "How much gold is Celia paying you, anyway?"

"Enough to put up with you," he said.

I waited for another volley, but he just sat quietly with me. Perhaps he'd said all he wanted to say back in the bell tower. Or he was keeping silent to avoid being seen by the guards. Either way, I was glad for the time with my thoughts.

"I hear what you're saying," I began after a moment. "But I disagree with your assessment of the situation."

"That's fine. You're wrong, though. But I ain't wasting any more energy on this."

"I—"

One of the three guards coughed, then pointed to a clock nearby. His compatriots murmured to themselves, then adjusted their swords and turned to walk away, leaving him alone.

Not three minutes later, a wagon rolled up to the dock.

"What is it?" Jax said, squinting in the darkness.

"Delivery of some kind," I said. "Maybe more ond?"

"If that's ond, we're in trouble," Jax said, his eyes widening.

In the dim light, I could just make out the shapes of men

walking off the docks. But unlike the previous night, where a single bag had been handed off, today's shipment contained large crates that required two men to carry.

My mouth went dry—a small bag was enough to level the gates in Neveri. That couldn't be ond, could it?

They offloaded the cargo in minutes, perhaps knowing that they were carrying explosives. Just as the last box was put on the wagon, the coachman snapped the reins and off they went.

"C'mon," I said to Jax.

I kept in close pursuit, marveling at how the wagon driver seemed to know when a Severian guard would be patrolling so they'd stop in an alley and wait them out. But perhaps Beswick had ingratiated himself with the Severian guards as he'd done with the Forcadelians.

When the wagon stopped in front of a familiar building, a grin grew on my face.

"This is one of Beswick's old clubs," I said to Jax.

"Seems odd he'd use a known place," Jax said. "If I were him, I would've bought a new building and stashed whatever I was smuggling there."

I couldn't disagree. When the cargo was offloaded inside the building, all seven guards jumped back on the wagon and rode off into the night. By the looks of it, the place was completely unguarded.

"Wait," Jax said, taking my arm. "It may be—"

"If it's a trap, we'll get out," I said. "But something's off about this. I want to see where they're going."

I patrolled the perimeter for a moment, listening. When I was positive it was safe, I worked the lock while Jax kept my crossbow pointed above my head. The door creaked open to reveal...

A room filled with boxes. And nothing else.

"Odd," Jax said, handing me the crossbow.

The faint metallic smell of ond was missing, but they could've just packed it tightly. "Maybe the ond is buried in one of these boxes," I said, craning my neck to take in the stacks.

"Only one way to find out," he said, walking to the first box.

My hands shook with anticipation. Would I even know what it was? Or would it be like ond, a simple weapon but potent under the right circumstances?

I cracked open the top of the first crate and found...bread? Thick, brown, crusty loaves that were just a little stale, but still edible.

"Huh," Jax said, holding up an apple from his crate. From the color, they appeared to be Kulkan.

I dug to the bottom of the crate, but there was nothing but more loaves.

"What in the Mother's name is going on here?" Jax said, pulling out a large potato from another set. "Did Beswick grow a heart or something?"

"I sincerely doubt that," I said, shaking my head. "He doesn't do anything without it benefitting him first. I bet there's ond in here somewhere. Why in the Mother's name would he go through all this trouble to smuggle in food?"

"Because food's illegal now," Jax said slowly. "That queen just put out another edict. All shipments of food go to the east, toward Severia. Ain't nothing supposed to come here first."

I barked a laugh. "Sure. That's a smart move."

"Nobody said she was smart, but Beswick sure is," he said, tossing the potato back in with the others. "If he's here doling out food like a saint, the people might be more likely to follow him into a rebellion against Ilara."

"But why would Ilara cut off food to Forcadel?" I asked, more to myself than him. "There are hundreds of Severians here, too. That's a recipe for disaster." I shook my head. "There has to be ond in here somewhere."

"You're free to spend the night opening every box in here," Jax said. "But the writing's on the wall, if you ask me."

There was no sign of the food in the market square for the next few days. Both Elisha and Jax reported nothing but moldy and overripe produce. But I'd expected that. The guards were quick to arrest anyone who had anything that looked remotely edible.

So what was Beswick doing with it all?

"He's got to move within the next week," I said, pacing the bell tower. "Or all that food is going to rot."

Jax snored in response. Elisha had gone out again to watch the tenants, although even she was starting to question the brilliance of it. But I had no other good options. What I wouldn't have given for Luard's advice right now.

You know what he'd say. You should be up in the camp with your troops.

Jax snorted, waking himself up, then fell back to sleep. I glared at his sprawling body, annoyed that he wasn't being more helpful. But every time I asked for his advice, it was more or less the same. He wanted me to go back up north. Clearly, he considered this investigation a dead end. I wondered when the sum of gold Celia had promised him would be less tantalizing than putting up with me.

Footsteps echoed on the stairs below, followed by Elisha's whistle.

"She's early," I said to an asleep Jax. "You clearly care so much. Glad it wasn't anyone here to kill us."

"I would've gotten up if it was."

I took the stairs two-by-two, hoping Elisha's early reappearance merited something good for us.

"Is everything okay?" I asked. "You're back early."

"Kind of," she said, looking up at me. "I know you said to watch the tenants, and I was doing that, but I saw something odd.

A guy with a pencil-thin mustache came to visit the lawyer guy. He gave me the creeps, you know?"

My pulse skipped. Sounded very familiar. "Did you get his name?"

"No," she said. "But he really freaked me out, so I followed him."

"Good girl," I said with a smile. "Where'd he go?"

"He went to a couple other tenants, and some people who weren't on your list, too." She shifted uneasily. "I couldn't hear what he said to all of them, but I did sneak into one of their offices to listen. Was almost caught, but I got out."

"Glad you didn't get caught," I said with a half-smile. "What did you hear?"

"He said there was gonna be a meeting tonight," she said. "He said 'the usual spot' but I don't know if we know what that means. Do we?"

"No. Beswick had a ton of places all over the city during his heyday," I said, chewing my lip. "But we can follow the tenants. You go back to the lawyer, Jax and I will take another. Hopefully, we'll all meet up at the same place."

She nodded. "So I did good?"

"You did great, kid," I said with a smile. "You'll make a vigilante yet."

Chapter Thirteen

Jax and I went with Elisha to stake out one of the tenants she'd seen, which was a feat considering it was the afternoon and he lived on the other side of the city. But Jax threw a cloak over my head and pretended I was his old mother, so we walked by Severian guards without any trouble.

It was well after midnight when our target finally left his house, wearing a black cloak and leaving through his backdoor. We kept our distance, dodging the same soldiers he did, until he disappeared into a dilapidated bar that used to belong to a friend of mine.

After making sure the coast was clear, I crossed the street to the abandoned building. Luckily for me, I knew the inside well, having been in more times than I could count to interrogate people. The large dance hall was in the back, which was probably the site of the meeting, as the private rooms were too small.

I used my sticky gloves to climb the walls to a second-floor window. As carefully as I could, I pulled the drill from my slingbag and made a tiny hole in the wooden window pane. Then I slid the metal tube through the hole and pressed the cup to my ear.

"...very well. Captain Coyle is, if possible, more inefficient than Llobrega. So I have faith that our operations will continue undeterred."

"Excellent."

I actually smiled—finally, someone I recognized. Ignacio was Beswick's favorite second, and as ruthless as his boss. If he was here, this was almost as good as Beswick himself being there. Almost.

"Our supplier hasn't been able to get back into the city, however," the other speaker said. "We may have to obtain the material in Neveri and get it down some other way."

"Neveri?" Another man scoffed. "Good luck getting in there. The gates are closed."

"Not anymore," Ignacio said. "Apparently, someone claiming to be Princess Brynna destroyed them using ond. She then turned around and handed the city to the Kulkans. Prince Ammon is there now, running things."

"Claiming to be Princess Brynna?"

"Yes." Ignacio paused, and I could almost see him stroking his chin. "I don't believe it. The real Brynna is too noble, too upstanding to do anything like that. My guess is that it's a Kulkan spy made up to look like her."

I had to smile. I hadn't known that Ignacio thought so highly of me. But perhaps that wasn't a compliment, coming from him.

"I've heard rumors that she's back in Forcadel."

"I've heard the same rumors," Ignacio said. "But even if it is her, she's nothing but a nuisance. She's bumbling her way around and not making any progress. If she took the ond the other day, she's wading into deeper waters than she anticipated."

I scowled. So much for his compliments. Clearly, my attempts at making myself worthwhile were failing. I'd have to step up my efforts.

"In the end, whoever was responsible for the attack in Neveri, it's in our favor that it happened," Ignacio continued. "You are all here because you serve a purpose to Lord Beswick, and that purpose will be to deliver this food to the people of the city. We have bread, produce, even clothing and textiles, everything. You will bring the money as part of your rental payments, and we'll deliver your next shipment."

"These prices are...high."

"A whole gold piece for a loaf of bread?"

"I think you'll find that Lord Beswick's prices are more than fair compared to what's in the town square tomorrow. The people in this city are starving, and we're just doing what we need in order to keep them fed and clothed."

"Bullshit," I muttered. If he was, he'd be giving the food away for free instead of enriching himself. This was how he was bankrolling his operation. Son of a bitch.

"And what's Lord Beswick planning to do with all this money?" asked one of the male voices.

"That is, of course, Lord Beswick's business. And if you'd like to continue to conduct *your* business and live in your homes, you'll support him."

The meeting ended shortly after that, as no one could argue with Ignacio's threat. I pulled my listening cups and climbed down, rejoining Jax and Elisha on top of the roof.

"Sounds about right," Jax said when I told him what I'd heard. "Are you surprised?"

"Disappointed," I said. "But it appears working with Beswick isn't going to work. We'll have to figure something else out."

"Which is what?" Jax asked. "You, the kid, and I try to take down his empire?"

"No," I said, mulling over some options. I still wanted things to come into the city, but I didn't want Beswick to profit off it. A tricky situation.

"Ignacio's on the move," Jax said, pointing below where Beswick's second was climbing into a carriage. "What do you want to do?"

"I want to have a chat," I said.

"I think that's a bad idea," Jax said. "First of all, he's got more guards than we have people. Second, Beswick's not going to want to listen to you."

"I have to try," I said.

Ignoring whatever Jax might've said, I jumped to my feet and ran after the carriage. I had spent so long trying to find Beswick that I wasn't going to let the opportunity to find out where his second was hiding slip away. Even if it took me all night.

"When are you planning on engaging him?" Jax asked, bending over to catch his breath. "Now might be a good time."

"No," I said. "I want him to get to his destination."

"Why?"

"Ignacio's men might come looking for him if he doesn't show up on time," I said. He looked confused, so I explained, "Once, I tried to intercept Beswick before he reached his destination. But he —"

"Sent his goons and they beat the shit out of you?"

My cheeks reddened. "Almost."

Ignacio's carriage rolled through the front gates of a stately manor in the center of Mariner's Row—fitting for a man who pocketed too much from the citizens of the city. The carriage itself had its own house in the back.

"So…" Jax said, finally catching up with me. "We lost the kid a while ago."

"It's all right. She'll meet us back at the bell tower."

"Are you sure you want to do this? Especially after the aforementioned ass kicking the last time you did something like this?"

The concern in his voice made me pause. But the overriding need to have a win—any win—kept me going.

"Keep a lookout," I said. "I'm going in."

I gathered the edges of my cloak and jumped off the roof, floating gracefully to the ground. I stalked through the garden, waiting for the man himself to leave the carriage house. When he finally appeared, he was alone.

I stepped out of my hiding spot, making myself visible in the scant moonlight.

Ignacio didn't look surprised to see me—but he didn't seem pleased, either.

"Such a shame to see you," he said. "It was so much nicer around here when you were dead."

I smiled. "I want to speak with your boss. It's rather urgent."

"He doesn't want to speak with you, not after you got Ruby executed."

I started, my mouth falling open. "Ruby was executed?"

"Apparently, she refused to tell the queen anything about our operations, and Ilara's patience is rather thin." He showed no emotion as he spoke, but he'd lost his veneer of calm. "We'll be sure to take that out of your hide."

"Or, alternatively, why don't we talk about the ond that went missing a few days ago," I said, thinking quickly. "I'd be happy to return it to your boss, if he'll meet with me."

"You can keep it," Ignacio said. "We've made other arrangements. Water transport is evidently very unreliable."

"Probably because you keep killing your associates," I said darkly.

He smiled. "They failed to perform to our expectations. But it doesn't matter. We're already getting more ond in via alternative methods, and now, with our new line of business in food smuggling, we'll win the hearts and minds of the people in town."

"Yeah, except that you seem to be misinformed about some things," I said, blocking him from walking into his house. "I have very powerful friends of my own these days. I can get the Niemenians to cut off your ond supply, and I can have Prince Ammon stop all shipments from Neveri."

"And let your people starve?" Ignacio said. "The only person offering salvation is Lord Beswick. Surely, you wouldn't be so evil as to prevent that."

"Perhaps I'll just deliver the food myself," I replied, bluffing a little. "Cut out the middleman. *I'm* not in the business of gouging my own people for personal gain."

He laughed, his amusement grating on me. "And where, pray tell, are you going to find the money to move all this produce if you're just going to give it away? You seem to think the world works on hopes and dreams. It runs on money, my dear, and if you have none, you have no way to reclaim your throne." He shrugged and snapped his fingers. Two shadows appeared out of the darkness. "But perhaps Ilara will give us a nice ransom when we deposit your dead body on her doorstep."

The hair rose on the back of my neck as shadows moved toward me. I reached into my slingbag for something—knockout powder, anything that could grant me a hasty escape. But there was nothing except lint. Perhaps I should've prepared more for this trip.

"Oh," Ignacio said, reading the concern on my face. "Has the little princess vigilante run out of tricks? I never thought I'd see the day."

I removed my hand from my bag, smiling. "I have a few tricks yet, Ignacio. Don't—"

An arrow sailed through the air, landing inches from Ignacio's face. He stared up at a dark figure overhead, his eyes growing wide.

"Tell your goons to step away," came Jax's deep voice. "Or the next one goes into your heart."

"The Veil doesn't kill," Ignacio said.

"Welp." Jax adjusted the crossbow. "I'm clearly not her, am I? Tell your goons to step away. I promise you, I'm an excellent shot."

Ignacio stared at me then back at Jax. Then he shrugged. "Suit yourselves. Gentlemen, let's go."

His goons shared bewildered looks but followed their boss, bumping into me as they went. My face grew warm as I stood there, hating that I'd needed saving. Then, it was just Jax and me, and the echo of my failures.

Jax jumped off the rafters of the stable and landed in a crouch in front of me. "I hate to say, I told you so—"

"Then don't," I snapped, crossing my arms over my chest.

"I take it Beswick doesn't want to work with you," Jax said, clearly enjoying this. "I can't imagine why."

"No, but I didn't expect him to," I said, adjusting my slingbag and walking out of the stable. "What I wanted to do was put him on notice that I'm back in town and he can't just get away with hurting my people."

"I'm sure he's shaking in his boots," Jax said. "What with you trying to throw air at him."

"He should be," I said. "Because I'm going to show him that he can't screw with me. All those shipments? They end now. Up river, in Neveri, I don't know. But I'm taking them over for myself, then I'll be the one distributing them. And if he thinks he's bringing more ond into the city, he's got another thing coming."

"Ignacio said he wasn't bringing anything in via water, though," Jax said.

"However he's moving it," I said, waving my hand, "I refuse to let him get away with using my people to fund his little rebellion— and I refuse to let him hurt anyone else."

"Are you just going to annoy him into submission?"

"Um…excuse me."

I straightened, turning to see Elisha behind us.

"What's going on?" I barked. "Why aren't you at the bell tower? Did something happen?"

"Um, well…" She wrung her hands

"Sorry," I said, softer. "What's going on? Is everything okay?"

"Yeah, it's just… Those soldiers, Jorad and Aline? They're back. And they said it's important that they speak with you."

I didn't need to be told twice. We raced back to the bell tower, my worries and fears spiraling from one horrific scene to another. Could Ilara have found the soldiers? Had everyone disbanded in the interim? Had I done the very thing that Jax had been warning me about and sacrificed my army while screwing around with Beswick?

My heart sank lower into my stomach. I'd sent Beata to stay with the soldiers. If anything had happened to her, I would never be able to forgive myself.

I took the bell tower steps two-by-two until I reached the top, where I found Jorad and Aline sitting on the trunk, talking quietly to one another. They jumped to their feet, saluting me as good soldiers did, and I exhaled a little. At least they were still loyal.

"What's going on?" I said. "Is everything okay with the camp? Is Beata all right?"

"Everything's fine with the camp," Jorad said. "Everyone's training and preparing for your next move, whatever that may be."

My shoulders slumped. "Thank goodness."

"But it's not good news," Aline said. "Ammon let Maarit go."

Chapter Fourteen

Katarine

Luisa had proven a capable and brilliant spy for Ilara. More than once, I'd found my letters had been opened and resealed, and it was only thanks to Luard's training that I noticed the slight irregularity of the wax seal.

Ilara had declined to meet with me again for several days, and I was starting to worry that, with Luisa's presence, I was systematically being cut out of Ilara's inner circle. It had happened to Felix, after all. I couldn't see a way to prevent it, though. My fate was out of my hands. But, like Felix, I'd make the most of my time while I still had it.

At night, I worked through ideas, scribbling them down then burning the paper to ash in my fireplace. I was in the middle of one such burning when there was a hurried rap at my door. It was late, and I'd assumed the castle had gone to bed. After making sure the entire paper had been reduced to ash, I walked to the door, not even bothering to tie my long hair back.

I opened the door to a servant's pale face. "Pardon the late hour, m'lady, but the queen has requested you join her in her Council room. Immediately."

"I'll be there in—"

"No," he said, looking earnest. "Immediately."

I pulled on my dressing robe and some slippers and followed him out the door. A thousand scenarios ran through my mind. Had they found Beata? Brynna? Had Felix...no, I wouldn't go there.

When I walked into the Council room, Ilara was already waiting in her chair, a tight smile on her face. Luisa was in the corner—and Captain Maarit sat before them. I hadn't seen the Severian military leader since she'd left for Neveri several weeks ago, taking all Felix's recruits and one of his lieutenants with her. Her uniform looked a little worse for wear, and the dark bags under her eyes were more pronounced. Clearly, something had happened in our border city. I dared not speculate, lest it color my reaction.

"I'm glad you came quickly," Ilara said, offering me the seat next to her. "Very well, Maarit. Tell us what happened."

"Neveri has fallen," she began quietly, as if she knew her words would condemn her. "To the Kulkans. But first..." She swallowed hard. "To Princess Brynna."

I gasped—honestly. Brynna had taken Neveri? Well, that explained Jorad coming to take Beata and me out of the castle. Had she managed to collect all the other soldiers there? I had so many questions that it was easy to let shock and confusion rule my expression.

"Are you sure?" Ilara asked quietly. "Brynna is dead."

"Then perhaps it was a ghost, but...the soldiers swore fealty to her," Maarit said. "Riya Kellis turned on me. I don't think they would do that if it wasn't... If she wasn't really..." Maarit swallowed. "Her."

"I hope you strung up Kellis up in the town square," Ilara said, her knuckles growing white.

"Kellis is dead," Maarit said. "Killed by one of our arrows."

My heart stopped in my chest and I closed my eyes. Oh, Felix. He would be devastated. Riya had been one of his closest friends.

"As did a hundred other soldiers, both Severian and Forcadelian," Maarit said, gaining confidence as she spoke. "They used some kind of explosive powder on the gates and gatehouses. All that's left is rubble. Ships have been coming in and out of Neveri for weeks."

"Ond?" I said, shaking my head. "Clearly, my sister needs to reassess her security measures."

"Your brother Luard brought it into my city," Maarit said, her gaze accusing and clear. "I believe he was working with...with Princess Brynna."

"That's impossible," I said with a small laugh. "My sister would never allow ond to leave our borders. Especially not with Luard. He's...he'd barter it away for a night with the first woman he saw."

A lie, all of it. Luard might've played around, but he was as loyal to Niemen as any. If he had ond, it was because Ariadna had allowed him to have it. Perhaps the reason Brynna wanted me to leave the castle.

"I can only tell you what I saw," Maarit said. "Luard arrived with four guards. He had some tale about how Her Majesty had asked him to inspect our gates. A signed letter from...from you, Your Majesty."

Ilara exhaled through her nose. "A forgery, clearly. Or are you too stupid to recognize one?"

Perhaps not. Luard was the one who'd taught me how to mimic a signature.

"Then what happened?" Ilara asked, sounding more bored than angry.

"After he inspected the gates, he said he was leaving the town, but I fear he was merely stealing a boat to take the ond, as you call it, to the gates. It happened in an instant—the gates, the gate houses, a hundred-plus soldiers. All of it...gone." She swallowed. "I thought we could take on the small group—after all, it was a handful of people, but they had some sort of...powder that made us hallucinate. Horrible things—things that I..." She swallowed. "Then the Kulkans arrived."

"The Kulkans?" Ilara said with a thin smile. "My, my, what an international incident."

"Clearly, Prince Ammon had some agreement with...with Princess Brynna but he was trying to go back on it. He said he'd take the city for himself and not...help her anymore. But then..." She sighed. "Llobrega's Forcadelian troops arrived on another boat, outnumbering them. And the city was Princess Brynna's. Anyone who didn't swear fealty to her was thrown in the barracks."

Ilara licked her lips and swiped her glass of wine off the table, swirling the liquid around. "And how did you manage to escape your imprisonment?"

"It was odd," Maarit said. "One minute the city was in the hands of the princess, and the next...the Kulkan flag was waving in the town square. All my guards were Kulkan, and all the ships in the bay were, too."

Brynna agreed to give Neveri to Kulka in exchange for their help. Clever, clever girl. I kept my mouth shut, hoping I still appeared to be digesting this information instead of cheering it.

"And then?" Ilara asked.

"Then, Prince Ammon came to my cell," she said, sitting up straighter. "He said that he was reconsidering his alliance with the princess and asked if I thought...if I thought you might be amenable to a partnership. He sent me here with two of his councilors to negotiate—"

Ilara waved her hand to silence her. "The people who helped in Neveri's destruction want to negotiate with me?" She laughed. "The Kulkans must be ignorant or insane. Either way." She flicked her wrist at the two guards in the corner. "Arrest her for dereliction of duty and treason."

"B-but, Your Majesty!"

"You have spoken enough," Ilara said, her eyes flashing with fury. "And you will speak no more. Tomorrow at dawn, I want her swinging from the gallows."

My heart thudded in my chest as I saw the future, saw her saying those very words about me. She was so unpredictable, if I caught her on the wrong day, she might decide I was no longer worthy of being her attendant. Now that my sister had all but declared war on her, I was in a precarious position indeed.

Maarit's cries for leniency echoed down the hall, leaving me chilled. She had been Ilara's favorite military advisor, the architect of the fall of Forcadel. Clearly, she had failed, but it sounded like Brynna had pulled off a masterful surprise attack in Neveri.

"Thoughts, Kat?" Ilara said, casting a long look at me.

"Many," I said slowly.

"And they are?"

"I apologize," I said with a half-smile, "I'm still trying to wrap my head around what I just heard. Brynna is alive, Neveri has fallen…Luard was involved." I swallowed hard. "It seems so farfetched, I wonder if we should check Maarit for insanity."

"It sounds like a cause for war, don't you think?" Ilara said. "Against the Kulkans and the Niemenians."

Slowly, I shook my head. "I want to believe there's a reasonable explanation for this. Ariadna would never risk open war with Forcadel. Not with me here. Unless…"

"Unless what?" Ilara said.

I allowed the real fear I was nursing to seep onto my face. "I've been struggling to understand why Beata was keen on leaving so suddenly. It was out of the blue, and she was adamant. She'd said there was something beautiful waiting at the border with Niemen." I exhaled shakily as a tear fell down my cheeks. "I had a feeling when we parted unhappily that...that she might not come back. That she was headed to Niemen at the behest of someone else."

"And you didn't think to tell me?" Ilara asked.

"I thought, perhaps it was..." I sighed. "I don't know what I thought. But surely, I wouldn't have dreamed it would've been to Brynna, if that's even where she went." I ducked my head. "I thought maybe she'd grown tired of being in the castle."

I stared at my hands, holding my breath and waiting for her response. Since Beata had left, I'd been crafting this narrative in hopes that it would provide the foundations for trust with Ilara. But that had been with the assumption that my siblings hadn't destroyed Forcadelian lives and property. Now, I had no idea what to expect from her.

"And now?" Ilara asked. "Will you leave me and join forces against me?"

"My first duty is to my sovereign," I said. "No matter what my sister might be plotting, I won't betray you. This is my country, and has been for nearly a decade. My sincere hope is that we can resolve this misunderstanding without any bloodshed."

I looked up into Ilara's dark eyes, holding her gaze with all the confidence I could muster. This was the critical moment—if she didn't believe me now, all would be lost.

Finally, her eyes softened. "Thank you. This must be so hard for you."

I wiped my cheeks. "I have endured worse, my queen, and remained steadfast. We will resolve this newest problem and the country will be stronger for it."

Ilara reached across the table and took my hand. "We will, because I have Niemen's smartest mind at my side."

"Indeed," I said, squeezing her fingers.

"Now, I suppose I must figure out what to do with these Kulkan envoys," Ilara said. "Shall I string them up next to Maarit?"

I jolted. "My queen? If we're already at war with Niemen, it might behoove us to take the olive branch offered by Kulka. They've long been enemies, and it would be better if we had another nation on our side."

"Mm." She rose. "I will consider it. In the meantime, I would like you to find Coyle and have him personally lead a search party for our dear friend. When he finds her—and trust that I expect he will—he is to bring her to me alive."

"A-alive?" I asked. Even Luisa looked confused.

"Indeed." Ilara walked to the dark window. "I also don't want a word of this leaving the room. You may tell Coyle his new charge, but he's not to speak of it to anyone."

How Coyle was supposed to conduct a search without telling anyone whom they were searching for was beyond me, but I nodded. "Yes, Your Majesty. Anything else?"

"No." She softened her gaze. "I apologize for getting you out of bed at such a late hour."

"It is no trouble at all, Your Majesty," I said. "I am grateful I could be of assistance."

And that she still trusted me.

Chapter Fifteen

"W-*what?*"

My voice echoed in the cavernous bell tower. Ammon and I'd had a deal—he had Neveri, and he would keep Maarit prisoner until I sent for her. I'd had a mind to send her back to Severia when this was all over, but like so many other things, it was low on my priority list. And now, it seemed, it had jumped to the top.

I rubbed my forehead. "How long ago?"

"Not sure," Jorad said. "Our messengers found out about four days ago, and we set off almost immediately. Apparently, a few merchants saw her getting into a Kulkan royal carriage along with two envoys, and they all headed south toward Forcadel."

"So he not only let her go," I began slowly, "but he's sending an envoy with her? Is he reneging on our treaty or something?"

"Appears so," Jax piped up from the corner. "Can't trust anyone these days, can you?"

I scowled in his direction then turned back to the two soldiers.

"So...what does this mean?"

"We don't know," Aline said. "Except that as soon as she arrives in Forcadel, she's going to tell Ilara that you're alive."

"And that means you should get as far away from Forcadel as you can," Jorad said.

I sank down onto the nearby trunk with a heavy sigh. "This day's just getting better and better."

"Beswick's the least of your problems now," Jax said.

"Beswick?" Aline said, giving him a look. "What does he have to do with this?"

"He's the one behind the ond attacks in the city," I said. "We just met with his second, Ignacio."

"I'm familiar with him," she said, narrowing her eyes. "So Beswick is the reason Captain Llobrega is in prison?"

"Among other things," I said. "Now, he's smuggling food into the city and making the people pay an exorbitant price to fund his rebellion. Or line his pockets." I turned away from them, nursing a headache.

"If I might offer some strategic advice..."

"I sure hope Celia has a pile of gold on standby for you," I said, turning around to face Jax. "Well? Speak."

"The issue in Neveri is one that needs a queen's attention," he said.

"I'm so surprised," I drawled. "And what about Beswick?"

"That sounds like a job for The Veil."

I lifted my hand in confusion. "Unfortunately, the Nestori haven't yet figured out how to duplicate people, so—"

"Do you think you're the only one who can run around in a mask?" he said.

"Are you saying you want to take up the charge?" I asked, genuinely surprised.

"Not at all," he said with a grin. "But I see two strapping young soldiers who would probably be up to the task."

"No way, I won't—" Jorad began, but Aline was louder.

"I'll do it," she said.

I blinked at her. "You…will?"

She shrugged. "Sounds like fun. And I'm bored out of my mind up in the camp. At least here, I'll be useful."

I chewed my lip. "When Maarit gets to Forcadel, she's going to tell Ilara I'm alive and what we did. If they find you here, they'll kill you—"

"I'm willing to take that chance," she said, pressing her fist to her chest.

"I'll stay and help her!" Elisha piped up from the corner.

"Oh, great, that makes me feel so much better."

"It should," Jax said, surprising me yet again. "She's kept your ass away from the guards every night you've been here. But it'll be impossible to do if the queen's combing the city for you."

I didn't like this; not only was I putting the investigation in the hands of someone with very little experience, but she wasn't a vigilante. I doubted she could even run on a rooftop. I couldn't help but feel like this would end with her down in the dungeons with Felix, or worse.

Another argument was on the tip of my tongue, but that little voice that always urged me to listen to Jax kept me quiet. It was hard not to agree that my presence here suddenly became more precarious.

"Fine," I said after a moment. "But before we leave, we have to retrieve something. You two," I said to Jorad and Jax, "stay here."

"We're coming," Jorad said.

Jax began to snicker, and I just rolled my eyes.

It took us longer than I wanted to cross the city with four people, but it also gave me a chance to watch Aline. She kept her feet surely along the tiles and showed no fear as we leapt over alleyways. At least I was sure she wouldn't slip off a roof.

We made our way to Sailor's Row, stopping every few minutes to wait out a Severian patrol, until we came to the pile of rubble that was Tasha's butchery.

"Stay here, for real this time," I said to Jax and Jorad. "Aline, Elisha, come with me."

I walked to the edge of the roof and beckoned them to follow as I climbed down to the street.

"What is this?" Aline asked quietly.

"I used to live here," I replied. "Before Felix found me and brought me back to the castle. The people who died here were good people."

She met my gaze. "What happened?"

"Ilara's bombs," I said, looking back at the rubble. "Because I'd been focused on the wrong thing. I don't want to make that mistake again. I'm going to the camp up north because I think if I stay..." I sighed. "But at the same time, I don't want to leave this unresolved. I'm putting a lot of trust in you to finish what I started."

She nodded. "My parents were indebted to Beswick. He paid for my commission and they died working their asses off for him. Knocking him down a few pegs would be..." She smiled, devilishly. "Very nice."

"My preference, and I can't believe I'm saying this," I added with a grimace, "is an alliance. He's a dirty crook and a liar, but his network is vast and I can't even begin to think about taking this city without him on my side or out of the way. At least if he works with me, I can temper some of his less-than-stellar qualities."

"How will you get him on your side?" she asked.

"I hadn't quite figured that out yet," I said. "But Jax suggested annoying him into an alliance, so you could start there. He's smuggling food into the city, so start there. Whatever avenues he's using are few and far between. Shut one down, he'll have to try another. Eventually, if you close all his doors, he might be willing to talk."

"And if he is?" Aline asked. "What then?"

"Tell him that due to his unreliable employees, he missed his chance to speak with me," I said, a smile on my face. "But that I'll be happy to speak with him upon my return."

She grinned. "I'll pass along the message. With pleasure."

"And what do you want me to tell him?" Elisha asked.

I looked down at her. "You need to do what you've been doing. Keep an eye out from above, and make sure Aline has cover."

"Are you sure it's wise to leave her here?" Aline cast Elisha a doubtful glance. "She's so young."

Before Elisha could respond, I lifted my hand and shook my head. "It's going to be you two against Beswick, and Beswick has more muscle. Elisha will keep your exits open." I smiled. "You'll be thankful you have her, believe me."

Aline nodded and held out her hand. "Sounds good to me, partner."

Elisha shook it with a growing smile. "I guess I gotta teach you the whistle code."

"Whistle…code?" Aline looked at me.

"You'll pick it up quickly," I said with a short nod. "But the gist of it is when you hear a whistle, get the hell out of there."

Aline nodded and smiled, but her gaze grew somber. "I want to say…I appreciate you trusting me with this. Captain Llobrega was out here while you were gone, night after night, and none of us were the wiser. I want to do the same." She swallowed. "I don't want to disappoint you. And by the Mother, I won't."

The earnestness in her gaze touched something deep in my soul. So with a sigh, I unclasped my cloak from around my shoulders and pulled the mask off my face. It was lined with gold —Luard had given it to me back in Kulka.

"Here," I said, placing the cloth in her hands. "I want you to use these. The cloak will help you jump off buildings—just grab the edges and it'll slow your descent. May take you a few times to get the hang of it, so don't jump off anything too big too soon." I cracked a grin. "You might break your arm. Speaking from experience."

She shared my smile, but there was still reverence in her gaze. "I don't know if I can take these."

"I think Felix took my spare. And here..." I unclasped my slingbag from my back and handed it to her. "I'm running low on supplies, but Elisha can help you make arrows for the crossbow and there may be a few Nestori in town. There's a list in one of my notebooks back at the bell tower. You'll want to get on their good side, and maybe pay them off. There's a whole bag of gold cutlery in the bell tower you can use. Elisha can show you how to wield knockout powder and anything else you might need."

Aline swept the cloak around her shoulders and tied the mask on her face. It was strange to see someone else wearing my clothes, and my bare back felt odd. But from the grin on her face, I had little doubt she'd fulfill the role with her whole heart.

"Where's mine?" Elisha asked with a frown.

"You're not Veil material yet," I said, patting her on the head to her utter disgust. "Soon, though. Just keep Aline out of trouble and I'll have a mask and cloak for you."

"Are you ready to go?" Jorad called from above. "It's getting late, and we need to get you out before the sun comes up."

"One more thing," I said, walking toward the rubble. With care, I lifted a couple of the large stones to reveal the small bag of ond I'd hidden here a few nights ago.

"Is that..." Aline began softly. "How did you get it?"

"It's Beswick's," I replied, making sure the bag was tied tightly before lifting it up. "I thought taking it and hiding in the city might persuade him to speak with me, but that clearly backfired. I think it might be best for us to get it out of the city. Just in case."

Aline nodded then saluted, and Elisha attempted the same. "Best of luck, Your Majesty," Aline said.

I took them both in, praying I wasn't signing their death warrants. "And to you, as well."

Chapter Sixteen

The sun was breaking over the horizon when Jax, Jorad, and I arrived at the small city outside Forcadel's walls. While Jorad went to get the horses from the stable, I stood facing the south, watching the sun's rays fall on my city.

Something tugged at my heart—perhaps guilt, perhaps just anxiety at what I was leaving behind and also heading toward. If I'd had my preference, I would've been the one under the mask, and Aline would be on her way to the army camp to lead them.

"Your Majesty," Jorad said behind me. He had two horses by the reins and offered me the second. "If you're ready."

"And here I thought I'd be walking," I said with a grin as I climbed into the saddle.

"Why would I make you walk to camp?" Jorad asked with a curious look. "You are a queen."

I opened my mouth to argue that I wasn't technically a queen, but Luard's voice came echoing through the past.

"You're a queen. So act like it."

"Yes, I suppose I am," I said.

Jax, seated on a third horse, snorted. "Mother above, now your crown won't fit."

We rode over the dewy grass and misty stretches of plains as the sun slowly burned away the night's chill. The thundering hooves did little to shake loose the uncertainty in my stomach. It was easy to hide behind the mask, to disappear into the shadows and be a symbol. Taking the mantle of queen was to be at the forefront, to have an entire kingdom look to me to save them. To protect them without a mask.

Perhaps that was also why I'd been so intent on Forcadel. I'd focused on the easy problems—Beswick, criminals, disruption—and given myself some breathing room while I figured out what to do. But I was merely avoiding the hard decisions.

Around noon, fluttering flags bearing the Forcadelian symbol lifted my heart and brought tears to my eyes. It had been so long since I'd seen them in their full glory. Beneath them, stood a collection of white tents and soldiers. I'd forgotten just how many had left Neveri with me, and seeing them together on this plain was like a kick to the gut. What must they think of their queen who led them to victory in Neveri and then vanished?

As our horses approached, a pair of soldiers appeared with their swords drawn. Jorad called out to them, and they quickly moved to allow us entry into the camp.

"Your Majesty," the one closer to me said, saluting me and bowing. "It's a pleasure to have you back."

"Thank you," I said with a forced smile.

More soldiers had heard Jorad's call and were arriving to greet us. They saluted me, bearing grins on their faces, then followed as we walked our horses deeper into the camp. More shouts of excitement and cheers erupted from all corners, and half-asleep soldiers rolled out of their tents to join the ruckus.

Two boys who didn't look that much older than me took my reins and allowed me to dismount.

"*Brynna!*"

I barely had time to turn before a black-haired blur landed in my arms, holding me close and kissing both my cheeks with furious passion. I stepped back, laughing as Beata's tearful face came into focus.

"Where's Katarine?" she asked, looking behind me. "And Felix?"

"She..." My face fell. "I couldn't... She's still with Ilara. And Felix is still... I'm sorry."

"I had a feeling," Beata said, her disappointment firming into resolve. "Don't worry about them. My Kat's the smartest woman I've ever met. She'll keep herself safe. And Felix is strong. We'll get him out of there in no time." She gripped my face. "Your hair is a mess, and your clothes—have you been climbing walls again? You look nothing like a queen."

"Aren't I lucky you're here to take care of me?" I said, taking her hands from my cheeks and kissing them.

"She's been taking care of all of us," Jorad said with a warm smile. "Thank you for sending her here."

"Speaking of which, I've got to get back to the dining tent and get ready for supper," she said. "I've put together quite a menu for tonight, just for you. You will be staying for a while, won't you?"

Another forced smile as guilt nipped at my heels. "Yes. It appears I will."

"Good," she said, tapping me on the nose. "It's high time you showed up and resumed your role. You can't govern from behind a mask, Brynna darling."

Even though her words cut, I couldn't help but smile at them. "I missed you, Bea."

"When you've finished getting settled, come visit me and we'll catch up," she said, squeezing my hands before letting them go.

"Your Majesty," Jorad said. "If you'll follow me, we can speak about the events in Neveri."

"Sure," I said. "Lead the way."

As we made our way to the center of camp, I received more bows and shouts of welcome. It was odd to be immediately recognized after spending so many months incognito—and it made me a little uncomfortable. Still, I pressed on until we came to a large tent that bore the Lonsdale crest.

My tent, I supposed.

Inside, there was an older-looking soldier leaning over a map. He straightened, saluted, then his face broke out into a smile.

"Your Majesty, it's wonderful to see you," he said, walking toward me. "My name is Captain Tarvo Mark."

I nearly fell over. "Captain Mark? As in, the captain who let my brother and father be murdered? As in, the captain Felix replaced?" I was also fairly sure he'd been stripped of his rank, but I was going to let that slide. For now.

His mouth twitched, just a little, as he straightened. "The very same."

"What in the Mother's name are you doing here?"

"I'd been retired to a nearby town when I heard about a rogue group of soldiers who'd set up camp here. When I arrived, it was clear that these young men and women were in need of some guidance, so I offered my services. I've been monitoring the situation both here and in Neveri so I could assist you when you finally returned to us."

I tried not to look guilty for my initial outburst. "Please, tell me all you know."

"As Lieutenant Llobrega has told you, Ammon let Maarit go. I expect she'll return to Forcadel shortly, if she's not there already."

"And we're sure she went to Forcadel?" I said. "After all, I don't think Ilara's in the mood to entertain failure right now. Maarit might want to just disappear."

"The pair of Kulkan soldiers accompanying her might feel differently," Mark said. "I believe Ammon's sending Maarit with a request to forge a new alliance with Ilara."

"He's doing all this without his father's permission, then," I said. "I had an agreement with Neshua that once Neveri was in their control, he would help me take back the kingdom."

"Neshua's three days away by boat, and even longer by foot," Mark said. "Plus, he's advancing in age. Perhaps he's willing to let Ammon do more than he had previously." His expression warmed into a somewhat patronizing smile. "Your father did the same with August."

I forced myself not to respond to that. "How many soldiers do we have?"

"Seventy," Jorad said. "Additional soldiers came from the borders when they heard we were here."

"Let's hope our number continues to grow," I said, pressing my finger on the city of Neveri, thinking to myself. "What does Ammon gain from allying himself with Ilara? He already has Neveri. He can control the border. What more could he want?"

"Your Majesty, if I may," Mark began with an overly-large smile. "I don't know if trying to understand his motives is pertinent. It's not about what he wants, it's about showing him that going back on your agreement won't be tolerated. It might be worthwhile to ride into the city with our might and have a meeting. If you remind Ammon that you have the Forcadelian military behind you, perhaps he'll reconsider his decision."

What I needed was to buy myself some time. "Do we still have scouts in Neveri?"

"Two," Mark said. "We receive daily reports from the soldiers we have stationed there."

Soldiers were good at ferrying messages, but making people

talk, that required a different skill set. "See if Jax will go to Neveri. He can find out more information than they can—and faster."

"Who is Jax?" Mark asked.

"He's..." I glanced at Jorad. Somehow, I didn't think Mark would take too kindly to having a thief in his camp. "One of my best spies. He can get in where others can't."

"I've never heard of such a man. Is he from your royal guard?" Mark asked.

"No," Jorad said. "But he's been with Her Majesty for weeks now, and if she feels he's the best equipped to retrieve information, he is."

I offered him a small smile as thanks.

"I disagree," Mark said. "We have some of the best soldiers Forcadel has to offer."

I can see why my father and brother were murdered. I forced a thin smile onto my face as I buried that thought. Mark had come in my hour of need, and he'd clearly kept my troops together. So I kept my tongue.

"Jax is quick. We should know something within a few days. I'll go find him and send him off now."

"That's inappropriate," Mark said. "Jorad can find him and tell him what to do. Queens must delegate."

I sighed, feeling the beginnings of a headache in my temple. "Fine. Go get Jax and bring him back here."

Jorad saluted and left me alone with Mark. I turned back to the map of Neveri, hoping for a moment of peace, but I didn't get it.

"It's quite wonderful to see you alive," Mark said. "When the soldiers told me, I have to say, I didn't believe them. You were such a young thing when you disappeared. And when I heard Felix had found you mere blocks from the castle..."

"Yes, hiding in plain sight," I said, under my breath. Something about him made me uncomfortable, almost like I was having to prove I was supposed to be there.

"And where have you been these past few years?"

I glanced at him. "They didn't tell you?"

"Well, they said you were masquerading as a vigilante in the city, but that has to be a lie," he said with a laugh. "I mean—"

"Why is that so surprising?" I asked, putting my hand on my hips.

"You were a mischievous child, but a knife-wielding, cape-wearing hoodlum?" He tilted his head. "I suppose it's just hard for me to reconcile that with what I knew of you. Your father would've been horrified."

"From what I heard, he knew," I said, evenly. "At least, Felix knew. So I assume August did as well." I had an itch to continue that thread, but I swallowed it with a grimace. "In any case, I'm here now, so we can move forward."

"Indeed," Mark said. "Without guidance from you, the camp has been a bit restless. I hope we can make a decision soon on how to proceed. Neveri would be an excellent option. Many of our soldiers lost friends there. Seeing Ammon go back on his word has been unnerving to them."

Further conversation was blissfully cut short by Jax throwing the tent flap out of his way and sauntering inside. "What d'ya want?"

"Are you really going to allow your subordinate to speak to you that way?" Mark asked, stepping forward with his hand on his sword.

"Jax doesn't really work for me," I said, deciding to leave out the Celia's-paying-him detail. "I need you to go to Neveri and find out what Ammon's thinking."

"I think Ammon's a rat," he said. "And he probably thinks he can do what he wants, because you're going to fail in the larger goal of taking Forcadel from Ilara."

"Thank you for that observation," I said dryly. "Will you go, please?"

He rolled his eyes and sighed loudly. "I guess."

"That was highly inappropriate," Mark said as Jax left. "If he's going to stay in this camp, he'll have to show deference to you."

"You work on that," I said, patting him on the shoulder. "Let me know how it goes."

Chapter Seventeen

"Mark does have a point," Jorad said as we walked away from the tent. "Jax can't openly defy you like that. It's bad for morale."

I made a noise. "One person isn't going to make a difference."

"Well..."

"Well, what?" I stopped and turned to him.

"Well, you also just disappeared for several weeks," Jorad said. "We left Neveri and you just gave a general order to find somewhere to camp. Then you sent us away, promising you'd be back within a few days."

My face warmed. "I had to take care of Beswick."

"And I understand that, but some of the soldiers may not," Jorad said. "All I'm suggesting is that you should consider that they might have some doubts about your leadership abilities." He cleared his throat. "If I'm not overstepping."

"You aren't," I said, putting my hand on my hip. "Have there been any problems from Ilara's soldiers?"

"No," Jorad said. "She hasn't sent any troops up this way—there's barely any security in the town nearby, so we've been patrolling the town in exchange for food and supplies."

"Excellent," I said. "I was wondering where all this stuff came from."

"Some from Neveri," he said. "But most of it's come from the village. Perhaps you can join Lady Beata when she goes. The townsfolk were overjoyed to hear that you're alive."

I winced. "I was hoping to keep my location a secret as long as I could. If Ilara finds out where I am, she could send a bevy of troops and flatten this place. We're still mostly out in the open."

"We aren't helpless," he said. "Seventy strong, and we have scouts monitoring the roads for signs of troop movements. We can pack up and leave in an hour if we need to."

I nodded. "Sounds like you've thought of everything."

"It was Captain Mark, actually. He's brilliant."

"Mm." I made a face. "He doesn't seem to think I know what I'm doing."

"It's in your best interests to listen to him," Jorad said. "Mark has years of leadership experience—nearly twenty as Captain of the Guard. Your father trusted him."

"And look what it got him."

"Pardon?" Jorad asked.

"Nothing." I shook my head. Clearly, I was the only one in the camp who remembered recent history. "Listen to Mark, sure. What else?"

"Take some time to get to know your soldiers," Jorad said. "One of the reasons Felix was so beloved was that he knew all of us —our hopes, dreams, fears. He took the time to understand why we'd joined and why we stayed." His eyes grew a little starry, and the guilt at leaving Felix behind in Forcadel gurgled in my stomach.

"I think I can handle that," I said, looking away from him to hide my unease.

A bell clanged—dinnertime, Jorad said. The soldiers walked toward a large tent in the center of the camp, where Beata greeted them. She, at least, had learned their names. I'd have her quiz me later.

"Brynna, my love," she said, tutting at me, "have you been rolling in the dirt?"

"A bit," I said, using the bottom of my tunic to wipe my face. "Got my ass kicked a little. Always good for the soul."

Jorad shook his head as he walked on, but Beata just giggled. "The old Brynna didn't like to lose."

"She's changed a little." I took her hands. "You look good, Bea. I'm glad they're treating you well here."

"I don't know about that," she said with a laugh as she led me inside the tent. "But I'm grateful for the industry. It keeps me from thinking about Kat in Forcadel." The ghost of a frown flitted across her face, and she shook herself to clear it. "I thought I was going to go mad in the castle. Ilara thought I'd be happy sitting around in Katarine's suite and doing needlepoint. Unfortunately, I've never been any good, so..."

"I bet your room was the cleanest it's ever been," I said with a smile.

She beamed. "Come, I've made a delicious beef stew for dinner tonight. And I've set a special place for you."

She led me through the tent, which took a while thanks to all the welcoming from the soldiers. A gold plate, gold goblet, and golden silverware decorated at a table with a fine linen tablecloth. A bottle of Kulkan wine stood next to the goblet.

"Beata," I said with a sigh as I looked behind me. The soldiers were eating out of wooden bowls and drinking beer from wooden cups. "You can't expect me to sit up here, do you?"

"I told Mark it was a bad idea, yes," she said with a knowing smile. "Go on, then. Grab yourself a place. I'll get this cleaned up."

I took her hand and winked. "Take that bottle for yourself. Queen's orders."

"I'll save it for when Kat comes back," she said softly.

While Beata cleaned up the head table, I retrieved a bowl and some stew then walked through the soldiers until I found an empty spot. I plopped down unceremoniously and began to eat. The soldiers quieted around me, and I glanced up at their shellshocked faces.

"What?" I asked.

"Is it...true?" one brave soul asked.

I swallowed. "Is what true?"

"Are you really The Veil?"

The clatter around me stilled as all gazes in the room landed on me—a feat, considering I was in the middle of them.

I finished chewing on the gristle in my mouth and took a long swig of the beer. "Yep."

A cheer erupted then the deluge of questions began. Did I really sink a ship? Had I really fought Captain Llobrega in the castle? Had I really flown from one city to the other?

"I've done a lot of things, but flying isn't one of them," I said with a laugh.

I did my best to answer them, being vague when it suited the mystery of the story, and coming clean when it wasn't. We stayed in the dining tent for hours then ventured out to one of the many bonfires as I kept my audience riveted.

"All right, all right," Jorad said, coming to the table. "Her Majesty has had a long day."

I hadn't been tired until he'd said so, and a yawn escaped my lips. The past few days had finally caught up with me, and I followed Jorad to one of the nicest tents in the camp.

"It's not much but—"

I didn't hear what he said, falling to the cot and closing my eyes.

I slept better than I had in ages, and the next morning woke to the sound of the breakfast bell. I pulled myself out of the cot and washed my face with the water and pitcher that had been left for me. I couldn't recall the last time I'd had a real bath—perhaps Neveri. I took some time to wash the rest of me before changing into a fresh tunic.

Having been surviving on one meal, I wasn't hungry, so I bypassed breakfast to explore more of the camp. A line of clothes near a creek wafted in the breeze, next to that a vat with a fire underneath it. Closer to the center of camp, another fire smoldered in what appeared to be a smithing hut.

Beyond the mess hall, two bare-chested men fought with wooden swords, clashing and swinging with focused effort. If I hadn't known better, I would've sworn they were trying to murder one another. But once the match ended with one on the ground, a blade to his chest, friendly smiles broke out and the winner reached down to pick up the loser.

"You're looking good," I called out to them.

"Your Majesty!" one of the soldiers cried, calling his friends to join me in their circle. They introduced themselves one by one, but I could no sooner remember their names than any of the others I'd heard today. Still, their energy was infectious, and I still nursed the urge to beat something up.

"So, who wants to go a round with me?" I asked, walking to the open trunk on the edge of the ring. I frowned—only broadswords. Not my favorite weapon, as the weight made it hard to use in a fistfight.

One soldier let loose a belly laugh. "It wouldn't be very good for us if we beat our queen."

I pointed the sword at him. "You're first."

His name was Enos, and he clearly considered me an easy

match. But I had some energy to burn, and wiping a smug smile off someone's face felt oddly appropriate.

"Are you ready?" he asked.

I swung the sword. "Let's go."

He thundered toward me, and I blocked him just in time. My arms shook as he pressed down on me, clearly superior in strength. On my knees, I couldn't use my legs to knock him over again, and my arms were otherwise occupied.

But at the same time, he was pressing all his weight on me, so if I removed the weight...

In one move, I allowed his sword to come down on mine, scooting out from underneath it and letting the joined blades hit the ground. I left the sword and dropped to a crouch, swinging my leg around and knocking him over. A cheer erupted from the group as I rolled forward to my sword, but...it was still heavy.

Screw this. I reached behind me for my slingbag, but it wasn't there—it was back in Forcadel. I realized this just as the wooden sword landed against my neck.

"The bout is mine!" Enos cheered.

"Indeed," I said with a thin smile. "Seems I'll have to get used to being queen instead of The Veil."

"And it's a good thing you have so many soldiers at your back," Jorad said, reaching down to help me up. I hadn't noticed he'd arrived, but a group of soldiers had gathered behind him. "Perhaps you should get cleaned up? I'm sure Captain Mark wants to have more strategy sessions with you."

"I'd rather get used to fighting without knockout powders and my crossbow," I said, picking the sword up from the ground. "Who's next?"

I fought no less than twenty matches, with Jorad taking me on twice and Enos coming back for thirds. By the end of the day, I was dripping in sweat, but I'd successfully stopped reaching for my slingbag and become as used to the sword as I'd been with anything else. It was still a slower fight than I'd have liked with the heavy sword, but I couldn't be disappointed. Tomorrow, I'd get better, and the next day even better.

As I was finishing my last bout, I felt a pair of eyes on me. Captain Mark was standing in front of his tent, his arms folded across his chest and a look of dismay on his face. The look on his face was telling enough, so I brushed myself off and joined him inside his tent.

"You seem to be settling into the camp," he began.

"I am," I said. "The soldiers seem well-equipped and content. I suppose I have you to thank for that."

"Indeed," he said, bowing. "Unity is achieved with order and rigor. Which is what I wanted to speak with you about. I'm concerned about your decorum around the soldiers."

I quirked a brow. "My what?"

"You're too easy with your subordinates, too quick with your tongue. Sitting at the table with them, instead of at your rightful place before them...it may send the wrong message."

"Sitting with my troops sends the wrong message?" I asked. "I seem to recall Felix doing the same thing. He lived with them."

"Felix wasn't queen," Mark said. "Crowned or not, you're ours, and you'd better start acting like it."

And here I thought I was. "I will do my best."

"Good girl," he said.

It was all I could do not to deck him.

Chapter Eighteen

Katarine

As promised, Maarit was executed in the town square in the morning. Ilara had forbidden anyone from speaking about what she'd done, except to say she'd betrayed the country. And once Maarit's body had been removed from the town square, Ilara would entertain no more conversation about it.

The Kulkan envoys who'd arrived with Maarit had been expelled from the castle, but I'd asked Luisa to keep tabs on them. I didn't trust her as far as I could throw her, but if she wanted to pretend she was in my employ, she could run errands for me. She reported that they were staying at an inn near the water and had no intention of returning to Kulka until they'd met with the queen.

Ilara, however, entertained no conversation about them, even going so far as to cancel our last few weekly sessions. And I still had no clue why she'd given the order to bring Brynna back alive. I was losing my insight into the inner workings of her mind, and that was cause for alarm.

How I longed for Beata, and our nightly strategy sessions. She always had a way of keeping me out of my own mind. And problems seemed so much less complex when considered from the warmth of her arms.

Instead, I had to settle for Luisa and her fake friendship. She had taken to meeting me in the small dining area of my suite for breakfast every morning. It seemed every morning she arrived earlier and earlier.

"Oh, wipe the frown from your face, Lady Katarine," she said, her dark eyes brimming with excitement. "Today is a very special day."

"Mm." I took a long sip of my coffee. It hadn't tasted the same since Beata left. "Is it?"

"Of course!" She wore an honest grin, and it drew a smile onto my face. "Today is the start of the Geestig festival!"

"I apologize," I said. "I'm unfamiliar with the event." Then again, before Ilara invaded, I'd known nothing of Severian customs or traditions.

"It may not seem like it here," Luisa said, rising to her feet, "but in the desert, this is the time of year when the geestig flowers bloom. It's a celebration of Severian resilience and life. See, the flowers are small, but it seems the entire city is blanketed in their sweet smell. They crop up out of the clay stone roadways and between crevasses in walls. We make tea out of them, and it doesn't need a cube of sugar." She clapped her hands together. "Men and women wear crowns of flowers made by the children, and we dance and make merriment for days."

"How do you offer salutations?" I asked. "Happy… Gastig?"

"Oh, you'll get the pronunciation," she said with a laugh. "But yes, Happy Geestig."

The wistfulness in her voice eroded some of my carefully constructed walls. "It sounds magnificent."

"It is," she said. "Ilara told me she tried to grow the geestig flowers here, but the ground was too moist. Can you believe that?"

She turned and smiled at me. "A flower that can't grow in Forcadel's fertile soil."

"It seems a plant made for the desert," I said.

"But flowers can be trained to live elsewhere," she said, turning back to the window. "You are a mountain-dweller, made for elevations and snow. Yet you thrive here."

"With help," I said with a soft smile. "How will you be celebrating today?"

"Queen Ilara will be taking a ride in the city," Luisa said. "She's asked us to accompany her on horseback."

"I thought it was too dangerous to venture out," I said, genuinely curious. Ilara had barely set foot outside the castle since she'd invaded, thanks to the riots and unrest. There hadn't been a significant change, or so I thought. Perhaps she was just feeling more confident lately.

More concerning was that Ilara had planned an entire festival and I'd had no idea about it. I would have to start asking more questions of the servants.

"Today is a very special day for Severians," Luisa replied, walking to the window. "It wouldn't do for our queen to remain behind locked doors."

"Indeed."

Luisa helped me dress in a shapeless cotton shirt and wide trousers that hung to my ankles. On my feet, she tied on a pair of leather sandals, exposing my toes to the world. But she wore the same, so I accepted this new experience.

"You'll get used to walking in sandals soon enough," Luisa said.

"They seem to be giving me something of a blister," I replied, resisting the urge to adjust them again. "It's a good thing we're riding."

We came out to the courtyard, which was already bustling with people. Most of the servants wore the same trousers and shirts, but the soldiers were dressed in their finest dark brown uniforms.

Many of them wore medals on their breasts along with the Severian crest. A few were on horseback, but the majority were on foot. Coyle was among them, one of a small number of Forcadelians in the mix.

"Will they all be joining us?" I asked Luisa.

"Of course! There will be a mile parade around the castle, just like in Severia."

The soldiers eased some of my worry about venturing into the city, but I still worried so many swords with so much unrest was a recipe for disaster.

"Good morning, ladies," Coyle said, walking over to us and saluting. "It's a wonderful day for Geestig."

No issue with pronunciation there. "You seem well-acquainted with this tradition for a Forcadelian, Coyle."

"It's my job to know everything there is to know about my soldiers," he said, leveling an unfriendly glare in my direction. "They've been talking about this for weeks on end. You must get out of the castle more."

The meaning in his words was clear by the look in his eye. He knew that my position as Ilara's second was slipping, and he wasn't going to do a damn thing about it. But I wouldn't have expected anything less from him.

"Captain Coyle, you certainly wear a Severian uniform well," Luisa said, flashing him a smile. "We're so fortunate that you're here, leading our troops and keeping our city safe. Things have surely turned around as of late, haven't they?"

"Indeed they have," he said.

I kept my tongue, but questions exploded in the back of my mind. Surely, I would've heard if something had occurred in the city. My communications hadn't been cut off for so long.

"Excuse me," Coyle said, leaving us to climb the stairs.

At the top, he put his fingers to his lips and whistled loudly, catching the attention of the soldiers. They turned on their heel to face him, resting their hands behind their backs.

He cast a wary look out among the group. "Her Majesty, Queen Ilara Hipolita Särkkä of Severia."

Ilara appeared behind him, dressed for the occasion in a Severian military uniform adorned with medals. On her head was a crown that seemed almost out of place...I had to swallow a gasp. It was Maurice's. August and Brynna's father. The last I'd seen it was on his head as they closed the coffin at his memorial service.

It was all I could do not to be ill.

Ilara carefully walked down the stairs, her head held high and the heavy gold crown perfectly balanced on her head. Once she reached the bottom of the stairs and Coyle was there to help her into the open air carriage. The same one August and I had ridden in after we'd wed.

I kept my breathing steady as Luisa and I approached the carriage.

"You look magnificent, Your Majesty," Luisa said, beaming from ear to ear. "Truly, our queen is majestic and has no equals."

"Lady Katarine," Ilara said, catching me with her scrutinizing gaze. "You look a bit pale."

"Perhaps a bout of illness from being indoors for too long," I said, curtseying as well as I could in the trousers. "It's most wonderful to see you on such a special day."

"Indeed," she said. "Do you like my crown?"

The corner of my mouth twitched toward a snarl before I could stop it. "You wear it well, Your Majesty."

She smirked and smoothed her dress. "I'm ready to depart," she called to Coyle. "Open the gates."

Luisa and I retreated to the tacked horses behind her carriage. With the sandals on my feet, it was hard to climb on, but I managed without looking too much a fool. Before us, the main castle gates groaned as they opened, revealing the city beyond and...a crowd of people, all of them cheering.

Coyle's call to the military was a far-off echo, but soon the sound of their marching filled the small courtyard. They marched forward in lines of ten and rows of five, their hands resting on their swords. Once the front of the parade had left space, Ilara's footman snapped the reins of the horse, and Luisa and I goaded ours into a slow walk as we followed her out of the castle.

I hadn't been mistaken—there was a crowd in the town square. It was hard to tell Forcadelian from Severian, but I couldn't imagine this unbridled joy coming from those who'd been conquered. Each person wore a crown of white flowers as they waved to their queen. She offered them a gracious wave back.

"I thought the flowers didn't grow here," I said.

"They don't, but Her Majesty had a shipment of flowers delivered last week. The children have been hard at work putting them together." She beamed. "They were so excited to see visions of home."

But I didn't see smiling faces—I saw more problems for Brynna. Ilara had filled the town with her own people, with innocent lives. Men, women, and children seeking a better life for themselves in a land full of plenty. Based on the adoring way they fawned over Ilara, they had her to thank for it. Even if Brynna killed Ilara, these Severians wouldn't return to the desert willingly.

"You look concerned, Lady Katarine," Luisa said beside me. "Cheer up, it's Geestig!"

And like so many other worries, I put that in the back of my mind and forced myself to smile for the crowd.

The parade was short, perhaps thanks to the security concerns in the northern part of the city, and when we returned there was to be a large feast in Ilara's honor. One of the young children who'd been invited from the crowd gave me a crown of flowers, and I couldn't deny the smell was sweet.

"Thank you," I said to her as she placed it on my head. "Do you live here in Forcadel, now?"

"No, miss," she said, flashing me a toothy grin that was missing a few in the front. "I live in Aunela, at a boarding school Her Majesty chartered for us."

Aunela? That was an eastern port city—and I'd never heard of a boarding school there. "Well, you've done a magnificent job. Thank you for this."

"Look at you!" Luisa cheered when she saw me. "You look almost like a Severian."

"I am trying," I said, adjusting the delicate crown on my head. "I'm sure this festival is something to behold in Severia."

"It's never been so grand," she said, taking my arm. "Queen Ilara has invited all her favorite businesses from the city to attend. Look at them all, former Forcadelians becoming Severians."

I gazed out into the crowd in the ballroom. Once, I could've named every single one of Forcadel's most favored business owners. But now, every other person seemed brand new to me.

One new face caught my attention. A Forcadelian man with a pencil-thin mustache. He met my gaze and offered a smirk, strolling over with all the confidence of a man used to getting what he wanted.

"Evening," he said, bowing. "Lady Katarine, Lady Luisa. The festival is wonderful."

"Thank you," Luisa said, bowing in return. "I hope you're enjoying yourself, Mr. Cantwell."

"Who's that?" I asked Luisa once he left to speak with a woman nearby.

"Oh, just a local businessman," she said with a bright smile. "He's been helping Her Majesty with some of her new business ventures in the eastern side of the country."

"She seems quite busy with that," I said.

"It has certainly taken a lot of her time," Luisa said. "But you can see it in the faces of our countrymen—they are grateful for her attentions."

"I thought most of Severia had moved here," I asked.

"Oh, no," she said with a bit of a giggle. "Severia is a vast nation with hundreds of thousands of souls. They couldn't possibly all fit within the walls of this city. Most of them are settling in the city of Aunela. I passed through on my way here. It's truly becoming a magnificent city."

"With a boarding school, I hear," I said.

She made a sound. "There's so much happening in that city. I can hardly keep it all straight. Boarding schools, libraries, new water systems. It's been under heavy construction for nearly six months now."

"I would like to see it," I said.

"You may, sooner than you know," Luisa said with a smile. "But for now, let us toast to this happy day, and the celebration of life!"

I toasted to her, but the knot of anxiety in my stomach grew harder as the reality of my position in the castle became ever clearer.

Chapter Nineteen

It was easy to fall into the routine with my soldiers. We rose at dawn, ate a light breakfast, then set to training, preparing, mending, laundering—all the things that were required of an active camp. Everyone pitched in, whether it was to chop wood for the bonfires or bring in water from the nearby stream.

I did as much as Mark would let me. Whether it was training in the ring with the soldiers ("It's bad for morale for them to lose against you") or where I ate ("If you aren't going to eat on gold, you should at least be at the front of the table"), I couldn't win with him. I still wasn't wholly comfortable pushing back against him, not when all the soldiers in camp seemed to follow his every move. So when Beata asked if I'd join her on a jaunt into town to pick up some fruit, I jumped at the chance.

"Please, get me out of this camp," I said, sitting on the trunk as Beata flitted around the mess tent. "If only for a few hours. I feel like I'm back in that tower, with Katarine putting me in that stupid posture contraption again."

Beata walked by and poked my side, forcing me to sit upright. "You be nice to my Kat. She was only trying to help."

She disappeared into the back room then returned with something dark. A velvet, Forcadelian blue dress with gold-trimmed sleeves.

"Beata," I said with a sigh. "Where'd you get this?"

"I remembered your measurements," she said. "Had it made for when you finally showed up. But you've been too busy rolling in the dirt to be bothered with it." She winked as she pressed it against me. "The people in town will be thrilled to see you, so you'd better fit the part."

"Thank you," I said, not altogether pleased to be wearing a dress again, but touched by the thought.

"And here," she said, handing me a black box. "Jorad said you'd given it to him for safekeeping, so he gave it to me."

I opened the box, revealing the gold circlet Luard had had made for me in Niemen. Last I'd seen it, it had been covered in muddy fingerprints from our battle in Neveri, but someone had cleaned it.

"I never thought I'd be happy to see this thing," I said, sitting down on a nearby chair. "Will you help me put it on?"

She unbraided and brushed my hair then reassembled the plait, twisting it around my head. Watching her in the mirror brought back memories of Forcadel before the invasion, of how I'd hated seeing her and Katarine watching me in the mirror and how miserable I'd been to be forced into this role. I took Beata's hand after she set the gold circlet and kissed it.

"I'm so glad you're here," I said, looking up at her.

"Be careful," she said, tapping my nose. "I am a taken woman."

I laughed and followed her out of the tent. The soldiers stopped what they were doing and bowed as I passed—even Enos, who offered me a small wave. I was starting to remember their names, although it would take me a few more days yet.

At the front of camp, Mark and Jorad were waiting near the wagon we'd be taking into town with a smattering of soldiers, all dressed in Forcadelian blues to match mine. Unsurprisingly, Mark look disgruntled.

"Glad to see you look the part of a queen," he said, glancing at my head. "But I must protest this trip. It's safer for you here in camp. Who knows what you might find out in the village?"

"Then it's a good thing I have my knives," I said, climbing onto the wagon without help.

"Can you fight in that?" Beata asked.

I shrugged. "I'd prefer not to. You did such a good job with my hair."

She giggled, and I turned to my two consternated soldiers. "I promise, Captain Mark, I'll get into no trouble on this journey. But if you feel strongly about it, then you can send Lieutenant Llobrega in your place."

In the end, he did give us an extra five soldiers, but he and Jorad remained back in camp. I was honestly grateful for the break, as it gave me a chance to get to know the soldiers accompanying us. Most of them had been in Neveri, but a couple were the defectors from the border. Malka, a tall Forcadelian woman, had fought me in the training ring the day before.

"I swear, she was a cat," she said to her compatriots. "I've never seen a person bend that way before."

"Practice," I said. "Maybe I'll teach you some things."

For the most part, the soldiers talked while I absorbed the small details they let into their conversations. Mentions of home, of Felix, of Neveri. Their uncertainty about where we would go from here, their pride in being the queen's soldiers, and their gratitude to people in town.

"They've taken us in with open arms," Orman, a defector from the border, said. "Especially when Lady Beata showed up."

"Oh, I did nothing," she said with a soft smile.

"Then what are these clothes in the back of the carriage?" I asked, looking at her.

"The seamstress in town is getting on in age," she said with a shrug. "I may have offered to make a few dresses for the townsfolk in exchange for some gold."

My face fell. "Bea…"

"I told you," she said. "I like the industry. I'm not sleeping anyway."

Guilt reappeared, and I let it eat at me as we continued toward the small town. A gaggle of children ran out to meet us, all under the age of ten. The oldest of the bunch stopped and gaped at me.

"T-the queen!"

The other children stopped their chattering and stared openly. I offered a little wave as we passed, uncomfortable with the unabashed shock on their faces.

"Get used to it," Beata said, nodding to the town, where more people were gathering.

The reaction was almost instantaneous, and before I even knew what was happening, I was surrounded. The expressions ranged from jubilation to hysteria, some even sobbing into their hands as I passed. My soldiers kept a tight perimeter, but I didn't sense anyone intent on hurting me.

"Hello, hi, how are you?" The words tumbled from my mouth as we pressed into the village. The crowd remained thick, even after we stopped and Beata disembarked to bring her wares to the tailor. Two of my guards stayed beside me as the crowd shouted too many questions for me to hear.

"All right, all right! Give the poor queen some air!"

A woman came ambling through the crowd, her low voice echoing through the din and quieting everyone. She wore a smile that said she ran the town and I instantly took a liking to her.

"Your Majesty," she said with a flourished bow. "My name is

Tamra, and I run the inn and tavern in town. It would be my honor to have you dine there." She gestured to the crowd. "At least you might get a word in edgewise."

"Sure," I said with a grin. "Lead the way."

Tamra cut a path through the crowd with ease, although I still had a few stragglers try to speak with me. She led me to a rather large building in town called The Flying Fish, and once I was inside, she shut the door on the crowd.

Tamra offered me a seat at the table. "If you'd like to receive people, I can let them in."

"I don't know what I can do for them," I said, glancing out the window. "What do they need?"

"Right now, just a little hope," she said, placing a tankard on the bar. She beamed at me. "I have to say, I was convinced they were lying. How in the Mother's name did you survive?"

I gave her the abridged version of my story, but she'd already heard the part about Neveri from the soldiers who'd been in town. She was clearly impressed with the lengths I'd traveled, and as I recounted my tale, I was a little impressed with myself, too.

"And now?" she asked, refilling my tankard.

"Now, I'm setting the pieces for the eventual retaking of Forcadel," I said, wiping the suds off my upper lip. "But it's not going so well."

"These things never do," she said as the door opened and Beata walked in. "You seem a capable person. I'm sure you'll figure it out. Especially if you've got Lady Beata by your side."

"They wouldn't let me in, so I had to threaten not to feed them," she said, sitting on a stool next to me. "Thank you, Tamra."

"My pleasure," she said, placing a tankard on the bar for her. "You get prettier every time I see you."

Beata blushed. "Katarine's going to be jealous with all this attention I'm getting."

But I glanced at the two of them, at the way Tamra leaned on the bar, the way Beata leaned toward her. There was definitely a flirtation going on. Not that I thought Beata would be unfaithful to Katarine, but clearly, she'd been doing whatever she could to further the cause.

Tamra excused herself to the back, and I nudged Beata playfully. "Look at you, flirting with bartenders."

"Katarine will be so jealous when she finds out," Beata said with a sad smile. "Or proud, I'm not quite sure which." She gazed down at her hands. "If I ever see her again."

My heart twisted for her. "Every day, I think about them and wonder if I could've done more."

"I know you did your best."

"The thing is, I didn't." I swallowed hard. "I could've gone into the dungeon. I could've fought my way through all the guards, maybe used some hyblatha to get him out. Instead, I let Jax tell me it was more important that I stay out of trouble. More important that I live."

"But that's the thing, Brynna. You aren't just a person. You're a symbol." She gestured to the town behind us. "Look at how they reacted when you came here. They didn't even have to be told it was you—they just assumed. The people are starved for hope. If you got captured..." She shook her head.

"I know," I said. "But it's hard to be the one who gets saved when everyone else gets left behind. Especially when those people..."

"Heavy is the head that wears the crown," Beata said, tapping the gold circlet on my head. "I don't envy you at all."

"Me neither." I stared into my tankard. "Especially since I'm wearing the crown, but I don't seem to be calling the shots."

"Then call them," Beata said. "You have a village full of people outside hungry to hear your words. And you ducked in here to hide out. I say you get out there and speak to your people." She shrugged. "You're going to have to get used to it anyway."

"Excuse me, Your Majesty." Enos ducked his head inside. "I hate to interrupt, but Captain Mark wanted us to have you home before sundown, and it's getting to be that time."

Beata quirked her brow at me, but I said nothing as I rose.

"Leaving already?" Tamra said, her arms laden with bottles of wine and rounds of cheese.

"Unfortunately, duty calls," I said. "But as soon as I'm able, I'll return."

The mood was the same when I walked out of the tavern. The crowd opened a path for me, anticipation plain on their faces. They'd wanted more from their queen, and I hadn't delivered.

"I have nothing to say to them," I whispered hastily to Beata.

"They don't need much," she said. "Just a bit of hope. Surely you can offer that."

Enos helped me climb onto the back of the wagon, where I sat facing the crowd. I gazed at the crowd—old and young, tall and short. Some lighter skinned, some darker. All desperate for something they could take with them.

"Wait a second," I said to Enos as he picked up the reins. I climbed on top of the wagon to look at the crowd.

"I wanted to thank you all for your hospitality," I called. "You've shown my soldiers such kindness in our hour of need. I wish I had more to give you than hope, but that's all I have at the moment." I paused, racking my brain for something else to say. "We will be retaking the kingdom in the next few months. And Ilara will wish she'd stayed to watch me die."

An eruption of cheers echoed from the group, and I waved as I plopped back down next to Beata. Enos cracked the reins, and we jerked forward.

"Well?" I asked.

"Not too bad," Beata said, brushing a stray hair out of my face.

"We'll make a queen of you yet."

Chapter Twenty

"I think that was a mistake," Mark said over breakfast the next morning.

"Color me surprised," I muttered. "Please, enlighten me?"

"You announced yourself to a town. What's to prevent Ilara from sending soldiers up this way? Word will travel." He cleared his throat. "Perhaps you should consider my suggestion to move camp. West would be a good option."

It was hard not to roll my eyes. "We aren't ready for Neveri," I said. "Not until Jax gets back with word. But I don't disagree that we should move."

To where, I had no clue. The map of Forcadel was vast, but nearly every part of the country was a day's ride from the capital. It was far, and yet it wasn't. I wouldn't put it past Ilara to assemble an army that could massacre mine in a single night. It didn't seem there was anywhere we could go that would offer more protection than what we had now.

"Skorsa could be an option," I said, pointing to the eastern city. "Ariadna surely has her forces in place now. They might be able to house us temporarily."

"I wouldn't want to move our troops so far from Neveri, though," Mark said.

It was hard not to roll my eyes. How many times could I tell him we weren't ready for Neveri? "What if I don't want to send troops to Neveri?"

"I can't imagine why you wouldn't."

I straightened and flashed a thin smile. "I think I'm going to take a walk to clear my thoughts. Keep coming up with alternatives."

As I left the tent, I had no doubt that every one of Mark's suggestions would be on the western side of the country. The man was nothing if not stubborn, but he'd surely met his match with me. I just wished I had something to tell him other than "No."

A cloud of dust rose up from the entrance of the camp, and I heard raised voices, so I jogged in that direction, curious. There, I found a gaggle of soldiers with their swords raised and one very irate Jax.

"Oi! Larissa! Brynna! Whatever the hell your name is now," Jax barked when he saw me. "Tell these idiots to let me through!"

"Stand down," I called, pushing through the crowd. "He's with me."

"Your dogs need to learn some new tricks," Jax barked, wiping the dust from his face. "Nearly got stuck with an arrow on my way in."

"Glad to know the security's working," I said with a half-smile. The young soldiers still wore looks of uncertainty. "Run to Lady Beata and get some food and water. Bring it to my tent."

"*Your* tent. You seem to be taking to this queen thing again." Jax said with a snort, following me deeper into the camp. Mark was waiting for us inside *my* tent, but I waited until the soldier had brought Jax something to eat before I peppered him with questions.

"Neveri's kind of in an uproar right now," Jax said. "The citizens seem to have soured on Ammon a little. There's a curfew again, all that."

"Okay, but what about Ammon?" I said, leaning forward. "What did you find out about him and Ilara? Why'd he go back on our deal?"

"Because he's a rat."

I sighed. "Jax."

"Fine, fine." He wiped his lip. "Basically, from what I gather, he doesn't want to be the only country without an explosive powder. So he sent an envoy to Ilara to give her Forcadel back in exchange for whatever she used during the initial invasion of Forcadel."

"And he thinks Ilara will agree to that?" I looked at Jorad. "Does she even have any more of it?"

"I don't know," Jorad said. "We didn't hear of it if she did."

I sat back in my chair, comparing what I knew of Ilara's temperament to this new information. I was playing a card game but could only see half the cards I'd been dealt. It was hard to make decisions that way.

"My queen?" Jorad asked. "What are you thinking?"

"I think there are two possible scenarios," I began slowly. "The first is that Ilara doesn't ally herself with Ammon. It's the least possible outcome, but the best one for us. Ammon will be back to where he started, and we could potentially return to our original arrangement."

"And the other?"

"Less fortunate for us," I said. "Ammon and Ilara become allies. We lose the Vanhoja river, and we're down all the artillery they promised us. And Ammon has Severian ond to use against us."

"What do we do if that happens?" Jorad asked.

"I don't know," I said softly. "Aline and Elisha are back in Forcadel, hopefully getting through to Beswick. If we can get him on our side, then we'll have a stronger footing inside the city. But losing Ammon and the river support leaves us vulnerable." I didn't want to think about what would happen if I lost Ammon *and* Beswick.

"Do we have more ond?" Jorad asked. "Maybe we could use it to barter with Ammon?"

"A bag," I said. "Not enough to sway Ammon, I'm sure. And I don't think Ariadna would be too happy about that. I'm not in the business of selling ond to foreign nations."

"Beswick isn't, though," Jax said.

I turned to him. "I'm sorry?"

"I heard a rumor while I was there," Jax said. "Beswick's still trying to get ond out of Niemen into Forcadel somehow. But Skorsa is all but closed now, and Neveri is crawling with soldiers. So what they're saying is that instead of bringing it through the major cities, he's using an alternate route through the forest."

My eyebrows shot up. "You think he's using Celia's forest?"

"Celia the forest pirate?" Mark did a double take.

Jax ignored him. "The point is: if Beswick is using the forest pass to get through the border, that means he's gotta take the ond through Kulka. So I say you tell Ammon where to get ond in his own country. You'll cut off Beswick's supply and appease Ammon in one fell swoop."

"But it's basically giving the Kulkans the ond and betraying Niemen's trust, just without getting my hands dirty," I said. "I can't jeopardize my only remaining alliance. If they found out, Ariadna might pull her support—or worse."

But it did present a new opportunity. "What if, instead of giving it to Ammon, we just send it back to Niemen? Catch it when it comes through the forest. Mark's been telling me to move our camp. Why don't we just move a little closer to the border?"

"I'm absolutely sure that Celia would be fine with you and a hundred of your closest friends camping out in her forest," Jax said with a firm nod. "That sounds completely reasonable."

"It might if we ask her to help us," I said. "You said yourself that she's very interested in helping me get back on the throne."

"Yeah, but...not that much."

"She sent her second to babysit me," I said. "That's pretty invested if you ask me."

He made a face, but Mark finally spoke up. "I'm lost here. Are you suggesting that we move our camp to *Celia's* forest?"

"I'm saying that we ask her for an alliance," I said. "She can provide spies, food, even some weapons. And we can intercept the ond, thus cutting off Beswick's supply." I paused, smiling at him. "And we'll be within half a day of Neveri, so you'll get what you want, too."

"I must strongly protest. Celia isn't our concern. Neither is Beswick. Besides that, she is a *dangerous* criminal," Mark said, rising to his feet. "She would sooner shoot you with an arrow than let you inside her camp."

I stared at him, pursing my lips a little. "Are you unaware that I lived there, Mark?"

He started. "You...what?"

"When I ran away from the castle," I said, sizing him up, "Celia took me in and taught me everything I know about being a vigilante. And when Ilara stabbed me, Celia's the one who rescued me. So yes, I do believe she would be interested in an alliance. Especially if I demonstrate that I've been successful in gathering other forces."

"And how have you been successful?" Mark asked. "Ammon betrayed you, Beswick won't meet with you, and your soldiers are barely holding on by a thread. Thank the Mother that I showed up when I did, or your entire operation would've fallen apart by now."

My brows shot up to my hairline.

Jax snorted. "Where is the lie?"

"We don't need thieves and criminals on our side," Mark said. "It's time that you move on and move up from those people. Beswick is easily dealt with, after all. He's a businessman; if you bribe him, he'll go away. And this idea of going to Celia's camp and asking her to be friends? It's ridiculous. The best thing to do is to march on Neveri tomorrow and reclaim your alliances by force."

"In your opinion," I said.

"It is the best option, and we all agree," Mark said, gesturing to Jorad. "You were a passable vigilante, but you don't know the first thing about leading an army, or strategy, or anything of that sort."

I sat back, surveying him. "Is that how you really feel?"

"Yes," he said, a smile growing on his face. "If you want, I'll give the order for the troops to prepare for an assault on Neveri. We can prove to Ammon that we aren't to be treated as such—"

"I do not want."

"I— What?"

I rose, tapping the map. "As it stands, I don't actually believe that you're in the majority here. And even if you were, it isn't up to you. It's up to me. And I say we take our chances with Celia. If all else fails, we can camp nearby and catch the ond as it comes into Forcadel. And we'll figure something else out with Ammon."

Mark exhaled. "I feel like you might not be in the right mind to be directing the troops. Perhaps you've got some lingering vendetta against Celia and Beswick, and that's what's coloring your vision, but you're not fit to make this decision."

"Not fit?" I said slowly. "And you are?"

"I am," he said. "Your father trusted me—"

"And you got him killed," I snapped. "Along with my brother. Within weeks of each other. Not to mention, you let Beswick grow his empire right under your nose. Perhaps it's you, Mark, who isn't fit to make this decision." I quirked a brow. "What, does Beswick have something on you? You did such a bad job managing him. It wouldn't surprise me."

Mark got to his feet, his cheeks growing ruddy with anger and his chest puffing with indignation. "I have never been spoken to this way. Your father would—"

"I think it's time for you to leave."

His eyes bulged. "What?"

"While I'm grateful that you showed up to help my soldiers when you did, I've grown tired of always being questioned. Clearly, you don't trust that I'm making the right decisions, so it's best that we part ways." I kept his gaze firmly. "I was a passable vigilante, but I was also responsible for the plan to take down Neveri. And in this case, I feel strongly that another assault on that city would fail —and I would know, as I took it once before. Patience is the name of the game with Ammon, and I intend to play it well."

"These troops won't listen to you," Mark said. "I am the only thing keeping them here."

"We'll just have to see about that," I said.

"You're going to fail."

"Then I'll fail," I snapped back. "But at least I won't have to listen to you."

The room went silent as Mark waited for the next volley. But I had nothing further to say to him.

"Your Majesty?" Jorad said.

"Pack up the camp," I said. "I'll take a group and ride ahead in the morning."

Chapter Twenty-One

"Captain Mark has been relieved of his command," I said the next morning over breakfast.

Surprise, and a little anger, rippled through the soldiers as they stood before me.

In truth, as I'd lain awake the night before, I reconsidered my haste. Arguments happened, and Mark was just trying to do the best he could. But him constantly disagreeing with me, even trying to go over my head, was too much to bear. I had enough voices criticizing my decisions; I didn't need to add another voice to the mix. In either case, my decision was final; Mark had left sometime in the night. And now I had to deal with the consequences.

"I've asked Lieutenant Llobrega to take over his duties for the foreseeable future," I continued. "I hope you'll treat him with the same respect and deference as you treated Captain Mark. His word is as good as mine."

I paused, waiting for arguments. None came.

"We'll be packing up camp and moving north," I said, deciding to leave out exactly where we were headed. "I'm riding ahead with scouts, and we'll send for the rest of you after we've found a suitable location."

I stared at them, unsure what to say next, and the seconds drew out between us.

"Dismissed," Jorad muttered beside me.

"Right," I said. "Dismissed."

The soldiers saluted in unison then broke into murmuring groups, some casting looks toward me. It was clear that for some of them, Mark was the reason they'd stayed. Would they defect, as Mark had predicted, or would they remain at my side?

"You don't need to worry about that now," Jorad whispered. "Just keep moving forward, and the soldiers will follow."

"Will they?" I sighed as I received dirty looks from a pair of female soldiers walking by. "It seems he was pretty popular."

"He was," Jorad said. "Most of us grew up with him as captain. When he arrived, we were heartened—some of us saw it as the Mother's intervention."

I cringed. "Great."

"It may take time, but the soldiers will learn to love you as they did him," Jorad said. "As long as you keep demonstrating leadership, making strategic moves, and showing them what you're capable of, they will fall in line." He cleared his throat. "And on that note, what should I tell the soldiers who are staying behind? We should leave someone in charge of moving the camp."

"Right," I said. "Erm…who do you recommend?"

"Enos would work," Jorad said. "He's still quite loyal to you and has the respect of the soldiers. Shall I fetch him to discuss the next move with you, or do you want me to do it myself?"

"Go ahead," I said. "I'm going to prepare for the trip."

Needing distraction and a friendly face, I ducked into the mess hall. Beata was in the back, already preparing her kitchen to be moved. Two soldiers were helping her, but they saluted and ran off when I showed up.

"Great. Nobody wants to be around me now," I said with a grimace.

"Oh, they're grousing a little, but I told them to hush up about it," Beata said with a kind smile. "I've packed you a bag of bread and dried meat to take with you. It's over there."

I pulled the bag off the shelf and stared at the mostly empty stores. "There should be more food at Celia's. She always has three weeks' worth on hand. And we'll figure out how to get more once we're there."

"Brynna, do you really think you can pull this off?" Beata asked quietly. "Celia's a dangerous woman. She might kill you before you can get a word out."

"She hasn't yet," I said. "I'm taking a calculated risk that she wants me alive, on the throne, and owing her favors."

"Even if it means giving up her camp?"

"I'm not going to ask her to do that," I said. "I'm going to ask her to join my cause. There's a difference."

"And all the people she's stolen from their families," she said softly. "All the children. You're just going to leave them there to be ransomed?"

I looked down at my hands. "I don't know."

"Well, you have some time to think about it," she said, forcing a bright smile onto her face as she handed me the bag of food. "I'm sure you'll come up with a brilliant solution. You always seem to."

With the bag of food slung over my shoulder, I walked through camp, feeling the gazes of soldiers on me as I passed. More than once, I caught a wisp of conversation about my plan, and how I was either insane or idiotic to attempt such a thing. Clearly, Celia had done well to instill fear into the hearts of even the bravest

Forcadelians.

The forest was about half a day's ride northwest of our camp, and I wanted to get there before night gave the spies in the trees the advantage. I didn't think Celia would order them to fire on sight, but one could never be too sure. I'd asked Jorad to assemble ten of his best soldiers to come with me. It was more to appease him—I'd wanted to ride alone. After all, if things went according to plan, I would meet with her, she would agree to my terms, and we could peacefully integrate the camp.

"I hope you're gonna say pretty please." Jax walked up to the group with a horse and wearing traveling clothes.

"What are you doing?" I asked him. "Are you here to knife me or something?"

"If I knife you, I don't get Celia's gold," Jax said.

Jorad made a move beside me, but I held up my hand. "Why are you here then?"

"Why wouldn't I go?" He climbed into his saddle and shrugged. "Unlike the rest of these morons, I know how Celia thinks. And if, as you say, you're coming in peace, you'll need all the help you can get."

Our group set off into the afternoon sun, none of us saying much. We passed small villages and carriages on the main road, but no one seemed to recognize me in a dark tunic and without flags. Around midday, the menacing forest appeared. I halted the riders near a creek to water the horses and ourselves, and to make a plan for approaching Celia.

"I say we go in together," Jorad said. "A group of ten soldiers —"

"Would get arrows through their bellies before they got two steps in," Jax said, leaning against a tree. "She goes in alone."

"I refuse to allow that," Jorad said.

"Then isn't it so grand that you ain't in charge? Celia won't kill the brat. She owes too many favors."

Jorad got to his feet, but I pressed his arm to quiet him. "Very well, genius. What do you suggest?"

"No idea. This is your crazy scheme."

I looked at the other soldiers and forced a tight smile onto my face. "Give us a minute."

Jorad glared at Jax before rising to his feet. He led the others back down to the creek where the horses were tied up, out of earshot.

"Want to try that again?" I asked.

"Nope."

"Jax." I shook my head. "You rode all this way just to be an asshole?"

"Well, you rode all this way to fail, so…"

I released another loud sigh. "I'm listening. Say what you want to say or shut up about it."

"You're giving Celia way too much credit here," he said. "If you walk in there and ask her for an alliance, she'll laugh you out of the forest."

"What do you suggest, then?"

"You've got a hundred soldiers. Use them."

I shook my head violently. "I'm not marching on the camp. There are too many innocent lives there. Kids, Jax."

"Which is exactly what Celia's banking on," Jax said, a smile curling onto his face. "Nobody wants to raze a camp filled with children. That's why your father let her grow her little kingdom within his borders."

"That's ridiculous," I said. "If a contingent of guards showed up, the kids would—"

"Turn tail and run," Jax said. "It's a clever game Celia played with all of us. She made the royals think she'll force children to fight and die for her camp. And she made the children too scared of the real world to leave. But in reality, the only thing keeping her camp together was a pack of lies."

I'd never thought about it that way before. Celia's camp had always been this terrifying monster, a giver of food and beds, but who could take it away just as quickly. But Jax was pulling the curtain back and revealing the monsters were just trees.

"Which brings me to your current idiotic plan," he said. "Celia's always been terrified *of you* because you have the power to take everything away. Even before you were back on the throne, she knew you could've told that Captain Llobrega fellow exactly where to find the camp, and how to infiltrate it. So she's been working hard to plant a loyal seed in your mind ever since you arrived. Make it an impossible notion that you'd ever betray the camp." He flashed a grin. "That's why you keep going back to her to ask for help. And why, instead of taking over the camp for yourself, you've got this ridiculous notion of alliance."

I sat back, running through my memories in light of what he'd said. "So what do I do?"

"Remind her who you are and what you know, and she'll drop her sword faster than you can say that ridiculously long name of yours."

I stared at him a long time. Jax had never been so honest with me, especially about what Celia was thinking. "What about your gold?"

"The way I see it, taking over Celia's camp gets you closer to that goal. So even if I have to take it from the camp myself, I'll get my reward." He flashed a smile. "One way or another."

Chapter Twenty-Two

Katarine

Geestig lasted a full week, and soon enough, the revelry died down to normal activity—and I was returned to my life of semi-imprisonment. Still, I had plenty of time to think about what Ilara had said about the eastern side of the country, and what it might mean. It was the closest to Severia, of course, and where she had routed all the food and ships. But what else was she doing out there?

Clearly, my position as Ilara's strategic advisor had eroded. I needed to take drastic measures if I wanted to maintain my position—if not for myself, than for Felix.

The Kulkan envoys were still in town, so my servants told me, and I hoped that the gaiety of Geestig would've put Ilara in a better mood to receive them. After all, she was making great strides to cement herself as the ruler of this land. Surely, she could meet with the Kulkans now. Or, better yet, send me in her stead, and I could discover why they'd reneged on their agreement with Brynna.

In the end, I was grateful just to have her accept my invitation to chat. To lure her in, I requested time to discuss some options for her winter wardrobe—absolutely beneath me, but it was innocuous enough that she couldn't decline my request.

When I arrived in Ilara's office, Coyle was already there providing his weekly update. He looked much less confident than he had during the festival, and his voice shook a little as he spoke.

"As I was saying, the smugglers have a new tactic now," Coyle said, casting me a curious look as I sat down on an empty chair. "They're flouting your latest edict and smuggling crates of food in from Neveri. We've been unable to discover where the breakdown is happening. I've had soldiers on the docks for days and...well, I think they're getting paid off."

Ilara skewered a grape with a pin. "I see."

"We believe that with the gates destroyed and Neveri in the hands of the Kulkans, supplies are moving easier from the north. We've set up a blockade south of Neveri, but..."

"Then we should refuse all ships into the bay," Ilara said with a saccharine smile.

"We..." Coyle looked confused. "Refuse all ships?"

"Yes, dear, it's quite simple. If the ships can't get into the bay, they can't offload their cargo," She smiled. "Blockade the bay."

"With all due respect," he began slowly, "if we cut off all shipments to the city, we'll no longer have food and supplies for the castle. Surely there's another way."

"I'm sure there is," she said. "But since you haven't been able to find it, clearly, we have to try something else." She paused, giving him a look. "And what of the other task I've given you?"

He cast me another, curious look, then turned back to Ilara. "There's no sign of her anywhere in the city."

"Really?" Ilara leaned forward. "No sign? Then why did three of my guards report seeing a masked vigilante in the streets last night, hm? And last week, there was a vigilante throwing bread and apples down from a rooftop. And three weeks ago—"

He paused, breathing out through his nose. "It appears to be more than one person, so it's hard to say if it's Brynna—"

"Don't say her name," Ilara said with a tight smile. Coyle opened his mouth to speak again, and she waved him off. "Clearly, this is a job too big for you. I will have to seek alternative methods if I want her taken care of."

"But—"

"Why don't you see if you can't manage to blockade the bay, hm?" Her smile was bright, but her eyes were cold. "Maybe if you aren't a complete screwup, I'll let you keep your job."

"Yes, Your Majesty."

Coyle bowed and hurried from the room, his cheeks pink with embarrassment, and I couldn't help the shaky exhale that left my lips.

"Oh, don't fret, Kat," she said, turning in her chair to face me. "Tough love always seems to work with our lovely Coyle, doesn't it? Now, we were going to discuss my summer wardrobe?"

"Yes," I said with a nod. Something told me she wasn't in the mood to entertain conversations about the Kulkans. "I have some very lovely fabric swatches I'd like you to see."

Clearly, if I wanted to speak with the Kulkans, I'd have to go a little outside my purview. I paid one of Beata's friends a solid gold coin to find out exactly where the Kulkan envoys were staying and to keep her mouth shut about it. I ordered a carriage under the auspices of visiting my favorite dressmaker, one of a handful still in town.

"Shall I accompany you?" Luisa asked.

"I think I would prefer to go alone," I said, forcing a smile onto my face. "It's been a while since I've been out of the castle, and I'm not sure I'm fit for company." I forced a lonely smile onto my face. "It's been weeks since I've heard from Beata and I fear..."

Luisa patted my shoulder. "I understand. I'm here if you ever wish to talk about it."

"Today, I think I just want to be alone."

Luckily, she took the bait and ordered me a carriage. Three Severian footman would be going with me—I just hoped I had enough coin to keep their silence.

"Will you wait here for me?" I said, once we arrived at the dressmaker's. "I'd like to stretch my legs before I go in."

One of them opened his mouth to argue, but I flashed him a gold coin. "As a personal favor. I'd like to visit a favorite spot of mine." The other two took their spoils and turned the other way.

Confident I'd managed a bit of espionage, I disappeared around the corner toward the small inn where the Kulkans were staying. Like most of the buildings in town now, it was a little run down and needed a fresh coat of paint. Inside, there was a faint musty smell and the tables needed a good dusting.

I walked the empty hallway until I heard voices. The two Kulkan envoys were reading in the small study and enjoying a dusty bottle of wine—perhaps the only one the innkeeper had on hand with all the shipping restrictions.

"I understand you two would like to meet with Her Majesty," I said, by way of announcing myself.

I recognized one of them as the Kulkan envoy named Melwin, who'd been sent for Brynna's coronation, but not the other gentleman with only a ring of hair left, who glanced up with a frown.

"Lady Katarine of Niemen?" the one I didn't know asked.

"Indeed." I walked into the room and shutting the door behind me. "I'm here on behalf of Queen Ilara to gather more information to help her understand the situation. She may not think it's useful to meet with you, but based on current events, I'd like to know all the facts." I rested my hands on the table. "So please, tell me what you plan to offer."

They shared an uncertain look. "It's highly unusual for us to be talking to a Niemenian royal about Forcadelian business."

"Consider me a Forcadelian," I said. "My loyalties are to this country and this flag. And if you would like an audience with Ilara, I'm the best you have"

"Prince Ammon would like to offer the city of Neveri back to Her Majesty," Melwin began. "In exchange for a shipment of ond."

"Ilara has no ond," I said, my blood pressure spiking at the thought of the Kulkans with Niemenian's precious natural resource.

"Then how did she destroy Forcadel?" the other envoy asked. "There were rumors of explosions and buildings demolished during the initial invasion. How was that accomplished if not with ond?"

"It was a Severian ore—similar to Niemen's, but not the same," I said.

"Then that's what we want," he said. "In exchange for reverting Neveri to Forcadelian control."

I sat back, curious. "If you just obtained this bargaining chip, why are you so eager to give it away?"

"I'm not comfortable discussing Kulka's strategic goals with a mountain-dweller," Melwin's partner said, casting me a look.

I let the slight roll off my shoulders. "Maarit told us Brynna had given you Neveri in exchange for your help. How can we trust a man who goes back on his word?"

"Princess Brynna reneged first," Melwin said. "She walked out on an official treaty."

"What...her marriage?" I barked a laugh. "Is Kulka really so proud that they'd fault a young girl for deciding a life of freedom was better than being shipped to a foreign country?"

"You were in the same position," Melwin said. "Yet you upheld your end of the bargain."

"I am not Brynna," I said. "And I find it heinous that you

would hold a grudge against a decision she made as a child—even to the point of betrayal."

"You were her sister-in-law," Melwin said. "Haven't you also betrayed her?"

"As I said," I got to my feet, "I am loyal to this country and this crown. Which is why I'll take your request back to Ilara. I think an alliance between Kulka and Forcadel would be beneficial, especially in the weeks to come. But be warned: Ilara won't take kindly to betrayal."

"Perhaps some advice you should take for yourself," Melwin said. "Good day, Lady Katarine."

When I returned to the castle, I headed straight for Ilara's office, rapping impatiently on the door until she opened it.

"Lady Katarine, this is highly unusual," Ilara said, curiosity on her face. "I don't believe we had a meeting scheduled for today."

"No, but we need one," I said. "May I come in?"

She stepped back and offered me entry, and I perched myself on the edge of the seat, waiting for her to settle down.

"Please, do tell me what's got you so troubled," she said, resting her chin on her folded hands.

"I just met with the Kulkan envoys," I said. "And I believe it's very important that you meet with them."

"Oh, is it?" She smiled, but not kindly. "Please, continue to tell the sovereign of this nation what she needs to do. And do remind me when I asked you to pay them a visit."

I swallowed; perhaps I hadn't thought this through. "I apologize for going outside my position, but I didn't want you to miss an opportunity for an alliance we so desperately need."

"Desperately, hm?" Ilara sat back.

"Yes," I said, not liking the look on her face. "The Kulkans would like to return the city of Neveri to you."

"I know." She tilted her head to the side, as if I were an amusing child. "In exchange for the Severian ore I brought to take the city."

I swallowed. "So you knew?"

"I sent Luisa to speak with them weeks ago," she said. "Or didn't they tell you?"

"They didn't," I said, my pulse spiking.

"Well, my dear, that's because no one needed to tell you," she said. "As it was none of your concern. I didn't think the Kulkans would like speaking to a Niemenian anyway. Aren't your countries constantly at war?"

I nodded, feeling faint and idiotic. I'd forgotten the one thing I had promised I wouldn't—that no matter how many despotic decisions Ilara made, she was a strategic thinker.

She laughed a little, as if she could read my mind. "Sweet Kat. I know you mean well. And while I would be happy to ally myself with the Kulkans, I've asked them to do one thing, and they have yet to accomplish it." She rested her chin on her hands. "I want King Neshua—or whomever decides to sit on the Kulkan throne—to acknowledge me as queen. And yet..." She shrugged. "I have no use for Kulkan internal politics. If Ammon wants to destroy his father, he will have to go somewhere else for it."

"If Ammon's looking for weapons, then he might try other sources," I said. "He may even go to Ariadna and ask for ond."

"To what end?" She laughed. "Would he try his hand at the city of Forcadel?"

"He might."

"I'm no slouch, Lady Katarine," Ilara said. "I have studied the very same history books that you have. I know this city benefits from a wide range of natural defenses—rivers that can be blockaded, a bay with cannons to prevent an ocean intrusion. And the main road to the city is filled with outposts. It was impossible for your ancestors to invade three hundred years ago, and it will be impossible now."

I couldn't help but agree with her.

"Besides that," she said. " I don't have any valo to spare, and especially not for a city with a destroyed gate. What remains of our supply is being otherwise used in the east."

"The...east?" I asked. I'd not heard of any activity, other than where the food was going. What would she need with exploding powder in Severia?

"Nothing to concern yourself with," she said with a coy smile. "I've barricaded the Vanhoja river at its narrowest points, and things are back to normal." She sighed. "Except for those damned smugglers. I suppose that we'll be eating a bit lighter at the castle until we can move."

Another flash of curiosity and concern crossed my mind. This was all new information—and I didn't like the sound of any of it.

"Oh, sweet Kat, you know that not everything I do requires your input, right?" She tilted her head. "Don't concern yourself with any of this. I promise all will be revealed in due time."

"Of course, Your Majesty." I rose and bowed. "If you'll excuse me."

I was almost to the door when she called my name.

"Oh, and Kat?" Her eyes glittered dangerously. "If I find you've gone over my head again, you will join Maarit in the town square."

I nodded. "Yes, Your Majesty."

Chapter Twenty-Three

The whistles began the moment I set foot in the forest. *Someone's coming. Woman, young. Brown hair.*

Larissa? came the whistled response.

Who's Larissa?

My heart pounded in my chest, but I kept walking, keeping my head up as Jax's words circled between my ears. I'd always thought Celia might've been a little nervous about me. It certainly explained why she'd never branded me and why she'd offered me a place as her deputy instead of dragging me back by my ankles when I'd run away from camp. No one else had received such special treatment from her.

It crossed my mind, especially as more whistles joined me in the trees, that Jax might've been setting me up. But there was something in his eyes lately that begged me to trust him. He was still an enigma, and I wasn't convinced he was only offering advice because he thought he might get paid.

The gates came into view and I exhaled a little—they were still open. And more importantly, the woman herself was standing in front of them, her arms crossed over her chest with an amused smile on her lips. Her black hair hung around her ears, framing sharp eyes that seemed to see right through me. On her hip, the bejeweled knife that she'd worn since the day I met her. As usual, all my confidence evaporated at the sight of her, but I was reminded of my soldiers, and my purpose.

"What do you want?" she called to me.

"I'm here to talk," I said.

She made a noise. "You don't look like you're queen yet. Why should I talk with you?"

I kept my pace until I stood right in front of her. "Because, queen or not, I hear you're bringing something dangerous into my country. Getting into the smuggling business now?"

"I've always been in the smuggling business," she said. "Your knowledge of my business operations has always been woefully inadequate."

"Then educate me," I said, leveling my gaze at her.

"Get out of my forest," Celia said. "I have no more patience for you."

I licked my lips, gathering my courage. "Very well." I turned around, giving her my back as I walked away. "It seems I have no choice. I'll be moving my army in at sundown."

I walked three steps before I heard. "Army?"

"Yes," I said, looking over my shoulder. "You didn't hear?"

Her eyes were a mask of uncertainty and she glanced up at a nearby tree. "Go investigate."

The girl in the tree nodded and jumped down, running past me with a curious look. Celia, however, had returned to her usual stoic demeanor.

"So you have an army now?" She shrugged. "Why move it here? This isn't Forcadel. You won't gain any strategic footing with

Ilara."

There it was—the smallest hint of fear in her voice. "My reasons are my own," I said as a whistle echoed out of the forest. *A hundred soldiers on their way.*

Celia's eyes widened as she looked at me. "Yours?"

"Mine," I said with a smile. "Loyal to me and to Forcadel. I don't think you want to pit your soldiers against mine. Most of your children would run, and even more would cower in fear and surrender. Those who remain are too few and would assuredly lose their lives."

"Would you really do such a thing?" Celia asked, more concern seeping into her voice. "I didn't take you as the sort of person who'd kill so mercilessly. There are those here who you once considered family."

My grin widened as Jax's strategy seemed to have paid off. "Which is why I'm asking you to lay down your weapons and surrender to me. I don't want to burn down the camp. But if you take up arms against me, I will have no choice."

She pulled her knife. "You can't possibly think I would surrender to you so…"

Her eyes widened and I followed her gaze. Jorad and the ten soldiers had disobeyed me and followed me inside. Jorad called my name and took off running toward us, pulling his sword.

"Will you call off your dogs?" Celia asked. "Or will you let them kill me?"

"I don't want to," I said. "Lay down your weapon and surrender."

"I don't think so," she said, gripping her knife. "I think I'll just let you kill me."

"I'm not going to kill you in cold blood," I said, my pulse pounding in my ears as Jorad came closer. He might actually kill her, even if I told him not to. "Put down your knife. There's no need for it to end like this."

"A stronger woman would've gutted me," she whispered.

And to my surprise, she tossed her knife onto the ground just as Jorad appeared by my side.

"You win," she said, holding her hands up in surrender. "Feel free to take me wherever you deem necessary."

"Your Majesty?" Jorad asked, panting a little. "What is your command?"

I didn't like the smile that had grown on Celia's face. She had given up entirely too easily, and something told me she'd just out-maneuvered me. But how, I had no idea.

"There's a small hut in the back of camp," I said to two of the soldiers behind me. "Take her there and make sure she doesn't leave."

"I wouldn't dream of leaving camp," she said as they moved to restrain her. "Why would I, when there will be so much entertainment?"

And with that, she allowed herself to be restrained and led through the gates.

"Is that..." Jorad looked between her and me several times. "I'm confused. Did she just surrender?"

"Yes." I reached down and picked up the knife, finding it much heavier than I'd anticipated. It felt much like the gold circlet when I'd first put it on—a symbol I'd seen my whole life, but I'd never once thought I'd wear. "The camp is ours."

He offered a nervous smile. "I can't believe she gave up that easily."

"The numbers scared her," I lied. "She made a calculation, same as me. She always said to value your own life first. And against a hundred soldiers, she would've lost."

"A...hundred soldiers?" Jorad rubbed the back of his head. "Did you lie to her or...?"

"The scouts at the border said there were soldiers coming," I said with a frown. "I thought the camp soldiers had made double time and reached here."

"No, I haven't seen them," Jorad said. "And our numbers are closer to eighty, not a hundred."

"You're welcome," Jax said, walking out from behind the Forcadelians. "Amazing what kids'll believe these days. So did it work?"

"Thank you," I said, avoiding his gaze. "Go ring the bell and call everyone to attention. We've got a few announcements to make."

"You ring the bell," Jax said, waving me off. "I'm going to make sure nobody touched my stuff."

"We really have to work on his subordination," Jorad said, watching him walk away.

"He just tricked Celia into giving up her camp," I said, walking toward the bell in the center of camp. "I'd say he's earned his keep."

Word spread quick as wildfire that Celia had been frog-marched into her cabin by a pair of soldiers and was missing her knife. By the time I rang the bell, everyone in camp had most assuredly heard the gist of what I was about to say. Unlike my soldiers, they clumped in haphazard groups and leaned over fences. Some of the older trainers seemed disinterested—angry, even—but the younger crowd sat cross-legged with wide eyes, pointing at the bejeweled knife at my hip. None of us had ever seen anyone but Celia hold it.

"Evening." This was my second speech in a day, but this crowd was more familiar. "As you probably heard, Celia's no longer in charge of the camp. She has surrendered herself and this place to me and my soldiers."

"A hundred of 'em, right?"

"Where are they?"

"On their way," I said, holding up my hand. "I—"

"Why should we listen to you? Celia's in charge!"

"Can I go home?"

"Yeah, can I?"

"I want to go home, too!"

"Silence!" Jorad bellowed, but it did little good. The crowd was now inching closer to me, all of them asking questions and talking over one another. Some of the older thieves had their hands on their weapons, grumbling and looking at me as if they meant to take the camp for themselves.

"*Enough.*"

Jax's bellow echoed through the space, silencing the conversation. He walked in front of me, his dark eyes stormy.

"You shut your mouths. Celia's gone. Larissa's in charge. That's all you need to know. Any one else makes a peep, and you'll have to answer to me." When no one did, he turned to me and nodded, walking back to where he'd been standing.

"I understand you have questions," I said. "As Jax said, some of you may know me as Larissa," I said, nodding to Locke and a few others I'd known since my first stint in the camp. "But my real name is Brynna-Larissa Archer Rhodes Lonsdale. The rightful queen of Forcadel."

Nobody looked impressed, but I hadn't expected them to.

"In the coming hours, the rest of my soldiers will be arriving. We'll be using this as a home base for our operations as I try to retake the kingdom." I paused, offering a smile. "We'll need manpower—spies, thieves, and people to help around the camp. If you choose to stay, you'll officially be part of the Forcadelian royal army. Once we retake the kingdom, we'll help you get back to your homes and families."

I turned to my left, where Nicolasa had appeared through her doorway. The Nestori healer wore a soft smile as she wiped her hands on her apron.

"I know I'm asking a lot of you," I said, turning back to the crowd. "And if any of you wish to go now, you are free to do so."

I waited for them to get up, but no one did. I still wasn't used to this much respect, especially from these kids.

"Very well," I said. "If you wish to claim your bedrolls, I would do it now. By sunup, we'll have more people than beds. I'll give you your new assignments in the morning."

The kids rose to their feet, talking amongst themselves. I had no qualms that they'd be able to make themselves useful—after all, it was what we did. But I did have some trepidation about including them in a war they had no business being involved in.

"You're getting better at giving speeches," Jorad said. "At least to this crowd."

"I watched Celia give a million of them." I put my hands on my hips, watching the camp disperse. "It's going to be weird for a few days as the soldiers mesh with the thieves."

"Do you think they'll stay?" Jorad asked, eyeing a pair of kids who were lingering in the open area. When he nodded toward them, they dashed away.

"I have no idea," I said. "We'll lose the newest, I'm sure, and those who have families who're paying their ransom. Probably the older thieves with the means to make new lives." Jax ducked into one of the sleeping huts. Would he be one of them? "But those who stay will be useful."

"They're so young, though," Jorad said.

"Some would say the same about you, Lieutenant," I said. "Come, I'll give you the tour."

Chapter Twenty-Four

My soldiers arrived in waves just after midnight, their Forcadelian flags held high as they came through the front gates. They craned their necks in amazement, seeing the famed thief camp for the first time. Most of them were similarly surprised by the children who gathered around the houses to watch the soldiers come in—and who'd ignored all my orders to go to bed. Soon, the camp was abuzz with new and old faces, each too wary of the other to speak.

"How long are we planning on staying here?" Jorad asked as we patrolled the camp. "Surely not indefinitely."

I shook my head. "No, not indefinitely, but... At least until the ond shows up."

"Once we have that, will we march on Neveri?" he pressed. "Or will we begin preparations to move into Forcadel?"

"We're not ready for Ilara yet," I said. "And as for Ammon, I'm still trying to decide how I want to handle him. We still don't know if Ilara's allied herself with him, and I can't make any decisions until I know whose side he's on."

"And you don't think it's smart to take a group of soldiers into the city?" Jorad asked. "I know you and Captain Mark had your differences, but I think he might've had a point. We can't let Ammon get away with betraying you like this."

"We won't," I said with a thin smile.

"I'm not just saying it for pleasantries. Some of us lost loved ones in Neveri." Jorad said. "Finding out that Ammon had gone back on his word...it almost feels like those soldiers died for nothing. And with the hasty dismissal of Captain Mark, not to mention your decision to allow Celia to remain in camp..."

I cleared my throat, hoping I sounded surer of myself than I felt. "If I let Celia go, she could go straight to Ilara and we'd be in serious trouble."

"Then kill her," Jorad said. "With as much trouble as she's caused over the years—"

"We're not killing anyone in cold blood," I said.

"It wouldn't be..." Jorad exhaled. "Whatever you think is best, Your Majesty. I just worry about what the soldiers might think."

I stopped, putting my hands on my hips. "I know that I made a mistake letting Mark go, but I can't bring myself to just...kill Celia. Besides that, she could be useful in some capacity. She might know when the ond is coming, or she could provide some strategic advice."

"I suppose I can understand that," Jorad said slowly.

"But I can't lose the respect of the soldiers—but I don't have any good answers for them right now. I need your help keeping morale high." I offered him a half-smile. "They seem to respect you. Maybe you can help provide me some cover with them."

My honesty seemed to have worked, because he nodded solemnly. "We'll fill their days with training, and they'll be too exhausted to question you. I'll have them make weapons, too.

There's more raw material here than we had before."

The surety in his voice lessened my anxiety. "That sounds like a good plan. And whatever thieves remain can join in."

"Well, with all due respect," Jorad said with a grimace. "I'm not sure that's the best plan. Many of these thieves are barely past their fourteenth year."

"So?"

"So it would be bad for our soldiers to train directly with them," he said. "Can you imagine the sight of children being beaten in sparring matches by fully grown adults?"

"I think it might be the opposite," I said. "These children aren't weak. Some of them have been in this camp since early childhood."

"They can wield weapons, but they are certainly not trained, not in a way that can be useful to us." He placed his hand on his pommel. "I also lack confidence in their loyalty to the cause. Many of them are here because they have nowhere else to go."

"Yes, and that makes them loyal."

He shook his head. "With your approval, I'd like to implement a training program similar to the one Captain Llobrega led in Forcadel. Teach them the ways of the royal guard."

I quirked a brow. "I don't think we have the time or energy for that, Jorad."

"We need to make time for it." He fidgeted a little. "Captain Mark drilled the importance of structure and unity. Soldiers who train together stay together on the battlefield. We've just doubled our numbers. It could get unwieldy quickly. And training your new recruits under the same flag…it sends a message. It would help your older soldiers see you're taking their contributions seriously."

"By training Celia's thieves to march and salute?" I shook my head. "If you're worried about the resolve of these thieves, I promise you they're up to the task. Here, everybody earned their keep, or their keep was taken out of their hide."

"I don't propose we put them into a six-year program, but a

few weeks of training could do wonders for them. It would help some of the soldiers see measurable progress while we're waiting for news on our next steps." He gave me a half-smile. "It's a rather elegant solution to the problem, in my opinion."

I chewed my lip. The thieves were already highly trained, but they did lack the discipline that Jorad spoke of. And if he thought putting them in formation would be enough to keep the other soldiers on my side, I would have to trust that he knew what he was talking about.

In the distance, the bell clanged, signaling that breakfast was ready. The thieves stared at one another curiously, as they'd never gotten a second meal before.

"Go on," I said to a pair of nearby kids. "I'm sure Beata's been at it all night long."

They whispered to their friends, who whispered to another set of friends. Soon, the young thieves were coming out of the woodwork, cautiously approaching the mess hall as if they weren't sure it wasn't a trap. They gave the soldiers a wide berth, too.

"See what I mean?" Jorad said. "Once they know we're all under the same flag, there will be more unity. And it won't hurt to have half the camp learning how to salute you."

"Very well," I said with a sigh. "Make it happen."

Jorad left me to make arrangements, and I continued on into the mess hall. There, Beata was serving gruel out of a large vat and a queue of soldiers was waiting for it. Bleary-eyed children sat at the tables watching the food get ladled into wooden bowls. I watched them for a minute before realizing why none of them had queued up behind the soldiers.

"It's okay to eat," I told them. "Just get in—"

My words were drowned out by the sound of little feet scrambling over themselves as they crowded behind the last soldier.

Beata shared a look with me as she nodded to the second ladle behind her, and I jumped in to help. With the two of us, we got through both the soldiers and the children in about half an hour, and there was a happy rumbling from the crowd.

"Eating together should help," Beata said, wiping her forehead with a towel. "These kids are really young, though. What will you have them do?"

"Jorad thought he might train them. The rest will be put to work."

She made a noise, looking at a smallish kid, perhaps seven or eight years old. "But Brynna..."

"Things are already better than they were," I said. "Two meals a day is unheard of."

"We have the food for it, but I'm not sure how long it will last," she said. "I can stretch it a bit, but we'll need to find a more regular source of fresh food. Surely, Celia has some gold lying around we can use to buy it."

I shook my head. "Whatever she did with her spoils, I have no idea. But I do know she had regular deliveries of food from farmers nearby. I think they were threatened and bullied into contributing."

"Then perhaps we continue what she started," Beata said. "They're bringing it anyway. They won't know the difference if it comes to your soldiers or to Celia."

"I can't just do that," I said. "It's stealing."

"Jax said Celia keeps tabs on everyone who owes her, and what they owe her. Once you get back on the throne, you can pay them all back."

I didn't like Jax discussing things with Beata—or that she agreed with him. "It doesn't feel right, though."

"Would you prefer your soldiers defect because they haven't eaten?"

"No."

"Then you'll have to learn to like it," she said. "It's not my preference, but your army is growing, and you have no gold. At least you know you can pay it all back."

Jorad walked into the mess hall, with Jax following. Jax, at least, looked annoyed to be there, whereas the younger man seemed ready to take on the world.

"Former thieves," Jorad bellowed. "My name is Lieutenant Llobrega. I am your new trainer. You will go outside and wait for me so we can begin your regimen."

Nobody moved.

Jax crossed his arms over his chest. "Get off your asses and follow him."

Slowly, the children rose from the tables, leaving their bowls and spoons as they filed outside, casting Jorad a curious look. Once they were all outside, Jorad pressed something into Jax's hand—a gold coin.

"Clever," I said to Jorad as he walked up.

"It's clear that Jax doesn't do anything for free, and that these kids believe him," Jorad said, handing me a list. "I took a headcount as they came in for their meal."

"So we're close to two hundred," I said, scanning the numbers. "Are you sure they didn't just stay to get fed and will be on their way?"

He smirked and nodded to Beata. "As much as I love Lady Beata's cooking, I don't think so."

"Let's hope not," I said, looking through the names, ages, and cities of origin. At the bottom were two I recognized, Jax and Locke, but none of the other trainers. While I couldn't argue with a hundred new bodies, most of them were under the age of fifteen. It seemed to be more mouths to feed without a whole lot of benefit to me—especially if Jorad wasn't going to let me use them.

"If you'll excuse me." He saluted and bowed deeply. "I'm off to our first day."

"He looks happy," Beata said, as he walked out of the mess hall. "What kind of training is he implementing?"

"He seems to think they would be better used learning how to fight with swords."

"And what do you think?" Beata asked, putting her hand on her hip.

"I think he's got a point about unity," I said, averting my gaze. "And I think until we get some action on either front, it's good to keep everyone occupied."

She gave me a sideways glance and shook her head. "Well, I was hoping some of those kids would help me do the dishes..."

Chapter Twenty-Five

It took Beata and me several hours to work through all the dishes, but eventually, we managed to get everything cleaned. She shooed me away when I offered to help her begin preparations for dinner that night, claiming that I was hiding from my own troops.

"They need to see you out and about," she said. "Go on."

It would've been useless to argue, so I let her be, intent on finding her some help for the evening. But I wasn't two steps out of the mess hall when a group of twenty young teenagers came jogging around the corner. Red-faced and panting, they kept pace with Enos barking behind them.

"Halt," he said when they saw me. "Salute!"

They spun in no particular hurry, some of them pressing their left hands to their breast, and some of them pressing their right. A few kids just stared blankly ahead then jumped to attention when they found their compatriots saluting.

"We can do better," Enos said, casting the kids a scathing look.

187

"We have done better."

"It's fine for a first day," I said, offering the kids a reassuring smile. "You don't want to scare them away."

"Turning and saluting is the least of their problems," Enos said. "Turn! And march!"

To my surprise, some of them actually fell in lockstep with him, although the rest certainly needed more work. But they seemed eager to please him, which, I supposed, was a good thing.

"Pfft."

I turned to the sound. Jax was seated against the weapons hut, peeling an apple with a knife.

"What?"

"These kids, trading one master for another," he said, plucking a slice from the apple with the knife and popping it into his mouth. "Sheep."

"You're the one who told them to go," I said.

He flashed me the gold coin. "I'll do anything for money."

"Clearly." I crossed my arms over my chest. "I would've thought now that Celia's out of power, you and your opinions would've taken your gold and left."

He shrugged and ate another slice. "She's still in camp, ain't she?"

"For the moment," I said.

"Why?"

I hid a cringe from him. "Because I thought it would be better to keep her here."

He shook his head. "I knew you were still soft. You've got over a hundred soldiers at your command and you're scared of one woman." He snorted. "No wonder these people think you're a failure."

"I'm not scared and I'm not a failure," I said, my face flushing at his honesty. "I just think it's smarter to keep her where I can see her. What's to stop her from walking down to Ilara's castle and giving us all up?"

"You." Jax ran his finger across his neck. "Problem solved."

"I'm not going to kill her," I said with a frown.

"Well, you gotta do something," Jax said. "Besides kicking these soldiers' favorite person out on his ass, you've done nothing except dither and stall. They ain't stupid."

The group of young thieves turned the corner and jogged by, stopping to salute me again. This time, more than half of them got it right the first time, even if they did press their fists to their chests at different times. Jorad, however, was unimpressed, and barked at them to keep running.

"That was ridiculous," Jax said. "What do you care if they salute you?"

"They're learning skills they'll need to fight Ilara and Beswick," I said.

"They have skills. Or else they would've been kicked out of the camp." Jax shook his head. "Felix Junior is acting like they're all soft children. Most of them have seen more battles than he has. Why aren't they in the trees? Why aren't they practicing with real swords instead of those baby wooden ones?"

"Firing Mark was hasty, and as you said, the soldiers clearly liked him more than me," I said, flushing. "I'm trying not to rock the boat any more than I have. So if Jorad wants to run these kids around, then I'm going to let him. It's not doing any harm right now."

"Who's watching the border, hm? Who's keeping an eye on the southern plains to make sure Ilara's not on her way?" Jax tilted his head back. "How are they gonna get a message to you if the ond comes waltzing through the forest? They don't know the whistle code. By the time they tell you where it is, the ond'll be halfway to Forcadel."

The little voice in my gut agreed with him. "I'll readdress it in a few days."

"Well, I'd tell you to make the young master listen, but you also haven't told Celia to hit the road," Jax said, pointing to the back of the camp. "So I'm not going to waste my breath offering advice you won't take."

Jax certainly had a way of getting under my skin, especially as he cared little for my ego and took great pleasure in bruising it. I didn't know whether to be grateful or displeased that he'd decided to stick around, but I did know that it meant there was still something in it for him.

I avoided the groups of new recruits who seemed bound and determined to salute me whenever they saw me, and made my way toward the training ring. There, the older soldiers who Jorad hadn't pressed into training services were sparring.

Unlike before, the soldiers didn't seem eager to come speak to me. Some of them even purposefully avoided eye contact, perhaps to keep me from striking up a conversation.

"Yer M'sty."

I turned at the sound of a familiar voice. Locke had been in camp nearly as long as I had. We were around the same age, and as a young teen, I'd nursed a small crush on him. But that had faded the day I'd killed the Forcadelian soldier. Now, he was a foot taller than I was, scarred and dangerous-looking. His path had certainly been a rougher one than mine.

Still, it was odd he'd stayed. Unlike Jax, no one had promised him gold if I returned to the throne. What was Locke after?

"I didn't think you'd stay," I said, after a long pause. "You know you're free to go. Whatever debts you owed Celia are expunged."

"Well, I 'member what you did for me," he said, the tops of his cheeks turning red. "How you gave me that stuff that..."

I nodded slowly. When I'd last been to Celia's, I'd asked her to provide soldiers and swords in exchange for a new weapon—hyblatha, a hallucinogenic plant. She'd wanted a demonstration and had chosen Locke to take it. His visions had been vivid and terrifying, leaving him a sobbing, trembling mess. It wouldn't have been so bad had it not been on full display for the entire camp.

The memory burned in my consciousness. "I'm sorry I couldn't have given you the antidote sooner."

"That's Celia," he said, glancing at the hut in the distance. "At least she let you."

I followed his gaze, almost reading his thoughts. "Still, thank you for staying. We need as many hands as we can get."

"Yer telling me," he said, looking to where two soldiers were facing each other with wooden swords. "They ain't even in real danger. Precious soldiers. They need to toughen up a little. Celia would laugh at them."

"They're tougher than they look," I said, hoping that was the case. I clapped to get their attention. "You seem to have found the training rings to your liking. If there's anything else you need, Locke will help you find it."

"Maybe I should find you some real weapons," Locke said, nodding at the wooden broadsword in the soldier's hand. "Do you think your enemies will have wooden swords?"

"That's not how we do things in a civilized world," the soldier barked back, gripping the sword. "We're not in the habit of stealing people from their homes."

"Neither am I," Locke said, leveling his gaze at him. "But I am in the habit of not being killed. Have you ever been in a real fight, or have you just trained with fake weapons?"

"Locke," I snapped. "That's enough."

"Who is this joker anyway?" another soldier said to me. "One of that pirate Celia's? Why isn't he behind lock and key?"

"And for that matter, why isn't she?" asked another one.

"Shouldn't she be out on her ass like Captain Mark?"

"And what are we doing here? Why aren't we in Neveri, taking the city back?" asked a female soldier.

"My brother died in the gate," said yet another male soldier. "And for what? What did we gain by destroying the gate if the Kulkans aren't going to work with us at all?"

"We gained Ammon's alliance, as well as the Niemenians," I said, but my heart began to thud against my ribcage.

"We ain't got shit from them," the first soldier said. "Just wandering around the countryside. Meanwhile, that desert-dwelling bitch has a stranglehold on the country. And you're just hiding out."

"What in the Mother's name is going on here?" Jorad and a group of young soldiers came jogging by. He must've sensed I was losing control because he stopped his cadets in mid-stride. "Everything all right, Your Majesty?"

"Fine," I said with a tight smile. "Locke was just offering to help the soldiers train."

"Then get to it," Jorad said with a steely glare. "And quit pestering Her Majesty with inane questions. When we have something to share, we'll share it with you."

To my surprise, everyone in the group saluted him and returned to their posts without another word.

"Ygritte, take the cadets for a loop around the camp," Jorad said to a nearby soldier. "I'll catch up."

The new cadets trotted away under her careful eye, and the other soldiers were soon sparring with their familiar wooden weapons. Locke gave me a look of surprise before turning to watch the matches. I hated him seeing me unable to control my own forces. I hated *being* unable to control them.

Jorad took me by the arm and led me away, out of earshot of the soldiers. "What happened?"

I heaved a sigh. "I'm terrible at this, that's what happened. I can't even talk to my soldiers without them questioning everything

I do."

"Don't let them question you. They should just wait for orders and follow them." He frowned. "Why were you over here anyway? Shouldn't you be getting the camp in order?"

I licked my lips. "I'm trying to repair the damage I caused. But I think I just made it worse."

"Repair how?"

I shrugged. "Last time I got into the ring with all of them, they seemed to like it. I thought I could do it again."

His expression was somewhere between patronizing and respectful. "With all due respect, Your Majesty...as much as you disagreed with Captain Mark's assessment of your leadership skills, he had a point. Sparring is nice every once in a while, but it's not what a leader does. They need leadership, not to be beaten in matches."

"What should I do?" I asked, helplessly.

"Just let me continue to lead them in your stead," Jorad said. "In time, they'll adjust to your rule. And when we've got news to share, they'll be happy."

It sounded like he wanted me to step aside and let him take command, much like Mark had. Still I didn't want to argue too much. Jorad was the only thing keeping half the soldiers from walking out the front gates. And he'd already proven himself to be loyal to me.

"Fine," I said weakly. "Do what you must."

As clearly, I had no idea what I was doing.

Chapter Twenty-Six

Katarine

I'd strayed out of line with the Kulkan envoys, putting not only myself, but also Felix, in danger. It had been a stupid risk, and I couldn't believe how completely I'd misread the situation. To make matters worse, Ilara had all but restricted my movements, leaving two Severians in the hallway outside my room under the auspices of "security." Luisa was now an infrequent visitor; I only assumed she'd taken my spot as Ilara's advisor. Even the servants had been instructed to keep to themselves, barely offering a good morning when they arrived to clean my study.

It was a lonely place, made lonelier by the constant reminders of Beata everywhere. Without being able to leave, I paced the rooms that we'd once shared, worrying about her and Felix and Brynna and all the other things I couldn't control.

Finally, I could take it no longer, and I penned a request to Ilara, asking if I might be allowed to attend the weekly church sermon. The response was flourished and vapid, "Of course, my dearest Katarine, whatever you need," but when I opened my door, two Severian guards were there to escort me.

Spiritual solitude, I surely wouldn't get.

With my shoulders back and my head held high, I traveled the short distance to the church on foot, eager to stretch my legs. My gaze drifted to the bell tower, and my heart ached. Seeing Brynna there all those months ago had been like taking the first breath after being under water. But now I was back in the murky depths, and running out of air.

The church was the same as ever, lit up with the candles of those who were in need of prayers. I walked the long distance to the front, feeling the gazes of those already seated. The congregation was a mix of Severians and the few Forcadelians who remained in the city.

I settled into the cushion in the pew and closed my eyes. Although past kings and queens had joined the service on a weekly basis, Brynna hadn't been interested and clearly Ilara wasn't either. I hadn't ever seen her at a service, although she regularly spoke about the Mother's grace. Perhaps if she'd been to one of Fishen's sermons, Ilara wouldn't be so hellbent on making the wrong decisions all the time.

But in this sacred space, those thoughts fell flat in my mind. I wouldn't waste my only Ilara-free moments thinking about her. So with a soft breath, I cleared my mind and prepared myself for the sermon.

"Evening, Lady Katarine," said a male voice behind me.

I tilted my head to acknowledge whomever it was, and my heart stopped. Johann Beswick sat behind me. He was much thinner than I remembered him, but his sharp eyes remained the same.

"Evening," I said, after a moment.

"You're looking well," he said. "But I suppose life in the castle is easy compared to ours."

I exhaled slowly as three more men took the pews behind me.

"I suppose one could look at it that way. But being in the castle has its own challenges."

He chuckled darkly. "I'm sure being a spy for Princess Brynna is not without its dangers."

It was all I could do to keep a straight face. "I have no idea what you're talking about. I haven't seen her since...since Ilara stabbed her."

"Pardon me if I don't believe you. Your girlfriend mysteriously disappears around the time a trio of masked vigilantes begins wreaking havoc in the city?" He made a noise. "Timing is suspect."

"Beata knew, but I was unaware," I said, thinking it best to stick to my lie as I'd been telling it. There was no knowing which master Beswick served—even if it was himself. "It was the reason our parting was so strained." I looked back at him. "Have you... seen her lately? Beata?"

"Can't say that I have, but I assume she's with your Princess Brynna," Beswick said. "It must be hard to know they're so close and to not be with her."

"Close?" I couldn't believe that. "What do you mean close?"

"There's been some disruption of my business lately. Your princess seems to delight in causing me trouble." He narrowed his gaze at me. "She needs to back off, or there will be dire consequences."

"Whatever Brynna is or isn't doing, or wherever she is, I have no clue," I said, finally turning to look at him fully. "I've had no contact with Brynna in months. If you would like to deliver a message, you should perhaps do it yourself."

He simply smiled, sending chills down my spine. "As you say. But I would reconsider whether coming to church every week is the safest idea for you. Then again, it's clear that your position in the castle is becoming more precarious. Perhaps Ilara's hoping the mob will do to you what she lacks the spine to do herself."

I stared into his dark eyes, mustering all the confidence I'd seen in Brynna. "I would think that you have more important things on *your* plate than to threaten me, Lord Beswick."

I felt his gaze on the back of my neck and did my best not to fidget. If he was trying to intimidate me, he would fail. I was a princess of Niemen, and a lady of Forcadel. He would have to do more than smile to scare me. Still, if Brynna was in the city, I wished I could give her his message. Not that she'd listen.

One of the other sisters climbed onto the dais to open the service, offering a litany of prayers that had been requested. We rose to our feet and sang a hymn of the hope, joy, and comfort of the Mother's love then gave our offerings. Then, finally, Fishen rose to speak, offering the smattering of attendants a warm smile that reminded me that not everything had changed.

"Good morning," she boomed, and the congregation returned the greeting. "I'm glad you're here."

I closed my eyes and let her good sermon run through me. The constant theme over the past few months had been of finding light in the darkness, of leaning on one another, of welcoming challenges with grace and humility. She was a master of weaving in anecdotes and scripts, landing at a central theme and making us all think. When she finished, we stood to sing one more hymn, filling the church with the beautiful sound of a hundred disparate voices.

Fishen closed the service and the congregation rose, some moving to the confession boxes to speak with the sisters. I wanted to take advantage of the brief respite, so I made a beeline for Fishen as she worked her way through the crowd. She had a patience about her that I'd always admired, fearing no one who came into the church, no matter how disheveled.

"My lady," she said, nodding to me. "You look troubled."

"I am," I said. "May we take a walk?"

She offered her arm and we began to walk, when I felt the presence of the Severian guards behind me.

I paused and looked over my shoulder. "Surely, you will grant me the privacy to speak with my spiritual leader."

They blushed and looked down as they took a seat in the pew. At least they still had some semblance of decency and reverence.

"Come, my child," Fishen said with a small chuckle. "Let's go to my gardens."

Although the gardens weren't as nice as the royal gardens in the castle, Fishen and the sisters took great pride in their green space next to the abbey. Here, instead of roses and hedges, there were fruit trees and rows of vegetables that were given away to the poorest in the city. But now, the vines were picked clean.

"We can barely keep up," she said. "Her Majesty must have some idea of what she's doing, but she's starving the population in the meantime. Those who can leave, have. And those who can't... well, they are here."

"I think she's up to something," I said. "But I can't figure out what it is. There are so many mysteries I'm trying to unravel, and so much worry in my mind. I haven't seen Felix in weeks, and I fear... every day I fear I'll hear that he's died. Or that there will be irons for me."

"Place your fears in the Mother's hands," Fishen said. "She will take your burden."

"I can't," I said, tears coming to my eyes. "My place in the castle is slipping, and I'm the only thing keeping Felix alive right now. I wish...I wish we could both just leave."

"But where would you go?" Fishen asked. "Your sister has all but declared war on Forcadel. Would she take you back?"

I bit my tongue rather than speak the truth. "We will go somewhere else, perhaps. Somewhere no one knows our names." I shook my head. "But that won't happen unless I can get Felix out of that prison."

Fishen was silent for a long time. "I have heard a rumor that

Lord Garwood isn't long for this world."

"I have heard the same," I said, curious about the change in topic.

"Ilara has allowed him a lord's burial outside the city," she said. "You'll recall the preparation of the body."

How could I forget? After August's death, Fishen had brought a white shroud lined with gold thread and placed it over his body as it was carried out.

"It would be easy to put a different body under the blanket, you know," she continued, giving me a look.

"I don't—" I stopped, my eyes growing wide as I realized what she was saying. The shroud was sacred, not to be removed for at least a week, in most cases. But for Garwood, it would remain on him until his body was delivered to the cemetery outside of town.

"I'll send word once Garwood's taken a turn for the worse. You are his only living kin here, even if it is by marriage, and it would make sense that you're there for his death."

"Thank you, Mother, for convincing Ilara to honor him this way," I said, taking her hands and kissing them.

And for giving me the opportunity I'd been waiting for. Because when Garwood died, Felix and I would be making our escape.

Chapter Twenty-Seven

By the second day of our integrated camp, the initial friction seemed to have died down. The thieves had taken to the regimental training with ease, and the other soldiers were heartened by the sight of new recruits. Farmers brought their daily wares to Jax and Locke, and Beata had more than enough to keep everyone fed and happy.

Everything was running smoothly. I just didn't seem to be the one running it.

I spent most of my time helping Beata in the kitchens. It was menial work to peel potatoes and wash dishes, but at least it kept me out of sight.

"And how long, exactly, do you think you'll be able to hide in here?" Beata asked, wiping her brow as she stirred a large spoon. "Sooner or later, people are going to wonder what they're doing next."

"Just waiting for the ond to arrive," I said, avoiding her gaze.

"You do know there's someone in camp who might know when that is, right?" Beata said, opening the flap to the kitchen and peering out into camp. "And where the hell are those children Jorad promised me?"

"Hm?"

"He's got all these babies in the middle of training," she said with pursed lips as she scanned the houses. "They can't even pick up a sword. I told him to send them in here to help me. They can peel potatoes. He better not have ignored my request."

"We need everyone to be useful," I muttered. "Maybe he has a better use for them."

"Really?" She put a hand on her hip. "Everyone, Brynna? What about that woman sitting in the hut who's twiddling her thumbs? Is she useful?"

My cheeks warmed as that old familiar guilt gnawed at my gut. "I doubt she'd tell me anything."

"She's your prisoner," Beata said. "Make her. Aren't you a princess vigilante? What are you so scared of?"

Failure? My childhood monsters? Being told that I'm soft? Take your pick. "Things are going great right now. I don't want to rock the boat any more than I already have."

Beata released a sigh of frustration and shoved a bowl of stew in my direction. "Fine. But I'm not bringing her food anymore. If you want her to eat, you get to deliver her meals."

I left the kitchen holding the bowl, feeling the gazes of everyone in the camp on me. I forced my shoulders back and head high, even though I certainly didn't feel confident. A few younger thieves stopped and watched me walk by them, but their superior officer barked at them to keep moving.

Celia's hut was in the very back of camp, a small building nestled against the back wall. A twirl of smoke rose from the chimney, although the curtains were drawn. Two guards stood on the front porch, though I wasn't sure why I'd put them there. Celia had been clear—she was sticking around to watch the show.

"Give us a minute," I said to the guards. I didn't want an audience for this.

They shared a look. "I don't think that's wise. She's dangerous."

"Not to me," I said with a half smile. "I have food."

They hesitated, but finally saluted and left the front porch. I made sure they were a some distance away before ascending the final few steps and standing on the porch. I shifted the bowl into one hand and waited, staring at the sky and praying to the Mother.

Then I raised my fist and rapped on the door.

"Who is it?"

I snorted. She'd surely seen me walking up the path. I opened her door and found her seated at her desk, reading a book. It was the first time I'd seen her without any papers or maps or plans. It was like seeing a fish on the banks of a river.

"Can I help you?" she asked. "I'm clearly busy running my camp."

I took a seat across from her and placed the bowl on the table. "A peace offering."

She glanced at it then returned to her book. "I hate stew."

"When is the next shipment of ond coming?" I asked, since she clearly wasn't in the mood to talk. "And what's coming with it?"

She shrugged and flipped the page on her book. "I daresay I have no idea. My job was to keep the path and border clear. That is what I did."

I leaned back in my chair, watching her for a moment before I spoke again. "How long have you been working with Beswick?"

"I wouldn't say working with," she said. "Partnered? Allied with? He seemed like a capable fellow. He's making more progress than you are."

"Do you still feel that way?" I asked.

She chuckled. "After seeing you in action? Absolutely." She paused. "If you can call the last few days action. Peeled many potatoes, Larissa?"

"I've done a lot," I said, my face heating up. "I captured Neveri with nothing but a prayer and a few soldiers. I walked over the mountains in Niemen to Linden. I'm up to nearly two hundred soldiers—"

"And what are you doing with all that you've gained? Nothing." She sat back. "Content to sit around and let that young soldier run your camp. It's no wonder I saw three soldiers leaving last night."

Was she bluffing? I'd have to ask Jorad. "I'm working on it."

"You're soft," she said. "It's the very reason I'm still here, in my house while you play leader in the mess hall. You can't bring yourself to kill me, even though it's most certainly warranted." She smiled. "And so here we are, stuck in a stalemate because you lack conviction."

I opened my mouth to argue, but there was a hurried rap at the door.

"Well?" Celia said. "You might as well answer it. I doubt they're here to speak to me."

I walked to the door and flung it open, looking into the face of one of the soldiers.

"Pardon me, Your Majesty," he said. "But you need to come quick. There's about to be a brawl."

I ran to the front of the camp where Beata, red-faced and angry, was pointing her finger at Jorad, who seemed just as put-out. Having never seen either of them so emotional, I hurried over to break up whatever fight they were having before Beata beat the crap out of Jorad.

"Okay, okay," I said, holding up my hands. "What's the problem here?"

"Brynna, I must object to this...this...*child slavery!*" Beata said, putting her hands on her hips as Jorad made a scoffing sound.

"Slavery?" I blinked. "What are you talking about?"

"Jorad has these poor babies up before dawn, running around the camp and saluting empty spaces. Then he has them sword fighting until dusk, with barely any time to rest. These are *children*."

I could've argued that these children had been used to far worse treatment prior to our arrival, but Beata wouldn't listen to that. "I'm sure Jorad's using good judgment here."

"Indeed, I am. They are no younger than I was when I started," he said. "They're not babies."

"They can't even read."

"They don't need to read to fight."

"Enough," I barked. "Beata, I understand that you're upset, but we have to use the bodies we have."

By now, a crowd had gathered, drawn to the loud voices.

"They're children, Brynna," Beata said. "Surely, you don't condone this."

"We'll compromise," I said, hoping to resolve this quickly before a bigger audience showed up. "Beata, you will take charge of the youngest in the bunch. If they can't hold a sword aloft for more than five minutes, they go with you. Otherwise, they stay with Jorad."

Beata's face screwed up in anger. "That's ridiculous, Brynna, and you know it."

A hush fell over the crowd, and I realized two seconds later that she'd openly defied me. Not me, Brynna. But me, the queen.

"Bea," I said quietly. "You might want to calm down before you make me have to do something I don't want to do."

"You lack the courage to do anything," she said. "That's why

Celia's still here, and that's why you're letting Jorad walk all over you! Maybe we should put him on the throne instead, since you can't even manage to keep the camp together."

She glared at me and grabbed the hem of her skirt, storming off in the other direction. The sound of the kitchen door slamming echoed across the camp, followed by a quiet murmuring from the crowd.

"Get back to work," I snapped at the gathered soldiers. "Jorad, a word."

The soldier followed me out of earshot, but when I turned to face him, he still wore a look of utter fury.

"You can't let her talk to you like that," he said.

"She was just hot. She's under a lot of stress."

"As are we all," Jorad said. "It looked bad."

"I know it looked bad."

"You should discipline her."

I gave him a look. "What, like, a slap on the wrist?"

"The punishment for open insubordination is twenty lashes," he said.

"Yeah, right." I barked a laugh. "Kat would never forgive me."

"And your soldiers might never respect you again," Jorad said. "I don't care who she is or what she means to you, you've got to establish some order here. You can be merciful, but what you did just now was soft."

There was that word again: *soft*. I'd never thought it would be used to describe me. Still, the thought of ordering a punishment for Beata was sickening. "She was warned, and she backed off."

"Did she? What's to stop her from doing it again?"

"She won't."

"If you punish her, she won't." He took a step toward me. "You need to show some leadership."

Chewing my lip, I turned away from him. I was tired of the chorus of criticisms, from both inside my head and outside. Celia's smirk burned my consciousness, and her words echoed in my brain. I couldn't argue with them, either. Every second I hesitated, another soldier lost faith in me.

Finally, I nodded.

Chapter Twenty-Eight

We walked back into camp, my stomach churning at the thought of what I was about to do. Jorad called for the soldiers to assemble then did his best to round up the younger children. They stood at attention, some of them staring off into space, as the rest of the camp gathered. The second to last to arrive, unsurprisingly, were Jax and Locke, who leaned over the fence.

Beata appeared in the doorway of the kitchen, defiant, but also somewhat resolved. Perhaps she knew what was coming. That didn't make it easier.

"Earlier," I began slowly, my voice carrying across the silent green, "there was an incident at the front of camp. Lady Beata had a disagreement with Lieutenant Llobrega. These things happen, of course, especially when it comes to something we care so deeply about, such as the welfare of our soldiers."

A ripple of discontent echoed across the Forcadelian soldiers.

"However," I said, turning quickly, "it is not appropriate for anyone in this camp to disrespect me. I am your queen, and as such, you've given me the burden of making decisions. You believe I'll do the right thing, and that includes meting out punishment when it's called for."

I turned to my left where Beata stood. She stared into my eyes with little emotion.

"Beata, you were disrespectful to the crown," I said, willing my voice not to shake. "For that, you will be punished."

She nodded. "I accept my punishment."

"Lieutenant Llobrega, what should be the punishment for insubordination?" I asked.

He stepped forward, clearing his throat. "Captain Llobrega gave us five lashes for speaking out of turn. I believe that should be applied here."

I cast him a short look—earlier he'd said twenty. *Is he giving her a reprieve?* "Very well," I said. "Lady Beata will be whipped five times for disrespecting the crown."

I retreated to the edge of the green while Beata walked to the center post. She'd clearly been expecting such an event, as the back of her dress was loosely tied. Two Forcadelian soldiers undid the binding, leaving her skin bare to the world. The two soldiers bound her hands gently to the post.

Jorad walked up to her with his riding crop and whispered something in her ear. Then he stepped back and let the first one fly.

I flinched when it landed on her back, but she didn't cry out. The second landed, then the third. At the fourth, she released a yelp of pain. And finally, with the fifth, it was over.

Jorad untied her hands and helped her dress. She straightened gingerly, then walked away from the post, headed back to the kitchen. Jorad turned to me, clearly expecting me to say something.

I swallowed the bile in my throat and turned to my troops, who looked almost stricken. "I will not tolerate insubordination. Is that clear?"

A wave of salutes followed, even from the youngest recruits, who seemed more interested in saluting correctly than I'd seen before.

"Continue your training," I said. "And watch your tongues."

I turned on my heel, walked out of the camp, and promptly emptied my stomach onto a tree.

That evening, there was a tense silence in the mess hall. Beata had still overseen the food preparation, but she was nowhere to be found during dinner. Jorad ate on the other side of the hall from me, and none of his soldiers would look me in the eye as I sat down at the table. I'd thought they would be happy I'd gone through with it, but I got the distinct feeling that they blamed me for Beata's outburst.

In Neveri, I presumed to understand what it was like to be a queen. But this...this was another realm. Even during my short stint on the throne, I'd never had to lead an army of soldiers. I'd had General Godfryd for that. And, well, Felix.

Who was currently rotting in jail.

The food tasted like ash in my mouth, and it was hard to swallow. After forcing half my bowl down, I gave up and left the hall, seeking refuge from my thoughts.

Unfortunately, they came roaring back at the sight of the candle in Celia's hut, the sound of her whispering *soft* in my ear. I turned on my heel and marched in the other direction. But that would lead me toward the mess hall, where everyone hated me.

I spun in another direction, finding myself at a wall. Appropriate. Another direction, the door to the camp. I was spinning in place now, and the camp was closing in on me. I needed to talk to someone, but the only person in camp who might listen was currently furious at me.

Then there was a light—not in Celia's house, but Nicolasa's. I hadn't seen her name on the list and assumed she'd left with Callum. But as I came around the corner, I found her on her knees, digging in a patch of flowers under the moonlight.

"Nicolasa?" I asked. "What are you doing out here?"

"I felt the unease in the camp," she said, staring at the night sky. "It's quite thick and made my stomach upset. I thought I might spend some time in the peppermint plants to soothe my fears." She looked behind her to smile at me. "And you?"

I shook my head and gazed up at the stars. "I really wish I knew what to do. It seems like everything I do fails."

"Not everything, I'm sure."

"I'm completely out of my depth," I murmured, a lump of emotion growing in my throat. "I'm supposed to lead an army, but I can't even keep my most loyal soldiers from fighting each other. How can I lead them to victory?"

"I'm sure you'll figure it out. The Mother's hand is strong on your shoulder," she said. "Otherwise, you wouldn't have made it this far."

"The thing is, I don't disagree with Beata," I said, leaning against the fence. "There are some kids who are too young to see war. They need to be protected and allowed a childhood. But they're here, eating our food and taking up space. I can't afford to feed people who don't contribute." I winced, again thinking of Celia. "I can barely afford to feed the people who do."

"Then let them contribute," Nicolasa said. "The swords used in war must be sharpened. Those who carry them need to be fed. Is it not better to use a child to deliver a message than an able-bodied soldier?" She paused and shrugged. "Merely my opinion."

"It's mine, too," I said. "But it's not the opinion of my military leader."

"He's young, the same as you. But he has a good soul." She smiled. "He would listen if you spoke to him."

"I have spoken with him. He didn't want to listen."

"You don't seem the kind of person to take no for an answer," Nicolasa said.

"It just feels like everything I've earned is precarious," I said. "The one thing I'm holding onto are these soldiers. If I lose them, I have nothing. And right now, Jorad is the only one they listen to."

"They're here because they believe in what you stand for," she said, her voice losing some of its ethereal quality. "It's why I stayed, why Jax stayed. You're the kind of ruler who debates and weighs the costs of human lives, not one who mercilessly hacks and slices her way toward victory."

"Celia says I'm soft," I said.

"And what does a queen care for the opinions of those she conquered?" Nicolasa mused with a smile on her face.

"I also just let my scullery maid disrespect me in front of my soldiers," I said dryly. "Then...flogged her in front of all of them."

She smiled warmly. "I'm sure she'll forgive you."

"But can I forgive myself for letting it happen?" I asked. "If I'd been a stronger leader... if I'd been able to put my foot down and know I was doing the right thing..."

"Sometimes, the only way to know how to do the right thing is to do the wrong thing enough times," Nicolasa said. "The trick is to trust your own experience, instead of listening to others."

The sound of hurried footsteps drew my attention, and Jorad nearly tripped over his feet as he came up to me. "Your Majesty, we just got a message. A wagon's come through the forest."

I couldn't believe my ears. "What? Where? When?"

"It passed through our scouts about twenty minutes ago."

I stopped, the blood draining from my face. "Twenty minutes? It took you twenty minutes to get this message to me?"

"Well, we had to get it from the scouts at the border, then we had to find you, and—"

I ran my hands through my hair. Twenty minutes was a lifetime—it only took forty to get from one end of the forest to the other.

"Larissa," Nicolasa said with a pointed look. "You know what to do."

Screw it. "Go find Jax and Locke. Tell them to meet me at the southern border in ten minutes."

"I'll send them and five others—"

"No," I said, turning to face him. "I need thieves, not soldiers."

"But—"

"I don't have time to argue," I said, running by him. "Do as I say."

After a quick stop at the weapons hut for knockout powder and a crossbow, I ran as fast as my feet could take me, a thousand different thoughts running through my mind. Mostly, that my movements weren't accompanied by the telltale whistles. We had no scouts in the trees, and so I had no idea what had been passing through my forest. Oh, but if we'd missed our one chance to catch the ond… All because I was too chicken to tell Jorad what to do.

I'd berate myself later; now, I needed to focus.

I arrived at the southern border, the dark open fields of Forcadel behind me. I shimmied up an old oak, resting in the branches and letting the foliage hide me. I settled in and waited, listening for the sound of hooves and carriages.

Instead, I got a pair of whistles. A shadow in the tree behind me, and one in front. Jax and Locke, just as I'd asked for. Finally, something had gone right.

The familiarity of this situation wasn't lost on me. Up in the trees, Locke in the next tree over, Jax whistling at me to pay attention. We'd all been here three years ago, the night I'd killed for the first time. It had been my first mission, and it had gone terribly wrong.

But as Nicolasa said, doing the wrong thing enough times

taught me how to be different. I was confident that I could subdue whomever was in this carriage without killing them. I was confident in my aim. Confident in myself.

Jax's whistle echoed through the forest. *Pay attention, idiot.*

I cast him a look then readied the crossbow on the tree branch. I sent a silent prayer that there would be only a few guards, and we could resolve it without too much of a fight.

The sound of squeaking wheels reached my ears first, then the carriage made its appearance. There was one coachman on top with two large horses pulling what appeared to be a massive wagon. It could've been laden with ond, or it could've been filled with soldiers.

Jax whistled for me to prepare for my shot, and I caught his eye, nodding. With care, I aimed for the spot above the coachman's shoulder and released my arrow. The knockout powder did its job, and the man slumped over, even as the horses kept walking. Jax jumped from the tree to grab the reins, and Locke and I landed on the ground.

The carriage stopped and my heartbeat quickened as the door opened. I held up my crossbow. "Turn around and go back to Niemen. Your ond isn't wanted here anymore, and I doubt Queen Ariadna gave you permission to send it."

A familiar face popped out. "Brynna?"

I blinked. "Luard?"

The prince of Niemen—blond, handsome, tall, and mischievous—stepped out of the carriage, wearing a look of confusion. "You're the one accepting ond?"

"No?" I said. "You're the one bringing it to Beswick?"

"No?"

At that, we both grinned and walked toward each other. "Seems as though we had a similar mindset about these things," Luard said. "Shall we have a chat?"

Relief of all kinds swam in my mind, especially as his other guards Ivan, Asdis, Nils, and Hagan appeared from behind the carriage, too. "Nothing would make me happier."

Chapter Twenty-Nine

Luard and I walked arm-in-arm into the camp, much to the surprise of Jorad and the rest of the soldiers. Where there were small gatherings of Forcadelian soldiers still awake at this hour, I introduced them to Luard. They saluted him with the appropriate reverence and seemed pleased that he was there. More manpower was surely welcome in this idiotic scheme we were undertaking—and it was hard to be mad around Luard.

"I don't have princely accommodations for you," I said with a small grimace. "I can find you the softest bed, though."

"What about that place?" Luard asked, pointing to the hut with the smoke curling out of the top of it.

"That's Celia's hut," I said. "She's still in there."

"Why? Didn't you say you took over her camp?"

"I did, but..." I shook my head. "I'm trying to limit my liabilities."

"Is she cute?"

I did a double take. "What?"

He shrugged. "I'm not above sleeping with criminals."

"She's a bit old for you," I said with a frown. Was he seriously considering this or just messing with me?

"Brynna, my love is for all women, young and old," he said, covering his heart.

"You are certainly welcome to try," I said with a nervous laugh. "But I have a feeling she wouldn't go for it."

"Fine, fine. The sleeping house it is." He cast a curious gaze at the hut. "But I do find it odd that you're leading this rebellion, yet letting your defeated foe sleep in what's rightly your place. At the very least, put her in a prison."

"She's out of the way," I said quickly. I already knew what Luard would say if we delved deeper into this subject, so I was hoping we could avoid it. "C'mon, let's go to my office so we can talk further."

I hadn't seen Beata since the lashing. But when she laid eyes on Luard, she dropped an entire bucket of water on herself. Even though she was dripping wet, Luard swept her into his arms, kissing her on either cheek as if they were blood-related.

"I shall make such a feast tomorrow morning," Beata said, smoothing her dark hair, which had dislodged from its tight bun. "Niemenian delicacies. All of them. We just found a stash of flour and yeast in the back of the pantry, and Nicolasa says there's a blackberry bush nearby that's still producing. A blackberry tart, for my favorite prince."

"Beata," I said with a small sigh. "I understand you're happy to see him, but we need to save our food for when we really need them."

"And I disagree," Beata said, clearly forgetting the lesson she'd learned about watching her tongue. "The soldiers in camp are weary. We're all in need of something to celebrate. A small party will be good for the soul. And it's a tart, *Brynna*."

The use of my first name and the sardonic tone that came with it drew my eyebrows up. "Well, that settles it, then. Bake away, Lady Beata."

She kissed Luard on the cheek then returned to the kitchen, muttering to herself about all the things she had to do before the dinner tonight. I had a feeling she'd break out that wine I'd given to her, too.

"Did it just get chilly in here?" Luard asked, once she disappeared.

"It's a long story," I said, sitting down at the mess hall table.

"Well, we have a few minutes to talk," he said, reaching across the table to take my hand. "What's going on?"

"She and Jorad got into it this morning," I said. "And when I tried to break it up, she...well, she was rather rude about it. Which, of course, I don't mind, but it was in front of the entire camp. Jorad said I shouldn't allow such insubordination, even if it is from Beata."

He made a face. "That's tricky. How did you punish her?"

I winced again. "Five lashes."

"Oh, well, then she got off easy," Luard said, waving his hand. "In Niemen, it would've been two days in the stocks for disrespecting a superior officer."

"It still hurt," I said. "Her more than me, I'm sure."

"Being a leader is tough," he said. "But you can't play favorites. Even if they are the ones who you love the most."

"I already feel like everyone's losing faith in what I can do here," I said. "Hell, I'm losing faith in myself. We're just waiting for things to happen and reacting to them." I cast him a sideways glance. "I'm really glad you're here. I've missed you and that big brain of yours."

"Well, now you're just buttering me up," he said with a laugh. "Fine, tell this big brain of mine what you've been up to since we parted, and I'll see if I can't help."

I gave him a quick summation of the past few weeks, including Ammon's betrayal, the discovery of Beswick as the source of the ond, and how I'd made the strategic decision to come to Celia's camp to try to intercept it—and take over the camp while I was at it.

He nodded at the end of my story. "You're doing all right so far. That Mark sounds like an insufferable dick."

"He was, but the soldiers liked him," I said. "And it's hard to ask them to trust me when Ammon's undoing all the work we did in Neveri."

Luard tapped his chin. "You said you had a bag of ond that Beswick fellow had smuggled into Forcadel, right? Why not use that to barter with Ammon?"

"It's not mine to barter with," I said softly. "But...you wouldn't have minded?"

"Of course I would've minded," he said. "And Ariadna would've been furious. But it would've been an understandable decision." He shook his head. "You're still too noble for your own good."

"It's not noble. It's about survival," I said with a bit of a laugh. "All of my alliances are falling apart. I'm not about to jeopardize the only one I have left."

"Tell me more about this Beswick," Luard said. "Do you know who he's been working with from the Niemenian side?"

"There was a Niemenian merchant, Goossen, who we came across in Forcadel. He'd met the business end of a club then found himself in the middle of an ond explosion," I said with a grimace.

Luard shook his head. "I'm unfamiliar with the name. Once all this is said and done, we'll unfortunately have to investigate who within our country has been selling our state secrets."

"And when I'm back on the throne, I'll assist in whatever capacity I can," I said.

"Ah, there's just the little problem of getting back on that tricky throne." He looked around. "Although it looks like you're doing a lot better than the last time we spoke. You're up to what, two hundred soldiers?"

"Nearly," I said. "Not enough to take on Ilara. Now that she knows I'm alive, she could send her forces out to try to meet me head on. I'm not ready for that yet."

"Mm, I doubt she'd do that," Luard said with a shake of his head. "Ilara's forces are mostly water-based, and you're way up here in the country. She's left herself vulnerable by thinking her borders are secure. She'll have a fairly rude awakening when she finds out what happened in Skorsa."

I grinned. "And what, exactly, did?"

"My sister dispatched her forces," Luard said. "As expected, we took the city within an evening. The poor Severian she'd put in charge folded like a deck of cards." He shook his head.

"Casualties?"

"A few, unfortunately, but nothing near the numbers in Niemen," he said. "Thanks to the efforts of your Lieutenant Lesley."

"Joella?" My smile widened. She was one of Felix's inner circle, like Riya had been. "She was in Skorsa?"

"Indeed. I was able to make contact prior to the invasion, and she and her Forcadelian soldiers helped us keep the peace as much as possible."

"And how is Joella?"

He grinned. "Happy you're alive and ready to assist in whatever capacity you need her."

At least someone had faith in me. "What will you do next?"

"We're going to continue into Forcadel to find whoever was responsible for this heinous crime against the kingdom of Niemen," Luard said. "And take the perpetrator back to face criminal proceedings."

"Sounds like fun," I said with a grin. "Can I join?"

"Shouldn't you be more concerned about your troops?" Luard said.

"It would be something to show them that we're moving forward," I said. "And besides that, as much faith as I have in your guards, I think you're woefully underprepared for what Beswick will bring. It would make me feel better to send reinforcements with you."

"Yes, but...does that mean you have to go?"

"Perhaps I just need something to occupy myself, too." I exhaled. "The first time I felt like myself was sitting in that tree, waiting for you. That's what I know. I know Beswick, too."

He gave me a look. "I suppose it couldn't hurt to have the expert with us. But please be advised that I have orders from my queen. Whoever we meet is coming back with us. No matter what."

"You have my word."

Chapter Thirty

Katarine

Clearly, Fishen worked miracles, or the Mother's hand was at work, because Ilara granted my request to spend Garwood's final days with him. I bore the smell and cries of anguish to wipe his forehead and tell him stories about August and anything else I could think of. I hoped Felix could hear my voice from the next cellblock over and prayed that when Garwood drew his last breath, I could set in motion a plan that would free us both. Fishen had already given me the shroud that would cover his body, the only pristine item in this grungy place. I brought it with me every day, along with the few earthly possessions I'd be taking with me when the time came. There was some gold buried between my favorite silk scarf, and the Niemenian crest my sister had given me on my wedding day. But everything else would be staying behind. If it was there when Brynna reclaimed the kingdom, so be it.

When I arrived one rainy morning, Lord Garwood was already dead. The chill on his skin said he'd been gone for several hours now. But the guards hadn't noticed. A good sign.

I went to the prison door. "Bring Captain Llobrega to me."

"Why?" the Severian barked back.

"Because Ilara told you to," I said with a steely-eyed glare. "My word is as good as hers."

He looked skeptical, but didn't argue. A few minutes later, Felix was deposited in the room unceremoniously. He cried out in pain when they dropped him on the floor, and I rushed to his side. He looked much worse than before, his cheeks even paler and some of the cuts on his face beginning to fester. As morbid as it sounded, Garwood's death couldn't have come at a better time.

"Listen very carefully to what I'm telling you," I said, lifting his chin to peer into his eyes as the door closed behind us. "I need you to be very still and quiet."

He nodded. "What are you doing?"

"Just stay here and rest."

I left Felix on the ground and tended to the corpse. With care, I pulled Garwood's body to the wall next to Felix, shrouded in darkness. It was a gamble—a large one—that they wouldn't check who was leaving and who was staying. But the Mother was on my side, and I'd prayed for days that She would watch over us.

I sat Garwood against the wall and gently positioned him. Then, I bowed my head. "I pray that you find your sister and August with the Mother and rest in peace." I looked up at his lifeless face, already losing whatever color was left. "Thank you for this one, final sacrifice."

I rose and returned to Felix, helping him to the center of the room where Garwood had lain. I placed him face-up on the ground then covered his body with the shroud.

The door opened—Fishen was there. She entered the room and knelt beside Felix under the shroud.

"Lord Garwood," she whispered, pressing her hand to his forehead. "You have lived a good, honorable life. Your service to the Mother as a man, husband, and caretaker of Forcadel will not be ignored. Go now, in peace, and receive your blessings at the Mother's side."

A shiver rolled through me. She'd said those same words over August's body, dead in his bed.

She took my hand and whispered, "Take care, Katarine. May the Mother offer her protection until you return to safe shores."

I squeezed her hand and swallowed the lump of emotion in my throat. "Brynna is alive, and we are returning to her."

"I know," she whispered with a half-smile. "The Mother told me as much."

Our conversation came to an abrupt end when the guards arrived with the cart that would carry Garwood's body out of the city. My heart pounded in my chest as they walked inside. One went to the sheet to lift it, but I cried out in horror.

"You do not remove the shroud from a dead man," Fishen gasped, as if what they were doing was the most offensive thing she'd ever seen. "Have you no shame, sir?"

The man jumped back as if the body were on fire, and his partner hissed at him. With care, they gently lifted Felix by his head and legs, grimacing as they did so.

"He's still warm," one of them said.

"He's only just passed," I replied, my heart pounding against my ribcage.

They said nothing more as they placed the body on the cart. Fishen squeezed my hand and followed me out of the cell. The prisoners had gone quiet as we passed, knowing someone important had died. Some of them bowed their heads in reverence, others whispered their love to Fishen.

We reached the end of the long hall—a dead end. I swallowed hard, praying that this wasn't a trap and we weren't about to be slaughtered. But a loud grinding sound echoed from somewhere far away, and what was once a solid wall tilted backward, revealing a torch-lit passage.

I could scarcely believe my eyes. Another entrance to the castle? I kept my head bowed as we walked up the long ramp, counting the steps in my mind, and trying to orientate myself.

"Hold," the Severian said, walking to a large door. There were several locks, ones that would take more than a skilled vigilante to crack. Four keys went in, turning in a particular order, before the door opened. A rush of warm air hit my skin, as did the stench of human excrement and Mother knows what else.

"We usually just dump them here," the guard said.

"We're not dumping anything," I snapped. "We will take him to the cemetery."

After the words left my mouth, I regretted them. If they'd just dumped the body, I could've come back later and retrieved Felix. But now, I would have an escort to the cemetery. Then we'd have to wait for a burial. Mother, I'd made a horrible mistake.

"I hear there's been a death."

My back went straight as Coyle joined us.

"Yes. Lord Garwood," I said. "It is so terrible."

"It's a shame he couldn't swear his fealty to the queen," he said. "If you'll allow us, we will complete the burial."

"No," I said, looking up at him. "I'm his only relative in town. I will be the one to oversee things."

Coyle stared at me long and hard, as if trying to understand why I was acting like this, but Fishen cleared her throat.

"It's unseemly to stand out here with the dead," she said. "Shall we?"

My hands shook as we left town, but I buried them in the folds of my dress. Four Severians walked with us, plus Coyle and Fishen. I could use a sword, and I'd had rudimentary training in hand-to-hand combat, but against four trained guards, I would be useless.

No, don't think like that. Felix's life depended on me not giving up hope.

But my options were running low as the wagon rolled under the iron gate of the cemetery. Statues and plaques of lords and ladies who'd lived decades or even centuries ago littered the green, rolling hills bathed in moonlight.

"Where shall we bury him?" Coyle asked.

"Near his ancestors," I said, thinking quickly. I had no idea where that was, so it might buy me some time.

"I think here is fine," Coyle said, turning to me. "After all, it's a mercy that we're burying him at all." He nodded to his soldiers. "Start digging."

With every shovelful of dirt, my dread grew. Would they lift the shroud? Would Felix forget himself and make a sound? Or worse—would they bury him alive?

Mother Fishen walked to the front of the wagon, pressing her hands to either side of Felix's head as she began to pray for Garwood and his soul.

"Oh Mother. Giver of life. We pray that you receive the soul of Lord Leandro Garwood, servant of Forcadel and the crown. Please place your hand on Lord Joseph Garwood, his husband, and Lady Katarine during their time of grief, and continue to guide us as we —"

An arrow sailed across the sky and landed in the wood of the cart. A guard and Fishen leaned in closer to look then fell forward almost in unison. My heart beat faster as another arrow hit near the second pair of soldiers and they, too, slumped.

Coyle turned, his eyes wide with fear as he pulled his sword. "C-come out."

The person who appeared wore a cloak and a black mask but it wasn't Brynna. She was skinnier, her skin a lighter brown. Still, it appeared Coyle would see what he wanted to.

"You will go," she said, holding up her sword. The voice was unfamiliar. "And you will not breathe a word of this to anyone."

Coyle scrambled over his feet and ran off. Perhaps he would return, lie down, and pretend he'd succumbed to the knockout powder as well. However he saved his own skin, I didn't care.

"You…" I said with a soft sigh. "Who are you?"

"We're friends of Princess Brynna." A young voice echoed from behind the grave, followed by a tiny girl, no older than thirteen. "My name's Elisha."

"Mother damn it," the masked woman cursed. "What did I tell you about announcing yourself?"

"Princess Brynna does it all the time," Elisha responded, putting her hands on her hips. "Besides that, this lady's her friend, ain't she?"

"Yes, but…" The masked woman shook her head.

"I don't understand," I said, after a moment. "Where's Brynna?"

"She's with the rest of the camp," the masked woman said. "She asked us to stay behind. We were watching the streets for Beswick's activity when we saw Coyle grab the guards. He said there was a death in the dungeons and you were requesting Mother Fishen." She swallowed and looked at the wagon. "I feared the worst. Is that…Captain Llobrega?"

"Yes, but he's alive," I said with a small smile. "Lord Garwood passed, so we… Well…it was my best option to get him out of the dungeons, so I took it." My knees grew a little weak as I exhaled. "And I'm grateful you came to my rescue. I confess, I didn't think this through very well. An oddity for me."

"We were glad to do it," she said. "Elisha found a Nestori in town who made knockout powder and replenished our supplies."

"I'm surprised Brynna let someone so young take on so much responsibility," I said to the girl.

"I'm not young," Elisha replied. "Am I, Aline?"

"Aline," I said, looking at the masked woman. "How did you come across Brynna?"

She pulled her mask from her face, revealing herself as Forcadelian. "I was a soldier under Captain Llobrega's command. Assigned to Neveri when Her Majesty arrived."

I had to smile. "Felix will be very proud of you." I gestured to his still body. "When he wakes."

"Where are you going next?" Aline asked.

"Wherever Brynna is," I said. "Or wherever's safest. Felix needs to heal and recover from his ordeal."

She nodded in understanding. "If you continue along this road, you'll come across a small town called Veeblen. From there, take the northwestern road."

She gave me more directions—towns and villages, and roads I should take. I remembered every name, cementing them into my mind as if my very life depended on it.

"I wish we could escort you, but Her Majesty gave us a mission," Aline said. "We're here disrupting Lord Beswick's operations." She perked up. "But I've been unable to get a message out, so perhaps you could deliver it for me?"

"I will," I said with a nod.

"Tell her that we've kept all ond out of the city so far." She grinned proudly. "I've been dumping it into the bay, as instructed."

I winced at the precious material being destroyed so unceremoniously. "I suppose that's good?"

"And we've also been disrupting the food supply, delivering the goods directly to the people and preventing him from profiting off it," she said. "Any day now Beswick will break and be willing to deal."

"He gave me a message as well," I said, unease sliding into my voice. "He wants you to back off and leave him alone." I glanced at the little girl, barely a teenager. "Are you sure you're safe here?"

"Yes, my lady," Aline said. "We can handle whatever trouble Beswick brings. His operation is hanging by a string. But now you need to get going. The patrols will be back, and they'll be wondering what happened out here."

"I understand," I said, picking up the cart handles. "If you'll just point me in the right direction."

"You're going to carry him like that?" Aline asked.

"He's my best friend," I said. "I would carry him to the ends of the earth. But I just need to know to which end I'm going."

Chapter Thirty-One

Luard's cheerfulness was infectious, and by the morning, whatever dark clouds had gathered over the camp seemed to have dissipated. The Niemenian guards ingratiated themselves with my soldiers very quickly, and the mess hall was the liveliest I'd seen it in probably…ever.

Beata was practically glowing as she handed Luard a large blackberry tart for breakfast the next morning. It didn't escape my notice that she had nothing for me.

"I do think that woman has a crush on me," Luard said, taking a big bite. "This is the best pastry I've ever had."

"I think she's going a bit crazy being away from Katarine," I said, my mouth watering at the thought of fresh blueberries and sugar. "As are we all."

"Hopefully, whomever we're meeting with in Galdon will illuminate us on events in Forcadel," Luard said, breaking off a piece and handing it to me. "I have faith in Katarine's brilliance.

She's much stronger than she appears, I promise you. And what she lacks in physical strength, she more than makes up for in intellect and strategy."

"Good morning, Your Majesty," Jorad said, bowing low. "Prince Luard, we're glad to have you with us once again."

"And I'm glad to be back," Luard said with a smile. "I always love getting into trouble with our favorite princess vigilante."

"If I may," Jorad said, gesturing to the empty seat in front of us. I nodded and he sat down. "Ivan tells me you'll be continuing down to Galdon to intercept Beswick's contact this afternoon."

"Hopefully Beswick himself," Luard said.

"And which soldiers will you be taking with you?" he asked. "If any?"

"I'm going," I said. "With Jax and Locke. Perhaps a few others, just in case. Beswick does like to bring an entourage."

"Your Majesty," Jorad began with a hesitant smile. "Shouldn't you be conferring with me on these matters? I don't know if it's smart for you to be putting yourself in the middle of this. Send me and my best soldiers. We can do the job."

Luard nudged me under the table.

I took a breath, gathering my thoughts. "There's a place for soldiers, Jorad, and there's a place for thieves. Right now, I need thieves."

"The Niemenians aren't thieves—"

Luard nudged me again.

"It seems we may be better served having this discussion with the entire group," I said. "Perhaps after breakfast?"

"As you wish." Jorad saluted and walked away.

I let out a hiss of annoyance. "See what I mean? I can't even get Jorad to listen to me."

"People are always going to argue with you," Luard said, wiping crumbs off his tunic. "What makes you effective is how you deal with dissent. With a man like that, all you need to do is to pull rank, and he'll fall in line."

Once the mess hall had been cleared, I asked Jorad, the Niemenian guards, and a few others to stay to discuss the plan for the afternoon. I'd been building one in my mind, eager to get back into the sorts of strategies I knew. Surprise would be our best weapon against him.

Locke walked up to the table, a young girl in tow. "Erm...Miss Larissa, my lady."

"Yes," I said, trying not to smile at his fumbling of my title.

"I thought Florie might be useful," he said, his cheeks reddening. "See, she's from Galdon, and she can tell us all about the town."

"I know all of it," she announced proudly.

"Excellent," I said with a nod to Jorad, who seemed a little uneasy at the concept.

"Are you sure she knows what she's talking about?" he asked.

"I'd trust her," Luard said, kicking back. "Look how eager she is. And I hear these kids are used to canvassing cities and such, right, Brynna?"

I'd never been more thankful for the prince. "Thank you, Locke. Florie, what can you tell us about the city?"

The girl sat down at the table and described it in almost perfect detail, naming streets and businesses, and helping Ivan sketch a map of exactly where the stakeout was going to happen. Both Luard and Jorad seemed surprised by her knowledge, but I wasn't. Once she'd completed her task, I sent her off to get some rest, as she'd be going with us in the afternoon to help scout. I expected a protest from Jorad, but didn't get it.

"Our contact is supposed to meet us here," Ivan said, pointing to the inn Florie had described. "It's big enough for around thirty people."

I nodded, letting my Veil instincts come out. "We should infiltrate the tavern early in plainclothes, and let Ivan do the handoff. He's the least likely to be recognized, and they'll be expecting a Niemenian."

"And what do we do once they know we don't have the ond?" Jorad asked.

"We surround and disarm them, hopefully without too much of a fight," I said. "It's a small space, so we can't have swords. Knives, crossbows, things we can wield quickly." I glanced behind me at the four Forcadelian soldiers Jorad had picked. "Are you capable?"

They nodded. "We're skilled in all manner of weapons, Your Majesty."

"Excellent," I said, sharing a smile with Jorad. "We're glad to have you here." I turned back to the map. "I want Florie and another scout watching all the exits and entrances. They know the code and can alert Jax and me when trouble is coming. I want them in place before any of this starts, so they'll ride ahead with the first group."

"Group?" Jorad asked.

"Yes, so as to not arouse suspicion. First, I want Hagan, Nils, Jax, and the scouts to get in town early in the morning. Canvass the city, keep an eye out for the contact."

"He's supposed to be wearing a red handkerchief," Ivan said to Hagan. "Though I doubt he'd be wearing it during the day."

"Still, keep your ear to the ground," I said. "If anything feels funny, send Florie or the other scout back on your fastest horse. You're going to be our security team, so I want you inside the tavern no later than quarter past seven. Use your discretion, but don't come in as a big group."

Hagan nodded. "Will do."

"Asdis, you and Ivan will take the carriage mid-afternoon," I said. "Your job is to look like you're in town to make the contact, so make sure to get a room at the inn like you're planning to stay. I want you in place in the tavern at eight, no earlier."

"Will do," she said.

"Finally," I said, "Luard, and I will arrive after sundown with Locke. We'll get in place around quarter 'til."

"And me, Your Majesty?" Jorad asked. "What will you have the soldiers do?"

"Stay here," I said, rising to my feet. "Keep the fortress secure until we return. And keep an eye on the border. I don't trust this isn't the last shipment."

The room began to empty, but Jorad remained in place. "Your Majesty, could I have a word with you in private?"

"Sure," I said, already guessing what he was going to say. Luard, still sitting at the door, put his hand to his chest as if to say, *Pull rank*. And while I supposed I could throw my queenly title around, I got the distinct impression it wouldn't mean a whole lot to Jorad at this point.

We were barely outside the camp's walls when Jorad started. "I'd like to understand why you keep choosing Jax and Locke instead of my soldiers. Is it because of Lady Beata? I spared her; she was supposed to get twenty and she only got five."

"No, it's not that," I said. "I appreciate your leniency, as does Bea, I'm sure."

"Was it because we delayed in getting you the message? We moved as fast as we could—"

"No, *we* didn't," I said. "Because *we* have eighty scouts at our disposal that we aren't using effectively."

"Who? The cadets?" He stepped forward.

"Yes, our scouts who have been sitting in these trees and spying for Celia for years," I said, finally speaking aloud what I'd been mulling over these past few days. "Otherwise, she wouldn't have let them stick around."

"And you don't think our soldiers can do a better job of

supporting you in Galdon?" he asked, sounding more hurt than annoyed now.

I put my hands on my hips, staring up at the dark sky. "Listen, what you're doing here, what you've done, is more than I ever could've asked for. I appreciate you and every person who's dedicated themselves to this cause. But if I'm going to be queen, I have to start trusting my own instincts. I may not know much about battle strategy or tariffs, but I know Beswick. I know how he operates and who he sends. I need people who know how to get in and out of places without being seen."

"Then teach us how to do that."

I lowered my gaze to his in surprise. "What?"

"Teach us your ways," Jorad said. "You have soldiers here who are yearning to prove themselves to you. "

"They aren't yearning to prove themselves. They hate me," I said.

"They're frustrated because they haven't had any clear direction from you." His eyes lit up. "Why don't you have Locke stay behind and send me in his place to Galdon? He can begin training your troops so they can be more helpful to you. I'll bet you by the time we get back, these soldiers will be well on their way to becoming formidable vigilantes."

"I don't know…"

"Your Majesty," Jorad said with something of a bashful smile, "All we want are marching orders. So give us some. I don't know what you're afraid of."

Nicolasa's guidance floated between my ears. I couldn't be afraid of making the wrong decision anymore. "Fine, give the order to Locke and the troops. But they will be training with real weapons—just like we did. No complaints."

"Yes, Your Majesty."

Boldness returned to my voice. "And I want the kids to show the soldiers a few things about fighting dirty. Until everyone's trained up, I want the youngers in the trees, watching all the routes into the forest. I don't trust that Beswick won't send another shipment in, and I want us ready if he does." I hesitated. "And I want someone to make a schedule to help Beata with the care and feeding in camp. She can't continue to do everything by herself." I paused. "And I want you to work with her to figure a way that she can work with the littles. Find a compromise that works for the both of you."

I took a breath, waiting for argument.

Instead, Jorad saluted me. "Thank you, Your Majesty. I will convey your orders at once." He marched away without a second look.

"I'd give that a passing grade," Luard said, walking out from behind a hut. "You sounded a little unsure at the beginning, but you definitely cleared it up in the end. Well done."

"Are you just eavesdropping on all my conversations now?" I asked, putting my hand on my hip.

"You seemed like you were in need of a little feedback," he said. "Or encouragement. I'm not sure which."

"A little of Column A, little of Column B..."

Chapter Thirty-Two

Later that afternoon, Jorad wore a bright smile as he brought a pair of horses for Luard and me. The rest of the group had departed as instructed, and so far, no word of any trouble had come back to us. It was hard not to feel nervous, though, especially with the number of unknowns ahead of us.

As we rode out, we passed Locke and a group of ten Forcadelian soldiers—and a few younger kids, too. They were sparring without weapons, and the kids were making quick work of the soldiers. As one particularly large man fell backward, I cringed.

"They'll get better," Jorad said with a smile that faded as the last of the soldiers ended up on the ground.

"Don't get me wrong, the thieves could use some discipline," I said, as one nearby spit on the ground. "But helpless, they are not."

"Yeesh," Luard said, watching the kids celebrate their victory. "Agree on both points. It's like you have a little army of vigilantes."

I glanced at him, a smile coming onto my face. "Indeed I do."

As we exited the camp, a chorus of whistles echoed from above. I gazed up at the trees, filled with a mix of soldiers and teenagers. The thieves waved, whistling to their scouts ahead that we would be passing through.

"What did they say?" Jorad asked me.

"Good luck," I said. "Or the code for good luck."

"Is it more a code for words or letters?" Luard asked, glancing up at them.

"A little of both."

Luard craned his neck back. "Fascinating."

"I'd be interested in learning," Jorad said, nudging his horse even with mine. "You did say you wanted everyone in camp to know it."

"Excellent idea," Luard said, winking at me when Jorad wasn't looking.

We had time, so I spent the ride to the city teaching both Jorad and Luard the basics of Celia's whistle language—starting with the warning codes, numbers of riders, friends, foes, and everything between. Before the first hour was over, Jorad was able to correctly identify each combination I gave him, while Luard was hopelessly lost.

"Why do you have so many options?" he said. "What do you care if a friend is coming into the forest?"

"Celia liked to know what was going on at all times," I said. "If anyone set foot in the forest, she'd know about it."

"You'd probably also want to keep all the other scouts apprised of it," Jorad said. "So there's no mistaken identity."

"True," I said. "As much as I disagree with Celia's overall philosophy, she did have the right idea on how to use the youngers. They're practically invisible when they want to be." I cast my gaze southward toward Forcadel, where Elisha and Aline were hopefully still causing trouble. "It's why Elisha is so invaluable to Aline, as well. But I don't like that we haven't heard from them."

"I'm sure it's difficult to get messages in and out of the city," Jorad said. "And with only two of them, I don't think Aline would want to lose Elisha's help just to send messages."

"Perhaps I should send more down there," I said, chewing my lip. At the time, I hadn't anticipated that I'd be gone long. But it had been a few weeks now. With thoughts of Elisha and Aline came the now familiar wave of regret over leaving Felix and Katarine in the castle. I had no clue what the latest was down in Forcadel. Felix could've been...

I exhaled shakily. No use in thinking that way until I knew for sure.

"You couldn't have picked a better person than Aline," Jorad said, breaking the silence. "I've known her since we arrived at the castle for training as children. She's probably the most capable, brilliant, feisty soldier I've ever met. A hair too rebellious for my tastes, but she was always looking to prove herself."

"Do you know what Beswick had her family doing?" I asked.

"Aline never said, but I don't think it was anything criminal." He shook his head. "Perhaps just criminal adjacent. She always felt guilty that they'd given up everything for her, and never seemed to get ahead with him."

"Beswick's victims never do," I said. "At least she can get a little revenge."

"If I know Aline," he said with a grin, "she's enjoying the hell out of it."

The city of Galdon was on the Ash river, which connected Niemen to Forcadel. As we crested another hill, the Niemenian mountains became visible to the north. We were getting close.

"This seems awfully convoluted," Jorad said. "The Niemenians took the ond out of the mountain, but instead of bringing it down the river through Skorsa to Galdon, they brought it via the underground road, over the border with Kulka, then through the forest, and now back to the river? Doesn't that seem odd to you?"

"Not particularly," Luard said. "See, it may be a longer path, but it's the one of least resistance. Once they're out of the mountain, they just have the Kulkans at the Niemen border to contend with, and they're easily bribable. Plus, they thought they had an easy path through the forest. If they'd gone through Skorsa, they would've had to deal with the influx of Niemenian soldiers."

"The hard part is getting into Forcadel city," I said, looking south. "I'm not sure how Beswick's planning to get it through the docks. Unless he has a ton of gold."

"Doesn't he?" Luard asked. "He seems like a rich fellow."

"Not as rich as he used to be," I said with a devilish smile. "Especially after Aline gets through with him."

We came into Galdon as dusk fell, stabling our mares near the city entrance and continuing on foot. Here, there were no curfews or increased security measures. The guards were the local sort, Forcadelians who knew everyone in the town. Children ran through the streets as dusk fell, none of them worried about what might happen once the darkness arrived.

"What a quaint little place," Luard said with a smile. "I can see why they would've wanted the handoff to occur here. I don't see a Severian amongst them."

A girl came running up to us, a smile on her face—and it took me a moment to realize it was one of the two scouts we'd sent ahead, Mab.

"Hi," Mab said, grinning at us. "Mister Ivan told me I had to come greet you and tell you what we're expecting."

"Excellent," I said with a smile.

"I..." She made a face. "Hang on, I forgot."

"Perfect," Jorad grunted.

"Take a breath," I said, used to the exuberance of the youngers. "See if you can't remember."

Her eyes lit up. "Oh yeah! He told me to tell you that they're in position. They haven't seen any other travelers in town that've asked about the ond. But he said you guys should get into position in the tavern, but that Misses should hide her head."

"Why?" I asked.

"Because." She pointed behind me to a poster of my face, surrounded by candles and flowers. "They know who you are."

"Thanks," I said slowly, walking toward the poster with a mix of curiosity and awe. It was from my coronation, the one where the artist hadn't quite figured out how to draw my nose. The surrounding homages seemed a mix of old and new—candles that had been burned to the bottom had been replaced by newer ones, flowers that had died lay underneath fresh ones.

"You're missed," Luard said, coming up next to me.

I nodded and followed him, pulling the hood of my cloak over my head. It wasn't my vigilante one, but a regular traveling cloak, and I still felt naked. Jorad peeled off to watch the front door of the tavern, and Luard and I continued inside.

Almost immediately, I recognized our team already in place. Hagan and Nils were seated in a back corner. Jax was at the bar, making conversation with the tender. The other two Forcadelian soldiers I'd sent with them were playing cards. No one in the room had a red handkerchief in their pocket, but they probably wouldn't display it until the exact meeting time anyway.

"Shall we?" Luard asked, pressing his hand to the small of my back.

I followed him to an empty table and he went to the bar to get us some drinks. I glanced at the clock on the wall—nearly eight. My pulse quickened and I licked my lips in anticipation. Who might Beswick send? Ignacio, his favorite lieutenant? Someone who'd been caught in his web and unable to escape? Or a new player?

Luard placed the tankard of beer beside me and took a long

swig. "This is disgusting," he said. "What I wouldn't give for a dark Niemenian brew right about now."

"Don't drink too much," I said, glancing at the door as it opened. Ivan and Asdis walked in, keeping their gazes down. They sidled up to the bar and ordered a meal, Ivan glancing behind him as if to look for his contact. He locked eyes with me for a second then looked away.

Beside me, Luard kicked back, taking my untouched beer and starting on it. "You look like you're about to be sick."

"I just hope all of this wasn't for nothing," I said. "Otherwise, we'll be—"

The door opened once more. It didn't even matter that he wiped his brow with a red handkerchief. I would've known it was our target even without the signal.

Without a word, I walked over, pulled him off the barstool, and punched him square in the nose.

Chapter Thirty-Three

Kieran fell backward out of his seat, and Sarala reached for her weapon to protect him. But I was faster, pulling my knife and pressing it against her throat.

"Back. Off." I snarled, baring my teeth at her. She dropped her weapon and took several steps back, falling right into Ivan and Nils' grip.

I turned to the pirate, still stunned and staring up at me from the ground. A red trickle of blood was coming from his nose, and he gingerly tapped it. Finally, he caught up with himself enough to look at who had socked him and his eyebrows went up.

"What the...? Veil?" He sat up. "What in the Mother's name was that for?"

"Take your pick, you son of a bitch," I said. "You sold out Felix. You brought that garbage ond into my country. And now you're here bringing more?"

"I don't understand," Kieran said as Hagan and Jax pulled him to his feet. "What are you doing here? Are you…?" His eyes widened. "Oh."

I pointed my knife at his throat. "You have exactly one minute to start talking about ond and Beswick or else I start cutting off bits." I dropped my knife to his groin. "Starting here."

"Yes, I'm the one who's here to get the ond for Beswick." He cracked a grin tinged with blood from his nose. "But as for your precious Captain Llobrega, I had nothing to do with his arrest. I didn't even tell Beswick who he really was. Cross my heart."

"And what are the promises of a pirate?" I snapped, advancing again. "That ond killed people in the city. Innocent people. And for what? Trying to make a living?"

"I also had no idea what the ond was for," Kieran said.

"It's an explosive Niemenian ore. What the hell else was it going to be used for?"

He worked his jaw, buying himself some time. "I had no idea."

"Bullshit."

"Well, holy Mother, what do you want me to say?" he said, anger flashing on his face. "I did it. I brought the stuff into the city. But I sure as shit didn't use it on your people. That, you're going to have to take up with Beswick."

"Oh, you bet I will," I said. "Where is he?"

"Back in Forcadel," he said.

"How many other shipments are coming?" I asked.

"I don't know."

"Kieran, I swear—"

"I'm telling the truth, promise," he said, holding up his hands. "All I know is that Beswick was having a lot of trouble getting it, which is why he paid me handsomely to do it myself. Apparently, it makes it all the way into the city before disappearing." He tapped his nose gingerly. "To be honest, I thought you might be the one causing all the problems. Supposedly some masked vigilante is pissing him off."

Some of my anger ebbed away. *Way to go, Aline and Elisha.* "No, I delegated that to someone else."

"Look at you, being all queen-like." He grinned, then wilted under my murderous stare. "I'll tell you everything I know about who brought it here and who I was supposed to meet. Just please… lower your weapons. And tell your guards to do the same."

I glanced behind me. There were no less than ten swords pointed at Kieran.

"Stand down," I said. "I think it's time we have a little chat, pirate."

Working with Beswick once, I could understand. Kieran dealt with criminals all the time, and he could've brought the ond in without knowing what it was. But now, clearly, he knew what it was and was still complicit. That I couldn't forgive.

I had my soldiers tie him up and let him sit while I considered what I'd do to him. He, like always, seemed completely unbothered by all of this, and was cracking jokes to the Forcadelian soldier with a sword pointed at his neck.

"Brynna?" Luard asked quietly. "Would you like to begin? We probably shouldn't sit here all night."

"Yes, Brynna, Veil, Princess," Kieran sang from his perch in the center of the tavern. "Queen? You look like a queen now."

"Quiet," I snapped at him. Then, in one fluid movement, I stormed from the position at the window and pushed him backward in the chair, pressing my knife to his throat. "Now, talk."

"But you said…" He gulped when I dug the blade in deeper. "Fine. What do you want to know?"

"Everything."

"Be more specific, please."

I growled and let him go. "Start with Beswick and the ond. How long has he known about it?"

"Ages," Kieran said. "I mean, we all have. It's one of those beautiful myths that exist in the criminal circles. You didn't think I got all those Nestori Veil goodies for you through legal channels, did you?"

"How did he get it into the city the first time?" I asked.

"Well, after Ilara invaded, Beswick got it into his head that he wanted to fight fire with fire, so to speak. So he set wheels in motion to get some ond past Niemenian defenses in the mountain. It took him a while to figure it out, but he did."

"How?" Luard asked.

"No idea, Prince," Kieran said. "Assume his usual methods of bullying, bribing, and stealing. Once it was out of the mountain, he had to contend with Queen Ilara's lovely border closings on both sides. Getting anything past Skorsa was impossible, thanks to Mayor Kelsor."

"Wait a minute..." I said slowly.

"Yes, dear Veil, you unwittingly had a part in this," Kieran said with a sheepish grin. "A few months ago, Beswick's man offered me a large sum of money if I'd be willing to pick something up from the northern climes of Niemen. Normally, I would've jumped at the opportunity, but I was completely out of gold to pay my way out of the docks. Then a little princess vigilante showed up and begged me to take her to Niemen."

I worked my jaw, resisting the urge to deck him again. "So you used my gold to get yourself out of the docks?"

"It wasn't just the gold, Veil. Skorsa was impassable unless you had Kelsor's special favor. But you, of course, have a way of getting anywhere you want." He flashed a smile. "And you didn't disappoint."

"So after you dropped me off in Aymar, you continued upriver," I said coolly. "Picked up the ond then came back through Skorsa?"

"And not a moment too soon," he said. "The day after we

passed, Ilara had a new mayor installed. Poor Kelsor was hanging in the square by midday. No more nightly border crossings."

I tried not to think about that. "What about Felix? How does he play into this?"

"Ah, well." He cleared his throat. "See, we brought the ond back to the city, but I wasn't going to give it up without assurances that I could get as far away from Forcadel as I could. Again, I was stuck in the docks, but this time, I needed signed exit papers from Queen Ilara herself. Then your Captain Llobrega showed up during a routine inspection."

"And you forced him to help you?"

"Forced? I wouldn't call it that." He shrugged. "More like... I told him that I'd help him if he'd help me. He was mucking everything up, asking the wrong people the wrong questions and not making any headway. I thought you might want me to do him a favor."

"As long as he did you one in return," I reminded him. "What was the favor?"

"I got him in touch with John from Stank's Bar," Kieran said. "Who was massively unhelpful, by the way."

John, too? "But you still got your exit papers and got out of town, leaving Felix to be arrested."

"Again, I wasn't the one who handed him over to Coyle," Kieran said. "How that happened, I have no idea. I didn't tell John who he was. I merely facilitated a meeting and allowed them to have a chat."

"And now?" Luard asked.

"I told Beswick's man where I was going to be next, just in case he needed me to get another shipment into town. About a week ago, I received a message from him asking him to meet a group in this bar so I might transport the ond into the city again. As luck would have it, I have a legitimate shipment of food that I'm bringing in from the border cities, so it would be easy to hide. But here you are instead..." He flashed me another smile. "Does that answer all your questions?"

I walked to the window, furious at my own unwitting role in the ond attack on my own people. But more furious that I hadn't been told any of this. Kieran had always had his secrets, but I'd started to trust that he was a good person. And it turned out he was just as crooked as the rest of them.

"So what now, Veil? Are you going to rough me up? Send me packing with my tail between my legs?"

"You'll be packing," Luard said. "But you'll be coming with us to Niemen. To stand trial for the illegal conveyance of ond."

"No," I said, narrowing my eyes. "He won't. He's going to continue down to Beswick."

"I'm sorry, what?" Luard straightened. "We had a deal, Brynna. You promised me a body."

"And a body you shall have," I said. "Beswick's the one behind all this. He's the one you should be putting on trial. Kieran's just the transporter. He's got no real stake in this, other than gold. And now," I turned to the pirate, "he's going to pay for what he's done by taking a message to Beswick."

Anyone else might've been terrified at the prospect of going to Beswick empty-handed, but Kieran simply smiled, as if he'd been expecting as much. "And what shall I tell our mutual friend?"

"Tell him that his supply of ond is permanently cut off," I said. "If he wants to negotiate, he can meet me in Celia's camp. I'm willing to listen, but my patience is growing thin."

"Yes, ma'am." Kieran grinned. "Look at you, being all queen-like."

"You don't get to speak to me again," I said. "What you've done is unforgivable. And if I ever see your face again, rest assured that it won't be connected to your body for much longer."

"I don't believe that was the smartest move," Luard said, catching up to me downstairs. "What's to prevent the pirate from wandering off? How do we know he'll even deliver the message?"

"He will," I said.

"How do you know that?"

"Because he wanted me to know he tried to help Felix," I said. "He knows he's on my bad side, and I think he'll do what he can to change my mind. He's still angling for pirate king."

"Pirate..." Luard shook his head. "This is an awfully big gamble. We're not sending anyone with him to ensure the information gets where we want it."

"It doesn't really matter," I said, casting a long look behind me. "Beswick doesn't have unlimited funds—not anymore. Aline and Elisha have been cutting off his supply down in Forcadel, and now we're cutting it off in Niemen. Even if Kieran doesn't make contact, Beswick will come to us eventually." I smiled at him. "Trust me on this. I know how he operates."

Luard made a noise. "That could take months."

"It won't. Beswick's clearly wanting to make a move, or else he wouldn't have asked Kieran. He's not cheap, so Beswick must be getting desperate. I'd wager we'll have news in the next two weeks."

He put his hands on his hips, staring up at the house with contempt and conflict on his face.

"Luard," I said softly. "Do you trust me?"

He turned, surprise on his face. "Of course I do."

"Then trust me when I say that if you let this small fish go, we'll get the big fish," I said. "And when he comes, we'll be ready."

Chapter Thirty-Four

Katarine

"He's my best friend. I would carry him to the ends of the earth."

Strong words, but after walking an hour, my arms were aching and my feet had developed blisters in my fine slippers. But I pressed forward. Felix had sacrificed so much for this country; it was time I offered my own.

We came to a small town north of the city, and I left the cart hidden behind a building. With the pace I was going, I wouldn't make it very far before dawn. And carrying a man on what was very clearly a wagon for the dead would surely draw attention.

I walked through the silent town until I reached the stables near the inn. There, I found a beautiful brown stallion who seemed friendly when I patted his nose. On principle, I didn't condone stealing, but for Felix, I would've stolen the crown off Maurice's head. So I picked the lock on the stable door—another Luard skill —and tacked the horse as best I could. With the reins in one hand and the rope in the other, I walked the horse back to the alley. Felix was where I'd left him and he groaned when I pulled him upright and threw his arm around my shoulder.

"Listen to me," I said. "I need you to climb onto this horse. Once you're there, you can relax."

He mumbled his approval and lifted his leg. I placed it in the stirrup then pushed him on top of the horse. My feet slipped on the ground, but I managed to get him up without falling flat on my face. I wrapped the rope around his hands, tying him to the saddle, then looped the rest around his midsection. I would have to go slowly, but he stayed put when I tested the horse on a few steps.

"Okay," I whispered. "We'll head to the north."

The horse provided some relief, but as the day wore on, my worry for Felix began to grow. My throat ached with dryness, and I was sure Felix was in more dire straits than me. But it was too risky to stop. So we pressed on.

I followed Aline's directions to the letter, guiding the mare slowly along the road and keeping to myself. Surely by now, Ilara was aware we'd escaped. Every so often, a thundering of hooves would echo from behind, and I'd feel the ghost of a touch on the back of my neck.

As the sun rose higher, I began to second-guess my decision to leave, or at least leave without food or water. Brynna wouldn't have made such a dumb mistake. She had a way of twisting her way out of any situation, or so Felix had said.

"What are you going to say to Brynna when you see her again?" I asked my silent traveling partner.

His head lolled and he snored softly.

I patted his thigh. "I think I'm going to ask Bea to marry me when I see her."

"Good idea."

I smiled, catching his half-open eye. But then he was asleep again.

We paused only briefly to water the horse and ourselves at a creek, as my thirst could be denied no more. I scooped liquid from the creek and brought it to Felix's lips, but he didn't drink much. So I helped him back on the horse and off we went again.

As the sun baked my skin, I allowed myself to daydream about holding Beata again, burying my face in her hair and resting easy in her arms. Knowing she would be at the end of this journey made my steps surer and resolve harder. As did knowing if I didn't get to the camp by nightfall, we would have to sleep in the streets.

Night eventually did fall again, but by the Mother's grace, the moon was bright and the sky clear. If Aline was to be believed, we would find the camp full of soldiers up ahead. But my doubts gnawed at the back of my mind, especially as there were no lights in the distance.

When the sun was a fireball in the east, I spotted the signs Aline had told me to look for. But as we drew closer, dread turned my stomach. There had clearly been a camp here, but it had since moved on. Remnants of fire pits dotted a wide-open field. No sign of the soldiers, no hints on where they'd gone.

The past few hours of hard travel caught up to me, and my head spun as I braced myself against the horse. There was a large shady tree nearby, so I walked the horse over to it and guided Felix off. He groaned at the movement, especially as I helped him to sit against the tree.

"Are we there yet?" he grunted, cracking open one brown eye.

"Not yet," I said, brushing my fingers along his forehead. I didn't have the heart to tell him the truth. "Just resting for the moment."

"I could use something to eat," he murmured.

"I know." My stomach was in knots, but also empty and gnawing. We had passed a small village to the south, perhaps I could find food and directions there.

I reached under my petticoat to retrieve my bag of gold coins and the small knife. "Here," I said, placing the knife by his fingertips. "Just in case."

"Be careful," he said. "And don't let anyone see your coins."

>————→

Walking by myself was a little unnerving. The soldiers and local guards all appeared Forcadelian, but I couldn't be too sure. My light skin and hair gave me away as a Niemenian, even as the sun reddened my arms and hands. Everyone outside was sure to give me a second glance as I passed.

In and out. Speed was the name of the game. If I only stayed a moment, perhaps the villagers would forget I'd ever been there.

The village didn't have a town square, so I chose a tavern. Inside, the darkness was cool on my burning skin, and my eyes took a moment to adjust to it.

"Howdy!" a booming voice called from the other side of the room.

I rubbed my eyes until they no longer saw spots then nodded to a heavy-set woman standing behind the bar. She wore a warm smile as she rubbed down the dark wooden countertop, but I reminded myself of my mission. Quick, quiet, and they would forget all about me.

"May I purchase some bread from you?" I asked, palming the gold coin in my hand. Perhaps I should've added some silvers—was it too obvious that I was rich? Was I now a target for thieves?

"You can sit your little pale butt down and eat, yes," she said, placing a large tankard of water and a plate full of bread and cheese in front of me.

I forgot all my royal upbringing and inhaled both in a few moments. Regret was instantaneous. My stomach was sated, but my best friend was still hungry and thirsty under a tree. I wished I hadn't eaten everything in front of me.

"Thank you," I said, pressing the gold onto the counter. "May I have some to take with me? And something to carry water?"

She nodded and set to assembling the items in a cheesecloth.

"You look pretty far from home."

I picked at the bar, hoping to avoid giving up more about myself. "I am."

"No horse?"

I hesitated, not used to spilling my secrets to new faces. If Ilara's forces were to come into town, she could very clearly tell them that I had been there, and where I'd gone afterward.

"It's all right," she said, resting her hand on my sunburnt arm. "You're among friends here in Forcadel."

"I'm sorry, but I don't know if that's true," I said. "I think I'll just take the food and be on my way."

But the woman was undeterred. "Maybe I can help point you in the right direction. If you're looking to head to Niemen, it's a ways away."

I exhaled, releasing my fear. "I'm not going to Niemen. I'm looking for..." I shook my head. "The camp that was here. Do you know where they went?"

"Can't say that I do," she said. "They were darling, you know? A group of young people who decided they'd rather serve the people of Forcadel than that damned desert-dwelling queen. They came from Neveri, saying the Kulkans had invaded and taken over. If you ask me, Neveri's in better hands."

I nodded, if only to keep her talking. "How many were among them?"

"Fifty, perhaps?" She shrugged. "They'd come into town and barter work for food, but we have fertile lands in these parts, so we just gave them what they needed."

I swallowed. "Was there...a woman named Beata amongst them?"

"Beata?" She beamed. "What a darling she is! Took care of all of those soldiers like they were her own, although bless her, she was barely twenty-five. Do you know her?"

I couldn't hold back tears any longer. Beata had made it to

Brynna's forces. She was safe and happy. I covered my face as I sobbed, earning me a comforting pat on the back from the bartender.

"Now I know who you are," she said softly. "Beata's love, the woman she left behind. She said you were a tall, statuesque Niemenian with eyes as blue as the sky."

I nodded, unsure how much Beata had shared about who I was or why I'd left. "I need to find her. Please, if there's anything you can do to help."

"First, though, you need rest," she said. "I'll see about finding you a room tonight—"

"No," I said, wiping my face. "No, I must get going. I have to find them. I have..." I trusted her, but not enough to speak of Felix. "I just need to keep moving. I won't be safe until I find them."

"Then I'd say go north," she said. "But steer clear of the thieves' forest. That Celia won't take kindly to you walking her pathways."

I paused, looking up at her. "Celia?"

"Notorious around these parts. She steals children and holds them until their parents can pay some sum of money."

"No, I know," I said. "But she's nearby?"

"I wouldn't say near. Another day's ride along this road. But you'd be wise to steer clear, as I said—"

No, I wouldn't. Something in my gut told me Brynna had moved her troops there—whether for more protection, more supplies, or some other purpose. From what I knew of the camp, it would be the perfect fortress to gather troops and hide from Ilara.

I got to my feet. "Thank you for all your hospitality. When I see Beata, I'll tell her you showed me kindness."

"Please tell her Tamra says hello," she said, squeezing my hand. "And allow me to send you away with a bag of food to take to her. Mother knows those soldiers can go through an entire farm in a day."

"I shall," I said, taking her hand. "Thank you."

I hurried back to Felix, the sack around my shoulder heavy with bread, fruits, and vegetables. My compatriot hadn't moved since I left him, though he did open an eye when I walked up to him. I used my knife to cut up pieces of an apple, feeding them to him slowly.

"Eat up," I said, feeding him another small slice. "We should be seeing our girls soon."

Or perhaps we'd be walking to our deaths. But if my trust in the Mother was firm, She would lead us where we needed to go.

Chapter Thirty-Five

I sent the rest of the soldiers back to Celia's camp, but I personally wanted to watch Kieran's ship disappear downriver, so Luard, Ivan, and I stayed behind in Galdon until the next morning. Ivan was similarly confused that I'd let Kieran go, but with one word from Luard, he quieted. It meant a lot that they trusted me so much, and I hoped I could repay that when Beswick showed up.

"And what do you plan to do when he does?" Luard asked. "From what I hear, the last time you went up against him, you were wanting."

"I learned," I said. "The reasons I failed before were threefold. First," I held up my finger, "I didn't see the whole picture. Beswick was covered by a layer of royal protection. My father gave him his blessing to continue duping the Severians so Forcadel could get cheap glass. But now, Beswick's operating under his own umbrella. No one's giving him protection anymore."

"Fair enough," Luard said. "And the other two reasons?"

"Second, I got cocky and impatient," I said. "I thought I was in a position to do something about him, and when I couldn't, I acted on impulse. And finally, I acted alone. I didn't ask for help or use my resources." I smiled at him. "And now, I have an army and a bevy of strategic thinkers to help me."

"Good to hear," Ivan said from behind. "Still not a plan."

"I'm getting to it," I said with an impatient wave of my hand. "The fact is, Beswick's going to be bringing his best. So we need to have our best, too. It's like you said the other day—I have an army of vigilantes. And I'm going to use them."

"You can't possibly be thinking about taking those kids to fight a criminal overlord," Ivan said with a stricken look.

"Oh, no." I shook my head firmly. "But I have a hundred soldiers who can be trained. I asked Locke to start teaching them a few things before I left. Once we get back, I'll put them through what I learned in Celia's camp. And when Beswick shows up, we'll be ready for anything."

"Hm." Luard wore a sly smile.

"What?" I shifted in the saddle. "Questions? Problems?"

"Just amused at the change in personality," Luard said. "The other day, you were hemming and hawing over the thought of telling your soldiers what to do. Now, you're changing their entire training regimen."

"Well..." My cheeks warmed. "I know what I'm doing with Beswick."

He wiggled his eyebrows. "You've got the makings of a great queen. Quit overthinking it."

A whistle broke my reverie. When I looked up, my young scouts waved. They whistled the code, *Welcome back*, but attached to it was a combination I hadn't heard before.

"What's that word?" I asked, looking up at the nearest tree. There I found both a teen and a soldier, working in tandem.

"Your Majesty," the soldier called back, bowing his head.

Jorad, who'd ridden ahead earlier in the day, was waiting for me at the camp's entrance. He bowed with a flourish. "Your Majesty, great news," he said. "Another twenty soldiers have arrived to bolster your numbers."

"Really?" I dismounted and handed the reins to a nearby soldier. "From where?"

"From the west. They heard that there was a group of Forcadelians in Celia's camp and came to pledge their support."

My brows lifted and worry fluttered in my chest. We were already stretched thin in terms of sleeping arrangements and food. Could I handle another twenty?

Luard cleared his throat. "Maybe you'd like to greet them and thank them for coming to your aid?"

"Oh." I shared a look with him. "Yeah. That sounds good."

Jorad bowed again. "I'll see to it right away."

Luard smiled warmly as he threw his arm around my shoulders. "Practice makes perfect, little princess. Let's meet your new troops."

Jorad assembled the soldiers in about ten minutes—a feat considering how spread out the camp was. They wore crisp Forcadelian uniforms with shiny crests that glinted as they stood at attention.

"You are all welcome here," I said with a firm smile. "Thank you for coming to our aid. Please find yourselves a place to sleep in the sleeping hut. Lieutenant Llobrega will see to your assignments in the camp." I paused then added, "Dismissed."

They saluted me in unison, then dispersed amongst the camp. Two or three of them hung around, whispering about how they owed each other gold. One pair came up to me, blushing.

"Pardon, Your Majesty," the one on the right said. "Were you really The Veil?"

"Yeah," I said.

"See?" His friend slapped him on the arm. "Now you owe me *two* coins!"

I kept a laugh to myself as they walked away arguing about whether they really wagered and how payment was going to be completed. Beside me, Jorad shook his head, but even he couldn't be bothered by their informality.

There was certainly a different energy than when we'd left a few short days before. Soldiers trained with thieves, grinning even as they were unceremoniously beaten by their younger counterparts. Near the weapons hut, a group of thieves were happily making arrows as quickly as their nimble hands could make them. Nearby, a group of soldiers had started the forge and were banging red-hot pieces of iron into swords. Another group—this one mixed soldiers and thieves—were busy sewing black fabric.

"You can thank Locke for all this," Jorad said. "He's the one doling out assignments."

"I certainly will," I said. "How goes the vigilante training?"

"He thought it prudent to wait until you returned," Jorad said. "Something about how the soldiers might listen better if the direction came from you. You are, after all, the vigilante."

I opened my mouth to argue, but thought better of it. "Then give the order that anyone interested in learning how to be The Veil should stick around after dinner in the mess hall."

We passed by Nicolasa's hut, where a group of six young children were seated cross-legged as the elder Nestori showed them the parts of the lavender plant. Beata sat nearby, taking notes in a leather-bound book with her tongue stuck between her teeth. I cleared my throat to get her attention, and she quickly jumped to her feet.

"Children, we have a guest," she said, interrupting Nicolasa. "What did we practice when the queen shows up?"

The children scrambled to stand up, some of them dusting themselves off quickly. Then, together, they bowed at the hip.

"Your Majesty," they chanted.

"Well done," Beata said with a beaming smile.

I was glad she seemed less angry with me. "You've certainly done a lot in a short amount of time. Are the children enjoying their studies?"

"More so than marching around camp," she said under her breath. I had to give it to her—she was stubborn. Maybe that was why Katarine liked her so much.

"We have worked out a schedule, per your request," Jorad said. "Lady Beata can teach the children in the mornings, and I get them for a few hours of training in the afternoons. I also have five soldiers rotating in the kitchens to give her time to do other things."

"And my thanks for that," she said to me. "I find my time is taken up by these littles more than I anticipated."

The children, now scrubbed and wearing clean clothes, certainly looked more like innocent angels than they had previously. "What's today's lesson?"

"Well, Jorad said you were teaching the soldiers how to be vigilantes," Beata said. "So I thought the children could learn how to make those little bags you're always throwing at people." She smiled coyly. "Locke said everyone needed to be useful."

My face warmed as she gazed at the hut at the back of the camp, the chimney smoke taunting me. But I wasn't in the mood to be goaded today. Before I did anything else, there was a fence that needed mending.

"Bea, can we take a walk?" I asked.

"I wanted to—"

"I'm sorry," Beata said, wiping her hands on her apron as soon as we were outside the forest gates. "I shouldn't have lost my temper and shouldn't have put you in that position to have to punish me."

"No," I said, shaking my head. "I should've been a better leader, and you shouldn't have felt the need to argue with Jorad like that."

"You should've seen my fights with Felix," she said dryly. "I suppose we both could've been better. I'm not sleeping lately and my temper isn't as controlled as it used to be."

"Bea," I said, laying my hand on her arm. "You don't have to kill yourself to keep us all fed. We can get others to help."

"I wouldn't be sleeping either way," she said, wiping her eyes. "I'm so worried about Kat and Felix. We haven't heard from them in weeks. They were hurting him in the dungeons, Brynna. How much of that is a man supposed to endure before he..."

"I know," I said, swallowing the lump in my throat. "Trust me, I know."

"I didn't mean to talk with you about this," she said with a watery smile. "You have enough on your plate without taking on my worries as well."

"After what you've done for us here, I always have room on my plate to listen to you." I took her hands. "Tell me everything."

It was a waterfall of fears, worries, anxieties, and even some details of their love life I wasn't sure Katarine would've appreciated Beata sharing. But there, beside the small creek in the forest, Beata poured her heart out to me, half-crying, half-laughing, and making my heart hurt for what she'd given up and for what she'd been holding back.

"I hadn't realized you two were so...serious," I said. "Or that you'd been together for so long."

"I always knew," Beata said with a warm smile on her face. "From the moment I laid eyes on her, she was the one. And your brother, oh, what a scoundrel!" Her entire face lit up. "I think he delighted in getting the two of us in compromising positions. I don't think I've ever cried harder than the day he died." She paused, pressing her hand to her chest. "I pray I never have to cry that hard again."

I took her hand. "They'll be here. One way or another, Felix is too stubborn to die, and Katarine's too…Katarine to let herself get captured."

"She is that," Beata said, wiping her eyes. "What do you think you'll say to Felix when you see him again?"

"Oh, I don't know. Perhaps yell at him for getting himself captured?" My cheeks warmed. "It's been…months since I've seen him. I don't think I'd even know where to begin."

She nudged me. "You won't confess that you love him?"

The lump in my throat reappeared and I swallowed hard to dismiss it. In truth, I hadn't thought much about it because I wasn't convinced our reunion would ever occur. My deepest fears I kept locked away, buried under a mountain of more pressing worries.

Beata graciously gave me an out. "Mother above, I've kept you so long. You've got to return to camp to lead things." She beamed. "Unless you feel like hiding in the kitchen and peeling potatoes."

I smiled weakly. "I think I can safely delegate that to someone else for a change. I just hope there's enough interest in this vigilante army."

"Getting to run around in a mask?" She shook her head. "I'd be surprised if the whole camp didn't sign up."

Chapter Thirty-Six

In fact, thirty soldiers remained in the mess hall after dinner. Some were ones I'd gone toe-to-toe with, like Malka and Enos. Others I'd seen around the camp. All of them eager to learn.

"It's going to be a lot," Locke said, scratching his nose with the tip of his knife. "I'm not sure I want to train fifteen at once. They may end up killing each other."

"Let's hope they don't," I said, rising to my feet.

I welcomed everyone and gave them a brief summation of what we were up against and why a vigilante army was the best solution to dealing with Beswick. I told them about Kieran and sending the message down to Forcadel, as well as how we had the only bag of ond outside the Niemenian mountain with us in camp. I felt Luard's gaze on me, and knew he was thinking of our agreement.

"My gut tells me Beswick will bring everything he has to reclaim the ond," I said. "Therefore, we need to be ready to meet him on his level. He won't be fighting graciously or honorably. His goal is to win at all costs. So we have to play the same game."

"With all due respect, Your Majesty," a lanky kid stood. "We've been training our whole life."

"And with all due respect, didn't I watch your ass get dropped by a twelve-year-old earlier today?" Jax strode into the room wearing a black tunic and holding a crossbow on his shoulder. "I wouldn't be speaking if I were you."

"Are you here to offer your services?" I asked.

"Do you really think you can do this without me?" he asked, his voice echoing across the room. "Who taught you everything you know?"

I quirked a brow at him. "Callum."

"And who do you think taught him?"

Celia. But I wasn't going to go there with him. With three trainers, we'd have ten soldiers each to take out into the forest. "Divide yourselves into groups," I told the soldiers. "And I pity whoever gets stuck with Jax. You're going to get very familiar with Nicolasa and her healing potions."

Unsurprisingly, I had to shoo away a few soldiers who wanted to go with me. The group that followed me out into the forest was comprised of a mix of familiar faces and new ones—including a couple who'd shown up not a few hours before. They'd left their swords in the camp in favor of crossbows and quivers, carrying them clumsily. And they certainly had a lot of complaints.

"I can't see."

"Where are we going?"

"I just dropped my arrows."

It was going to be a long night.

"We're going to the northern road from Kulka," I said. "Far enough from Jax and Locke that they won't interrupt us."

"And what, exactly, are we doing?" This was from Narin, an

eighteen-year-old from the capital. From the looks of him, he seemed more the type to have been volun-told into service, instead of being here of his own free will.

"It's creepy out here, Your Majesty." Orman also came from the capital, but looked a little less like he was of noble blood. "Are you sure we're safe?"

"We're trained soldiers," Narin shot at him. "Which is why it's insane that we're out here learning how to fight. We know how to —"

I reached behind for my crossbow and shot an arrow at him. It landed just above his shoulder.

"What the—? You shot me!"

"Are you bleeding?" I asked, turning around and lifting my crossbow.

"I…" He rubbed his shoulder. "A little."

"That's why we're out here," I said. "I want you to be able to fire off a shot like that. In the dark. Without looking. Purely based on the sound of his voice."

"That's impossible."

"She just did it."

"This is how Celia trained us," I said. "You can train all you want in the ring. Learn how to use weapons, perfect your aim. But all of that is controlled. In the thick of a fight, you have to trust your instincts. Move without thinking. The best way to do that is to put yourselves in as much danger as you can survive."

"Did anyone ever die?"

"No, but we surely got bloody," I said. "Everyone pick a tree. We're starting with target practice."

By the time the sky turned pink, my vigilantes-in-training were hitting trees instead of bushes. Even Narin, with a bloody shoulder, fought through the pain and found his targets. But more than their aim, they had improved in their confidence. They were no longer afraid to move in the dark, nor were they shy about their crossbows. It wasn't perfect, but it was certainly a good start.

"You all did exemplary work tonight," I said, leading the soldiers back to the front of camp as the gray sky grew lighter. "Tomorrow, we'll start working on target practice while up in the trees. Balance, of course, makes all this harder. So everyone get some breakfast and rest." I paused. "Dismissed."

They saluted then marched through the front gates, their prior stoicism gone in favor of excited discussions. A few moments later, the other two groups of bleary-eyed soldiers appeared from the darkness, followed by their trainers.

"How'd it go?" I asked Locke.

"They're a little too smooth," he said. "Need to rough them up."

"You said it," Jax barked, wiping a little blood off his ear. "Never seen people so respectful of trees before."

"I'm sure you'll break them of their delicate natures soon enough," I said, crossing my arms over my chest. "You certainly have a way with people."

He made an offensive gesture and walked toward the mess hall.

"Don't let him fool you. He likes it," Locke said, flashing me a toothy grin.

"Do you think they'll be ready for Beswick?" I asked. "Honestly."

"I think they'll do their best, ready or not," Locke said. "They all want to impress you. And I think they're excited to run around in a cloak and mask. They kept talking about the things you did while you were The Veil. I can't believe you took on ten guards at once."

"Five," I said with a look. "But good that they've got aspirations. This crazy idea might just work yet. Between the vigilantes and the soldiers, we'll have plenty of backup when

Beswick finally reappears."

"If we can be half the warrior that you are, he doesn't stand a chance." He pressed his fist to his chest and bowed. "Have a good night, Your Majesty."

"Impressive," I said with a small laugh.

"We're supposed to be your royal guards, ain't we? Gotta look the part." With that, he bowed once more and left.

"If I didn't know any better, I'd say he has a crush on you." Luard cracked a loud yawn as he appeared in the doorway of the sleeping hut nearby.

"What are you doing up so early? It's not even dawn yet." My gaze narrowed. "Are you sleeping with my soldiers, Luard?"

"Brynna, I'm wounded," he said, though his hurt was masked by another loud yawn. "Asdis has been keeping me on a tight leash."

"Oh? Has something happened between you?" I asked. "Finally consummated your long-running flirtations?"

"If only, if only," he replied with a sly grin. "No, my dearest guard tells me I should keep my irresistible charms to myself, so as to not distract your soldiers. As a personal favor to our budding queen."

"Well, I appreciate that," I said. "Why are you up so early, then?"

"Hard to sleep with all this fresh air." He inhaled deeply and made a face. "But while you've played vigilante all night, a message came from Neveri."

I took the paper from him and opened it. Inside was a short message—the envoys had returned, but nothing other than that. Ammon was fast becoming the thorn in my side I needed to deal with first.

"I think it's time to send some real spies into Neveri," I said. "Maybe I'll pay him a visit. Things seem to be functioning well enough here."

"Maybe you and some of these new recruits could go," Luard said. "They seem eager enough."

"They can barely hit trees. I'm not sure I'm ready to plunge them into true vigilantism."

"We learn best by doing," Luard said, putting his arm around me as he walked me into the camp.

"It's a possibility." I chewed on my lip. "But I—"

A whistle broke the night. Someone was riding on a horse through the forest—no, two people.

"What is it?" Luard asked.

"Someone's coming," I said, quieting him to listen for the next sound.

A Niemenian woman and a Forcadelian man.

My heart stopped in my chest. Without another word, I spun on my heel and took off toward the southern entrance of the camp.

Chapter Thirty-Seven

I almost didn't believe my eyes.

Katarine, wearing a dark tunic, her blonde hair falling out of a braid and her face smudged with dirt and sweat, led a horse through the forest. Riding the horse was Felix, bruised, bloody, dirty, and unconscious. She'd tied him to the saddle so he wouldn't fall, and his head lolled uncontrollably. But he was alive.

They were here. They were safe.

I took a hesitant step forward, a sob releasing from my lips.

Katarine looked up and she stopped, even as the horse continued forward.

"Brynna?"

I sprinted toward her, tears bursting from my eyes, and when we connected in a tight embrace. She sobbed, I sobbed, and before long, we were two red-faced, wet-cheeked messes.

"I'm s-sorry, I look t-terrible," she said, running a hand over her yellow hair.

"You're such a sight for sore eyes," I said with a laugh.

"You said it." Luard had joined us, his blue eyes shining with unshed tears.

Katarine pushed me away and ran toward her brother. He held her close, the relief and love shining on his face.

I turned to Felix, and my heart stopped in my chest. Scabs and fresh wounds lined his pale face and his tunic was ripped and bloody. What had those monsters done to him?

"He's very sick," Katarine said, wiping her cheeks. "I didn't know if you had—"

"We'll take him to Nicolasa," I said, untying his hands. He rolled onto me, his weight buckling my knees, so we fell to the ground together. I cupped his sallow cheeks and brushed the dark hair from his forehead. "You're safe now."

"You both are," Luard said.

Two soldiers came running from the camp, this time carrying a makeshift gurney. They rested Felix on it and carted him back into camp. I stood, watching him leave, torn between going with him and staying with Katarine.

"Go," she said. "I'm fine. Just in need of a stiff drink."

"I'll be back as soon as I can," I said. "Luard—"

"I will." He gathered her into his arms. "Go to your captain."

I flashed her one more smile then ran back into the camp. By now, the soldiers had all been roused by the breakfast bell, and most of them had seen Felix carried inside. They'd gathered around Nicolasa's hut and turned their furious questioning on me.

"How is he?"

"Is he all right?"

"He's not going to die, is he?"

"I don't know," I said, pushing past them.

"Your Majesty," Jorad said, his expression boyish and fearful. "That's our captain. Please, tell us what's going on."

I stopped, my mouth open as I remembered what Felix meant

to them—and my newfound role as their leader. For the moment, I pushed aside my own fears and relief and turned to the gathering crowd.

"Captain Llobrega is back with us," I began. "As is Lady Katarine. I don't know how they arrived, or by what miracle they escaped Forcadel, but the important thing is that they're here and safe."

"He looked like he was on the brink of death," Malka said, her eyes brimming with tears.

I smiled. "Nicolasa brought me back from the Mother herself a few months ago. I have faith that he's in the best hands possible."

"Can we see him?" Jorad asked.

"In time," I said. "But first, I need to assist her. I promise, as soon as I know more, I'll share it with all of you. For now, let's just be thankful they're alive and here with us. Go about your daily tasks. Dismissed."

With my final word, they disbanded quickly, although they didn't go far. They still wore their fear on their faces, none more than Jorad. He hovered in front of Nicolasa's hut, pacing the length of the small building, chewing on his nails.

"Jorad," I said, stopping him. "This isn't going to help him. Go do as I said. I've got to rest for the next training session tomorrow night so I need you to run the camp for me. Can you do that?"

He nodded, but didn't wipe the concern from his face. He wasn't afraid for his captain, but for his cousin. Their similarities had never seemed so great until that moment.

"Jorad," I took his hands, "he's going to be fine. Nicolasa will work her magic and he'll be back to ordering us all around in no time. But right now, you need to pull it together and keep a brave face for the camp. Everyone is worried for him, so I need you to be strong so they'll be strong."

He met my gaze. "Yes, Your Majesty."

⇒————→

I pushed open the flap to the hut and exhaled softly. The Nestori had already stripped Felix down and was cleaning his many, *many* wounds. My gaze landed on the large purple bruise marring his ribcage, as well as the festering cuts on his arms and back. His skin was sallow, and he'd lost considerable weight.

"Is he..." I asked quietly.

"He'll be fine, but it will be a while before he's fully recovered," she said. "They surely didn't spare the rod with him."

I balled my fists. If Jax hadn't pulled me out of the castle, if he hadn't changed my mind, perhaps Felix could've been spared some of these injuries.

"If I may," Nicolasa said, "instead of stewing, you could help tend to him. Four hands are better than two."

We carefully cleaned every one of his wounds, applying a special ointment that made him hiss. Once he was bandaged, Nicolasa gave him a large helping of liver oil and a few other potions to expedite his healing.

"I'm going to stay with him," I said to her, settling at his side.

"He may sleep for a while," she said. "And there's nothing you can do but let the Mother's healing happen."

"I know, but..." I took his bandaged hand in mine. "I don't think I can go back out there until I see his eyes."

She rested a hand on my shoulder and squeezed, then left me be.

This wasn't the reunion I'd hoped for, but at least they were here. For so long, I'd nursed the fear of the worst possible outcome, a simmering foreboding that one day, a messenger would arrive saying Felix had died in the dungeons and Katarine had been executed for treason.

Tears welled in my eyes again, and for once, I let them fall. I held Felix's hand, running the pads of my fingers along the calluses on his palms. His soft breathing was growing stronger and deeper now that he'd had a dose of Nicolasa's medicine. Some of his color had even returned. The anxiety I'd held onto for so long dissipated, and I rested my head on the bed. Before I knew it, I'd fallen asleep.

Chapter Thirty-Eight

Katarine

If not for Luard's tight embrace squeezing the life out of me, I would've thought this was a dream.

Since leaving the village, I'd been sick with dread, praying to the Mother that I wouldn't find unfriendly faces in Celia's forest. I almost turned around when the whistles started, but something kept me moving forward. We would see this through to the end.

Instead of arrows and swords, there was Brynna, standing in the center of the forest, her chest heaving up and down as she drank me in. I'd never seen her cry—not like that, anyway. And as if I couldn't have been more elated, I looked up to see my own brother's smile.

I didn't even care that I was a mess, or that my clothes smelled, or that my face was probably covered in dirt. All that mattered was Luard's firm grip around me, and the way he stifled his tears.

"I missed you so much," he whispered. "Thank the Mother you're safe." He backed up and took in my face. "How did you get here? And with Felix, no less!"

"It's been a long few days," I said. My brain caught up with me. "Beata! Is she here?"

"She is," Luard said. "And she'll be ecstatic to see you."

He walked me into the camp, which was about as rustic and bare as expected. But inside, I found a sea of happy faces, all Forcadelian, except for the four Niemenians who rushed up to me.

"Lady Kat!" Asdis cheered, kissing my cheeks before I could stop her. Behind her, Ivan's eyes twinkled with unshed tears, and Hagan and Nils stood arm-in-arm, sporting matching gold bands on their fingers.

"When did you two get married?" I asked.

"Oh, so much to catch you up on," Luard said.

"I missed you," I replied, unable to stop staring at their familiar faces. "I miss Ariadna and everyone back home. I wanted so badly to return, but..." My words failed me at the relief of seeing them. "I can't believe I'm really here."

"Of course you're here! I am wholly unsurprised you carried your half-dead friend across the country on your own two feet." He gave me a long look. "Mother above, Kitty Kat. I missed you."

I shared a smile with him. "You seem to have kept yourselves busy."

"You wouldn't believe what your little vigilante princess has been having us do lately. Climbing gates and bringing them down."

I stopped, mid-stride. "So it's true, then. You brought the ond into Forcadel."

"Well, if you want to play semantics," Luard said. "I brought it into Neveri. With Ariadna's blessing. A man named Johann Beswick is responsible for the rest of it. We're devising a trap to lure him to us, then we will take him back to Niemen."

"Good luck," I said. "Brynna's been trying to get him for months."

"I know," he said. "But she gave me her word that he's mine."

I might've asked if he trusted it, but clearly he did. Perhaps Brynna had grown into someone more worthy of the title of queen in the months since we'd parted. As I looked around the camp, I recognized Felix's favorite cadets, those that had been assigned to Neveri.

My gaze landed on a small group of children in the corner and...my Bea. She was seated cross-legged in the front of them, holding up a book and walking them through the words. There was a quiet joy on her face, one that said she was not only surviving in this camp, but had found her place. We'd often discussed of our dreams of becoming mothers, and seeing her with the children warmed my heart in ways I couldn't have imagined.

She glanced in my direction then back at the children. Then, she turned slowly to meet my gaze again. The book slipped from her lap as she came to her feet.

"Is it the queen?" one of the children asked.

Beside me, Luard pressed his hand to his lips as Beata slowly walked toward me. My heart pounded as more tears came to my eyes.

"You look..." she began softly.

"I'm sorry I've been traveling," I said, brushing a hand over my hair.

"Beautiful," was all she said before falling into my arms.

My knees buckled as I found her lips, soft, beautiful lips that tasted of home and berries. I pressed my forehead to hers, impressing this moment into my mind, sending prayer after prayer of gratitude to the Mother for allowing me to hold her once again.

"You're really here," she whispered.

"I'm here," I said. "And so is Felix. We made it."

"How?" Her large eyes, wet with tears, bored into mine. "How did you manage it?"

"I..." My words died in my throat. At the time, using Garwood to make our escape had been fitting, but now it just seemed grotesque. He wouldn't be returned to his husband like I had been to Beata.

"Forget I asked," she said with a shake of her head. "We'll get you a bath and a meal. Children," she turned to the children behind her, who were wearing looks of amusement, "we'll continue this lesson tomorrow."

"Oh, I can finish the lesson," Luard said, plucking the book from the ground. "You two go catch up. We'll be just fine here."

Beata took me through the camp, pointing out the houses that were used for different things as we headed toward what she termed the bath house. Clearly, she was proud of all she'd accomplished, but I couldn't help feeling she was shouldering everything in the camp herself.

"It's fine," she said with a wave of her hand. "I wasn't sleeping much. Too many worries on my mind to rest." She kissed my hands. "And these soldiers need me. When I arrived, they were wearing the same clothes day in and day out. Grotesque didn't even begin to describe the smell."

"And I'm sure you told them so." I beamed. "There was a woman in the village I stopped in—Tamra. She said you had them at your beck and call."

Beata's eyes lit up. "You met Tamra? I hope she gave you and Felix a good meal."

"Felix was too ill," I said. "And I was too afraid to bring him into the village. If Ilara had sent riders…"

"She doesn't know where you are, does she?" Beata asked, worry marring her features.

I brushed it away with my thumb to her cheek. "No, I don't think so. No one followed us. But surely the defenses are strong here, anyway."

"They're strong as long as our location remains secret." She shivered. "Besides the Forcadelian soldiers, all we have here are children."

"Thieves," I said. "The ones Celia takes from their parents, correct? I would've thought Brynna would let them go."

"She offered freedom to everyone," Beata said. "But those who had no home to go to stayed. Most of the camp are orphans, including the littles I was teaching. I fought hard to get them an education. Jorad would've had them marching around camp from sunup until sundown." She made a face. "We had a...little disagreement that got out of hand. Unfortunately, the camp was a witness to my disrespecting the queen."

"She probably deserved it."

"She did, but not that way," Beata said with a soft smile. "I did her no favors and let my tongue get the better of me. Jorad let me off easy, though. Only five lashes."

I nearly tripped over my feet. "You were *lashed*?"

"Oh, dear Kat," Beata said, taking my hands. "He could've given me twenty."

My blood boiled. "You shouldn't have received a single one."

Beata smiled and stroked my face. "Please don't blame Brynna for ordering it. It clearly troubled her and my disagreements would've been better resolved away from an audience."

I closed my eyes to her touch, and my anger disappeared. "She has taken good care of you?"

"She's kept me safe and given me a purpose. I'm learning Nestori potion-making as well," Beata said. "And she comforted me when I allowed myself to miss you." She leaned into me. "Every waking second."

I held her tight to me, taking in the feel of her, the scent of her hair. The sound of her voice. Every piece of her was so familiar in this unfamiliar place.

We reached the back of the camp where there was a small hut. Inside was a solitary metal tub already filled with water. I could tell just by looking at it that this would be a cold bath.

"It's quite rustic here, my love," she said, producing a bar of lye from beneath the tub. "Some days we have to make do with a dip in the river or—"

"It's fine," I said, pulling her to me. "I would jump in the frozen ocean if it meant I got to be here with you."

She flushed, allowing me to hold her. "Whatever happened in the castle must've been horrible," she said, running her finger up my arm. "You haven't ever been this... I mean, you kissed me in front of the whole camp."

"Perhaps I'm no longer afraid to show how I really feel," I said, running my hand along her back. "Why don't you stay?"

Her eyes widened. "I don't know if that's proper. People will talk—"

I kissed her to quiet her. "I don't care if it is proper. I've crossed an entire country to see you, and I don't intend to ever let you go."

Chapter Thirty-Nine

Someone was stroking my hair.

Slowly, I lifted my head, which protested from being bent over for so long. Felix's soft brown eyes met my gaze, his chapped lips turned upward in a tired smile.

"Is this a dream?" he murmured.

I cleared my throat. "I could punch you in the jaw again, to be sure."

His smile widened and I couldn't keep my lip from trembling or a sob from hiccuping from my chest.

"Tears?" he asked, weakly wiping my cheek. "I'm honored."

"Don't you dare make fun of me, Felix Llobrega," I said, sniffing. "Not with you looking the way you did. Not with..." I bit my lip, the old guilt blossoming in my chest. "I'm sorry I let this happen to you."

"Don't be," he said. "I was glad to sacrifice myself so Beswick would ally himself with you."

My mouth fell open, and I didn't have the heart to tell him otherwise.

But Felix could still read me. "He...is an ally, isn't he?" he asked, ducking his head to catch my eye.

"A lot's happened since we last spoke in Forcadel," I said, sitting up. "The long and short of it is that things aren't as bad as they were, but they still aren't great." I smiled and ran my finger along his cheek. "But right now, they're infinitely better. You and Kat are safe."

He closed his eyes to my touch until I reached a tender spot, earning a loud hiss.

I retracted my hand. "I'm sorry... I'll have Nicolasa bring you something for the pain."

"Nicolasa..." Felix shook his head, as if some of the fog was clearing from it. "Where am I? And how did I get here?"

"Celia's camp," I said. "And as for the how...all I know is that Kat showed up with you on a horse. I assume I'll get the full story eventually."

He blinked, staring at the ceiling. "I remember Garwood. Perhaps even...Aline?" He shook his head. "It's a blur. I'm sorry."

"After what you did for me, you never have to apologize to me again," I said.

"Is that a promise?" His gaze sparkled with mischief.

Despite myself, my cheeks reddened.

"I never thought I'd see you again," he whispered. "In this life, anyway."

"You aren't allowed to die," I said. "Who's going to follow me around and annoy me?"

His eyes opened wider, capturing me with seriousness. "I would've haunted you."

I snorted then burst into laughter. He joined me, our cackles echoing in the space until they drew Nicolasa's attention.

"You shouldn't be exciting my patient," she said, brushing by me with a bottle in hand. "Here, more liver. Will help you regain your strength."

Felix took his medicine, but not without a grimace. I'd had my share of the stuff when I was recovering, so I could relate. But however disgusting it was, it drew more color onto his cheeks

Once she disappeared, I took his hand in mine, squeezing it. "I have to go."

"No." He rested my hand over his heart. "Stay with me. I'll sleep better with you nearby."

I couldn't say no, so I laid my head back down on the bed, watching Felix sleep quietly until my eyes closed again.

I hadn't meant to sleep the day away, but next to Felix's quiet snores, I didn't shake myself awake again until least mid-afternoon. Nicolasa had apparently even given Felix another few doses of medicine while I slept, which I found to be highly embarrassing. Especially as I'd been drooling.

"Pssh," she said. "I've seen you in worse situations. Now hurry up and give those soldiers some news. I think they're wearing a hole in the ground outside."

I laughed and took the peppermint she gave me to perk up before walking outside. There, as she'd said, there was a gathering of soldiers, all of them waiting for news. I didn't have the heart to chastise them for disobeying my orders to get back to work—even Jorad was amongst them.

"He's resting comfortably," I announced. "I think he'll make a complete recovery, but we need to let him be. Please, return to your positions." I gave them a look. "And now I mean it. Dismissed."

Heartened by the news, they saluted and left. I stood with my hands on my hips, marveling at how comfortable I'd become with ordering my troops around.

"Brynna?"

Katarine had taken the space the soldiers had left. She'd clearly had a bath—her golden hair was wet and hanging by her ears, and she was wearing a clean dress. Her gaze kept darting to the hut behind me, as if she weren't sure whether to step any closer.

"Kat," I said softly, as if giving her permission.

"How is he?" she asked.

"He'll be fine," I said. "Already up and making jokes. All thanks to you, I might add."

"Thanks to the Mother," she said, looking at her hands. "He was so ill, and the journey was... But we did our best. I just hope..."

"Kat." I walked toward her. "You're here. It doesn't matter how you did it." I took her hands in mine. "I'm sure Beata was glad to see you, too."

She smiled, ducking her head. "Enough about that. We have much to discuss."

We walked, arm-in-arm to the mess hall, where Beata delivered a freshly baked blackberry tart and kiss Katarine on the forehead. It didn't escape my notice that Beata's hair was also wet, and she flushed bright red at the sight of Katarine, but I only allowed myself a sneaky smile.

"Thank you, my love," Katarine said, kissing Beata's hand. "Are you sure I can't help you?"

"You'd be more harm than help," she said, but there was nothing but love shining in her eyes. "I've got more than enough in the kitchens now. These soldiers may not know how to salt anything, but they can chop vegetables."

She pressed one final kiss on Katarine's forehead, then bustled back toward the kitchen area. Katarine's gaze never left Beata until she disappeared behind the flap.

"You two seem back in sync," I said, amused.

"And clearly, whatever disagreements you had have been resolved," Katarine said, finally tearing her eyes away from the door.

"Ah." My face grew warm. "I suppose she told you about that."

Katarine looked like she wanted to say something about it, but instead forced a thin smile onto her face. "You've certainly grown into your role, haven't you?"

"Fits and starts," I said. "I've just surrounded myself with smart people."

"You were surrounded by smart people before," she said. "The trick is to listen to them. That's a skill Ilara hasn't quite mastered yet."

"Good for me." I inched closer, eager to hear more. "So… What's happening down in Forcadel? Did the Kulkan envoys arrive? What did Ilara do with them?"

"Yes, they arrived," she said with a heavy shake of her head. "Horrible what Ammon did to you. They were surprisingly unhelpful toward me as well. I suppose old wounds fester."

"But did Ilara agree to work with him?" I asked, a little breathlessly.

"No," Katarine said. "She sent the envoys back to Neveri empty-handed."

I released a loud sigh. "Thank the Mother. Thank the *Mother.*"

"I don't understand," Katarine said.

I shared everything that had happened since I'd left Forcadel with a letter to Ariadna. She knew or had guessed some of it, such as my involvement in Skorsa, and was unsurprised to hear that her sister had given me a secondary task of asking Neshua to help. But when we got to the battle of Neveri, my chest tightened.

"What is it?" Katarine asked.

"Riya, she…" I looked at the ground. "She died when we took the city."

"Maarit said as much," she said softly. "Before she was executed."

The air left my chest. "Ilara executed Maarit? I thought they were close."

"I did, too. But apparently Ilara has little patience for failure." Katarine leaned onto her elbows.

"She sounds unstable," I said. "No wonder the country is going to shit."

"I don't think she's unstable at all." She gazed out the open door thoughtfully. "I confess that I lost my insight into her mind these past few weeks. She was making moves that I didn't understand, and I was no longer privy to her reasoning. But I do believe she knows exactly what she's doing. She was the youngest child and, within four years, managed to clear a path to the throne with seemingly little trouble."

"By killing her own family," I said.

"She doesn't have any regard to the how, that's for sure," Katarine said. "She's been focused on the eastern cities close to Severia, but why I have no idea. I thought, perhaps, that ordering all ships to deliver food and supplies there was just to spite the Forcadelians, but now I wonder if she isn't plotting something else."

"I can't see what else she would want to do," I said. "She already has the crown jewel of trade routes."

"Perhaps," Katarine said. "She isn't infallible, though. She tends to rule by emotion rather than intellect. Perhaps you can use that in some way."

"What do you mean?"

"She has this need for everyone to know she has absolute power. To her, that means keeping people who were once her enemies alive, just to prove a point." She looked to me. "She told me she wanted to bring you back alive."

I blanched. "Are you serious? Why? So she can hang me herself?"

"I haven't been able to figure that one out," Katarine said. "She certainly spared no expense erasing you from the collective memory. Then again, my understanding of her psyche changed nearly every time we spoke."

"I don't envy you," I said with a shake of my head. "So what changed? Why did you suddenly decide to leave?"

"Well, after she executed Maarit, it dawned on me that it would only take one slip to turn her opinion against me. And with odds like that, I couldn't possibly risk Felix's life." She looked at her hands. "And Fishen provided the perfect opportunity. Garwood was dying, so she told me that I could swap their bodies under the ceremonial shroud." She paused, closing her eyes. "I just hope Lord Garwood forgives me."

"I think he'd be honored to have helped you escape," I said. "How did you get out of the city? Surely, you had an escort."

She shivered. "I thought we'd get caught but...one of yours, Aline, came to the rescue."

"Aline?" I perked up. "And Elisha? How are they?"

"They've certainly taken the vigilante flag from you," Katarine said with a small chuckle. "Coyle about wet himself running away."

"I must've made an impression on them," I said, giddy at the thought of Coyle fearing for his life. But my happiness was fleeting. "I hope Fishen isn't punished for helping you."

"She was one of the first to succumb to the powder. Perhaps by design." She cast me a furtive look. "I can't believe you left such a young girl behind like that. Then again..." She glanced out the open door. "There seem to be younger children working here."

"They're hardier than they look," I said. "I gave them their freedom, but this is home to most of them. The older ones keep watch and are learning how to be soldiers from Jorad, and the youngest are learning to read. I would've preferred to have an army of fully-trained, adult soldiers but..." I shrugged. "At least I know they're loyal—as are your brother's soldiers. I'm so thankful they've come to our aid as many times as they have. I wouldn't have been able to take Neveri without them."

"I see now why you wanted me out of the castle so quickly," she said. "I could scarcely believe Maarit when she said Luard had brought ond out of the country.

"I don't understand how you were able to convince Ilara you were still on her side after that."

"I'd been preparing for it, though the details were a surprise," she said. "I wanted her to think she was the only person I had left, and that my safety was dependent on her good graces."

"I mean..." I made a face. "It was."

"But as I said," Katarine replied thoughtfully, "Ilara likes absolute power. So if she felt she was the only thing keeping me from the noose, she wouldn't send me there. She just wanted me to dangle, and know that she would determine my fate."

Again, I couldn't see a difference between what Katarine was saying and the truth, but still, I shivered. "I can't hide my emotions the way you can. Five minutes with Ilara, and she'd know every secret I had."

"It's not about hiding emotions, it's about using them to your advantage," Katarine said. "So yes, when Ilara asked about Beata being gone, I could dredge up the loneliness and be honest about how much I missed her. And when I found out about Neveri, I was honestly shocked and surprised—and also honestly scared for what it meant for my own place at Ilara's side."

"But what about when you had to lie?" I asked.

"For that, it's simply recalling a time when you felt a certain way," she said. "So, when it came down to making her believe Beata had abandoned me, all I had to do was think back to the day my father told me I was the one chosen to marry your brother." Her eyes grew wistful. "At the time, I was hurt and scared and betrayed. My other sisters were of marrying age as well, but I was the one who could be spared. That day I left, the last time I saw my mother and family..." She sighed mournfully. "That's a pain I carry with me to this day."

My heart began to ache from the pain in her voice, as I knew exactly where she was coming from. Then, I shook myself. "Damn. You're good."

"See?" She wiped the tears from her eyes. "In reality, while I was very lonely on that day, I found my home and my heart in Forcadel." She cast a look at Beata, a smile fluttering onto her face. Even though she'd just given me a primer in how to lie, there was nothing dishonest about the warmth in her eyes.

"I'm glad you're here, too," I said, rising from the table. "Your insight into Ilara's plans will be invaluable when we finally get around to dealing with her."

"Which will be...?"

I shrugged. "Working on it."

Chapter Forty

Dinner had passed in a blur, and I'd barely gotten a chance to swallow my food in-between the questions about Felix. I had nothing more to offer them than that he was in very good hands, and that he had woken up briefly and he seemed to be in good spirits.

When the crowd finally thinned, I was left with my ten vigilantes-in-training, and a long night ahead.

"I thought you said we couldn't train in the ring," Orman said.

"Good memory," I said, hiding my annoyance. "I want to try a little hand-to-hand combat. You know how to fight with swords. I want to see how you fare without them."

"So, beat each other up?" Malka said.

"Not too much," I said. "It's more about the upper hand. Once your opponent is on their back, the match is over. Then we'll try again. As long as you're on your feet, you can still escape."

"Escape?"

I nodded. "One of the most important lessons we learned was the art of escape. No one in the camp was asked to lay down their life—at least not needlessly. If you needed to run, you ran."

They stared at me as if I had two heads. "You're asking us to be cowards?"

"Not cowards," I said with a small sigh. "I'm asking you to survive. No one here should lose their life to Beswick. His men aren't going to stick around long enough to give up theirs." I licked my lips. "We always gained the upper hand by outsmarting soldiers —but also because we were fighting for ourselves. If things got too bad, we'd leave the mission and get home. Whereas the soldiers were trained to lay down their lives."

Slowly, they nodded, but more than a few had confused looks on their faces.

"I promise," I placed my hand on Malka's shoulder, "when we go up against Ilara, you'll all have a chance to fight to the death. But for now, all we need is for you to come out of this in one piece. Now pair off."

They did, but we were missing Narin, who couldn't quite fight with his bloody shoulder. So I matched myself up with his supposed partner, Orman.

"I'm quite uncomfortable with this, Your Majesty," he said. "I don't know if I should be fighting you. I could hurt you."

"You won't," I said with a grin. "Now come show me what you can do."

He ran at me and I dodged his first blow with ease. I tapped my heel against the back of his leg to remind him that he'd left himself open. He swung his fist around, but it was slow, so I ducked and tapped him on the inside of his ribcage. He came back around, but this time, I went in for the kill, flipping him over my shoulder. He landed in a puff of dust and a loud grunt.

"She fights dirty, doesn't she?"

Felix leaned against the fence, a knowing grin on his face. He wore a loose white tunic, and his complexion was still sickly, but the sparkle in his eyes had returned.

"Captain!" chorused the soldiers behind me. They rushed past me and up to him, bombarding him with questions about his health and about Forcadel. I stood back, watching the joy on his face as he deftly answered every query, our training session long forgotten.

"Ilara has to try harder if she wants to kill me," he said, catching my eye. I personally thought she'd come damned close, but I didn't want to dull his shine. "I hear you've been training hard in my absence."

"Princess Brynna has been showing us how to fight in the forest," Orman said. "She's an excellent teacher."

"I don't doubt it. Why don't you show me what you've learned?" His eyes flashed. "Why don't you take on Her Majesty?"

I laughed a little. "Does Nicolasa know her patient is walking around the camp?"

"She said the fresh air would be good for me," he said with a look that awoke a feeling of longing in me. Perhaps it was the way his lips quirked upward when something amused him, the low, gravelly sound of his voice. The color of his eyes and the way his hair fell against his forehead.

"Your Majesty?" Malka asked.

"Fine," I said, blushing as I made myself stop staring. "Let's show Captain Llobrega what we've learned so far. Pair off."

"I'd like to see them go up against you," he said. "Ten to one. Didn't you fight more than that as The Veil?"

"My best was five," I said.

"Then five," Felix said. "And don't go easy on her."

I cast him a dirty look, but walked into the ring, finding a pair of wooden knives that felt close enough to my usual weapons. After some finger pointing and self-selection, five of my guards joined me in the ring. They hesitated at the edges, none of them willing to make the first move.

Finally, I sighed. "Well? Let's get this over with."

Orman was the bravest, running at me with his sword up. I easily deflected it, but then was met by Malka's blade, which I parried. Emerick received an elbow to the middle, and Saral a kick to the back of the shins. Orman came back for seconds, and while I knocked him away, I barely missed Lileth's blade and lost my footing.

I landed hard in the dirt, the tips of the wooden swords coming for my neck. But I rolled out of the way, pushed myself to a crouch then swept my leg around to knock them both on their asses. I scooped up their swords and pointed them at their necks.

"Yield?" I asked, panting a little.

The first one nodded, but the second slammed his foot into the back of my knee, then pulled a real knife from his back pocket and held it to my neck.

"Yield?" he said with a grin.

"Yield." I held up my hands. "Well done."

Behind me, Felix clapped, and was joined by the rest of the group. "That was absolutely impressive. It takes a special talent to defeat The Veil."

"Keep practicing," I said to the rest of them. "I'm going to walk Captain Llobrega back to Nicolasa's hut."

"I can't help but feel you were setting me up. Or did you just delight in watching me get beat?"

"I was curious how well you'd taught them," he said. "Clearly, they're learning how to be a little less upstanding and a little more ruthless. They'll need that."

His gait was steady and the cuts on his cheek were already healing over. It had been less than a day, and he was already nearly back to the man who used to drive me up the castle walls.

"You look good," I said. "Nicolasa is a miracle worker."

"She is that," he said. "As are you, Brynn."

My name on his lips—not my full name, but the shortened, familiar version only he seemed to use—sent chills down my spine.

"Things are steady, at least," I said, shaking the feeling from my body. "For the moment."

"Kat stopped by this morning and told me what you've been up to," he said. "As I said, miracle worker. You went from absolutely nothing to an army nearly two hundred strong in the span of a few months."

My face grew hot once. "And you? Playing masked vigilante in Forcadel?"

"Unfortunately, I'm not cut out for that work," he said with a sad shake of his head. "I spent most of our time apart figuring out that Beswick was behind the fires, while also trying to balance keeping my guards—and myself—out of harm's way." He shook his head. "I can't help but feel like I failed you."

"There's no way you could've failed me," I said, covering his hand with mine. "You sacrificed yourself for me. I could never repay you for that. And trust me when I say that whoever was responsible for it will pay mightily. I already socked Kieran in the face."

"As much as I would've loved to see that," Felix smiled wryly, "he was actually quite helpful. Well, not helpful, but he did help me get a little further along. I just..." He sighed. "I suppose I was asking the wrong questions. As I said, not cut out to be a vigilante."

"I'm happy to have you as captain," I said, squeezing our joined hands. "Jorad's certainly been exceptionally helpful, but I know he's happy to see you."

"And his partner Aline?" Felix asked. "I haven't seen her."

"I left her in Forcadel with one of my best thieves," I said. "Once Maarit was freed, it was too dangerous for me to remain in the city."

"Hm." Felix made a face.

"What?"

"I'm just... That doesn't sound like the Brynna I know," he said. "Don't get me wrong, it was the right choice. But when have you ever let someone else do your dirty work?"

"What can I say?" I said with a small laugh. "I'm learning. It hasn't been smooth, though. I feel like half the camp's been ready to walk out at least three times already"

"Growing pains are to be expected," he said. "But they look up to you. They listen, they follow you. Whatever you did to keep them here, it's working."

Yet again, that familiar warmth spread across my face and chest. "I feel bad undoing all that you taught them. They're upstanding soldiers. I'm turning them into thieves."

"They'll be whatever we need them to be," Felix said. "And I don't think learning how to survive in a real battle is the worst thing. Sometimes, I felt like I was training them to be peacocks. Strutting around the castle in their finest uniforms and keeping the peace in what was already a peaceful city. Now, at least, they'll be battle tested when we go up against Ilara—or Ammon." Felix shook his head, disgusted. "No honor amongst the Kulkans, it seems."

"Some honor," I said. "But perhaps it's more that he thought he could get away with it. After all, what recourse do I have against him?"

"Plenty," Felix said. "You can't be precious with your soldiers, Brynn. They may not be ready to fight in a forest, but they'd be more than enough against Ammon. And you need him back on your side before you can even think about taking on Ilara."

"I know," I said heavily. "It's just hard to know the right move to make."

"You've made plenty of right moves thus far," Felix said as we arrived at the Nestori hut. "As long as you keep listening to the same people who led you here, you won't fail. You clearly have good council."

"Council, hm…" That gave me an idea.

Nicolasa appeared in the doorway of her hut, her eyes alight with indignation. "Captain, I don't believe I allowed you a full walk around the camp."

Felix shared a look with me, as if he'd been caught stealing sweets from the kitchen.

"Back inside with you," the Nestori said. "And I'll thank you not to keep him too long, Larissa. He's still got a long way to go to heal."

He mouthed 'Larissa?' to me before the Nestori hustled him inside. And I, eager to avoid any more lectures, turned and hurried away.

Chapter Forty-One

The next morning, I asked for my most trusted advisors to meet me in the mess hall after breakfast. Jorad arrived first, a little confused as to what he was doing there, followed by Luard, who seemed pleased that things were finally moving. Arriving next, arm-in-arm, were Felix and Katarine. I didn't miss how the younger Llobrega perked up when Felix came in the room. Some of his cuts were fading, and his color had improved. Still, he favored his left side, where his ribs had been broken, and he barely hid a wince as he sat down on the bench.

Finally, at the very last minute, Jax strolled in, taking a seat in the back and looking very uninterested in being there at all.

"Thank you all for coming," I said, offering each a smile. "Back in Forcadel, when I first showed up on the throne, I had a group of people who were supposed to advise and counsel me on matters."

"As I recall, you didn't listen to them," Felix said lightly.

"And that was my mistake," I said. "But also, I had no say in who was advising me. Therefore, I'm reconvening my official royal council—and asking all of you to sit on it."

"Technically, foreigners aren't supposed to sit on your Council," Katarine said, looking to Luard. "Are you sure you want us here?"

"Technically, I'm not queen right now, so we're both bending the rules," I said. "But you five are the ones I trust the most, so I'm asking you to help me make better decisions. I have a lot on my plate, and I need help."

I glanced around, waiting for someone (probably Jax) to stand up and walk out, but everyone remained seated.

"Excellent." I unfurled a map on the table, flipping it around to face the rest of those assembled. "Right now, we have three enemies. The first, of course, is Ilara. But in order to face her, we have to deal with the other two enemies. Ammon and Beswick."

I pointed to the western part of the country.

"Ammon is currently in Neveri. From what Katarine's told me, Ilara was unreceptive to his overtures. Therefore, we have an opportunity to reforge our alliance with him or, at the very least, keep him out of our way."

I slid my finger across Forcadel to where the Ash river met the Niemenian border.

"On the other side, we have Beswick. He's after the ond, and by now, Kieran should've delivered the message that I want to have a chat. I expect he'll send a messenger or a message in the coming days. To that end, I'm preparing the troops to be ready to take on his criminals. We've also got Jorad's younger cadets," I said to the younger Llobrega, "who can serve as lookouts and messengers."

"Some of the older ones will be ready for service soon," Jax said. "They're not terrible."

"So what's our next move?" Felix asked. "Ammon or Beswick?"

"We can't do anything about Beswick until he answers our message," I said. "Eventually, he's going to get frustrated with what

Aline and Elisha are doing and reach out. So our focus, for now, should be on Ammon."

"Our messengers say he's got a hundred soldiers in the city," Jorad said. "Plus additional warships helping to protect the ocean and river."

"I'm not looking to wage war just yet," I said. "Not unless I have to."

"I don't think it's necessary to go to war," Katarine said thoughtfully. "The forces move where Ammon tells them. So all you need is to convince Ammon to return to your original agreement."

"And how do I trust that he'll stick to it this time?" I asked.

Luard tapped his fingers on the table. "What we have to ask ourselves is why Ammon's gone in a different direction than his father. It's been months and Neshua won't accept Ilara as queen. But Ammon sent envoys to ally himself with her. What's to say they don't have differing opinions about everything else? Maybe Ammon's getting tired of waiting for his father to give up power."

I tilted my head toward him. "You don't think he was planning to use the Severian ore as leverage to get his father to give up the throne early, do you?"

Luard quirked a brow.

"Seriously?" I turned fully to him. "You think he'd try to blow up his own people?"

"I'm saying that if he showed up at his father's doorstep with it in hand, his father may take him a bit more seriously," Luard said. "I think he's ambitious, but I don't think he's a monster."

"So where does that put me?" I asked. "Do you think if I agreed to help him get on the throne, he'd stick to our original agreement?"

"I think it would be a mistake to get involved in Kulkan internal politics," Felix said.

"Exactly," Katarine said with a nod. "You have enough on your plate as it is. But I think knowing where he's coming from will inform how you deal with him."

"He's trying to prove to his father that he's ready to take over," Luard said. "Ergo, it would be highly embarrassing if he suffered a defeat in Neveri. So if you want him to work with you, I'd threaten to embarrass him in front of his people and father."

"And what might that look like?" I asked.

"If you were to take the city back from him," Luard said. "You did it before with fewer resources. I bet you could do it again."

I shook my head. "I told you, I'm not waging war in Neveri again."

"Yes, but *he* doesn't need to know that," Luard said. "Whatever Ammon's been doing, it's without the approval of his father. One hint that you'll blow the entire operation, and I'll bet he returns to your side."

"So you think I call Ammon's bluff, then?" I said. "Show up and threaten to retake the city, without having any real intent to, just so he'll remember who he's dealing with?"

"Then leave twenty soldiers behind to make him adhere to the agreement," Felix said. "You can spare those bodies. A small show of force would remind him you mean business."

I rubbed my chin, thinking through the plan. "I could take some vigilantes with me, too. It would give them some experience using the weapons we've been training with. But are we sure Ammon won't call *my* bluff?"

"When you were The Veil, you used to threaten to dismember lots of people," Felix said. "Whatever you do to threaten him, make it so terrifying that he'd never question your follow-through."

I glanced around the table, still unsure. "Is everyone in agreement with this?"

"Aye," Felix said, holding up his hand.

"Aye," Katarine and Luard said in unison.

"Yes, Your Majesty," Jorad said, jumping to his feet.

"You're on the Council, you can just say 'aye,'" Felix whispered to him.

"Aye!" he cheered with gusto. Felix shook his head, muttering to himself.

I looked at Jax, who hadn't said much, and who wore a disgruntled look on his face.

"Jax?" I asked. "I need the unanimous consent of my Council. If you have misgivings, you need to tell me about them."

"I'm on board with the plan, but I ain't on board with being on this stupid group," he said with a shrug. "You do whatever you want."

Jorad turned to me, as if to argue, but I shook my head. "That's why he's here. He gives it to me straight. He'd let me know if it was a bad plan."

"Always nice to have an asshole in the group," Luard said.

"Very well, Your Majesty, what's your command to the soldiers?" Jorad asked then gave Felix a nervous look. "I mean, Captain Llobrega can—"

"I'm still recovering," Felix said, holding up his hands in surrender. "This is your command, Lieutenant."

Jorad's chest puffed out even more.

"I want you to prepare twenty soldiers to come with me," I said. "And ask Locke to give me his best vigilantes. I'm hoping we won't need any of them but better to be safe. We leave in the morning."

"Yes, Your Majesty," Jorad said, saluting me before leaving.

"Is it just me, or is he a lot more eager since you showed up?" Luard asked Felix.

"Can't help it. Llobregas like to show off in front of each other," Felix said, as he stood gingerly. I rose to help him, but Katarine's soft touch landed on my arm.

"Would you take a walk with me?" she asked, her face the color of a tomato. "I need to discuss something important with you."

Felix snorted and muttered something I couldn't hear, and Katarine's face turned, if possible, more red. Even Luard was staring at her with a look of confusion.

"Now?" she squeaked.

"Absolutely," I said. The words were barely out of my mouth before she dragged me from the room.

Once out of the camp, I led Katarine toward a more dense part of the forest where there were no scouts. I wasn't sure what she was hoping to accomplish, but I didn't want to violate her trust by having a teenager listen in on whatever it was.

"I think that went well," I began. "It's nice to have so many people give their perspectives."

"They won't always go that smoothly," she said, a little agitation in her voice. "But yes, it seems like you've assembled a fine Council."

I stopped. "Is everything all right?"

"Yes, but..." She made a sound of frustration. "This was much easier in my head."

"What?" I took her hands. "You can tell me. Whatever it is, I promise I'll support you. After what you did, staying behind then getting Felix out—whatever you want is yours."

"The truth is..." she began softly. "I've spent the past few weeks regretting that I hadn't done more to show my love to Beata. And I don't want another day to go by without her knowing exactly what she means to me. Luard is here, you're here. This place is beautiful. And when we lay our heads down to sleep at night, we may not wake up. No time like the present."

"To...?"

"Marry her," Katarine said with a smile.

I blinked several times. Of all the things I'd thought she'd wanted to talk to me about, this wasn't one of them. "Uh...I mean..."

"Unless you think it's crass," Katarine said quickly, wringing her hands and walking away from me. "We're in the middle of a war, and Ilara's out there, and—"

"No, it's not that," I said. "It's just that... It's not my decision, is it? Maybe you should be having this conversation with Beata instead."

"Well, if we're adhering to the treaty," she said with a coy smile, "the Forcadel sovereign retains control over my nuptials, especially since my husband died." She took my hands in hers. "So, Your Majesty, do I have permission to marry the woman I love?"

I kissed her hands. "Permission and blessing. As long as I get to stand there with you."

"I'd have it no other way," she said. "Now I just need to drum up the courage to ask her."

"You just broke Felix out of the Forcadelian dungeons, and you're afraid to ask your girlfriend to marry you?" I asked, incredulously.

"One day, Brynna-Larissa, you'll be in this position," she said with a knowing look, "then we will talk about how easy it is."

Chapter Forty-Two

Katarine

If I were being honest, asking Brynna for her permission was merely a stalling tactic. I'd been thinking about this monumental question for days now, my palms growing sweaty every time I was in the same room as Beata. I had no idea how she'd react, or if she even wanted to start a life together. My heart, of course, was sure of her. My head was still steeped in doubt.

So I avoided the question as long as possible. Instead of finding Beata after Brynna's new council meeting, I caught up with Luard, who was playing cards with his guards. It was so positively normal to see him lounging near a bonfire as his voice carried through the camp. Two young female guards were nearby, although Asdis was keeping a close eye on them.

"Ah, Kitty Kat!" Luard called to me, throwing down his cards and jumping to his feet. "I delivered your captain to the Nestori with no issues."

"Much appreciated," I said, sitting down next to Hagan and Nils. "It's so wonderful to see all of you here. It seems you've managed to keep Luard out of trouble."

"Not since he started hanging out with Princess Brynna," Ivan grumbled. "My hair's going gray every day we're around her."

"It's distinguished," Luard said, swiping at the guard's hairline. "Women love a gray-haired man."

"Do they, though?" Asdis said with a giggle.

"Tell me everything that's happened back home," I asked. "Has Ariadna had her child yet? Has Erlina married?"

"I haven't received word about Ariadna," Luard said. "But it should be soon. I wish I could be there, but duty calls." He swiped the cards from the table, shuffling then dealing them to us. "Now, you may be skilled in strategic thinking, but it's been a while since you've gone toe-to-toe with a Niemenian at the game of skreet. I bet you're rusty."

I deftly picked my hand from the table and sat back. "We will have to see, dear brother."

I stayed and played a couple of games, allowing Luard to win some and taking Asdis for all her gold. But the pressing need to ask Beata the most important question of my life weighed heavily in the back of my mind and in my chest, making me antsy as I waited for the next hand to be played.

"Ah, Felix! Jorad!" Luard called over my shoulder. "Come join us for a round. My guards are nearly out of gold, and you look like a couple of rich fellows."

"I think we'll pass," Felix said. "Never get into a game of wits with the Niemenian royal family, Jorad. You'll lose everything you have."

"Noted." Jorad nodded firmly.

"Would you like to join us, Kat?" Felix asked. "Jorad's troops are ready for a drill and he'd like me to watch. It might be less expensive than playing with your brother."

"Yes, please join them, Kat," Asdis said, reaching across the table to take the pile of coins from me. "I'll play your hand."

The young soldiers were barely up to my chest, and many of them seemed too skinny for the work they were being asked to do. But they lined up as quickly as any other soldier Felix had trained, and their salutes to their captain were nearly perfect.

"Excellent," Felix said. "You've certainly trained them well, Jorad."

"I'm doing my best," he said, ducking his head reverently. "These kids are excellent already. It's not as if I had to do much. Not like you whipping us into shape back in Forcadel."

"I'd say your class of cadets did fairly well," he replied. "Especially showing up like you did in Neveri in the nick of time."

The younger cousin flushed, staring at the ground with wide eyes. Something was up. Felix wasn't usually so generous with his compliments.

With a whistle from Jorad, the soldiers paired off and sparred, clashing with wooden weapons. I waited on the edge of the training space while Felix and Jorad made their rounds. A few times, Felix interjected into the fray to show a pair how to do something then complimented his cousin.

Yes, something was definitely afoot.

When the matches were over, Jorad beckoned the young cadets to assemble before us.

"And, *salute!*" Jorad called.

They pressed their fist to their chest in unison.

"Dismissed!"

The formalities slid from their shoulders and straight backs, and they shuffled away, barking and cajoling like ordinary children. More than a few curses left their lips, and one particularly screechy girl sounded like she'd walked out of a gutter. I had to hide a smile —Jorad had certainly taught them well, but they were still thieves at their core.

"They'll make fine soldiers one day," Felix said. "I'm very proud of you. Dismissed, soldier."

Jorad saluted him with relish then marched away, the back of his neck still pink with embarrassment.

"I think you did that on purpose," I said with a coy look.

Felix actually attempted to look innocent. "Did what?"

"What do you want from him?" I pressed, putting my hands on my hips. "To give up his command?"

"Of course not," Felix said. "He's doing an admirable job. The trainees are doing well, too. I wouldn't dream of getting between them."

I narrowed my eyes. "Then what are you after?"

"Nothing."

"Felix."

He made a face, looking away. "Fine. I want him to convince Brynna to let me go with them to Neveri."

"Forget Brynna, I don't think *I'll* let you." I poked my finger into his ribcage, earning a wince from him. "You're still recovering, Felix."

"I'm better than I was," he said, rubbing the spot I'd poked. "Nicolasa says I can ride and travel."

"Did she now?"

"She will," he said. "Or she'll just see that I can."

"Stubborn ass," I whispered. "And why do you feel your presence is necessary? Brynna has an army to protect her."

I expected him to fire back a quick response, but he grew pensive, staring at the ground with a quiet reserve unlike him.

"I don't recognize her anymore," he said quietly. "The girl I plucked off the streets was a wild, violent thing who took too many risks and laughed in the face of danger. And now, Brynna is a queen—battle-tested, strategic, cautious." He shook his head. "And worse still, I don't know where I can help her. Going with her on this trip would help me feel like..."

"I understand," I said, softening a little. "But she's still our Brynna—she's just a bit more mature and cautious. And she's listening to us, which is a refreshing change. But that doesn't mean you need to put yourself in danger to prove anything."

"Kat, I don't think you understand," he said. "I got nothing accomplished. Clearly, Beswick feels the same as he did when I met with him. I made a mockery of my time as The Veil. I thought I was sacrificing myself for her, but instead all I did was cause her more pain and trouble. And if I hadn't been captured, you could've gone with Bea."

I covered his hand with mine. "I'm sure she doesn't feel that way. She's just grateful to have you safe. And she's failed many times as The Veil. It's apparently part of being a vigilante." When he didn't respond, I tugged at his hand a little. "I know it's hard to come into this place and not know where you fit in. But Brynna needs all the help she can get, whether it's strategic or physical or even just..." I smiled. "The love of a man."

His gaze darted toward me. "That's not what this is about."

"I'm sure," I said with a small shrug.

"This coming from the woman who hasn't asked Beata to marry her yet."

My pulse spiked as I sputtered. "I'm...sorry?"

"Oh, Felix," he said, drawing his voice higher to mimic mine, "when I see Beata again, I think I shall ask her to marry me." He grinned as my sputtering intensified. "Oh, Felix, I'm so smitten with her, I cannot even begin to—"

"What?"

Beata stood nearby, her eyes wide with surprise and her pink mouth open a little. How much she'd heard, I had no clue, but clearly she'd heard enough.

"Well?" Felix said, pushing me forward. "Go on."

"And you," I snapped, pointing at him, "Nicolasa is expecting you back. Hurry up."

He backed up a few steps then turned in the direction of the Nestori's hut, whistling a little to himself.

"Shall we...take a walk?" I squeaked to Beata. Then, clearing my throat, I asked her again. "In the forest?"

She smiled warmly. "Sure."

Our footsteps crunched on the leafy underbrush, a perfect accompaniment to my thundering heart. Perhaps she would say that marriage was in poor taste, or perhaps she'd lost her love for me along the way. Or, more terrifying, she might agree to marry me.

"It is quite lovely here," she said, breaking the silence between us. "I don't get a chance to walk out into the forest much."

"I didn't really notice when I came in, but yes."

A whistle echoed in the tree above us. At first I thought it a bird, but then a young teenager jumped from the tree.

"Beggin' your pardon, missus," he said, flashing us a grin that was missing a few teeth. "But Her Majesty asked us to keep watch over the forest. I—"

Another whistle echoed in the space above us, and this time I noted a pattern to it.

"Er..." He bowed awkwardly. "Never mind. I been told otherwise. Enjoy your walk." He took off on foot through the underbrush.

"Well, that was odd," I said, but Beata just smiled.

"Someone wants to give us some privacy," she said with a knowing look. "The whistles are a code the children use to communicate quickly from all parts of the forest. They've tried to teach me, but I confess, it's a bit convoluted."

I nodded, allowing the silence to stretch out between us. There was nothing around us, not even the whisper of a rodent in the leaves or a bird flapping its wings. It had been so long since I'd been out of the hustle and bustle of the city that the silence was almost alarming.

"Kat," Beata said quietly. "Was there something you wanted to ask me?"

I swallowed, my tongue like sandpaper in my mouth. "Yes, but I'm not quite sure how to phrase it."

"That's my Kat," she said, taking my hands in hers. "Always have to do things perfectly the first time, don't you?"

"It is a quirk of mine," I said, some of the tension loosening in my chest. Looking in her eyes, it was hard to remember why I'd been so terrified. She was everything I could want in a wife, and more importantly, she was everything I could want in a soul mate. I couldn't imagine life without her by my side anymore.

"Beata," I said quietly. "I've spent these last few weeks apart thinking about how much you mean to me. And if something should happen to either of us..." I ran my finger along her hand. "I have nothing to give you except my love."

"That's more than enough for me," she replied with a soft smile.

"Then if you'll have me," I said, a lump of emotion growing in my throat. "I'd love the honor of being your wife."

"Katarine," she said, stepping closer to me. "My Kat. My love. Nothing would make me happier in this life or the next than to be your wife."

With a soft sob, I closed the distance between us. Her skin was soft under my fingers, her cheeks wet with tears. She gripped my face, as if I might slip away if she let go. Sniffling, she rested her forehead against mine, closing her eyes.

"When shall we get married?" I whispered.

"Tomorrow, if you like," she said. "We'll throw a big party here in camp. I'll bake a cake. Everyone will be invited."

My heart leapt at the idea, but my mind tamped it down. "We can't go to such extravagance."

"Extravagance is exactly what is needed. We haven't had good news in weeks. Seeing love flourish in such dark times would do wonders for morale," Beata said, some of that familiar stubbornness coming back to her eyes. "But tomorrow is too soon. There's so much to do. I must find myself some white linens for a dress—perhaps even make a cake—"

I knew better than to argue with her. But before she dashed away to plan and prepare, I pulled her in for one long, final kiss.

Chapter Forty-Three

Word spread quickly in the camp that there would be a wedding in the coming days. Luard, of course, was overjoyed, and declared loudly that he would be helping Beata plan it. When we gathered for breakfast the next morning, he pressed each of the soldiers for hidden talents, determined to have music and dancing.

"Hagan can strum a lute, but Mother knows he's rusty," Luard said. "Everything must be perfect for my Kitty Kat's wedding."

I let him dither and pester people, as it seemed to lighten the mood. In the meantime, I busied myself with preparing for my trip to Neveri. It had been a few weeks since I'd felt the weight of a slingbag against my back, but I was eager to get back under the mask. It was grounding, almost, a reminder of all that I'd accomplished with it.

The problem was Felix.

"I'm going," he announced when I walked into Nicolasa's hut.

I barked a laugh. "Like hell you are. You're in no shape to ride, let alone help me in Neveri."

"I feel fine," he said. "And Nicolasa said I could go."

I turned to the Nestori, who was a few paces behind him. "Well?"

"He is well enough to travel, but not to fight," she said.

I put my hands on my hips, staring daggers at him. "Felix, I know you want to come, but I can't babysit you."

"I'm not asking you to," he said, walking over to me. "I promise I'll stay out of trouble. But I need to find something to do or I'll go crazy."

"You could help plan the wedding?" I said with a saccharine smile.

"Please," he said. "Let me help you."

I sighed, pursing my lips. It was hard to argue with his large, brown eyes.

"You stay outside the city," I said, pointing my finger at him. "If trouble rears its head, you run. Understand?"

"Yes, Your Majesty." He saluted me with all the gusto of his former position, but the smile on his face was nothing if not sarcastic.

I had a feeling I was going to regret letting him come, but I didn't have the heart to argue with him. So together, we joined the rest of the soldiers at the front of camp. I waited for Jorad to say something against him, but he just jumped onto his horse and nodded to me. The other riders included my vigilante trainees Malka, Orman, and Narin, whose shoulder had clearly healed. Their excited grins reminded me of Aline's grin when I'd left her in Forcadel.

I gave the signal and we took off, serenaded by the sounds of whistles from the scouts in the trees above us. It would be half a day before we'd get to Neveri, perhaps even longer with the leisurely pace of the horses. But for once, I wasn't in any hurry. There was a cool breeze, I had something of a plan, and Felix was riding next to me. It didn't escape my notice that the other riders gave us a wide berth, perhaps knowing that we hadn't had much time to catch up since his arrival. So I entertained us both with a recounting of my journey, making sure to embellish the more embarrassing moments, just for his amusement.

"Naked?" Felix said. "You fell naked in front of Luard?"

"My robe slipped," I said with a grin. "But he was gentlemanly about it."

"I'm sure he was."

"He's a very complex man, much more than I realized when I first met him back in Forcadel," I said. "I hadn't been able to see the resemblance between him and Kat. But now? Especially when he's urging me to think more strategically, I see it."

"I'm glad someone got through that thick skull of yours," Felix said. "Perhaps I'll have to ask him to teach me his ways."

"I think it had something to do with me being completely out of my depth," I said, remembering that first night in Linden, when I'd still been waffling on my path. "Kings and queens and wars are not my forte."

"They seem to be now," Felix said.

"Okay, now I know you're up to something," I said, glaring at him. "Why are you buttering me up? Trying to get on my good side?"

"I have no idea what you're talking about," he said, offering an innocent look. "I'm merely making observations."

"I'm not letting you go with me into the city," I said.

"Why? Afraid I'll show you up?"

"I don't want all Nicolasa's hard work to go to waste if someone knifes you."

He just laughed. "I noticed she still calls you Larissa. Surely she knows your name by now."

"Habit, maybe? Locke does the same," I said. "Sometimes, I even think of myself as Larissa. It feels better, you know? A name I chose for myself, not one I was given. Larissa was the girl who survived in Celia's camp, the one who returned to Forcadel and made a name for herself as The Veil. I guess I just like that version of me better."

He scrutinized me. "I can't see it. You'll always be Brynn to me."

There it was again, that shortened version of my name. "Why do you call me that?"

"What?"

"Brynn."

"It's your name, isn't it?"

"My name is Brynn-*a*," I said.

He knitted his brows. "Just a faster way to yell at you, I guess. If it bothers you, I can stop."

"No," I said. "Besides, when have you ever listened to me anyway? And you didn't answer my question. What are you up to?"

"I am merely enjoying a long ride with my queen," he said with another innocent shrug. "So what happened after Linden?"

I continued my tale of traveling under the mountain, seeing the ond stores, and the talk Luard and I'd had about making hard decisions. About Kulka, Neshua, and Ammon, and walking through the marshlands—earning me a whispered prayer from Felix.

"The Mother's hand was surely on your shoulder," Felix said. "And to have Riya and the soldiers there in Neveri, too."

I straightened in the saddle. "Did Kat—"

"She did," he said with a solemn nod.

"Felix, I'm sorry..." I looked down. "I didn't even have a chance to... It just..."

"She would've been proud to have given her life for you," he said. "At least her sacrifice wasn't in vain."

The doubt had returned to his voice, and I had nothing to say to erase it that wouldn't fall flat. I knew the sting of failure, of working hard to achieve something only to realize it had been for nothing. The only way I'd gotten out of my funk was when Celia had practically dumped me on the front steps of the city. Maybe it wasn't the worst thing for Felix to find some purpose again.

"You put your life on the line to protect the city as The Veil. That was brave," I said.

He made a noise and looked away.

I thumbed the necklace I wore, and the two Forcadelian crests that hung from the chain. "I've been wearing this since, just to remind myself of what I've lost."

He nodded, then did a double take. "Isn't the other one mine?"

"Um…" My face heated up, remembering what he'd said when he'd given it to me. *I'll dream of you every night.* Had he? "Do you want it back?"

"No, you can keep it," he said, wearing a knowing grin. "I'm just surprised that you still have it after all this time. Through the mountains and over Kulka, you wore my pendant. If I didn't know any better, Your Majesty, I'd think you had a crush on me."

I opened my mouth to argue with him, but all I could do was sputter idiotically.

"Wow, I didn't think that was possible," Felix said with a satisfied smirk. "I've rendered you speechless."

It would be easier to infiltrate the city at night, so we found a spot far enough from the city to set up a temporary camp. For once, I wasn't nervous about the impending mission—and neither were my soldiers. There was an infectious, excited energy that rustled between us.

"What's the plan, Your Majesty?" Malka asked, rubbing her hands together. "Are we going in together?"

"First, we need to case the city," I said. "Our scouts say he's taken over Maarit's old office, which I've infiltrated before, but I'm sure their security is a bit different. I'll be scouting first then coming up with an engagement plan. I want two of you on lookout —anything or anyone coming, whistle. The other three, I want nearby on buildings. I shouldn't need backup, but in case I do, you'll be it."

"And what if you need more than that?" Jorad asked. "We have swords. We can help."

"That's why we've got scouts," I said. "You know the code. Come if we call."

He smiled. "Will do, Your Majesty."

"But I won't engage unless I need to," I said, sharing a look with Felix. "Trust me, I'm not going to risk my life just to have a chat with Ammon."

"Very well," Jorad said with a frown. "We will stay and ready the camp for a hasty exit."

"Be careful," Felix said. "Ammon has an entire army, and I'm not convinced he's as much of a coward as Luard says."

"And you are—"

"Staying here."

I nodded. "Good. Jorad, I'm leaving him in your care. Don't let him try anything funny."

Jorad saluted. "Yes, Your Majesty."

Felix attempted to salute as well but grabbed the side of his ribcage with a hiss. "Just imagine I saluted you, okay?"

"Are you all right?" I asked, my hands itching to reach for him.

"Fine," he said. "Nicolasa sent me with some medicine. I should take it and rest so I'll be ready to ride back." He straightened, giving his troops a nod. "Good luck to all of you. I have faith that you'll be successful."

He walked away, limping slightly, leaving me confused. He wasn't forcing himself to go with me? Did that mean he was in more pain than I thought, or was there something else going on?

"Can I have a word in private with you?" I said to Jorad, and he followed me out into the open field. "I'm not convinced he's going to just stay put after coming all this way, so restrain him if you need to."

"I think he'll stay," Jorad said. "He and I agreed as much."

I quirked a brow. "You what?"

"We spoke before we left. I wouldn't say a word against him coming, and he wouldn't attempt to follow you to the city."

"That still doesn't explain why he came all this way for no reason," I said, frowning. "I feel like he's up to something."

"I think his reason for wanting to travel here was clear," Jorad said. "He's in love with you."

My face grew hot, even in the cool air of the night. He'd said it once, but that had been months ago. Although we'd been flirting, *love* was more than just stolen glances. And we'd barely spent a few minutes together. "I'm not sure that's the case."

"He went to jail for you."

"Yes, but…"

I shook my head to clear my thoughts. This wasn't a subject I wanted to discuss with Jorad about. Katarine, yes. Maybe even Luard. Besides that, I had other things to worry about tonight.

"As long as he stays here, that's all I care about." I reached into my bag and pulled the black mask from the slingbag. "We will be back before sunup."

Chapter Forty-Four

The river water and swampland smell awoke memories of my time in Neveri. I had become nearly as familiar with this town as Forcadel's capital city. But on this visit, the memories were tinged with sadness.

There, we passed Norah's farm, which had become a little overgrown. Her animals were gone, hopefully taken by neighbors in the aftermath of Neveri's downfall. Though it was dark, I could still make out the raised patch of dirt where she had been buried. I whispered a small prayer of thanks to her, and hoped wherever she'd gone, she could hear it.

We continued along the path, which had been once been patrolled by Forcadelian soldiers, but was now unguarded. Our messengers had said Ammon kept a tighter perimeter to the south, but I still told my team to be vigilant.

"I want to get to Ammon without being seen," I said. "Stay to the rooftops and only engage when absolutely necessary."

I guided them up a stack of crates, then we took off. We resembled a caterpillar, with me as the head jumping first, and the rest following. These vigilantes had truly absorbed all I'd taught them, because they kept up without any issue.

We came to the farmer's market, and there we hunched down as Kulkan soldiers marched through the streets. They seemed a little more approachable than the Severians had been—until my gaze found a poster on the front of one of the buildings.

"Climb down and get that for me," I said to Orman.

He returned with the rolled-up piece of paper. I unfurled it for the group and scowled.

"Anyone caught wearing a mask will be lashed twenty times in the town square?" I read with a scowl. "What the hell, Ammon?"

"I saw one a couple streets back," Malka said. "Should we take ours off?"

"No," I said, rolling up the poster and handing it back to Orman. "New plan. I want all of you to go out and get yourselves seen by the guards."

"But you said—"

"I know what I said," I said with a thin smile. "But I'm changing the plan. That's what you do as The Veil. Once you get new information, you adjust. Clearly, Ammon is having a Veil problem, and I think if his guards find five of them out in the city, it might stir them up."

"And you want that?"

"I do," I said. "It'll be easier to sneak into the barracks if all the guards are running around the city." I made eye contact with each one of them. "Don't get caught. Can you handle that?"

They all nodded, pressing their fists to their breasts and bowing. "Your Majesty."

"If we don't meet up, I want you back at the camp with the rest of the soldiers by sun-up." I grinned. "Go have fun out there."

They dashed off the rooftops and into the city. Within

minutes, the guards cried out and called for help. I said a prayer to the Mother that these new vigilantes would run faster than their guard counterparts then set off for the barracks.

Predictably, by the time I got there, Kulkan guards were few and far between. Most of those on duty had been reassigned, chasing after the five vigilantes who'd made their appearance. I didn't even have to use knockout powder to get past the two who were there.

I swallowed my nostalgia as I walked across the patch of grass toward the barracks. I pointed my crossbow at the roof and fired, wincing at the sound. This was a special arrow, Kulkan-made, ironically, designed to pierce a roof beam and hold in place as I climbed. Ivan had promised it would be perfect for this job, but I still made sure to take each step carefully as I walked up the side of the wall.

When I reached the top of the wall, I peered inside the dark office. It was covered in Kulkan crests—including those of the royal family. With one hand, I cut the glue around the window glass, pushed it through, and opened the window, landing on the plush carpet. The office was much different than when Maarit had been in here. Now Kulkan crests and paintings lined the walls.

With a smirk, I sat down on the leather chair and put my feet up on the desk. Then I waited.

About half an hour later, I heard voices down the hall. I adjusted myself in my seat, crossing my feet over one another on the desk. When the door opened, light flooded into the room from the hallway, and Ammon came marching in.

"Evening, Ammon."

The Kulkan prince went stick-straight and turned slowly. For effect, I pulled a green apple—similar to the color of his eyes—out of my bag and slowly peeled it with my knife.

"Pleasure to see you again," I said, as Ammon's gaze fixed on the apple. "How are things?"

He took a hesitant step into the room. It didn't escape my notice that his hand went to guard his manhood, especially as I continued sliding my knife along the skin of the apple.

"Things are good. Why are you here?" Ammon asked. "Why not send an envoy to pass along a message if you had one?"

"*Speaking* of envoys," I said, taking my knife and slicing the apple. "I hear a couple of yours were in Forcadel recently. And they had Maarit with them." I pulled one slice out and placed it on the desk. "I thought we had an agreement."

He licked his lips and his green eyes darted around, looking for a way out. "Merely checking all avenues."

I put the apple on the table and stuck the knife in the center of it. "You betrayed me, Ammon. You can pretty it up all you want, but you and I had an agreement and you backed out." I softened my gaze a little. "Not that I'm surprised, based on your past history."

"You're the first to run out on a treaty," he said.

"Oh Mother, will you *let that go*?" I said, glancing to the ceiling. "I didn't marry you. You're happy with your new wife. Why don't you just let bygones be bygones already?"

"Because it was highly embarrassing to my father and the court," he said.

"Do you know what else will be highly embarrassing?" I said, putting my hands behind my head. "Gaining Neveri, the stronghold you've been after for years, only to lose it to the very woman who took it for you."

"What are you talking about?"

"I'm talking about the army of soldiers I have waiting just outside the border of this city," I said, kicking my feet off the desk and coming to stand. "I'm talking about the bags of ond Ariadna's been kind enough to give to me for my cause. If you don't straighten up, I'll take a bag of ond and stick it on top of the barracks and light a candle."

His eyes widened.

"You know from the gates that it doesn't take much to make a big impact," I said, a grim smile coming to my face. "How many soldiers do you have sleeping in the barracks? Fifty? A hundred?"

The corner of his eye twitched. "You wouldn't."

"I don't want to," I said, making a face. "But you've put me in an odd position. You stabbed me in the back, and there must be consequences for it." I pressed my hand to my mouth. "What will your father say when he finds out you lost a hundred soldiers?"

I wasn't sure which would resonate—the father angle or losing the soldiers. By his pale face, perhaps both. "What can I do to make this right?"

"Our previous agreement was that you'd blockade the river," I said. "Now I want ships. Five of them—ocean-faring, too. And an additional hundred soldiers under my command."

"No way," Ammon said. "That's too much."

"You'll get them all back."

"I have another idea," he said, backing up a step. "*Guards!*"

"Oh, screw you, you giant asshole," I snarled, rushing him. But before I could get to him, three armed soldiers rushed in behind him. I didn't want to cause a scene, so I ran to the open window. And without thinking, I jumped...

...too late remembering that the cloak around my neck was just a cloak, and not the specially made one I needed to break my fall. I couldn't help the scream of fear as I braced myself for the pain of falling three stories onto the hard ground.

Except I didn't land solid ground—I landed in a pile of hay. It still hurt, but instead of broken bones, I just saw stars. Slowly, I pushed myself upward, shaking my spinning head.

"See, I told you."

I blinked and looked up at the grinning faces of Jorad and

Felix. "W-what are you doing here?"

"It doesn't matter," Felix said. "We need to get you out of here."

"Not yet," I said, crawling out of the wagon and onto the floor. "I'm not done with Ammon."

"*There she is!*" Ammon bellowed from above. "Surround her! In the courtyard!"

"Brynn, we—"

Like a swarm of insects, the Kulkan soldiers filled the courtyard, their weapons drawn and pointed at Felix, Jorad, and me. The younger Llobrega went to pull his weapon, but Felix held up his hand, shaking his head. He looked at me, nodding his head slightly.

Out of the corner of my eye, a torch flickered on the barracks wall. And an idea blossomed in my mind.

"Well, this was an exercise in idiocy," Ammon said, walking through the parting guards. "What were you planning on doing? Escaping? I have this city surrounded."

"Sure you do," I said with a low, Veil-like purr. I reached into my slingbag and pulled out a small pouch, holding it between my two fingers. "But I've got something you want."

Ammon's eyes widened in recognition. "You brought some with you?"

"Of course," I said, inching closer to the torch burning against the wall. "I'd had a mind to come to an agreement, but clearly, you decided otherwise."

"What are you—*Get away from there!*" Ammon cried, rearing back in fear as the bag came within a hair's breadth of the flame. "Are you trying to kill us all?"

"Ammon, I don't want to do this," I said, holding the bag aloft. "There's a hundred people in this building. This would knock out your entire army."

"And yourself as well," Ammon said. "You won't do it."

I moved the bag closer. "Others would continue in my stead."

"Your Majesty, don't!" Jorad cried, but Felix held up his hand.

"Trust her," he said. "She knows what she's doing."

"Does she?" Ammon said, fear creeping into his voice. "Or is she absolutely crazy?"

"A little of both," I said with a smile. "It doesn't have to end like this, Ammon. All you have to do is yield and give me what I want."

Ammon looked to his military advisors, all pale-faced and worried, then behind him to his soldiers. "You'd really kill your own people?"

"I did it once before," I said, bringing the bag closer to the candle.

"*All right!*" he cried. "All right. You'll get your soldiers and your ships. And my alliance. Just please, get that candle away from that bag."

I straightened, blowing the flame out. "Excellent. I'll be sending a contingent of fifty soldiers to make sure you keep your word this time. They'll have ond with them. If you betray me again, you won't get a warning." I looked at Felix and Jorad. "Let's go."

We walked by the Kulkans, who seemed too shocked to say or do anything. Wordlessly, the three of us climbed back onto our wagon and set off toward the rising sun in the east.

"I have to ask," Jorad said, after we were out of the city. "Were you really going to blow us all up?"

"I told Ammon I'd knock out his forces," I said with a sly look at Felix.

"W...wait..." Jorad said, turning in his seat. "Was that...?"

I lifted the bag of knockout powder and smiled.

Chapter Forty-Five

"Knockout!" Jorad cried to the vigilantes around him. "I couldn't believe it. I thought for sure she was going to blow us all up."

"Give me some credit." I shared a wry smile with Felix. "I'm not half as reckless as I used to be."

He, wisely, said nothing.

Our vigilantes had met up with us shortly after we arrived outside the city. For all his complaining about not being helpful, Felix wasted no time in ordering half of our vigilantes to remain in the city and await the arrival of a backup contingent. I was content to let him fall back into his old behaviors, and even Jorad said nothing about it.

Once I'd made sure Ammon had seen my soldiers, and impressed upon him that I was leaving them with plenty of bags (of what, I didn't say), the remaining vigilantes rode back to Celia's camp.

No, not Celia's camp. My camp.

"This will surely go down in the annals of Forcadelian lore. A princess vigilante fooled the prince of Kulka with simple knockout powder." Jorad hadn't stopped talking about it since we left. When he was barking orders and training cadets, it was easy to forget that he wasn't much older than I was. But all his boyish tendencies had come to the forefront.

Felix, on the other hand, hadn't said much since we'd departed. I could tell he was tired, but I hadn't even received a single chastisement for jumping out the window. It was an odd change—first allowing me to walk into the city, and now this.

"Thank you," I said to Felix, as Jorad continued babbling to anyone who was within earshot. "For saving my butt out there."

"It was a combined effort," Felix said. "Neither Jorad nor I felt right about you going in empty-handed. And I had a hunch you'd be going straight to Ammon."

"You don't want to lecture me?" I asked. "Surely, you've got an 'I told you so' in you, Felix."

"I've long since learned that doesn't work with you," he replied with a coy smile. "Besides that, you accomplished what you went to do. Ammon won't test you anymore and you're getting additional soldiers and ships. Clearly, you know what you're doing."

"Clearly!" Jorad said with a grin that made him look him ten years younger. "I still can't get over that knockout powder trick. How did you even think of it?"

"Well, somebody told me to channel the person I used to be as The Veil," I said, casting a quick look at Felix. "And that person delighted in making people think they were going to die. Did I ever tell you about the Niemenian ship?"

I amused the group with the tale of how I'd sunk a Kulkan vessel, but made everyone think it was a Niemenian one, which lasted the rest of the journey. By the time we got back to the camp, greeted, of course, by whistles of *Welcome Back, Your Majesty*, Jorad had taken over the storytelling, telling everyone about the recent events in Neveri.

"Sounds like you were successful," Katarine called. She and Luard were there to greet us at the gates. Her sharp blue eyes raked over Felix but seemed to find him well enough. "On all counts."

"Yes," I said. "Ammon will be giving me an additional hundred soldiers and five warships to help our cause."

"Five warships?" Luard said, his eyes bugging out. "You must've scared him good."

"She did," Jorad said, flashing me a smile. "He'd be foolish to betray you again."

"He was foolish to try anything at all," Felix said, wincing a little as he dismounted.

"You," Katarine said, pointing behind her. "To Nicolasa's. Now."

"Yes, ma'am," Felix said, saluting her, and wincing as he bowed.

"Did he fight?" Katarine asked.

"He sat on a wagon," I said, deciding not to elaborate and save him a lecture. "Perhaps did a little more than he should've. But he was oddly restrained. I think he's really injured."

"Perhaps," Katarine said with a knowing look behind her.

"Has there been any word from Forcadel?" I asked.

"Not a peep," Luard said. "But I confess I've been too busy planning the most beautiful wedding in the history of the four countries to pay much attention. Speaking of which, Katarine—"

"I promise, whatever you come up with will be perfectly fine," she said with a tight, but patient, smile. "As long as Bea's happy."

"But that's what she says about you," Luard said with a frown. "Fine. White flowers it is."

I shared a smile with Katarine as Luard left us. Even from a distance, the camp had already been transformed, with garlands hanging from the houses and bouquets sticking out of the torch holders along the walls. I had no doubt that Luard had pressed every pair of available hands into service.

"So when is the big day?" I asked with a grin.

"Two days," Katarine said. "I asked for a small, intimate ceremony, but—"

"I doubt Luard even heard," I said. "You know, it doesn't have to be so soon."

She made a dismissive noise. "Well, with Beswick due back any day now, Beata and I both thought it would be less worrisome for you if we kept it small and short."

"Oh, no," I said with a hearty shake of my head. "You, Lady Katarine, get the works. A long, boring ceremony. A huge dress that you can barely move in—"

"I had all that once before," she said. "When I married your brother. This time... This time I'm marrying for love, not ceremony. And speaking of romances." Katarine wagged her eyebrows. "Clearly, Felix got his way."

My face warmed. "How so?"

"He practically insisted on going with you on this journey," Katarine said. "Well? Did you kiss? You have to tell me everything. Or else I'll just have to get it from him."

"We didn't," I said, my face now as warm as the sun. "But I guess you could say we...flirted."

"It's a start," Katarine said.

"He seems different," I said. "Less insufferable, perhaps?"

"To you, perhaps. But you don't know Felix as well as I do—not the boy he was before he assumed his responsibility. He was upstanding, yes, but he used to be so much more..." She sighed. "Fun. But that was mostly August's doing. He liked to stir the pot, and Felix was usually the one behind him, half-trying to keep him from stirring, half helping." She tilted her head to the side. "I think the Felix you're seeing now is one who's stared death in the face and realized he probably shouldn't take himself so seriously."

"I think he still takes himself a little seriously," I said.

"Oh, of course, and once we move closer to taking on Ilara, he'll come back to the serious man we both know," she said, nudging me. "But he's allowing himself to love you. And I couldn't have picked a better woman for him."

At dinner that night, Jorad's retelling of my antics in Neveri had grown to epic proportions, and I finally had to step in.

"There were twenty guards in the courtyard, not a hundred," I said, placing a hand on his shoulder. "And all I had was a bag of knockout powder."

"It was still brilliant," he said, flashing a smile at me.

"You won't get him to quit talking about it," Felix said when I sat down next to him with my dinner. "He's never seen something so incredible in his life. Besides that, it helps morale."

"I suppose," I said. "I just don't want them thinking I'm superhuman or something."

"You aren't?" Felix said with mock surprise.

I swatted him with my spoon. "Has Nicolasa chided you for leaving?"

"Not as much as she probably wanted to. I do feel better— stronger, even. These ribs are the only thing that still give me trouble, but not as much as they did."

"Good," I said. "Because I hear you've got a big job in two days."

He flashed a smile. By virtue of his position in the royal guard, Felix was the only one who could under the Mother's teachings. Luard had said he could teach me how to do it, but my role in this ceremony would be secondary.

"I've been looking forward to this for years," Felix said. "I knew the moment Katarine laid eyes on Beata that they were going to be something special. I'd never seen her look so terrified in her life."

"How old was she?"

"Fifteen," Felix said. "Three years away from marrying August. And August knew, too. Wouldn't let her live it down until she admitted she thought Beata was cute." He looked down into his bowl. "I wish he was here to see this. He would've been thrilled."

I glanced at him, trying to picture him as the young, mischievous man Katarine had described. There were flashes of it, sure, but the man I knew had pushed me to be a better woman and queen. As much as Katarine may have missed the more fun version of Felix, I might've liked this one better.

"What?" he said, catching me staring.

"Nothing," I said, looking at my dinner and trying not to let myself blush.

"Excuse me, Brynna," Beata said, holding a bowl. "Could I trouble you to bring this to Celia? I've got my hands full keeping an eye on the cake for the celebration."

"Beata, you shouldn't be baking your own cake," I said with a frown.

"I would have it no other way," she said, thrusting the bowl at me as if I'd mightily offended her. She stormed back into the kitchen, leaving me holding the bowl.

"What are you going to do about her?" Felix asked.

"Who? Beata? Nothing, I—"

"No, Celia."

I sighed and palmed the bowl. "I don't know. Right now, I'm going to bring her some dinner."

"Evening," Celia said, yet again reading a book when I walked into her hut. "So the scullery maid is too good to bring me food now?"

"She's a bit busy planning her wedding," I said, placing the bowl on the desk in front of her. "I suppose you've seen the activity."

"I have," she said. "Seems odd to have such a happy celebration right before you go to war."

"It will be." I stared out the open door, which had a clear line of sight to the front of the fort. "Everyone will be occupied. Happy. Excited. Nobody will be paying attention to you."

"As if I care."

"No, but I do," I said, turning to look at her. "Tomorrow night, I want you to pack up your things and leave the camp."

She stopped and looked up at me. "Excuse me?"

"Leave." I crossed my arms over my chest. "No one would be the wiser. Just take whatever you need—supplies, weapons, food—and walk out of my camp."

"Your camp?" She leaned back in her chair.

"You said you were waiting for me to fail," I said. "But I don't think I will anymore. And so if I'm not going to fail, there's no reason to keep you in camp."

"You're willing to let me leave?" she said. "Why the change in heart?"

"I thought I was too scared to do anything about you, but that's not really it, is it? The fact of the matter is...you saved my life. And not just when Ilara stabbed me. You gave me a place to stay, food to eat, and a purpose when I had absolutely nothing. For that, I will be forever grateful."

She tilted her head up. "And now?"

"Now, I have an army. I'm growing my ranks every day. And whatever you think you can throw at me, I can handle. It's time to stop being precious with my forces—and time for you to quit wasting my time. So you have a choice: leave or help me reclaim my throne."

She sat back in her chair, looking honestly surprised. "You trust me that much?"

"Not at all," I said. "But I trust myself."
And with that, I slammed the door behind me.

Chapter Forty-Six

Katarine

The morning of my second wedding, I woke early, the butterflies in my stomach pushing me from bed. It was hard not to compare this event with my wedding to August. Then, I'd awoken at dawn to bathe and prepare for the morning wedding. My dress had taken nearly an hour to put on, requiring sewing and adjusting as the servants overlaid petticoats laced with diamonds. I could still remember the faint sadness in my heart as I watched Beata curl and style my hair, wishing I could tell her how beautiful I thought her eyes. Back then, I hadn't been brave enough to say how I felt, too focused on my duty to Niemen and my newly adopted country.

And now I was marrying her.

Instead of layers of petticoats, I was wearing my hair loose and a linen dress my bride had made for me. On my feet, the same shoes I'd been wearing when I left Forcadel. The young children who helped around camp had done their best to rinse the blood and mud from them, but they were hopelessly stained. I wore them like a badge of honor.

I did have one item from my first wedding, the beautifully sculpted brooch my sister Ariadna had given me to wear on my wedding day. It was one of the few things I'd refused to leave behind, and now I was glad for the foresight.

I settled on the cot I'd claimed the night before, running a comb through my long hair and thinking, oddly, about August. Our wedding had been all ceremony and no romance. But even though it lacked any romance, our marriage had been something special to me. I'd genuinely cared for him, and he for me. It was why he'd pushed me to be more forthcoming with Beata.

"All I want is for you to be happy here." I could still hear his low voice as we'd looked over the kingdom that we thought would be ours one day. We'd discussed our great plans for improving the infrastructure in Haymaker's Corner, and for relieving the tensions between Kulka and Niemen. About how we might parent our eventual children into becoming just and fair rulers, and once they took over, what we planned to do with our newfound freedom.

But the Mother, it seemed, had had other plans.

Still, there was a lot of August in Brynna. She had his tenaciousness, his fierce loyalty, and his rebellious streak. August would've made a great king, but he would've been comforted in knowing that his little sister was taking his mantle with pride.

I shook myself from those thoughts when Luard's laugh echoed in the distance. He and Ivan came into the sleeping hut, not caring if they woke the soldiers who'd been out training all night.

"Dearest Kitty-Kat." Luard's face was full of warmth and pride, his eyes brimming with tears. "You are the most beautiful bride I've ever laid eyes on."

"Just wait until you see Beata," I said, coming to my feet. "I'm sure she'll outshine me."

"As much as I love her, I only have eyes for you today," he said, taking my hand and spinning me around. He saw the brooch on the bed and made a noise, rushing toward it. "I remember this.

Didn't Ariadna give it to you?"

"She did." I gestured to my simple dress. "I don't know where I might wear it, though."

"Sit down," Luard said. "I think I can do something with your hair."

"You?" I glanced up at him. "I don't think I want to know where you learned such a skill."

He made a face as he picked up where I'd left off, running a comb through my locks. He gathered a section of my hair and braided it from my scalp down, fastening the pin to the point where it gathered behind my ear. A simple look, and perfect.

"Thank you," I said when he'd finished. "I'm so grateful you're here today."

His blue eyes shone with tears, and one dripped down his face. "I would be nowhere else."

Luard escorted me out of the sleeping hut into the bright morning. Birds chirped nearby, replacing the normal sounds of the camp. It seemed today our queen had given them a reprieve from training, or perhaps they had given themselves one. The blue sky was cloudless, and a cool breeze rustled the leaves of the nearby trees—almost as if it were sent from Niemen itself.

As we drew closer to the crowd, my brother's sniffles increased and I nudged him. "You can't cry like this. I'll be a mess. Just hold it together for a few more minutes."

A stringed instrument began to sing as we came into view of the gathering. Asdis's beautiful voice echoed across the camp, serenading us with a beautiful Niemenian song.

Between us was the entire camp, all wearing their dress uniforms or nicest tunics. Even the young children had been scrubbed and their hair combed—no doubt Beata's doing. They were split into two groups, leaving a path for Beata and me to walk. When the music changed, they turned in unison to face me, reminding me strongly of the first time I'd done this.

"Ready?" Luard asked.

I nodded.

He stepped into the space between the two groups, his arm steady as emotion sapped my strength. As we drew closer to the front, the faces became more familiar, the smiles wider, until I passed Nils, Hagan, and Ivan, the latter of which squeezed my hand as I passed. It was all I could do not to lose it there.

Luard stopped at the front of the group, releasing me. He pressed a kiss to my wet cheek.

"I love you, Kitty Kat," he whispered. Then, wiping his cheeks, he left me to join his guards.

The music changed once more, this time to the Forcadelian royal march. Down the makeshift aisle, Beata stood arm-in-arm with Brynna.

My breath caught in my throat as I took in the sight of my bride. She wore a simple white dress, her black, curly hair tumbling down her shoulders. She wore very little makeup, opting for a single flower in her hair, and her smile could've been visible from Niemen. Her gaze locked with mine, and her grin, if possible, grew larger.

She was the most beautiful thing I'd ever seen.

Brynna stepped forward, taking Beata with her, and my bride stumbled a little by the abrupt move. I stifled a giggle as she blushed, and beside her, Brynna ducked a smile. Their walk seemed both interminable and too short. Before I knew it, Brynna and Beata stood next to me.

"Here," Brynna said, giving Beata's hand to me. Then she kissed both Beata and me on the cheek, before retreating to Luard, wiping her cheeks hurriedly.

"Hey," Beata said softly.

"Hey," I replied.

"Are you two ready?"

Felix had joined us, wearing a dress uniform from Forcadel. It was empty of his usual badges and medals—and with a glance at Jorad, who was wearing plainclothes, I knew where he'd gotten it.

"Let's get married," I said, squeezing Beata's hands.

"Welcome," Felix bellowed, loud enough for those in the back to hear. "And thank you for joining us today as we celebrate these two beautiful people and the new life they're starting today."

Behind me, Luard began to sob, and Brynna comforted him.

"There are some who might think that this sort of ceremony is superfluous or unnecessary. After all, we are preparing for war. Our countrymen are suffering. Why should we celebrate?" His gaze landed on me. "Because even a small light in the darkness is still a light."

Beata caught my gaze and smiled, squeezing my hand.

"The brides have asked that I keep this short," Felix said. "So we'll get to it. Your Majesty, Your Highness, if you will."

Brynna nudged Luard and took his arm as they rejoined us at the front.

"I, Brynna-Larissa Archer Rhodes Lonsdale, do hereby give my permission for these two incredible women to wed," she said, her voice tight.

Luard inhaled deeply. "And I, Luard Aleksander Hasklowna, do hereby give my permission, on behalf of Queen Ariadna, for my baby sister to wed the love of her life."

Together, they handed Felix a pair of golden rings. Then Brynna helped Luard back to their place in the crowd, rubbing his back.

"Bea," Felix began, looking at my bride, "repeat after me: In the name of the Mother."

"In the name of the Mother."

"I, Beata, take you, Katarine, to be my wife, to have and to hold from this day forward. For better, for worse, for richer, for poorer..."

Her brown eyes sparkled and her voice never wavered as she promised herself to me. When she finished ("This is my solemn vow"), she smiled.

"Kat," Felix said, looking at me, "repeat after me: In the name of the Mother."

The words came out, but I didn't remember saying them. All I knew was I would never let anything come between us. Not distance, not politics, not even our differences of opinion on how to organize my sitting room back in Forcadel.

"This is my solemn vow," I finished.

"Let us pray," Felix said, covering our joined hands with his. "O Mother, please bless these two, and all of us, as we journey through these next few treacherous weeks. Help Bea and Kat speak in love and not anger and keep them safe from harm. In Your name."

"Amen."

Felix grinned at me. "Well, go on and kiss her."

I didn't need to be told twice. Gathering my new wife in my arms, I captured her soft lips with mine as cheers erupted behind us.

Chapter Forty-Seven

I'd never seen Celia's camp so light and full of love. Everywhere I looked, smiles and laughter echoed between the walls that had formerly been solely for stoicism and fear. It was what I hoped all of Forcadel could look like one day.

Watching Beata and Katarine exchange their vows had been one of the most moving experiences of my life. What they had, how they looked at one another—that was true love. The kind that lasted for decades, that was written about in song and fable. It was a terrifying concept to feel something so fully, and yet, it made me want the same for myself one day.

The crowd dispersed toward the mess hall, which had been similarly transformed by garlands and ribbons in every corner. A cake stood at the front of the room, with an entire roasted pig nearby. The soldiers had given themselves assignments to serve and assist, though many of them stopped to congratulate the new wives as they made their rounds.

"Brynna," Katarine said, coming to kiss me on the cheek, "thank you for this."

"I did nothing," I said, squeezing Beata's hand. "I'm just grateful that you two have found each other."

We were interrupted by Ivan and Asdis, and I took my cue to leave them to enjoy the festivities. I retreated to the back of the room to fill my goblet and watch the action. The music struck back up and the brides took to the floor, followed by a very emotional dance with Katarine and Luard. Then the soldiers joined in the fun, dancing fast and slow and everything in between.

Nils and Hagan proved to be the best in the group, dazzling all of us with complex spins and dips. Each took a bride for a turn around the floor, earning cheers—the loudest coming from Luard. When the music grew slower, the mess hall filled with couples once more.

"Ah," Felix said, sitting down next to me. "This is beautiful, isn't it?"

I nodded. "I've never been to a wedding before."

"That's not true. You went to your aunt's when you were a child." He chuckled. "And as I recall, you spent the whole time with a sour look on your face."

"Sounds about right," I said with a genuine laugh. "How are you feeling?"

"I'll be sore tomorrow," he said, rubbing his ribs. "But Kat's worth it."

Katarine and Beata came twirling by, laughing as they swayed together.

"I wish August were here," Felix said softly. "He would've been crying worse than Luard."

I cast a look at Katarine's brother, who seemed to have enjoyed his share of the wine as he wiped his moist cheeks. "I don't know if that's possible."

"Perhaps," Felix said, coming to stand. "Well, we can't have our queen sitting by herself all night. Come dance with me."

"Dance?" I shook my head. "I don't dance."

"I'll teach you. There's nothing to it."

Before I could answer, he snatched my hand and led me out to the center of the hall and gently pulling me toward him. The melody was still slow, and everyone on the floor seemed lost in their own little worlds.

"Relax," Felix said, sliding his hand around the small of my back, sending a zing of fire from his fingertips across my body. With the other, he threaded his fingers through mine. "Just let me lead you."

"When has that ever worked?" I asked with a smile.

"There's a first time for everything."

It was difficult to relax into his touch, but soon the slight movement of his hand against my back eased me into trusting him. We swayed as I found my footing in this new movement. His breath tickled my forehead, reminding me how close we were. But as soon as the tempo increased, he released my back and grinned devilishly at me.

"Felix, I don't think—"

"You run on rooftops. I'm sure you're very graceful."

I wasn't, but I gave it a good effort. Midway through the song, Nils broke in and took me from Felix, flinging me and spinning me with wild abandon. I could do nothing but laugh and let the Niemenian throw me around. When it was over, he handed me back to Felix with a kiss to my cheek.

"We'll have to practice," he said, tapping my nose. "For your wedding."

My eyes widened and I laughed nervously as Felix reappeared for another dance. He pulled me close, and our noses almost touched. Even though the music had slowed again, my pulse had not.

"What is it?" Felix asked. "You look upset."

S. Usher Evans

I shook my head, but caught Jorad's, who offered me a genuine grin and a thumbs-up. *Felix is in love with you*, he'd said.

"Why did you sacrifice yourself for me?" I asked softly. "Is it because you love Forcadel, or because…"

"I would sacrifice myself a million times for you," he said.

"But because I'm the monarch, or because…" My face was on fire. "Because you actually care about me? About Brynna the person."

"Can't it be both?" Felix said. "It's true, I would've done the same for August or your father, but you…I do love you, Brynna."

My heart skipped but I pushed my excitement to the side. "You know that if I get back on the throne," I said slowly, "you'll have the same problems we had in Forcadel. My role as queen, marriages as alliances—"

He tilted his head closer, his voice dropping to a whisper. "If you're willing to climb mountains and wade through swamps for the country you love, I know that if you want us to be together, you'll make it work." He pressed his forehead to mine. "And I was foolish to doubt you."

I fell into the rhythm of the music, allowing myself to smile as we swayed together, his forehead against mine, his thumb making circles on the back of my hand. I didn't care who saw us, who noticed the grin on my face. Nor did I worry about what might happen in the future. This moment was perfect.

"Your Majesty," Jorad said, bowing low. "I hate to interrupt."

Then why did you? "What is it?"

"Elisha returned. She brought this."

He handed me a note and my heart dropped into my stomach.

Bring the ond to Galden, and I'll give you the other girl.

"Brynn?" Felix asked. "What is it?"

"That son of a bitch," I whispered, balling up the paper. "You enjoy the festivities. I'm going to go deal with this—"

Felix grabbed my hand before I could run and pulled me back

to him. "What is it? What's happened? Is it Ammon?"

"No," I said. "Beswick."

"Beswick," Luard said, walking over. "What's happened?"

"Beswick?" Now Katarine and Beata joined our small group. Had my face been so easy to read?

"It's nothing to concern yourselves with right now," I said, forcing a smile onto my face. "Just stay and enjoy the wedding."

"Beswick's taken Aline, and he sent Elisha back with a message," Jax said behind me. "There, now you don't have to ruin anything."

Felix went pale, and Katarine shared a look with Beata.

"I'll take care of this," I said, backing away from them. "You all stay here and—"

"Not a chance," Beata said, ending any further arguments. "We all knew Beswick would resurface eventually."

I wanted to argue further, but that would just waste time I didn't have. "Meet me in my office in ten minutes."

"Do you want us to clear the mess hall?" Luard asked, looking around.

"No," I said, glancing to the hut out the front door, where the twirl of smoke had been absent since early this morning. "My office."

I changed out of my dress and into my tunic, already feeling more like the leader again. But before I joined the rest of the group, I went to Nicolasa's hut. I had a hunch Elisha was there—it was the first place any of us went when we were injured or scared. The younger girl wore a dark tunic and a blanket draped over her head and shoulders and the mug of calming tea steamed up to her red and tear-streaked face. She looked unharmed. For that, at least, I was grateful.

She gasped a sob when I walked into the room and ducked her

head lower.

"I'm s-sorry," she whispered. "I f-failed you."

"Oh, no," I said, crossing the room to sit next to her. "You did exactly the right thing. You brought me the message."

"S-she made me r-run, but t-they caught m-me," Elisha continued with a small hiccup. "They t-told me t-that if I didn't t-tell you that they'd…that they'd…"

"Shh," I whispered, cupping her wet cheek. "You did great. You're here, and we're going to rescue Aline. But I need you to take a deep breath and tell me everything you know."

She took another long drink of the tea to calm herself. She was scared, but Celia's training kicked in as she forced herself to calm down.

"We were doing what you said," she began in a clear voice. "Screwing up Beswick's business. Mostly, we were getting to his food shipments before he could and giving them to the people. That made him real mad."

"I bet," I said with a smile. "You cut off his money supply."

She nodded and took another sip of tea. "We had a good thing. I'd keep watch, Aline would do the Veil thing, and we'd both escape. But I guess…" She swallowed hard. "I guess he got smart. Last night, we were surrounded before we could… And I didn't…"

"It's fine," I said, rubbing her cheek before she lost it again. "Where are they now?"

"I don't know," she said. "But they want you to meet them in Galdon tomorrow night." She shivered. "I ran all the way. Didn't get tired once."

"Then you rest," I said, coming to stand. "You've done remarkably well, and more than I ever expected of you. I promise, we will get Aline home."

I helped her lie on the cot and tucked her in, giving her one final pat on the cheek for good measure. Then, I left her to find Nicolasa out in her mint garden.

"Thank you," I said. "She's resting now."

"She's strong," Nicolasa said. "One day, she will make a great warrior. Just as you did."

I put my hands on my hips, exhaling the tension from my shoulders. Although it was hard, I let go of the urge for revenge and focused on the problem at hand. Beswick had made his move —clearly, he wasn't in the mood for friendship. And if I wanted to defeat him this time, I needed to keep myself unemotional.

"Do we still have hyblatha around here?" I asked. It was a common herb in calming teas, but in powder form caused violent hallucinations.

She nodded. "Before you arrived, Celia was having me stock up. We should have nearly fifty bags ready for use. But there's no tinneum."

The antidote. It grew in Niemen, and Celia had been in the process of importing it to grow in Forcadel. "I have a few pieces left. We'll just have to ration it between all of us."

She looked up at the sky, something unreadable crossing her face. "There's a storm coming. A terrible energy gathering to the south. I fear it will come unrelenting and unmerciful."

I turned to her, a chill skittering down my spine. Nicolasa's predictions were never wrong. "How do I prepare?"

"Pray to the Mother," she said. "It's all any of us can do."

Chapter Forty-Eight

I walked into Celia's office, now very cramped with Luard, Felix, Jorad, and Jax...and Beata and Katarine already out of their wedding attire and in dark tunics, albeit holding hands.

"You two shouldn't be here," I said softly. "You should be off enjoying marital bliss. We'll handle this."

"That horrible creature has taken one of our own," Beata said. "How can we celebrate?"

"And I'm on your Council," Katarine replied. "There's nowhere else I'd rather be."

"How's Elisha?" Jax spoke softly and without his usual sarcasm. Clearly, he'd bonded more with the kid than I'd thought.

"Resting. She's in good hands." I sat down at the head of the table and folded my hands together. "Beswick wants to meet in Galdon tomorrow night. If we bring him the bag of ond, he'll hand over Aline."

"Or he's planning on killing you," Luard said.

"Probably, but he won't get that chance," I said. "What I would like to do is find a way to maneuver our forces into the city without him knowing. We did this before when we met Keiran in the city, but Beswick's bringing everything he's got. So we should be prepared."

"How many people are we talking about?" Luard asked.

I sat back, chewing my lip. "At one point, Beswick had hundreds, maybe close to a thousand, people working for him. But he suffered a blow after Ilara took over—nearly half the names in that notebook had either left town or disappeared. I'd wager his muscle force did the same." I hated having to peg a number when I didn't know, but I had to make an assumption. "Let's say he brings a hundred."

"I doubt a hundred people would fit in this tiny village," Katarine said, pulling the map closer to her.

"This is his last bit of ond," I said. "We'd better expect him to bring his entire operation. And then some." I glanced down at the map. "Forget Beswick's men inside the village, how are we supposed to move our troops? There's wide open fields on all sides. He'll see us coming for miles."

"Unless we invade in plain sight," Jorad said, taking the map from Katarine. "We have the benefit of the river. We could move soldiers in by water, masquerading as freight from Skorsa and Forcadel. Should Beswick bring the numbers you fear, we can quickly move into position to help."

"And we can acquire more soldiers in Skorsa," Felix said. "Joella's troops are still there, aren't they?"

"By the Mother, they are," Luard said with a grin.

"But they aren't vigilantes," I said.

"In this case, numbers beat all," Luard said. "That's nearly two-fifty—"

"No," Jorad said. "Only a hundred and thirty are fit for battle."

"Agreed," I said. "And I don't want to leave the camp

completely defenseless, so we'll leave twenty soldiers here."

"One hundred and ten, then, plus the fifty from Skorsa," Katarine said. "Still more than enough to quell his forces. We can take Niemenian fishing boats from Skorsa. They'll hold twenty-five soldiers each. We'll have one docked on the northern side of the city and one on the southern side. You'll take your thirty vigilantes into the city."

Luard grinned. "Beswick thinks you've come underprepared, and when he attacks, we'll overwhelm him with your forces. He won't know what hit him."

I chewed my lips. "I don't know if the vigilantes are ready for this. Beswick won't hesitate to kill them."

"Brynn, they aren't just vigilantes, they're trained soldiers," Felix said. "They know what they're getting into and can handle themselves."

"So what do we do?" I said. "Hope that Beswick doesn't shoot me the moment I set foot inside the city?" I shook my head. "There's far too many unknowns here."

"Then perhaps I meet with him in your stead," Katarine said. "As both an official Niemenian envoy and your representative."

"I'm not sending you in there alone," I said.

"I'll go with her," Felix replied. "I know Beswick now. It'll be nice to speak with him again."

"You aren't going, either," I replied. "You've barely healed."

"No, Felix should travel to Skorsa and handle the troops," Luard said. "We send my guard with Kat, they can protect her. And Beswick won't kill her until he's had a chance to chat. You can even promise to open an official channel of ond with him."

"So we make him think I'm still offering a peace agreement?" I asked, nodding slowly. "And when he inevitably declines it, we attack?"

"Exactly," Luard said. "My team will ensure Kat makes it to safety while the rest of you do...well, you do the rest."

I sat back in my chair, running through the scenario and all possible alternatives in my mind. If we could catch Beswick off guard for once—instead of the other way around—perhaps it might be enough to get the upper hand.

"How soon can you get the troops out of here?" I asked Felix.

"They can be ready within the next hour," he said. "They're trained for this."

"Then do it," I said. "Luard, you go with him to Skorsa to wrangle the troops." I looked behind him to Jax. "Can you manage the vigilantes? Get them into position and be ready?"

"I suppose," he drawled. "And the scouts?"

"I'll handle them." I rose. "Do we all have our assignments? Any questions, concerns, issues?" Silence. "Let's take out a crime boss then. Dismissed."

Within half an hour, there were four horses ready to ride east to Skorsa. I helped Felix climb onto one of them, watching his face for any signs of pain. I didn't see any, but that didn't mean he didn't feel it. Nicolasa had sent him off with a bag of medicine, but I still wished he'd stay behind and rest.

"Listen to me," I said, placing my hand on his calf. "I know you'll be coming in with the troops, but you're in no shape to fight. I want you to be my eyes and organize these troops, do you understand?"

He covered my hand with his. "I promise, Brynn."

"Tell Jo I'm looking forward to seeing her again," I said with a smile. "And make sure to keep Luard out of trouble as well."

"Oh, Brynna, I never get into trouble," Luard said with a charming grin. Ivan and Asdis, behind him, rolled their eyes in unison.

"I'll see you tomorrow night," I said, taking a step back. "Just...be careful."

And with that, they rode out of the camp, leaving nothing but dust and anxiety in their wake. I tried to find comfort in the fact that their destination was Skorsa, a friendly town, and that they would be providing backup. But it was hard to tell the tightness in my chest anything.

Midday, I assembled the next group—the vigilantes Jax would be leading into the city to infiltrate it. They stood before me wearing masks and cloaks identical to the ones I donned in Forcadel.

"You look good as The Veil," I said to Jax, whose mask was in his hand.

"Hmph," he said, stuffing it in his back pocket as if he were ashamed of it. "Locke tells me that he's confident these soldiers are ready to go."

"Then I am as well," I replied.

If I told him that I had confidence in him, it might've earned me a rude gesture so I kept it to myself. Instead, I addressed the line of soldiers.

"Those of you who went to Galdon before will be very familiar with this plan," I said. "We'll enter the city in waves. You twelve will be coming as weary travelers and buying a night at the inn. You ten, I want coming in under cover of darkness. The city is open to fields and roads to the north, west, and south, and accessible only by river to the east. Pick your route and don't follow anyone else. The rest of you, keep watch on the perimeter. Watch who comes and who goes—and who looks like they belong with Beswick. I'm sending along the younger scouts as well. They'll be placed between you and the tavern where we're meeting. If you're needed, you'll hear it."

I looked around at their faces, all cloaked in black masks. It was hard not to feel a little twinge of pride.

"Good luck. Dismissed."

They turned on their heels and split off to their assignments. Three rode into the darkness after Felix and Luard, and the rest, I had faith, would follow when they saw fit. Jax was the last to mount, the black mask stuffed into his back pocket.

"I'm surprised that he's bringing it," Jorad commented. "Seems like he's taken well to this new mantle."

"Captain of the Veils?" I said, trying the phrase out in my mind. "It's an interesting concept."

"I was wondering..." He cleared his throat. "I know you asked me to assist in the movement of soldiers to the south, but I was hoping for a different assignment."

I furrowed my brow. "What kind?"

"Since Captain Llobrega's returned and mostly recovered from his ordeal, I thought I might be of more use to you as the cadet trainer," he said. "It's the role I hoped I might take from the captain back in Forcadel one day. I've grown to like these kids and I'd like to stay behind and keep an eye on them. And when you get back, perhaps we can discuss that graduation ceremony."

"I'd like that," I said with a smile. "But are you sure Felix would like to give up that duty? I seem to recall it was one of his favorites."

"I have a feeling Felix may be otherwise occupied," Jorad said with a bit of a smile. "You looked quite cozy the other night. I felt bad interrupting."

"I'm glad you did," I said, blushing bright red at the thought of everyone seeing us dance. "But since you're staying, I'd like you to do me a favor."

"Anything."

"Keep a close eye on Elisha. She's a tough kid, but I know what it's like to feel like you failed everyone." I glanced at Nicolasa's hut. "Once we get Aline back, I'll need to pick her brain about Forcadel. So I need her to be strong enough for that task."

"I'll do my best," he said, saluting and bowing. "Good luck, Your Majesty."

Chapter Forty-Nine

I had a fitful sleep, partially because of my grinding nerves and partially because of the activity outside the sleeping hut. When I finally gave up, it was midday, and the final few riders were finishing their preparations. Nils and Hagan were escorting Katarine, and I would be riding with them for most of the way.

Before I saddled my horse, I ventured into the forest to retrieve the bag of ond that I'd left there. The bag was small and insignificant compared to all the trouble Beswick was going through to retrieve it.

I brought it back into the camp where Katarine was saying her goodbyes to Beata.

"You promise me you won't take any risks," Beata said, holding Katarine's face close to hers. "The moment things erupt, I want you to run as fast as you can."

"I promise," Katarine said, kissing her. "Are you sure I can't convince you to go to Skorsa?"

"My place is here." She winked at me. "Blackberry tarts when you return victorious."

"Thank you for staying behind," I said.

"Someone has to," she said, casting a coy look at Jorad and Locke, who was also staying to help guard the camp. "We'll be fine, I promise."

I hoisted myself into the saddle as Katarine's eyes grew misty. She twisted the gold band around her finger as she shared an unspoken conversation with Beata. The other woman patted the horse's rear and kissed Katarine's hand gently. And without another word, we departed.

We rode hard, my pulse pounding as loudly as our horses' hooves. We made good time, reaching the checkpoint just up the road from the city as the sun began to sink in the distance. Katarine had been silent the whole ride, but her nervousness was palpable.

"What do I do if he takes me?" she asked.

"Fight as hard as you can to get free," I said. "There'll be a swarm of soldiers nearby, and my vigilantes, so you shouldn't be in danger for long."

"But what if—"

"We can what if all day," I said, turning to her. "But all that will do is make you more nervous."

She exhaled and nodded. "I'm just not used to this sort of thing."

"What?" I made a face. "You lied to Ilara for months."

"That's different," she said. "Ilara was somewhat unpredictable, but at least she and I were on the same page in terms of consequences. I don't have the faintest idea how to deal with a criminal."

"It's more or less the same," I said. "All you need to do is find out what Beswick wants and figure out a way to make him do what you want instead. Just like you did with Ilara."

She gave a weak smile. "I wasn't very good with Ilara."

"Now's not the time to doubt yourself. You're a Veil now, and a married woman. When you go in there, think about Beata and all the happy times you're going to have when you get home. Let that focus you and remind you why you're there."

Finally, she nodded. "What should I say to him?"

"You're going to negotiate the release of Aline in exchange for the ond," I said, nodding to Nils, who had the bag in his hand. "Beswick may try to take it from you, but he won't harm you."

"And if he..." She paused and took a breath. "Never mind."

"I've authorized you to give him the ond and to let him know there's more coming if he agrees to my terms," I said. "Because I want to ally with him. But we both know he won't go for that. Still, I want you to try as if you think he might. And when things go south, you, Nils, and Hagan just need to get out of there. We'll take care of the rest."

She exhaled softly and squeezed my hand, the weight of her new ring pressing into my skin. "Thank you for trusting me to do this."

"Honestly, Kat, I wouldn't have anyone else," I said. "You're the best liar I know."

"I will assume that's a compliment."

I did have a lot of faith in Katarine, but absolutely zero in Beswick, so almost as soon as we parted, I raced toward the city. Katarine and the others would be coming in on the eastern road, whereas I would be joining Jax and the others to the south. There was a smattering of farmhouses and structures just outside the city, making it easy for me to sneak closer. Even before I got inside, I saw two of Beswick's goons standing watch.

A short whistle got my attention and I looked up toward the source. Malka waved at me from the roof of a barn, silently beckoning me to follow her. She led me to a wagon pushed up against the farmhouse, which allowed me to climb to the roof.

"Evening," I said, crouching down next to her. "You realize we can't get into the city from here, right?" The next house was at least a hundred yards away.

"Jax told me to wait for you here," she said. "We found another means into the city, but Beswick's people showed up and closed it." She pressed her lips together and whistled two short chirps. The response came back in the form of an arrow laden with knockout powder.

The guards slumped to the ground and before I could move, two dark shadows appeared. They tied up the guards and dragged them into a nearby building. A few moments later, the vigilantes reappeared dressed as guards.

I'd never been prouder in my entire life.

Together, we jumped off the roof and passed the guards, who saluted me as I went by. We hurried into a nearby alleyway, Malka leading me toward the stack of crates. Waiting for me on the roof was Jax.

He offered no snide remark, so I skipped the pleasantries. "How are we looking?"

"Not great," Jax said with a grimace. "Come with me."

He led me on a roundabout trip toward the southeastern part of the city—where a shipload of my troops should have docked. Instead, I found a large group of people gathered. I squinted to get a better look—there were women and children.

"What in the Mother's name?"

"Beswick's been here a while," Jax said. "He had his goons round up all the people and put them here. What he plans to do with them, I have no idea."

"They're hostages," I said. "I'd wager there's some leftover ond under the docks."

"Wouldn't put it past him."

I cursed softly. "Any sign of our troops?"

"Not here," Jax said. "But Felix is pretty smart. He'll work out another way into the city."

High praise, coming from Jax. "We don't have time to waste. Katarine will be getting into the city any minute now."

Under the cover of an overcast night sky, we moved into the city, staying out of sight of the patrolling guards. Jax's observation had been accurate; clearly Beswick had been planning this for a while.

When we paused on top of a building, I whispered to Jax. "Do we have a count of Beswick's people?"

"No," he said. "But it's more than a hundred."

Another curse rolled off my lips as we kept moving. The buildings and street names matched the map in my mind, and my pulse quickened as we closed in on the tavern where the hand-off would be occurring. Outside, there were at least ten bodyguards the size of large trees standing with their hands folded in front of them.

Jax grabbed the back of my neck and pushed me flat on the rooftop.

"What?" I whispered.

"There's someone on the roof of the inn," he said.

Putting my hood up, I peered over the arch of the roof to look on the other side. Beswick had gotten wise to my routes, it seemed. The guard didn't look to be paying too much attention to his post, but he would still sound the alarm.

Quietly, I assembled my crossbow and knockout powder and rested it on the ledge. When the guy on the roof wasn't looking, I let the arrow fly. The arrowhead embedded itself in the roof, and the guard turned to look at it.

My heart dropped into my stomach as he fell forward, sliding off the roof. But he was caught—by one of my vigilantes—Narin. He flashed me a thumbs-up and pulled the comatose body up the slope of the roof, disappearing onto the other side.

"That was close," I whispered.

"Your Majesty," whispered a male voice behind me—Orman. "If you want to get closer to listen, we're in position."

Jax made a face. "Maybe I trained them too well."

"I mean, I am impressed." I flashed him a grin. "I never had it so easy in Forcadel."

"Before you go," Jax said, reaching into his slingbag and handing me a small bag. "Here."

Inside was a pair of listening cups—not mine, but similar.

"I thought you said you didn't need Nestori tricks," I said with a smile.

"I didn't need *your* Nestori tricks," he grumbled. "But since yours aren't here…"

I hid my grin as I stuck the cups into my slingbag and followed Orman across the rooftop to the inn. I pressed my finger against my lips as I quietly bent over the eaves, looking into the dark room and searching for signs of movement. When I saw none, I let myself in with the glass cutter. As quietly as I could, I tip-toed across the room to where I knew Beswick would be meeting with Katarine and lowered myself flat on the floor. I dug out Jax's listening cups and drilled a small hole in the floor with my hand drill.

With the small metal tube stuck in the hole, I pressed the cup to my ear and waited.

Chapter Fifty

Katarine

I fidgeted with the gold ring on my finger as the carriage rattled through the darkening landscape. I tried to focus on everything except what I would be doing—the Niemenian carriage I sat in, the faint scent of Luard's cologne that permeated the plush seats, the idle chatter of Nils and Hagan above me. It did little to dispel my anxiety.

I pushed aside the curtain on the window to look at the gray sky above. Brynna had said the Nestori predicted a storm. It didn't help the flutter of nerves in the pit of my stomach.

The carriage came to a halt, and I swallowed hard as Nils's muffled voice spoke to someone. Smoothing my sweaty palms down my skirt, I straightened my shoulders and opened the door, ducking my head out with what I hoped was a look of annoyance.

"What's the hold-up?" I asked.

Five guards were blocking our path. They wore no colors; they most assuredly were Beswick's men.

"City's closed," one said. "Turn around or else."

"We're invited," Nils said, handing over a slip of paper—the note Beswick had sent to Brynna. The man reviewed it momentarily, then nodded to his compatriots. They shuffled out of the way, but he remained in the center of the road.

"Out of the carriage," he said. "You walk from here."

Hagan started to argue, but I was quicker. "Fine. I could use the fresh air."

I stepped out of the carriage and smoothed my skirts and hair while Nils and Hagan retrieved the ond from inside. They shared an unspoken argument about who would carry it, but in the end, Hagan won. He tied the bag to his hip and rested his hand on top of it.

"May we go now?" I asked the guard. With a grimace, he allowed us to continue.

Once we'd passed the initial guards, the city was eerily quiet, and it set my nerves on edge. It wasn't even that there was a curfew —it seemed as if everyone in the city had up and disappeared. Windows were open, doors swung in the light breeze, and signs declaring businesses open still hung in the shops.

"What in the Mother's name?" Nils whispered. "Where is everyone?"

"Stay sharp," Hagan said, keeping his hand on the ond. "Something smells wrong here."

"Take heart, Kat," Nils said, giving me a half-smile. "If all else fails, we can lob this stuff at his face."

"With all the torches around?" Hagan said, giving his husband a look. "We'd all be dead in seconds."

"I'm just trying to keep her nerves steady."

"Well, with you talking about blowing people up, I don't see how that's possible."

I smiled. "Is this the sort of wedded bliss I can expect from Beata?"

"She's Forcadelian," Nils said. "I assume it'll be much worse."

I twisted my ring again, exhaling to myself. "At this point, I'll just be happy just to see her again."

"You will," Hagan said. "The Mother will look after you. Put your trust in Her."

"As should we all," Nils said.

We turned a corner onto the main street and were met by another set of guards, this time in front of the inn where we were meeting Beswick. Nils and Hagan moved in front of me, Nils placing his hand on his sword.

"Who are you?" the man said, pointing his sword at Nils.

"We're here to meet with Lord Beswick," I said softly. "We have what he wants."

He eyed me uncertainly, but then stepped aside and let us continue.

Brynna had said there would be vigilantes on the rooftops, but I didn't even want to look. My anxiety might spin out of control if I saw someone. I whispered another prayer to the Mother that all would be well and kept moving forward.

The inn was exactly as Brynna had described it—thank the Mother for her attention to detail. There would be enough unknowns in this situation without having to worry about what color the paint was. I twisted my ring one final time before telling myself to put it down. From here on, I would be as still as a mountain.

The doors opened, and I nodded to Nils and Hagan. They allowed me to go before them, passing under the threshold and into the dark room first. There, I found Johann Beswick, just as I remembered him from the church.

"You're not the person I wanted to see," he said, leaning forward onto the table. "Was I not clear in my message?"

"You were." My voice was much stronger than I felt, and I let myself believe my own lie. "Unfortunately, Her Majesty is trying to reclaim her kingdom and couldn't make this meeting. Trouble in

Neveri with the Kulkans. She does send her most sincere apologies and her most trusted representative in her place. And she thought it fitting to send a princess of the kingdom from which you stole the ond."

Beswick made a face but offered me a seat. I crossed the room and sat down, but my two guards were barred entrance.

"Just us, Lady Katarine," he said. "Your guards need not stick around."

"I would feel better if they did," I said. "You are a man with a reputation."

"I have twenty swords at my command," he said, flashing me a menacing grin. "I doubt your two would do much to protect you."

This wasn't part of the plan, my voice whispered in my mind.

Brynna will figure it out came the other, more confident voice. The one that was beginning to sound more like the princess vigilante herself.

"Very well," I said, looking behind me. "You may wait outside."

Nils and Hagan opened their mouths to protest, but I cast them a stern look, with just a flash of pleading. The seconds passed like hours as they made their decision.

Finally, Nils nodded. "We'll be outside."

Hagan walked forward, earning a pair of swords to his throat. He lifted the bag of ond up. "I think you want this."

"Yes, yes," Beswick said, waving his hand. "Let him put it down."

The swords disappeared, and Hagan placed the bag onto the table, releasing a small whiff of metallic odor. He winked at me, hidden from Beswick, and my heart beat in my throat as I begged him silently to leave with his husband. Finally, he straightened and walked out the back door.

The door shut, and I couldn't help but jump.

"Calm yourself, Lady Katarine," Beswick said, snapping his

fingers. A figure appeared out of the darkness with a bottle of wine and two glasses. "You seem like you could use something for your nerves."

"Perhaps it's the twenty guards," I said. "Or that we're sitting in a room full of flames with a bag of ond."

Beswick pulled the bag toward him while his attendant poured the wine. He reached into it with his entire hand, running his fingers through the ond. It was unnerving to see him so flippant with such a precious material.

"It's all here," he said.

"Where's Aline?" I asked.

He flicked his wrist and the door behind him opened. A teenager was frog-marched in, her mouth gagged and hands tied in front of her. She had a light sheen of sweat on her forehead, but there was murderous intent in her gaze.

"She's unharmed. For the moment," Beswick said. "As are the citizens of this city."

I blinked. "The citizens? What citizens?"

"It's clear that I can't trust your little wannabe queen," Beswick said. "So I had to make sure she didn't try anything funny. I had my soldiers round up everyone in this little hamlet and relocate them to the docks. There's a bag of ond under the wood, just waiting for someone to strike a match."

I swallowed. "You have more ond?"

"Of course," he said.

But that made no sense. If he had more, why not use it down in Forcadel? "Seems like you went through a lot of trouble for just one bag," I said, hoping he'd share more of his thought process with me. "If you had more, why are we here at all?"

"It's not just about the ond," he said. "What I want is for your little princess flea to disappear. Be killed, lose her army, I don't care how. She has been annoying me for far too long, and I'm ready to send a message."

"She sent me here to ask for an alliance," I said. "Would you be interested if I promised more ond?"

He waved dismissively. "I don't need your promises. I can get my own material."

"Then why go through all this trouble to get one bag back?" Then, understanding dawned. "This is personal, isn't it?"

"It's always personal," Beswick said. "Which is why it's going to be so wonderful when I deposit your dead body on her doorstep."

My heart began to race. "There's no need to resort to that. You have the ond."

"But as I said," he said with a smile. "It wasn't about the ond. She needs to learn that—"

There was commotion outside and the mustachioed man by the window moved the curtain away. "The guards are gone."

"Check it out," Beswick said to the two by the door.

As I turned, cold steel pressed against my neck. My gaze went to Beswick.

"I knew she was listening," he replied devilishly. "And now she's walking right into my trap."

The door flew open and I was yanked to my feet, the knife still pressed to my throat. Brynna walked into the room, masked and beautiful. I'd never seen her in her Veil glory, but if she faced down criminals this way back in Forcadel, she'd been a truly fearsome creature.

And right now, all that fury was trained on Beswick.

"Let her go, and we can talk," she growled, her voice low and dangerous. "This is your last chance."

He laughed. "You're outnumbered."

"Am I?" She cracked a humorless smile. "I learned a few things from dealing with you over the years. Namely that you're a slime ball who can't be trusted."

"And yet you sent your envoy in here to talk alliances."

"I changed my mind. I think I just want you behind bars." She raised her sword. "So why don't we just skip all the crap and just get to it?"

"Fine by me."

The room filled with people, none of them Brynna's. And before I could say another word, Beswick's man pulled me out of the room and into the darkness of the night.

Chapter Fifty-One

"Kat!" I screamed as she disappeared out the door behind me. Before I could follow her, the ten guards in the room pulled out an assortment of weapons, all pointed at me. I turned to Aline, who was shaking and pale on the floor and stepped in front of her.

"Go," I ordered.

"What?" She looked up at me.

I palmed my knives. "Go. I'll take care of these assholes. You've done more than enough for me."

She gave me another look then scrambled out the door behind me. I expected some of them to go after her, but they stayed put. Clearly, I was who they wanted.

Slowly, I twirled my knives in my hands. "They keep telling me I've fought off ten at once. Let's see if I can actually do it."

They rushed me, but their coordination was their downfall. I dropped to the ground, allowing two of them to run each other through. In the confusion, I rolled forward, slicing through the calves of the two closest to me.

Before I could make another move, a hand closed around my throat, yanking me from the melee. I saw stars as my windpipe closed, but I brought my elbows down on his arm, freeing myself. My fist went to his solar plexus and he doubled over.

More hands grabbed me and threw me backward, and I landed hard on a chair that crumbled beneath my weight. Blinking, I looked up into the faces of the remaining five, ready to kill.

"Well?" I said, lifting my chin.

But they didn't come for me; rather, they dropped their weapons and held up their hands.

"Always coming to save your ass," came Jax's voice from the doorway behind me. I spun to find him, as well as ten others, with their crossbows aimed at Beswick's men. There were even more pointing their crossbows through the windows.

"What took you so long?" I said with a wry smile.

"Things are a bit hairy outside," he said, glancing behind him to his people. "You five, take these out to the field then return. We got a long way to go."

"What do you mean hairy? What do you mean, field?" I said, following him outside. There I found a smattering of my soldiers fighting with Beswick's. On the rooftops, the vigilantes were taking people down with arrows.

"Where's Beswick?" I said, spinning.

"I don't know, inside?" Jax said.

"He went with Kat," I said. "We have to find him before he leaves the city."

"He's not going far," Jax replied, but followed me as I climbed up to the roof. "The city's practically surrounded with our people."

"Except on the southern docks," I said pointedly.

"Then we'd better get there, and fast."

367

We took off along the rooftops, as the streets were clogged with fighting. There were more soldiers, but I couldn't tell where they'd come from. Were they the ones I'd brought from camp, or had Felix managed to find more somewhere? Either way, they were going toe-to-toe with Beswick's thugs, so I assumed they were on my side.

"Halt!"

Just as we jumped onto a rooftop, we were met by a gaggle of ten of Beswick's soldiers. Still more appeared, seemingly out of thin air, in the roofs around us. We were trapped.

"Oh, come on," I said panting a little. "Can't you guys just get out of my way for once?"

"Lord Beswick said we were to stop you at all costs," said the woman in the front. "And that he'd give us a nice reward if we brought you back to him alive."

I shared a look with Jax. Alive?

"But your friend can die," she said, walking toward him.

Jax pulled the knives from their sheaths and caught her sword before it fell. I jumped in to parry two of the others, but another slid down my cheek—too close for comfort. I elbowed the perpetrator in the face then kicked another body. But still more came.

"Jax, we need to go," I cried, as he pressed against my back.

"I don't think that's really an option right now," he snarled. "Unless you've got something in your bag."

I ducked a fist that landed hard on Jax's shoulder and he fell forward. I spun around to face the attackers—eight of them. Too many to take on without a little help.

"Jax," I said, digging in my slingbag. "Do you have the tinneum I gave you?"

"Ugh."

"I'll take that as a yes."

I threw a bag of hyblatha in the air then used my crossbow to split it, raining the hallucinogenic down on top of us. As quickly as I could, I stuffed the minty tinneum in my mouth, making sure Jax had done the same. It wasn't a moment too soon, as the guards started screaming and pointing at imaginary visions.

"Let's—"

A nearby guard's fist connected with the back of my head, and the wad of tinneum flew from my mouth. The hyblatha's sweet scent filled my nose, and the world around me faded away. What had once been a rooftop was now the forest—my forest. Celia's forest.

Lightning flashed overhead, and a deluge of rain came falling. The storm Nicolasa had predicted had arrived. It stung my eyes, blinding me to everything, and yet I could still see. I could see...

Ilara.

I staggered a step back. "What are you doing here?"

She merely smiled as she walked closer. Her dark hair swung to her hips, her dark eyes flashed with triumph. She sauntered toward me slowly, and I couldn't help backing up toward the edge of the roof.

"Oh, little princess vigilante," she cooed, her voice sounding far away. "Did you really think you could outsmart me?" She giggled. "You've always been destined to fail. Just look around you."

I turned and the bodies of the unfamiliar became familiar. Jorad, Beata, Locke—the children I'd left behind at camp. They lay scattered around me in horrifically gruesome positions, all of them killed by arrows. Elisha's dead eyes stared up at me from below. Beata's body covered hers in a vain attempt to keep her safe.

Ilara knelt before me and took my face. "Now, you'll take your medicine like a good little tool."

I clenched my jaw shut, shaking out of her grip, but someone else was holding me too. Together, they forced my mouth open and crammed something minty inside of it. Tears sprang to my eyes, and I began to cough. Slowly, the world came back into focus

—and Ilara's face faded into...

"Joella?" I croaked.

"There she is." My Forcadelian lieutenant grinned at me, a sight for sore eyes. "Welcome back, Your Majesty."

"That tinneum works wonders," Luard said behind her. "Probably should've had some before you threw that hyblatha at everyone."

They helped me sit up and I blinked in the darkness as the rest of the hyblatha left my system. The bodies faded into nothing, and Forcadelian guards I only vaguely recognized had Beswick's men secured in an alley. My mind cleared enough to see a cloudy, rainless sky above, but my nerves remained.

A storm is coming.

"W-what are you...?" I said. Then I shook myself back into my body. "Kat. Beswick has Kat. Where is he?"

"We didn't see him," Joella said to Luard's stricken face.

"Southern port," I said, rubbing my face. "Let's go."

Luard had clearly brought reinforcements. As soon as Beswick's men showed up in my path, more Forcadelian soldiers popped out of the alleys and side streets to fight them off for us. And when they were late, the vigilantes above cleared a path.

There were boats down at the docks, and if Beswick got on one, we might lose him and Katarine forever. Beata would never forgive me if her wife didn't come back—and I would never forgive myself, either.

"Where's Felix?" I said to Joella.

"No idea," she said. "He left before we did, but I didn't see his ship in port."

My heart seized, but I kept running. Felix wouldn't let me down. I had to have faith that he was on his way as fast as he could.

The docks became visible in the distance. Where I'd expected to see civilians, I saw nothing but open ports. Perhaps they'd all escaped in the confusion. I just hoped anyway. I didn't think Beswick would've had his men kill an entire city full of people.

"There!" Jax called, pointing to the street below. Beswick and two of his guards were half-dragging Katarine down the street. She was making a valiant effort to fight them off, until Beswick hit her in the back of the head. She slumped and the guard tossed her over his shoulder.

"That son of a bitch will pay for that," Luard snarled next to me.

"Stay here," I snapped at him. "I don't want you in danger either."

"Like hell—"

"Luard," I snapped. "This isn't a place for a prince. Let me do my job."

Despite the fury in his eyes, he nodded, and I left him on the rooftops. I jumped off, landing in a roll and then sprinting toward the docks. Beswick was nearly onto the boat, so I doubled my speed until my boots clacked on the wood.

"Beswick!" I called, coming to a stop. "You can't go any further. Give Katarine back to us and surrender."

He snorted. "I'm standing next to a boat that will take me down to Forcadel. Do you know the ransom Queen Ilara put on this woman's head? It rivals yours."

I licked my lips. I hadn't heard anything about a ransom, but that didn't mean it wasn't true.

"Whatever it is," Luard said, stepping forward. Clearly, he hadn't heeded my order. "I'll double it. As long as you give me my sister back unharmed."

"And hand myself over to you, Prince?" He laughed. "The way I see it now, I've got all the cards. You can let me go, or—"

Beswick's eyes bulged as he swayed on his feet for a moment before tipping forward. His two guards lost their footing and fell into the water. Behind them, Felix, dripping wet, caught Katarine in one hand while letting Beswick's guard fall face-first onto the wood.

"Finally," Luard said, scrambling over to the boat and taking his sister. To be sure, he pressed his finger to her neck. "She's fine. Just unconscious."

"Why are you wet?" I asked, narrowing my eyes at him.

"We thought we'd go for a swim." He grinned and nodded toward the murky water. Four vigilantes waved at me, two of them holding Beswick's guards.

"And you said you weren't a good vigilante," I said to Felix with an appraising look.

"It wasn't my idea," Felix said, looking behind him to where Aline was climbing out of the water. Some of the color had returned to her face, but she still wore a sheepish grin.

"I thought I told you to run." I said to her.

"That's not what The Veil does," she said. "You taught me that."

"Can't argue with that logic," Felix said.

Chapter Fifty-Two

With Felix's additional forces, plus those civilians who'd decided to stick around and help, we quickly subdued Beswick's forces and herded them to the field just outside of town—Jax's idea.

"You're so precious. I didn't think you'd take too kindly to us killing all of Beswick's men," he said.

The captured men and women sat in the open field, hands bound, surrounded by the Forcadelian soldiers and the vigilantes with swords pointed at their faces. I wasn't worried about them fighting back. Once they knew Beswick had been taken prisoner, most dropped their arms and surrendered immediately.

Those who hadn't, I'd had placed on the Niemenian fishing vessel Felix had come in on to await their interrogation.

"Why are we interrogating them?" Luard asked. "And what are you planning to do with them afterward?"

"You're taking Beswick," I said. "But he can still be useful to me. Even if in name only."

"What do you mean?"

"Maybe I learned a little something from Celia," I said. "Or I'm less noble than I used to be after accepting stolen food in her name."

I opened the door to the quarterdeck where Ignacio sat tied to a chair, bound and gagged. He snorted in my direction as I sauntered inside but gave me a curious look as I gently undid his gag.

"Good morning, Ignacio," I said, standing in front of him with my arms crossed over my chest. "You're looking well."

He made a noise. "I ain't talking."

"Aren't you in luck?" I said with a smile. "I don't want you to talk. I want you to work."

Ignacio shifted in his seat, trying not to look interested.

"See, Beswick's got a great thing going in Forcadel right now," I said. "He's got people who fear him and people who want to ally themselves with him for power. I want to harness that."

"Good luck," he said. "Nobody in Beswick's operation wants to work for you."

"They won't be working for me. They'll be working for you, and you now work for me."

He tilted his head up, confused.

"You told me once that rebellions aren't run on hopes and dreams. That they're run on money. And you're right. I need money if I'm going to win against Ilara."

"But—"

"The story you'll tell is that Beswick's been taken, but you managed to escape," I said, waving my hand to silence him. "And took up the mantle of his operations in his stead. You're his closest ally, so clearly this is what would've happened anyway. Take all the rent, threaten all the people, just keep on as if you reported to your old boss. But instead, all the money will be going toward my cause." I smiled. "And, of course, you now take direction from me."

"Thought you had a moral code and all that," he said.

"I do," I said. "Which is why once I'm back on the throne, I'll be using the royal treasury to pay it all back. And as thanks for your help, I'll wipe the considerable number of crimes from your ledger. You'll be a free man to start your life over as you see fit."

"That's a big if," he said. "Ilara's pretty entrenched in the city now. You think you have a chance?"

"Are you really asking me that after what I did tonight?" I asked.

"And what happens if I don't want to work for you?"

"Then you'll join your boss on a one-way journey to Niemen," I said with a smile. "Luard tells me they'll plunge him up to his neck in ice until he freezes to death." I shivered. "Sounds quite unpleasant. I'd take my chances with Ilara myself."

He swallowed hard. "Beswick has people in Niemen."

"Beswick picked a fight he couldn't win," I replied. "He's out of funds, out of friends, and right now, out of chances. He'll go to Niemen to be put to death for his crimes, and the people in Forcadel will be better for it." I got to my feet. "I suggest you think long and hard about who you want to support right now."

I was halfway to the door when he cried, "Wait."

"And you trust he'll do what you ask?" Felix asked as we walked through the town.

Two of his guards flanked us, and on the rooftops, my vigilantes were keeping an eye on things. In the stores and businesses, people were opening doors and getting back to work.

"Not in the least," I said. "Which is why I'm sending a couple of my vigilantes with him. If he so much as sniffs in the wrong direction, they have my permission to gut him."

A group of children stopped in front of us. I quirked my brow at them, waiting for them to move, but instead, they bowed and scampered away. My traitorous mind brought me back to the hyblatha vision, of all the children back at camp dead. I shook it away. Just my worst fears, a trick of the weed. Nothing more.

"The people are grateful for what you did here," Felix said. "I wouldn't be surprised if some of the younger townsfolk come back to camp with us."

I smiled and waved back at a woman who'd opened her front door. "Maybe. But there are a lot of people in camp now. I don't know how I can house them all."

"Then perhaps it's time to consider moving," Felix said. "Beswick's taken care of, Ammon's on board. The only thing left to tackle is Ilara."

"Indeed," I said, as we came to the outskirts of the city and what I hoped would be the new additions to my army. Joella stood at the front, her eagle-eyes watching those seated for signs of unrest.

"What about them?" Felix asked. "We can't take all of them back to Niemen to stand trial. Most of them aren't even guilty."

"I have a plan for them, too," I said, leaving him to walk toward Joella. "How are the prisoners?"

"They aren't talking," Joella said. "But we've been bandaging their wounds and tending to them. Hopefully that kindness will loosen some tongues. Some of them I recognize from Forcadel. They're shop owners and merchants. Not soldiers. Seems like Beswick rounded up every able-bodied person he could to fight."

"Whether they wanted to or not," I said darkly. "Thank you."

I continued toward the group, asking the two guards in the front to move aside so I could address them. I straightened my shoulders and raised my voice.

"Good morning," I called.

A few heads perked up.

"Some of you may not recognize me," I said. "My name is Brynna-Larissa Archer Rhodes Lonsdale. The rightful queen of Forcadel."

Those who'd been avoiding my gaze looked up, and a few squinted in my direction. I gave them all a minute to take a good look before I continued.

"I know most of you are here because Beswick's holding something over you," I said. "And if given the chance, you would gladly return to your homes and families. I'm happy to say that Johann Beswick will no longer be in Forcadel—he's on his way to face justice in Niemen."

A ripple of surprise ran through the group, and more than a few gasps of relief erupted.

"I know you're all eager to return home. But I'd like to ask you to put that on hold, if only for a few more weeks. We will be returning to Forcadel. And I need as many willing bodies as I can get to defeat Ilara and her forces."

The relief turned to surprise, and even a little anger.

"You'd be joining members of the Forcadelian Royal Guard, thieves from the forest pirate Celia's camp, and others that have joined my ranks. If you stay, you'll be expected to fall under my colors, under my command, and those who I've delegated. And I promise that I will make sure all your crimes are expunged, and all that Beswick took from your family is set right. You have my word."

I waited for someone to ask what would happen to them if they chose not to join with me, but no one did. Instead, the closest to me rose to his feet with some difficulty.

"Your Majesty," he said, dropping to one knee.

One by one, they got up then fell to their knee. As they did, I motioned to the Forcadelian guard to cut their ties and allow them freedom. At the end, only ten remained seated, and those I told the guard to bring to their feet.

"They'll be coming with us," I said. "I'll figure out what to do with them later. Maybe we can finally put together a real prison."

"Or they'll change their minds," Felix said with a knowing smile.

"Hopefully," I said. "I hope you're ready to assume command of them."

"Wait...me?" Felix blinked.

"My army's getting rather large now, Felix," I said. "With these sixty, we're getting close to two-fifty. I need someone well-versed in military leadership. And as much as I like Jorad, he's just a kid. You are my best military advisor." I held out my hand. "General Llobrega."

"Quite a leap from captain," he replied.

"I think you've earned it," I said. "And not just because you're cute."

With the town back to normal, and my newly minted troops under Felix's command, all that was left was to deal with the man himself. Beswick had been sequestered on Luard's boat since his capture, guarded by both Niemenian and Forcadelian forces.

When I climbed onboard the ship, Luard was drinking a goblet of wine.

"Not my favorite vintage, but it'll do for celebration," he said, offering me a glass.

I took the glass and sipped it. "How's the prisoner?"

"Swearing up and down that he'll be able to get out of his binds," Luard said. "But what he doesn't understand is that I have more money than I know what to do with, and anyone who tries to get him out will be offered triple what he's promised."

"Triple nothing is nothing," I said with a grin. "I think he's finally done for."

Luard rose. "Thank you for letting us have him. I know how

much you wanted to bring him to justice yourself."

"I don't care much about that," I said. "What I care about is that he can no longer hurt anyone. Besides that, it'll be a few months before the Forcadelian courts are back up and running. I think I can let Niemen take care of him for me."

"That we can," he said. "And when I get back to Skorsa, I'll send ships down to your aid."

"Wait on that," I said. "I'll send a messenger. It's been a while since I've been to Forcadel and I don't know quite what I'm getting myself into down there." I cleared my throat. "Would it also be all right if I sent Joella and her forces back to Skorsa? I'm not sure we have room for them at the camp just yet."

"I suppose," Luard said with a mock sigh. "Shall I also send some funds your way? Seems like you're constantly in need of them."

"If all goes according to plan, Beswick's operation should be providing all the funds we need for the foreseeable future," I said. "Hopefully."

"Would you like to say goodbye to the prisoner?" Luard asked, walking to the door.

"Oh, I really would," I said with a grin.

When the door opened, Beswick was sitting on a stool in the corner of a small prison cell. He looked older than the last time I'd seen him, but just as confident. If I hadn't known what was in store for him, I might've thought he'd won, instead of being the one in chains.

"This is nice," I said, exhaling. "I like seeing you behind bars."

He snorted. "As I told your Niemenian prince, prisons can't keep me. I have friends in Niemen who can sway Ariadna to let me go."

"Mm, I don't think she'll listen," I said. "You've pissed her off, and that's a hard thing to do. The Niemenian royal family don't get mad easily. I'm afraid this is the end of the road for you."

He made a face.

"Defiant until the end, I can respect that," I said.

"Why are you here? Just to gloat?"

"I wanted to imprint this in my memory," I said. "The day you finally released your death grip on my city and people."

"Death grip." He snorted. "I barely had a finger on them. Ilara's the one you should've been focused on."

"I am focused on her," I said.

"Are you? You've spent a lot of time with me," Beswick said.

"A day. I spent a day on you," I said, but it unleashed a flurry of anxiety in my chest. "And only because you wouldn't cooperate. I wanted to be allies, but you ignored my overtures."

He just smiled and sat back. "It's nearly sundown."

Something twinged in the back of my mind. "What does that matter? What did you do?"

"Me?" He shook his head. "Nothing. Others, though..." He shrugged. "I always have a contingency plan. Surely, you should know that by now."

Chapter Fifty-Three

"We have to leave. Go back to camp," I said, running out onto the quarterdeck. "I don't know what he did, but he did something."

"What?" Luard said.

"Slow down." Felix put both hands on my shoulders. "What are you talking about?"

"Beswick, something... He did something. The way he was talking." My heart was pounding, and I couldn't wipe the vision of the kids back at camp from my mind. But what could he have done? His forces were here.

"Brynna," Felix said, cupping my face. "Are you sure he's not just messing with you? We've won. He's in our custody. There's nothing more that he can do."

I pushed him away. They didn't understand Beswick like I did. If he had a contingency plan, if he was still wearing that smirk, he'd planned something else.

My gaze fell on Ignacio, who was sitting on a crate in the back of the ship, along with the others who'd agreed to help me.

Lip curled, I marched over to him. "You," I said, pointing my finger at his chest. "What's your boss planning?"

"W-what?" He made a face. "What are you talking about?"

"He said he had a contingency plan," I said. "What is it?"

"I…don't know," he said, shaking his head. "He didn't tell me what it was."

"But it's coming."

"I have no idea."

I pulled my knife from my hip and pressed it to his neck. "I will bleed you dry here and now if you don't start talking."

"I have no idea," Ignacio said, raising his hands. "He didn't let me know half of what he was up to lately. Too paranoid that someone was going to leak his plans."

"Brynn—" Felix began but I hissed at him.

"He knows more than he's saying."

"She's right," Katarine said behind me. "I saw him at the castle. During the celebrations. Luisa said you were helping Ilara with something."

Ignacio went a little pale. "I was merely ferrying messages from Beswick."

My heart fell into my stomach. "What kind of messages? Why was Beswick talking with Ilara? What—"

"Insurance," Ignacio said, as I pressed the knife harder into his skin. "On the off chance you were successful. He wanted to have an in with the queen."

"*What is his plan?*" I snarled.

"I swear to the Mother, I don't know!" Ignacio said.

I nearly threw a punch, but instead I turned back to Felix, who finally looked appropriately worried. "We need to get back to camp. *Now.*"

Every second we wasted was another knife to my gut, but finally, after some wrangling, a group of soldiers, including myself, Felix, Katarine, the Niemenians—with Beswick locked in their carriage—and a smattering of other Forcadelian guards set off north. Joella remained in the city to organize the chaos we'd left behind, including moving the rest of Beswick's forces north to meet us. I had no idea where I was going to put all of them, but that was a faraway problem for now.

"There are no reports of any armies in any direction," Felix said. "If she promised him backup, it never arrived."

But my fear wasn't that something was coming, it was that something had already happened. I had an uneasy feeling in the bottom of my stomach, a sense that something had gone terribly wrong. Beswick was a man who dealt personal blows—he didn't kill you, he killed your entire family and made you watch.

As we left the main road, veering north across the plains toward the forest, the grass below looked trampled. More so than normal —like an army had just come by. I kicked my horse to move faster.

"Brynna, we can't keep this pace up," Felix called, coming up beside me. "The horses need a rest."

"They can rest back at camp."

"They won't make it there," Katarine called, a little further behind me. "Felix is right. We can spare ten minutes."

They could stay behind. I wouldn't be able to breathe until I saw the gates of my camp for myself.

Finally, as the moon appeared on the horizon, the forest came into view. The butterflies turned to a swarm of bees in my stomach. It looked normal, but something whispered to me on the wind that what I would find inside was anything but.

"Wait," Felix said, as I dismounted and started toward the forest on foot. "You can't go in there by yourself. We'll all go."

"It could be an ambush," I said. "Let me go in—"

"Brynn."

"Ilara wants me alive," I said, remembering what Beswick had said. "If I'm not out in ten minutes, come after me."

"I'm going with you." Felix drew his sword. I should've argued more, but I didn't have the energy. I just needed to see my camp.

As soon as I set foot inside the forest, dread filled my entire being. It was silent. No whistles, no rustling in the trees. Whether it was my fear or foreboding, the energy had shifted.

"Brynn..."

I looked behind me at Felix, who'd gone pale. Slowly, I turned around and my eyes adjusted to the darkness. What I'd thought was underbrush at first was actually...

Bodies. My scouts had been shot out of the trees.

My knees went weak as I stumbled toward the nearest child. Barely thirteen, she stared up at me with lifeless, terrified eyes, her arms twisted unnaturally behind her. An arrow had been shot into her chest, and blood pooled beneath her.

"Oh Mother," I whispered, stroking her cold face.

The air left Felix's chest in a gasp as he passed me, kneeling in front of another body ahead of me.

Locke, sweet Locke.

His bruised and bloodied body had been trampled, but some kind person had seen fit to move him to the tree. Or perhaps he'd been slowing them down. Next to him was another kid, perhaps sitting next to him in the canopy. I'd thought they'd be safe in the trees. But clearly, whoever had come for the camp had known what they were doing.

Sickness rose to my throat as the fort came into view.

A mixture of soldiers and children lay in the front of the camp, some of them barely in their uniforms. The soldiers had brandished their weapons, as had some of the children. But all of them had met the same grisly fate. They had been woefully unprepared for this massacre.

And leading the charge was Jorad.

I fell to my knees in front of him, the air leaving my lungs. His brown eyes—the same as Felix's—stared over my shoulder into nothing. He'd fought valiantly—no less than three arrows stuck out of his stomach and shoulder. But the gash in the center of his chest had been the killing blow.

"No."

Felix stumbled over to kneel next to me, his hands remaining at his side, perhaps afraid if he reached out to touch his cousin's body, the vision would become real.

I turned to my right, to Nicolasa's hut. The Nestori had been dragged out of her house and slaughtered in her mint field.

A storm is brewing in the south. And I'd left a paltry twenty soldiers. Would she have told me if I hadn't left enough? Had she even known, or had the Mother merely warned her that death was impending? *All we can do is pray to the Mother.*

She seemed so far away right now. All these lives taken in an instant, mercilessly slain for no reason other than that they were here. These were my soldiers, my people. And I'd allowed this to happen.

Not me, Beswick.

I balled my fist. There would be one more life taken this day. One that truly deserved it.

⇨————

The army had started to trickle in behind me, but I ran past them. Once I left the forest, I broke out into an all-out run toward the huddle of people surrounded by a halo of torchlight. The outline of the prison carriage was my focus, and I let my boots slide across the wet grass as I skidded to a stop in front of it.

Beswick smiled from behind the bars. "Something amiss back at camp?"

"Let him out," I snarled, pulling my knife. "I want to gut him myself."

"Brynna, what happened?" Luard said. "What's going on?"

"They're dead!" I cried, my voice growing higher as my rage boiled my mind. "All of them. Every single person. Because of *him*."

Silence echoed from behind, but that slimy son of a bitch just chuckled.

"I wish I could take credit for this. But if you have a problem, you'll have to take it up with Queen Ilara." He crossed his arms over his chest, as if bored. "She and I have been in contact, you see."

"I'm well aware of that, you traitor," I snarled.

"Businessman," he said. "I never close the door on an enemy, so I kept tabs on her in case there was ever a chance I could get what I want."

"I thought you wanted her off the throne," Luard said.

"I did, but I wanted my own kingdom back more," Beswick said. "Being a rebel leader is an underpaying gig, you see. And as luck would have it, a chance appeared, right after your sister left Ilara's good graces. A ransom, a rather large one, was placed on her head, as I said. So I offered my services to the queen, along with the promise that I could also deliver the princess." He laughed. "When I told her that, she said I could do whatever I wanted in her city as long as I brought you back alive."

I shook my head. "Why the hell does she want me alive?"

"Why, I have no idea. Perhaps she just wanted to kill you herself."

"But this..." I gestured at the forest behind us.

"I told my messenger to expect me back by sunup, and if I didn't arrive, to go to Ilara and tell her exactly where to find your people." He smiled. "Should've worked a bit faster, princess."

My stomach churned. "All this...for money?"

"I thought you would've learned your lesson the first time. You don't ever take your eyes off your main enemy. You—"

I slammed my fists against the iron. "*Shut up!*" He jumped back, fear finally appearing on his smug face as I clawed at the bars. "You shut your Mother-forsaken mouth. I'm guilty of a lot of things, but this—this is your fault. I gave you the chance to be my ally. And you walked away just so you could keep your little kingdom. You have the blood of every person in there on your hands. And I will make sure that you pay for it." I thumbed my knife. "Open the gate, Luard."

"Take a breath," Luard said, pulling me away. "You aren't going to mutilate him."

"Watch me," I growled. "He deserves it—"

"He deserves justice, and that's what we'll provide in Niemen," Luard said. "Trust me. We can dig into the archives of old Niemenian lore to find the most fitting end for him."

"Luard, they're all dead," I whispered, pressing my face to his chest. "Everyone is dead. They're all dead." I could say nothing else, repeating it as my brain finally broke from the exhaustion and grief.

And just when I thought it couldn't hurt any more, I heard a soft question.

"Where's Bea?"

I froze, my eyes opening wide as grief and pain came anew. I lifted my head to look into Katarine's bright blue eyes and was rendered speechless.

She backed up three steps then took off.

Chapter Fifty-Four

Katarine

Mother, please. Don't take her away from me.

I prayed harder than I'd ever prayed in my life. The Mother wouldn't be so cruel as to give me only a moment of happiness. Had I not been a faithful servant? Had I not tried to do the best I could as princess and steward of my adopted homeland?

But as I came down the path, perhaps the Mother had forsaken us all.

The sight of children's bodies lining the forest floor drew sickness to my lips, but I kept walking. They were a silent witness to the numb understanding enveloping me, as I prepared myself for what I might find through those open gates.

In the center of camp, Felix sat hunched over the body of his cousin, holding him as if he were a child. He took no notice of me, whispering soft words to the young man who he'd taken such pride in training.

"He's gone, Kat," Felix said as I walked by. "Who did this?"

I couldn't find the words, not until I knew where my wife was.

My brain couldn't reconcile the happy place I'd known a few hours ago with the gruesome picture before me. Children lay strewn about, their blood staining the dirt where they'd played. Our small wedding altar was now covered in arrows.

My feet moved beneath me, forcing me to explore every inch of this massacre. Everywhere I looked, more bodies, more death. More innocent lives cut short by unyielding cruelty.

A loud gasp drew my attention to the front. Jax, Brynna's surly friend who'd never shown any emotion other than annoyance, paled as he took in the sight. Tears spilled down his face as he ran to the Nestori healer.

"Nicolasa," he whispered as he cradled her. He pressed her eyelids closed and bowed his head in prayer. "Be with the Mother."

I had no words of comfort to share with him. All that I felt was numbness. And fear of what other terrors I might find in this place.

Slowly, I turned to the mess hall, knowing I needed to look, but not wanting to. Perhaps if I stayed in this spot forever, I might never have to know. But a stronger voice pushed me to walk toward the hall, to face the reality as bravely as Beata had. So I let go of Felix's hand, and steeled myself.

I pushed open the door to the mess hall, finding it blessedly devoid of death. All the tiny soldiers had scrambled to protect the camp, no cowards among them. Still, the tables were overturned, and even Beata's large vat was on its side. The decorations from our wedding had been left alone—perhaps a small miracle.

I slowly walked toward the back, my heart thudding in my ears as tears spilled down my face. If she was gone, I prayed it had been quick. That she hadn't suffered long. My lip trembled as I pushed aside the small curtain separating the main hall from the kitchen area.

Light spilled in. All the food had been thrown on the ground and smashed, the bags of flour ripped and spilled everywhere. In one fell swoop, they had destroyed what had taken Beata a few weeks to assemble.

My love, however, was nowhere to be found—and a new fear blossomed. What if they'd taken her back to Forcadel?

I turned and ran from the mess hall. I threw open every door and cabinet, calling Beata's name. Panic rose in my chest as I thought of her in the dungeons. She was strong, but against the whips and chains, how soon would she break?

When I came running out of the sleeping hall, I nearly ran into Felix. His wordless stare conveyed his fear, and undid me completely. With a heaving sob, I collapsed into his arms, allowing him to catch me.

"She's not here," I said. "She's gone."

"We'll find her."

"Felix, they're going to hurt her. I don't know if she can handle that."

"We'll get her out. Brynna won't stand for this." He took my face in his hands. "Are you sure she's not…"

"I've looked everywhere," I whispered.

"Kat?"

My shoulders dropped along with my stomach. Beata's soft voice echoed from behind me. Against my will, my body turned, ready to see the final moments of my love's life.

Instead, I found her sitting atop a wagon pulled by an old mare. Beata's face was streaked with dirt and tears and there were leaves sticking out of her hair. But she didn't seem to have a scratch on her.

"B-Bea?" I whispered, walking toward her. "Are you…"

"Oh, Kat," she said, jumping off the wagon and rushing toward me.

I fell to my knees as we connected, pressing my face into her neck and sobbing in relief. It was selfish, but I thanked the Mother that I had been spared in this massacre.

"How?" I whispered. "Oh, Beata…"

"Celia," she said, looking over my shoulder to where the forest pirate had her last stand. She was beautiful, even in death, her black hair fanned around her head. Four arrows had felled her, including one to the heart. In her hand was a bejeweled knife.

"She came back," I whispered.

"She wasn't far," Jax said, walking past me to her. He knelt beside her and gently tugged the arrows from her flesh, throwing them away. Wiping tears from his cheeks, he bowed his head in prayer as he took her hand.

"I don't understand," I said, turning back to Beata.

"She heard the troops coming up from the south..." Beata wiped her eyes. "She told the camp to clear out, but...but they wouldn't. They vowed to stay and protect it."

"Oh, my love." I wiped her tears. "Tell me you didn't stay."

"I did, at first," she said. "But when the soldiers arrived and..." She swallowed. "Celia told me I had to go. Take the babies and go, is what she said." She sniffed hard. "I didn't want to but I could see it in her eyes. I could see...this in her eyes."

"The babies?" Jax croaked behind me.

Beata nodded and pointed to the wagon she'd come in on. "It's all right, children. You can come out."

A child's head appeared, wide-eyed and terrified. Followed by another. Then another. Six children in all. And...

"*Elisha*," Jax cried. He ran to the wagon to pull the girl from it, crushing her small frame to his body. The girl seemed surprised at first, but eventually closed her eyes and leaned into him. "Thank the Mother you're all right."

She made a sound, looking at the devastation around her.

"She didn't want to go," Beata said, nodding to the young girl. "But Nicolasa told her to."

"I don't know why," Elisha whispered, tears leaking down her face. "I shoulda died here."

"Holy Mother."

Luard had his hand over his mouth, looking green, and still others behind him filtered into the camp. Some couldn't take the sight, turning and running from the devastation. Others merely fell to their knees in front of the thieves and soldiers they'd called friends. I held Beata closer.

"All of you, on your feet."

Brynna was back, too. Although her cheeks were stained with tears and dirt, she seemed more in control of herself. Her fury, it seemed, had focused her. Or perhaps she'd realized that, as queen, she didn't have the luxury of anger right now.

"We will not let this defeat us," she said, walking to the center of camp. "We will bury and mourn the dead this week." Her gaze landed on Celia and widened with shock. "But we can't linger here." She turned to Joella behind her. "Order a camp to be set up in Kulka, north of here. Once we have that, I want volunteers to help with burials." She narrowed her eyes. "Make sure Ignacio's front and center to all of it."

Joella nodded and began barking orders to those behind her. Some in the camp got up, but others remained on their knees. Those that did, Brynna helped up and led them from the carnage.

"We should go, too," Luard said, holding the hands of two of the littles. "It's not right for them to see this."

With difficulty, I nodded and took two small hands myself. Together with Beata, we left the devastation behind and continued into the dark forest.

Chapter Fifty-Five

We began the burials immediately, starting with the twenty brave soldiers who had stayed behind and laid down their lives and ending with the children who'd been the last line of defense. Between Joella's soldiers from Skorsa and Beswick's former charges, we managed it in half a day. Those of Beswick's people who'd been reticent to join us seemed to have a change of heart at the sight of little bodies littering the forest floor. Some of them sobbed as they helped carry the smallest bodies to their final resting place—even the ones who'd been reticent earlier in the day. Even Ignacio helped, ducking his head and refusing to look anyone in the eye.

I had no more tears. All I had was rage. But my people needed a leader, so I swallowed my fury and got to work.

Joella oversaw the construction of temporary tents, helped build bonfires, and relocated the stores of food. Ten soldiers from Skorsa stepped up to cook for the camp, and even more offered to serve. As I looked out amongst those seated on the grassy plains, it was hard to tell a difference in my forces.

Once the soldiers were settled with rotations and sleeping arrangements, I finally allowed myself to return to the graveyard. The moon was high overhead, and I couldn't remember the last time I'd slept. But even half-delirious, I wanted to pay my final respects.

I passed through the silent forest, along the road where we'd accosted Luard and his carriage. I paused briefly at the fork—one path leading into the camp, the other continuing to Forcadel. I'd been asked several times what I wanted to do with the camp, but I had no response yet. Burning it seemed like a fitting end, but…I'd said so many goodbyes lately, I couldn't stand another one.

As I left the forest, I crested a small hill and came upon the newly dug graves. Under the full moon, they were well-lit. Seventy plots, each of them facing north-south, in the Forcadelian military tradition. Someday, I would return and place the crest of the Mother and of Forcadel on each of them, honoring their service to my kingdom.

But they hadn't stayed because they believed in the cause. They'd stayed because this was their home. And they'd protected it at all costs.

Below, a figure stood in front of a grave. I hadn't seen Jax in a few hours; he hadn't been through the food line. I'd wanted to grieve in private, but his pain was palpable. He, like me, had lived at the camp, had known the kids there. And today, he'd buried his family.

I came up beside him, saying nothing. Jax held his hands behind him in reverent silence. I didn't have to guess which three graves lay before us.

Celia, Locke, Nicolasa.

"I can't believe she came back," I said.

"I can," Jax said. "This was her home. We were her family."

A family she'd held hostage. I'd never quite understood Celia.

Not when I'd first arrived at her camp at thirteen. And not at fifteen, when she'd said she wanted me to take over for her. Certainly not now.

"Take the babies and go."

Perhaps I didn't need to understand her. For now, I would just be grateful to her for getting Beata and the others to safety.

Locke had been laid to the right of her, his knife resting atop the overturned dirt. He'd been one of the handful of Celia's best who'd stayed—all because I'd shown him kindness. He'd thrown himself into training my soldiers, teaching them everything he knew about being a good thief. That training had been worth its weight in gold in Neveri, and in Galdon.

And on the other side, with a sprig of lavender, was Nicolasa. She was innocent—had never raised her hand in battle or anger. And the way she'd been killed... I swallowed the bile rising in my throat.

"Think she knew this was coming?" Jax asked, his voice low and gravelly.

"I think she had an inkling," I replied. "But as with most things, feelings aren't... Well..."

A storm is coming from the south. Twenty soldiers. Surely, she would've told me if she knew they'd need more.

"Perhaps this is just as the Mother wanted it," Jax said, wiping his nose with a quick movement. "For what reason, I have no damn idea."

"I guess you're free now, hm?" I said softly. "You don't have to work for me or Celia anymore."

"I bought my freedom from Celia five years ago," he said.

I turned to him, surprised. "Then why did you stay?"

"Because I believed you could win," he said. "And maybe I wanted to do something right for a change."

"And now?"

"That desert-dwelling bitch destroyed my home and killed my

family," he said, balling his fists. "She's going to pay for that. As is that son of a bitch Beswick."

I glanced to the east. Luard had sent Beswick away with his guards sometime in the night, presumably sensing that his prisoner might not see the light of day if he stuck around much longer. But the prince himself had stayed to help.

"I'm just thankful we didn't lose everyone." Jax glanced over his shoulder to where another small figure curled into a ball next to a grave. "She's tough, but...this is a lot."

I squeezed his shoulder and left him, walking along the edge of the graves. Elisha was silently crying, looking at a grave as if it held her best friend. It probably did.

"Hey," I said, kneeling in front of her. "You shouldn't stay here long, okay? Go back to camp and eat something."

"I shouldn't have left," she whispered. "I shoulda stayed and died with them."

"And what would that have done?" I asked, taking her hands. "We'd be burying you. At least now you can stay and fight." I squeezed. "Remember what Celia taught us. Better to survive than to die, even if it is honorably."

She nodded.

"You did a good thing," I said. "The Mother wanted you to survive."

"That's what N-Nicolasa said," Elisha whispered, wiping her eyes. "She said my story wasn't finished. What do you think that means?"

"It means..." I reached into my back pocket, where I'd stashed the black mask Aline had given me back in Galdon. "It means that you're ready for this."

She took it with wide eyes. "But this is..."

"I need you to be strong. You're officially in The Veil's army now. That means...we mourn the dead, but we can't stay here forever." I stood and held out my hand. "We have to keep fighting and keep living. For them."

She took my hand and came to her feet, stepping forward into my arms and pressing her wet face against my shoulder.

"I just miss her so much," she said.

"Why don't you tell me about her?" I said, turning to walk her out.

I brought Elisha back to camp and took her to Luard to feed and put to bed with the rest of the remaining children. He'd stepped up to keep watch over them while Katarine and Beata recovered from their shock and grief, and for that, I was thankful.

"I wondered where you'd run off to," he said to Elisha as I walked her up. "Go on and get some rest."

She nodded, offering me one final half-smile, then ducked inside the tent.

"Poor thing," Luard whispered. "Was she out by the graves?"

I nodded. "It's going to take a while, I think. How are the others?"

"They're resilient little buggers, I'll tell you that." His eyes warmed, giving me some hope. "I think if anyone's going to pull us back from this grief, it's them. I can't be sad when they're running around."

"They don't know what happened?" I asked.

"Bea seems to have shielded them from most of it," he said. "She's... well, she's doing as well as can be expected. And I don't think Kat's let her have a moment alone since they were reunited."

One small mercy. "Tomorrow, we'll reconvene the Council, whatever's left of it. I think forcing people back into normalcy will help. We have to decide what to do next."

"I agree," Luard said. "Any ideas?"

I could honestly say I didn't have any. My focus these past few days (had it been days?) had been in maintaining, in keeping everyone afloat as we navigated this dark and stormy river of grief. Ilara seemed a long way away.

"Don't forget to mourn, too," Luard said, wrapping his arm around my shoulder and kissing the side of my head. "Even the strongest of us need to break once in a while." He paused. "Speaking of, I haven't seen Felix in a while. You may want to make sure he's all right."

I canvassed the camp, but no one had seen Felix all day. I returned to the graveyard and found it void of anyone except ghosts.

Walking back toward our new camp, I came to the fork, but instead of continuing straight, I took a left, headed to the one place where I hadn't yet said my goodbyes. There were still bloodstains on the ground, and I could still see every life that had ended there. I paused once where Locke had given his life, praying to the Mother. There was an odd feeling to the air, like someone had desecrated a church. In my soul, I knew nothing would ever be the same in this place again.

A figure stood in the center of camp—Felix.

"I don't know how I'm going to tell his mother," Felix whispered as I came up beside him. But there was more than the grief of his lost cousin—Jorad had been one of Felix's cadets. Felix had spent years with them, training them, molding them. Knowing and caring for them. The same way Jorad had grown to care for his cadets.

"She'll be proud to know he died protecting his wards," I said. "As am I."

The longer we stood there, the more something itched in the back of my mind. Perhaps it was the Mother's hand on my shoulder, or the need to formally say goodbye to the camp. But I walked to one of the dead bonfires near the kitchen and ignited a torch.

The warm glow cast a shadow on Felix's face, and he followed my lead, finding another torch setting it aflame. Together, we lit every building in the place, the flames and embers rising up toward the open night sky. I prayed to the Mother as I caught fire to Nicolasa's home and walked through her green garden. The scent of flowers and herbs drew tears to my eyes, and I could almost hear her voice whispering that it was all right. This was the way it had to be.

As the buildings burned, I walked to the back of the camp, to Celia's hut. I left the torch in a holder outside, amused at how afraid of this door I'd once been.

"Brynn?" Felix asked, holding his torch. "We should go."

I nodded and pressed my hand to the desk, offering one final prayer of gratitude to the woman who'd sat at it. And as I exited, I took the torch and lit the thatched roof. It caught fire quickly then spread to the back wall. Calmly, I left the torch on the front desk and returned to Felix, taking his hand.

We said nothing because there was nothing more to be said. At least that night.

Chapter Fifty-Six

In truth, I waited a week before convening my Council. The sheer numbers in the camp meant things moved slower. Joella had put Beswick's former bodyguards into soldier training, having them jog around the perimeter, learn how to fight honorably, and serve meals. It was oddly reminiscent of Jorad, although the bodyguards were less disciplined than the young cadets had been. The rest of the soldiers segmented themselves into groups and continued to train, if only to burn off their energy. Slowly, smiles returned to some faces, although there were still echoes of loss admits the laughter.

One early morning, as the fog rolled over the green fields, I asked my Council to join me in the main tent. Beata arrived arm-in-arm with Katarine and Luard came right after. I hugged them together, lingering for a while with Beata.

"We'll be all right," Katarine said, putting on a brave face. "We have each other."

All Beata could do was nod and wipe away tears. But that she'd come at all was a good sign.

Felix was the next to arrive, a light sheen of sweat on his forehead from putting the soldiers through their paces. With him was Aline, who seemed nervous to have been asked to join us at all.

"Nonsense," I said, when she protested. "You were in the city. You know what's on the ground. I need your expertise."

She flushed and sat next to Felix.

The tent flap opened and Jax stormed in, his eyes lit up with unbridled fury. "This asshole says he was invited." He thumbed behind him to where Ignacio stood, stripped of his former bluster. I almost felt bad for him.

Almost.

"Let him in," I said with a nod.

"You don't sit near me," Jax snapped, taking a spot on the other side of Luard. Ignacio sat as close to the door as possible.

"First," I said, placing my hands on the table that had been moved inside for me, "I just want to say..." I'd had words prepared for this moment, but somehow, they escaped me. "That bitch is gonna burn for this."

There was a weak attempt at smiles and nods, but everyone was too tired to conjure any fury. Except Jax, who just scoffed.

"I've been thinking a lot about the next move," I said. "How we want to tackle Ilara. So I asked Aline to come talk to us about Ilara's forces." I looked at her. "Anything you can tell us would be helpful."

She cleared her throat and stood with her hands behind her back. "At last count, there's close to three hundred in the city. But as we all know, she's got the upper hand in more than just people. The city itself has a wide range of natural defenses, from the river to the mouth of the bay. It'll be difficult to move a large number of people inside without her knowing."

I nodded. "Has anyone ever successfully taken Forcadel?"

"No," Katarine said. "Not until Ilara. And I doubt we'll be able to replicate what she did."

With a sigh, I sat in my chair, running my hand over my chin. Just because it hadn't been done before didn't mean I couldn't figure a way. But my mind was spent, and sitting here strategizing was the last thing I wanted to do.

"What if we work backward," I said, forcing myself to sit upright. "What do we have to do to get the Severians out of Forcadel?"

"Kill Ilara," Felix said. "She's the one giving the orders."

"And if we kill her, the Severians will just…leave?" I asked.

"She certainly hasn't built a strong succession line," Katarine said. "But I don't think so. The land they come from is harsh and unforgiving and they might not want to return. Not to mention, we still don't know what she's doing in the east."

"Ignacio," I said, looking at Beswick's second. "Anything to add?"

He cleared his throat. "No. All I know is that she was building schools and libraries. She was very interested in moving supplies there. Beswick said he'd arrange it."

"So it could be nothing," Luard said to me.

"If anything, it's helping cement Ilara as a goddess to her people," Katarine said. "If we make a move on her without accounting for their perceptions, we risk them turning against us as well. And there may be more of them than us at this point."

"Which goes back to the impossibility of moving an army big enough to defeat her into the city," Luard said. "And we're back to where we started."

"It's not impossible if Ilara did it," I said.

"She's not…" Katarine cleared her throat. "She's a bit more perceptive than you were. She would see trickery coming from a mile away."

I glanced at her, the wheels in my head finally turning. "But you said she didn't always make the most strategic decisions, right?"

"Yes, but she'll always do the thing that keeps her in power."

"Will she, though?" Felix asked. "Making the citizens of Forcadel angry with her edicts and curfews didn't sway her."

"But the citizenry didn't do much, and she was confident in her own forces," Katarine said. "She's not going to let us do to her what she did to us."

"But what if she did?" I said slowly.

Katarine shook her head. "I don't see how that's possible. She has the upper hand."

"What if she doesn't have the upper hand? What if she only thinks she does?"

"I don't follow?" Katarine said.

"It's just something that Beswick said to me," I said, rubbing my chin. "She would've let everyone live as long as he brought me back to her unscathed. And Katarine, you said she told Coyle the same thing. Why would she want me alive?"

"So she can kill you herself," Felix said.

"You told me Ilara delights in showing people she's won," I said to Katarine. "If she has me in her possession, she'd be able to parade me around the city and brag to the world that she's bested me. She'll think she's won. And while she's gloating—"

"We move into position," Katarine finished slowly.

"No way," Felix said with a bit of a laugh. "You can't possibly think that's a smart idea, Kat."

"Actually..." Katarine said softly. "It might not be the worst. Brynna's correct that Ilara seems to have some odd fascination with her. I don't believe she would kill Brynna—at least not right away."

"But how does that help us move an army inside the kingdom?" Felix asked. "She has all the odds in her favor—soldiers, defenses, funds. Forcadel itself."

"And we have Brynna," Luard said. "I'd say the odds are evenly stacked."

"We have enough soldiers to split up," I said. "If we come in through different directions—the north, the south, and on the rivers, we might just be able to manage it."

"But is Ilara really going to believe that Brynna would allow herself to get caught?" Felix asked.

"What she did just now was heinous," I said. "She murdered innocent children. It would be reasonable that after something like that, I'd make a mistake. It's happened before."

"And what's to say you aren't making one now?" Felix said.

"Because I trust Katarine's judgment," I said. "If she believes Ilara won't execute me on sight, then I believe her."

"She will, eventually," Katarine said. "But not until she's done with you."

"Then you four will have to make sure things are ready before that time comes," I said, unfurling a map of the four countries. "Felix will take half the soldiers, including the new recruits, and join the soldiers already in Neveri. Ammon promised me a hundred troops and five ships. You go make sure he keeps his word then help them get into the city." I turned to my right. "Aline, I want you to go with Felix and help him. You know the city inside and out now. You'll need to share your knowledge."

She nodded, her eyes still red-rimmed from crying. "I'll do Jorad proud."

"Kat, you and Joella go with Luard to Niemen." I nodded toward them. "We'll gladly take whatever forces Niemen's willing to provide."

"You have my word," Luard said.

"Ignacio," I said. "Are you with us on this?"

He rose to his feet, then bowed. "Whatever you need, Your Majesty."

"You'll do as I told you before," I said. "You are now the new

Beswick. Make sure you keep good notes about who we owe money to when this is all over. If you can continue your alliance with Ilara, so be it." I paused. "I'm sending a babysitter along to make sure you don't screw me. He'll have orders to kill you otherwise."

Ignacio nodded, pale.

"Jax," I said softly. "If you're up for it, I'd like you to lead the vigilante army. Pick up where Aline and Elisha left off. Except this time, you're going to be causing trouble for Ilara, not Beswick. You're going to be my eyes and ears on the ground. And... hopefully, get messages to me in the castle if Ignacio can't."

He nodded. "I'll see what I can do."

"But we have no idea how to get our forces from Skorsa and Neveri into position," Katarine said. "If we were to pull this off, it would be quite an achievement."

"Then aren't I so lucky that I have Niemen's best minds behind it," I said, standing. "All this time, people have been telling me I need to delegate. So I'm delegating. I'll go in and be the distraction. You four come save my ass."

"Brynna..." Felix started.

"Look, I'd be leaning on you guys anyway for the military know-how. So let's cut out the middleman," I said. "I'm giving you full control of my army and the ability to make strategic decisions as you see fit. However you can get them into position...that's what you'll do."

I waited for more arguments, more discussion. Instead, they merely looked nervously at one another, as if they were waiting for the other to be the first to argue.

Jax stared me down. Then, to my utter surprise, he pressed his fist to his left breast and bowed. Ignacio followed suit, then Aline and Felix. Beata, even, broke from her reverie and bowed. Katarine and Luard rose more slowly, neither one of them saying anything.

"I need unanimous consent," I said quietly.

"I don't like the thought of sending you into the lion's den alone," Luard said. "But if there's anyone in this world who could come out without a scratch, it's you." He pressed his fist to his chest and nodded. "I'm in."

Katarine stared at me, her blue eyes rimmed red and her cheeks pale. "If Ilara finds out what we're doing, she could use you as leverage."

"She didn't when you were there."

"That's because I made her believe we hadn't been in contact," Katarine said. "And that you didn't care about me."

"Then I'll just have to tell her that you and I haven't crossed paths," I said with a grin.

Katarine crossed the room and took my hands. "I'm not losing you, Brynna-Larissa. So you damned well better become a better liar in the next few days." She bowed her head. "I'm in."

Chapter Fifty-Seven

I was to set off the next evening. The troops would be told that I'd gone to Forcadel on a spying mission, made a mistake, and that they would be continuing under the direction of Felix and Katarine once word came to them that I'd been taken.

"I leave it to your discretion what to tell the vigilante army," I said.

"Veil army," Jax said with a look. "Heard you say that to Elisha. I like the sound of it."

"Thank you," I said, holding out my hand. "There's no one I trust more to handle this mission than you."

He took my hand and shook it. "Don't take any unnecessary risks in there. If the opportunity comes to get a message out, take it, but don't—"

"I got it," I said with a nod. "Back in Forcadel, there's an archive directly across the street from the castle. In the archivist's office, underneath the desk, you'll find a complete map of the castle. There are some Ilara knows about, but others, including the one behind the barracks, she doesn't." I licked my lips. "It's supposed to be a state secret only seen by the royal family."

"Then I'll just assume you've given me a dukedom," he said, flashing me a devilish grin. "I told you I'd get paid one way or another."

"What is? Where are you going? Can I come?" Elisha popped up next to us, wearing the black mask I'd given her.

I gave Jax a nod and put my arm around Elisha, walking her away from him. "Listen, I'm going on a little mission for a while. But I need you to get your things ready to go."

"Back to Forcadel," she said, puffing out her chest. "With Jax. I heard you."

"No," I said with a shake of my head. "You'll be going to Skorsa with Lady Katarine and Lady Beata."

Her face fell. "But you said—"

"My army's getting split up," I said. "Jax will be taking some of the troops, but there'll be no one with Lady Kat who knows how to be a scout. You're the best one I have."

"I'm the only one you have." It should've been said with more disdain, but the loss of her friends at the camp had hit her hard. "I'll do my best."

"Whatever Lady Kat asks, I need you to do without question," I said. "Same for Lady Beata. I'll tell them to trust you as they trust me." I patted her cheek. "I'm really proud of you. And I'll see you in a few weeks."

As the sun began to set in the distance, I said my goodbyes to Luard, Katarine, and Beata. I found them in a tent on the outskirts of camp, watching the youngest survivors chase each other in a game of tag. Luard's comment about the children bringing light back to Beata's face seemed true, as both she and Katarine watched them with a mix of joy and caution.

The children stopped short when they saw me, scrambling over themselves as they queued up before me. With a flourish, they bowed in unison then stood upright, giggling to each other.

"Very good," I said, catching Beata's eye. "You've certainly got the best teacher."

"Go wash up for dinner," Beata said to them, walking over to me.

The children nodded with a chorus of "Yes, Lady Beata" and ran toward the small river in the distance.

"You'll bring them with you to Skorsa, won't you?" I asked, watching them disappear. "They'll be safe there. Or maybe even send them up to Niemen—"

"They'll be safe in Skorsa," Luard said. "As will Kat and Bea. You have my word that nothing will happen to either of them."

I took Beata's hands and kissed them. "I wish I had more time to spend with you and Kat. But know that I am grateful every day that..."

"I understand," she said softly. There was nothing more to say that hadn't already been said, so I hugged her tightly and kissed her cheek.

Luard took her place, pulling me in for a tight hug that could've lasted forever. "Remember everything we've talked about," he said, pressing a small bag into my hand. Tinneum. "If you ever get scared or worried, just chew on this stuff. It seems to clear your head."

"Give my love to your sister if you see her," I said. "And make sure Beswick hurts before he dies."

He kissed my cheek and released me, and I was face-to-face with Katarine. Her eyes had filled with tears once more as she came toward me, and when we embraced, it was hard not to feel like a child against her taller frame.

"You've become quite the queen," she said. "It takes a strong leader to know when to step back."

"I'd better not see you in Forcadel," I said as a tear splashed down my face.

"We'll make sure of it," Beata said with a knowing look.

But the determination in Katarine's eyes told a different story. "We'll gather as quickly as we can. You can hold Ilara off for weeks, but months is doubtful."

I nodded. "Any tips?"

"Speak the truth as often as you can," she said. "If she asks if you know what we're doing, you can honestly say that you don't. If she asks if we've seen each other—"

"I'll think about when I thought you guys had abandoned me," I said with a smile. "I do listen to you, Kat."

She kissed my forehead. "Soon enough, we'll be having tea back in your room on the day of your coronation."

With a heavy heart, I took a step back, gazing at the three of them and imprinting them on my mind. We would be reunited, but in which life, I had no idea.

"I'm riding with you."

Felix stood behind me, holding the reins of two horses already tacked and ready to go.

"You can't," I said, turning to him fully. "I need you in Neveri."

"I've already delegated command to Aline until I return." He shook the reins. "It's getting late. We'd better hurry if you want to get to Forcadel before sunup."

I opened my mouth to argue, but there was nothing to say. "Fine."

$\Rightarrow$———→

We rode in silence, neither of us looking back once. The moon was bright overhead, casting an ethereal glow on the plains and on Felix's face. He was stony, serious, and the sword at his hip had me wondering if he was going to ignore my command and whisk me away to safety. Perhaps tie me up and leave me in a house until they'd completed their plan.

When he slowed his horse, I tensed for a fight.

"The horses need water," he said, pointing to a small creek in the distance. "Let's rest here for a moment."

I dismounted and walked my horse over to the creek, allowing it to drink and eat an apple from my saddlebag. Then I joined Felix by the banks of the river as he looked out on the plains of Forcadel.

"This really is a beautiful country," he said. "I hate that it's taken this for me to see it."

"Niemen was magnificent," I said. "Mountains taller than you'd ever think possible. Snow—"

"You saw snow?" Felix asked with a smile.

"I walked through it," I said. "Up and down a mountain. Wouldn't recommend it."

A smile teased at the corner of his mouth. "You certainly worked hard to get to where you are. If I'd have known the girl I pulled out of that butchery would turn into this magnificent woman..." He quieted. "No, I knew you had this inside of you. I'm glad I picked a queen—"

"Under a mask," I finished for him.

"Are you scared?"

I frowned. "No, I'm not. Recently, I've gotten into the habit of trusting myself—of knowing that whatever mess I get myself into, I'm capable of getting out of. Whether through my own wits or..." I glanced up at him. "Because I've got an amazing group behind me."

The sound of the creek rushing over the river pebbles lulled me into a calm sense of peace. Being here, with Felix, was the last bit of truth I would get for a while, and I was grateful for the opportunity to revel in it.

"Felix, I—"

"I love you," he said, looking down at me. "And that terrifies me."

I blinked. "What?"

"It would be easier to let you walk back into Ilara's castle if I didn't love you so much," he said, looking at the ground. "Because then I could listen to my head, who knows that you've been in worse situations and come out alive. My head trusts you implicitly and has never doubted your abilities once. But all my heart wants is to keep you safe."

"Felix, I—" I shook my head. "You can't stop me from doing this."

"I'm not going to." He brought me closer, caressing my face with his fingertips. "But damn it, this hurts. Letting you walk into danger, even though I know you can handle it…it hurts. Letting you out of my sight hurts. Not being…" He closed his eyes. "Not being with you hurts."

"I know," I said, pressing my forehead to his. "I wish we had more time."

"Then let's have more time," he whispered. "Right now."

He kissed me, and there was nothing gentle about it. We fell to the banks of the river, tearing off clothes and seeking some joy amidst all this sadness. I'd been with men before, and even some who'd made me soar to the heights of pleasure and happiness. But with Felix, it was different. There was no rush, no need to get to the end. His touch was slow and his kisses lingered on my skin. My body was his church, and he lit every candle on my wall.

When it was over, we lay together, wrapped in each other's arms and we spoke about everything and nothing. We reminisced about the months he'd followed me, and the moment he realized he'd fallen for me, and how much his first kiss had surprised and confused me. He apologized once more for his cowardice and breaking my heart, and I apologized for punching him in the jaw when we saw each other in Forcadel again.

"I feel like we wasted months," I said, running my finger down his chest. "If I'd have known what was coming, I would've come to my senses sooner."

"Everything happens according to the Mother's plan," Felix said, kissing my forehead. "If this is the end, I'll be grateful I had this time with you now."

Tears pricked the corner of my eyes. "It had better not be the end, Felix Llobrega."

"Promise me you'll be careful."

"As long as you promise the same," I said. "You're not the only one worried about the person you love."

He cupped the back of my head, pulling me close. "Say it again."

And I did. Again and again and again.

Chapter Fifty-Eight

The city of Forcadel lay before me like a gem. I stood on the rooftop near the city square, gazing down on all the familiar buildings. The church where I'd stashed my vigilante things. The castle where I'd felt a prisoner. To the south, the bars and haunts where I'd found information. All of it had changed so drastically since the first bomb appeared on my shores. As had I.

In my hand, I had the mask Luard had given me. Fine black cloth lined with gold markings. I'd asked for it back from Aline, giving her one of the other Veil masks that Beata had made. For Ilara to believe I'd been the one causing trouble in the city, I needed to be in full costume.

The wind whipped my cloak behind me, my slingbag felt at home against my back, and my knives were a comforting weight at my hips. Bathed in moonlight, I truly felt my name—The Veil. Brynna. Brynn. Larissa. Her Majesty. All were me, and I was an amalgam of the different titles I wore. Soon, though, there would be one more added to the mix. Prisoner.

I reached for the two coins at my neck, thumbing Riya's for a moment before returning to Felix's. Would Ilara be so cruel as to take them from me? In case, I said my final goodbyes, kissing them both and promising I would fulfill this next role with all the aplomb of The Veil.

I let the coins fall and closed my eyes, allowing all the pain and misery of the past few weeks to fill me with unyielding rage. Katarine had said I could be an effective liar by feeling real emotion when I lied. And today, I was to be a grieving princess who was out of options, driven mad from loss. Tears gathered in the corners of my eyes as I thought of Locke, Celia, Nicolasa, and the children I'd buried, imagined their fear as they faced death. And when I opened my eyes, my hands shook with the need for revenge.

Footsteps echoed on the street below, and I gathered the edges of my cloak and took a deep breath. I jumped off the building and landed in a crouch before the Severian soldiers.

"Evening," I said with a smile as I pulled my knives. "I'm in the mood to make some Severians bleed. And you look like good candidates."

They came for me, swords out, and I deflected them. I could've easily knocked them both out within seconds, but I pulled my punches. Only a little, as I needed them to believe I hadn't let myself get captured.

I hissed as a sword tip sliced through my cheek. "Great," I said, running my finger along the cut. "Now you've made me mad."

I kicked him in the stomach, sending him flying toward the brick wall behind him. He slumped to the ground, out cold. His fellow soldiers kept their distance, infuriating me more.

"You should leave," the second Severian said, sounding almost hopeful. "The queen won't have any use for you. It's suicide for you to even be here."

"Then I suppose I'll just have to die," I said, swinging my

knives in my hand. "It's the only thing I have left."

I took a step toward him, but more soldiers arrived in the alley. Two, four, six—I lost count. A maniacal grin spread on my face. I'd taken down five with Beswick; perhaps six would be my new record.

"Let's do this," I said, running toward them. I swung and hacked, and when my knives were kicked from my hands, I used my fists and feet. Just as I was making headway, something large and heavy barreled into my midsection, sending me crashing to the ground. And before I could say or do anything else, a fist came toward my face, and everything was dark.

I awoke in a familiar room—the posters on the bed still bore the scuff marks from the night I was handcuffed to it. For a moment, I wondered if the past few months had been a dream. Had I just imagined that Ilara had taken over my kingdom? Had it been one long, tortuous nightmare?

I slid my hand across my stomach, finding the scar there. No, definitely not a dream.

"Good morning."

My pulse spiked as I rose slowly. Ilara sat in a chair across the room from me. It was the first time I'd really gotten a good look at her since the day she'd given me the scar. Her eyes were colder than I remembered, her smile wide but calculating. Perhaps it was just because I knew better, but I couldn't find the girl who'd befriended me.

"Well?" she said. "Aren't you going to say good morning back?"

"I'm surprised I'm not in the dungeons," I said slowly. "Or dead."

"Clearly, killing you doesn't work," Ilara said with a knowing look. "Instead, I thought I might show you a bit of mercy. After all, the Brynna I know wouldn't get captured by a pair of guards. You're better than that."

"I made a mistake," I said, forcing myself to look angry.

"Katarine should've provided better guidance, then."

"And I'm sure she would have, if I'd seen her," I said with a glare. "Isn't she here with you?"

"No. Unfortunately, she absconded with Felix a few weeks ago," Ilara cast me a curious look. "You mean to tell me they didn't away to your side?"

I dug through my memories to when I'd been convinced that Katarine and Felix had forgotten me. The pain was as fresh now as it had been then.

"No," I said. "I don't even think they knew where to find me."

"Beswick did," she said with a look. "Oh, I'm sure that must've stung. Getting bitten by the same snake twice." She tapped her nose. "You took your eyes off the main enemy to focus on the one you wanted."

"Are you just here to gloat?" I snapped. "Or are you going to have me executed?"

"Oh, dearest Brynn," she said, sending a surge of white-hot fury through my veins, "I'm not going to kill you. At least not yet. You see, there seems to be a pernicious rumor around that I don't have complete and total control of my kingdom. But now, I have you. So I'm sure I can put those silly rumors to rest."

"So, what?" Curiosity—real this time. "You're just going to let me stay here?"

"For a bit." She stood. "How long you remain alive depends on how nicely you play with me. I have to say, I'm honestly excited to see just how long you last." She walked to the door. "I'll have someone come up with some breakfast. I do hope I don't have to handcuff you to the bed like Felix did."

She winked and walked out the door.

Once it was shut, and her footsteps had faded, I flung the

sheets off me, running to the window to catch my breath. Five minutes in, and I was already sweating bullets. This lying thing was going to take some practice, and I didn't have much time to learn.

I closed my eyes and said a prayer to the Mother. It was up to my army now to keep on the path toward victory. All I had to do was trust that they'd get to me before Ilara's patience ran out.

Brynna's adventures will conclude in

Arriving Winter 2020

Acknowlegments

Thank you to Kristin and to Alice for helping me beta read and get this one just right.

Thank you to Dani, my magnificent line editor, for always helping me make things better.

Thank you to my QA checker, Lisa, who always manages to find the small little details that I miss. And in this case, helped me make sure I didn't write myself into a hole.

Thanks, as always, to my support network: My folks, my Hadley, and my dogs, for reminding me when it's time to get up and go for a walk.

And thank you to my magnificent reader group, the Sushis, for keeping me going, even when I was sure I was going to fail.

Also By the Author

Lexie Carrigan Chronicles

Lexie Carrigan thought she was weird enough until her family drops a bomb on her—she's magical. Now the girl who's never made waves is blowing up her nightstand and no one seems to want to help her. That is, until a kind gentleman shows up with all the answers. But Lexie finds out being magical is the least weird thing about her.

Spells and Sorcery is the first book in the Lexie Carrigan Chronicles, and is available now in eBook, paperback, audiobook, and hardcover.

The Razia Series

Lyssa Peate is living a double life as a planet discovering scientist and a space pirate bounty hunter. Unfortunately, neither life is going very well. She's the least wanted pirate in the universe and her brand new scientist intern is spying on her. Things get worse when her intern is mistaken for her hostage by the Universal Police.

The Razia Series is a four-book space opera series and is available now for eBook, Audiobook. Paperback, and Hardcover.

Also By the Author

THE MADION WAR TRILOGY

He's a prince, she's a pilot, they're at war. But when they are marooned on a deserted island hundreds of miles from either nation, they must set aside their differences and work together if they want to survive.

The Madion War Trilogy is a fantasy romance available now in eBook, Paperback, and Hardcover.

empath

Lauren Dailey is in break-up hell, but if you ask her she's doing just great. She hears a mysterious voice promising an easy escape from her problems and finds herself in a brand new world where she has the power to feel what others are feeling. Just one problem —there's a dragon in the mountains that happens to eat Empaths. And it might be the source of the mysterious voice tempting her deeper into her own darkness.

Empath is a stand-alone fantasy that is available now in eBook, Paperback, and Hardcover.

About the Author

S. Usher Evans was born and raised in Pensacola, Florida. After a decade of fighting bureaucratic battles as an IT consultant in Washington, DC, she suffered a massive quarter-life-crisis. She decided fighting dragons was more fun than writing policy, so she moved back to Pensacola to write books full-time. She currently resides with her two dogs, Zoe and Mr. Biscuit, and frequently can be found plotting on the beach.

Visit S. Usher Evans online at:
http://www.susherevans.com/

Twitter: www.twitter.com/susherevans
Facebook: www.facebook.com/susherevans
Instagram: www.instagram.com/susherevans

CPSIA information can be obtained
at www.ICGtesting.com
Printed in the USA
LVHW091941151020
668918LV00017B/475/J